The Cities

THE JEWEL OF TURMISH

Mel Odom

THE JEWEL OF TURMISH

©2002 Wizards of the Coast, Inc.

Distributed in the United States by Holtzbrinck Publishing. Distributed in Canada by Fenn Ltd.

Distributed to the hobby, toy, and comic trade in the United States and Canada by regional distributors.

Distributed worldwide by Wizards of the Coast, Inc., and regional distributors.

Cover art by Eric Peterson
First Printing: February 2002
Library of Congress Catalog Card Number: 20010897463

9 8 7 6 5 4 3 2 1

UK ISBN 0-7869-2725-9
US ISBN: 0-7869-2698-8
620-88545-001-EN

U.S., CANADA,	EUROPEAN HEADQUARTERS
ASIA, PACIFIC, & LATIN AMERICA	Wizards of the Coast, Belgium
Wizards of the Coast, Inc.	P.B. 2031
P.O. Box 707	2600 Berchem
Renton, WA 98057-0707	Belgium
+1-800-324-6496	+32-70-23-32-77

Visit our web site at **www.wizards.com/forgottenrealms**

The Cities

The City of Ravens
Richard Baker

Temple Hill
Drew Karpyshyn

The Jewel of Turmish
Mel Odom

Into the Streets of Evil
The Taker's War has left the cities on the coast of the Sea of Fallen Stars reeling, but there is no rest for the weary.

Haarn Brightoak
A druid of the Emerald Enclave, sworn to protect the balance of nature against the encroachment of civilization, Haarn has no love for cityfolk.

So what is it about the beautiful mercenary who comes into his forest to hunt wolves that makes him help her?

What evil force has a group of naive clerics unleashed in the city of Alaghôn?

What could bring Haarn Brightoak to the streets of the Jewel of Turmish?

CHAPTER ONE

Blood stink fouled the air.

Haarn Brightoak followed the scent through the thickly forested land near Evenstar Lake with a sense of trepidation, knowing that ultimately he would find yet another body only a short distance ahead. He'd been finding them for the last three hours.

Despite the heavy foliage covering the land, Haarn moved gracefully, not leaving a quivering bush in his wake. Twilight laid a soft hand on the harsh terrain, etching shadows where the land dipped and opened.

The men Haarn pursued would stop soon for the night and he'd catch up with them. Nothing would stay his hand from the justice he would exact.

Only a few yards farther on, he spotted the gray goose fletching of the ash arrow jutting from an elm tree. He went to it, knelt, and grabbed the shaft. His arm knotted with muscle as he pulled the arrowhead from the tree trunk.

The fletcher had used ash to make the shaft, and Haarn could feel the slightest tingle of spellcraft that clung to it. Ash arrows marked a serious hunter. It was one of the hardest woods to work—unless someone used magic to shape the wood. The shaft was fully three feet long from fletching to heavy iron arrowhead. The iron had been hammered into a shape designed to create a wound that would remain open, allowing the target's life's blood to trickle out until the heart pumped dry.

The arrowhead carried the identifying mark of the fletcher, signed so that others who encountered the arrow would know whom to ask for when they reached market.

Haarn memorized the mark, snapped the shaft in half, and put the iron arrowhead into the pack he carried high across his shoulders.

Though he would never allow the arrowhead to be used again as a hunting weapon, there was a dwarf who traveled through Morningstar Hollows to whom Haarn could trade it. The dwarf would use the metal for trinkets that he smithed to trade at small towns throughout the realm of Turmish.

Haarn stood again, his ears cocked for the sounds coming from the forest ahead of him. He sniffed the air, smelling the stronger scent of blood nearby. Small carnivores gathered in the forest, drifting in from the shadows.

Another fifty paces farther on, he crossed a stream where the victim had tried to elude her pursuers. Haarn knew the victim was a female now; he could scent her pheromones in the air.

He also scented the female among the hunters.

The waning twilight giving over to full night turned the blood on the grass ahead almost ebony. Still it was fresh enough to gleam.

Haarn ran his fingers across the blades of grass. The victim had run hard and well, but she hadn't been able to elude her pursuers. He crouched in the tall grass beneath the swaying bows of an old oak tree. His practiced eye read the story with ease.

The victim had hidden in the tall grass off the well-worn game path that wound through the trees to the north. Forest creatures used the game path to trek down to the artesian well that created a spring only a quarter mile away.

She had waited, Haarn knew, and hoped that her pursuers

would follow the game path and miss her. She was canny, and Haarn regretted that she was too soon taken from the world before she could contribute to the balance. He had no doubt she was dead.

Despite her craftiness, she'd been found. The hunters had followed her blood spoor from the earlier wound and stayed on track. Judging from the amount of blood that had littered the forest, Haarn doubted she would have lived anyway. The blood had misted across the grass blades in places, almost too fine for even Haarn's keen eyesight to detect, but it had indicated that at least one of the hunters' arrows had taken her through a lung.

It had only been a matter of time till she'd drowned in her own blood.

Haarn stayed on course, following the thin trail, racing through the forest as starlight filtered down through the thick canopy. He ran fast enough that his breath rasped against the back of his throat, but still he made no sound the hunters would hear.

If the hunters had found their victim so easily, it only meant that they were armed with a magical talisman of some sort. It was the only way they could have found her in the forest. After all, she was at home there, and the hunters were interlopers. They should have been her prey—or at least been toyed with and abandoned in the forest.

Haarn touched the scimitar hanging upside down behind his back and under the pack. Silvanus willing, his blade would drink the blood of the hunters before morning. Only a little farther on, he found her.

Her body lay in a tangle of flattened grasses and brush where she'd fought her tormentors with her last breath. Blood stained the ground and foliage around her.

Creeping and flying insects from the forest drank of her blood from the grass and brush. A clutch of green-glowing fireflies, drawn by all the activity around the corpse, swirled in the air over the victim's head like a ghastly ghost-light.

She was young. Haarn saw that at once, and she'd left

a litter somewhere behind her. Her body, even torn and savaged as it was, showed heavy with milk. She hadn't been part of the pack the hunters had trailed through the forest; she'd just been another target that had crossed their sights. Wherever it was, the litter was too young to take care of itself. Without help, they would become casualties, too.

Haarn studied the wolf sprawled out in the forest. The signs showed her struggles against her foes, and he hoped she had given a good accounting of herself before being executed.

Quietly, Haarn mourned the wolf, though he had not known her. She was small in stature, barely more than five feet in length and just over a hundred pounds, covered in yellow-red fur flecked with black. Evidently she'd been on her own with her cubs because they had sucked her down over the last few tendays. Game was hard to come by for a solitary wolf, and much of what she had caught had probably been regurgitated for her cubs. Her eyes held round pupils that stared sightlessly into the darkening sky as the insects and small carnivores tore her to pieces.

Haarn didn't try to stop any of the savage feasting. It was nature's way, an unexpected bounty for those that had found her. He slipped his hunting knife free of his moccasin and stepped forward.

A trio of raccoons and a lynx gave ground reluctantly, hissing and spitting. Even the insects retreated somewhat before him.

The hunters had scalped the wolf before they'd left her. Her skull shone brightly white at the top of her head, and the blood had already started to coagulate.

Haarn rolled the wolf over and cut quickly, praying as he did so. "Silvanus, Keeper of the Balance, thank you for the table you have set before me. Watch over me now as I seek to right the imbalance her death has wrought."

The knife sliced the wolf's flesh cleanly. Haarn cut four steaks from the body, cutting out the best meat. Even that, he knew, would be tough and stringy, but it would save a brace of rabbits that he would have taken for his dinner later.

Finishing his prayer, his voice soft and low in the forest, Haarn wrapped the steaks in leaves from the broad-leafed box elder trees where the wolf had made her last stand. When he had the steaks protected and masked somewhat by the scent of the crushed leaves, he stored them in his pack.

Then he took up the trail again, knowing the slight delay wouldn't keep him from catching up to the executioners. He kept his stride long and measured, crossing through the forest with the silence of a shadow. Where a more civilized man would have seen only dense brush and near-impenetrable walls, his trained eyes discerned a dozen different trails through the forest, all with different benefits and costs.

The executioners had primarily stayed with the game trail. Bent grasses and twigs on either side offered mute testimony of the passage of the men.

And the woman, Haarn reminded himself.

He loped through the forest, occasionally hearing his traveling companion pass through the brush behind and to the left. Broadfoot was nearly five times as big as Haarn, and his greater bulk wasn't built for stealth. That was why Haarn had gone alone. Still, Broadfoot remained nearby, ready to come to Haarn's aid at a moment's notice.

As he intersected then crossed the game trail the hunters followed, Haarn catalogued the different strides and mannerisms he could identify by the marks they left in the soft earth as well as their passage through the brush.

There were nine different members of the party. Two of the eight men were heavy and tall. Haarn judged that by the length of their strides. They were also confident, and he knew that because they were consistently in the lead. They also had similar mannerisms, which marked them as brothers or perhaps students of the same teacher.

The woman was interesting. She moved confidently,

but she seemed to stay in a position that sometimes placed her apart from the eight men in the party. Her stride was long, and when Haarn measured it, he guessed that she was about his height and weight. She was also the one who left the least in the way of marks to point to her passage. Haarn knew she would be dangerous.

One of the men carried pipeweed, meaning that he seldom traveled in the woodland areas far off the beaten path. Anyone who spent time in the woods knew better than to carry pipeweed, perfumes, or soap because it stood out against the forest scents.

The other five hunters showed varying degrees of familiarity with the forest. They were accomplished hunters—for city dwellers. One of them had a habit of stopping occasionally to check their back trail, always starting off the next step with his right foot. Another had a slight limp. Still another continually marked the trail by twisting small branches together so he could find it easily. Haarn untwisted the branches as he passed so the trees would grow as Silvanus and their nature had intended.

In only a few more strides he was close enough to hear them.

With the deepening night falling full bloom across the forest, the light of the lanterns carried by the hunting party stood out sharply. The golden glow didn't travel far and was partially masked by the trees and brush.

Haarn slid his scimitar silently free of its sheath. The blade was blackened so that it wouldn't reflect the light that lanced through the trees in places. He crouched lower to the ground, his eyes moving restlessly, but he kept moving forward.

"It's getting too dark," one man said. "You keep hunting in these woods this late at night, you're only asking for trouble."

"These damned wolf scalps are worth gold, Ennalt," another man said, "but not so much that we can be lollygagging about this piece of business."

"Aye," another man agreed. "Forras has the right of it,

I'm thinking. Better to be into this bloody work quickly and out of it just as quickly."

"It's only a little farther to Evenstar Lake," the woman reasoned. Her voice was soft and low, holding a throaty rasp that made it sound deep. "We can camp there for the night and take up the hunt again in the morning."

Less than fifty feet from his quarry, knowing Broadfoot would slow as well and await his signal, Haarn turned to the right and went up the slope of the wooded hill. He stayed low so the hunters gathered in the brush below couldn't skyline him against the star-filled night. As he moved, he caught brief glimpses of the eight men and the woman as they clustered within the small glen below.

Scimitar still in hand, Haarn sat on his haunches beside a thick-boled maple tree and watched the group.

"Me," another man said, "I'm all for bed. The sun will come up early enough tomorrow and we can set to hunting them damned wolves again."

"They're nocturnal feeders," still another said. "I'm telling you, with or without that enchanted charm the shepherd gave us, this is our best time of hunting wolves."

"It's also the most dangerous," Ennalt argued. "While we're hunting them, they can be hunting us." He was a small-built man who had a habit of lifting the lantern he carried and peering into the forest. "Especially that scar-faced bastard the shepherd's promising to pay the bonus for."

"We've killed nine of those wolves," one of the earlier speakers said. "I say we've done enough for the day—and the night—to warrant a rest."

Another man laughed. "You're just wanting to get next to that jug of elven wine, Tethys."

"And what of it?" Tethys snapped. "I'll drink the wine to replace the blood I've been donating to feed all these damned thirsty mosquitoes." He slapped at the back of his neck. "At least the bottle will numb some of the itching and put back some fluid into my body."

"That's what you've got water for," the woman replied evenly, but her voice held steel. "I won't abide any drunken fools on this mission."

" 'Mission,' she says," Forras said. He was the one with the limp. Even now as he stood in the glen, the man favored his weaker leg. "Spoken like she was a sellsword guarding the Assembly of Stars or Lord Herengar himself."

The woman met the man's gaze and he turned away.

"We were hired to kill wolves, Druz," Tethys said, "not to give our lives to some noble cause you might imagine up."

Haarn stared at the woman with interest. As solitary as his work and commitment was, he seldom saw others, and he saw women even less. He sometimes found them interesting, as his father had laughingly told him he would, but there was always the heartbroken side of his father that kept Haarn in check. Feelings between men and women, the elder Brightoak had pointed out during the time Haarn's education had touched upon the subject, were not as simple as the mating seasons that drew on animals. Liaisons between men and women were lasting things that Haarn had seen emulated between wolves, who tended to mate for life.

The woman was a few inches short of six feet, and her form was filled with womanly curves the leather armor she wore couldn't hide. Her red-gold hair was bound up behind her in an intricate knot, and the lantern light turned her beautiful features ruddy, though dirt and grime stained them. She carried a long bow slung over one shoulder, a long sword at her hip, knives in her knee-high, cracked leather boots, and a traveler's pack secured high on her back.

"Trust me," Tethys said, "this is a lot quicker work and will pay more handsomely than guarding some fat merchant's caravan from Alaghôn bound for Baldur's Gate, Calimport, or even Waterdeep."

Haarn turned the names over in his mind as he listened.

Baldur's Gate, Calimport, and Waterdeep were all famous cities of the Sword Coast known to him through stories he'd heard as a boy growing up under his father's tutelage. Ettrian Brightoak had been more socially driven than Haarn had turned out to be. Though he had no desire to go see those cities, thinking of them still fired his imagination.

He had yet to see even Alaghôn, the so-called Jewel of Turmish, and it lay within three days' travel of Morningstar Hollows where he spent much of his time. The idea of being in a place that housed so many people was at once exciting and terrifying.

Still, his father's descriptions of the Throne of Turmish, as the city was also known, held fascination, especially when Ettrian Brightoak waxed eloquently—an art Haarn had never acquired—about the history of the city that included stories of Anaglathos, the blue dragon that had ruled the city for a time, or of the Time of Troubles when Malar himself—also called the Stalker and the Beastlord—entered the Gulthmere Forest to destroy the Emerald Enclave.

"Gakhos, the shepherd," Tethys continued, "is a rich man, and he's drawn to vengeance. In my experience, a man drawn to avenge—even by proxy, which is what he hired us for—will pay until there is nothing left of his gold or his anger. We can kill a lot of wolves for the gold he's paying and not have to worry about taking one of those damned overland trips to the Sword Coast."

"Or maybe you're wanting to begin a new career as a sellsword aboard one of those new ships that are being outfitted for the Sea of Fallen Stars," another of the young hunters said. "Since the Serôsian War and the destruction of the Whamite Isles—not to mention the unleashing of the sahuagin throughout the Inner Sea—there's plenty of call for sailors that don't mind getting bloody."

"Mayhap you can even sign up to join the forces guarding the trade negotiations of Myth Nantar," another of the young hunters said. He was one of the two largest men in the group. If they weren't twins, they were at least brothers. "I hear that after pulling a tour of duty down in Myth Nantar, you can breathe the ocean waters just like the air itself."

"Standing here talking," Ennalt grumbled, "isn't going to put us any closer to our beds for the evening, or to hunting wolves, if that's what we're going to do."

The reminder pulled Haarn from his inclination to watch the hunting party rather than deal with it. Broadfoot shifted restlessly in the forest to Haarn's left, but the noise he made wasn't something the hunters in the group below would have noticed.

Haarn laid his scimitar across his knees, the flat of the blade resting easily, then cupped his hands before his mouth. He blew gently, making the sound of a bloodybeak, one of the small birds in the forest that fed on the mosquitoes that lived around Evenstar Lake. He hit all four notes perfectly, and a chorus of responses came from the darkness as nearby birds answered him, but Haarn knew Broadfoot would recognize his call and be alerted.

Whisper-quiet, Haarn stood and walked down the hillside toward the hunting party. His arrival startled them, stepping as he did from the trees into the circumference of light from the lanterns.

"Tymora watch over me," one of the men snarled as he turned to face Haarn. "What the hell is that?"

All of the men and the woman reached for their weapons, baring blades in a heartbeat. Two of the men lifted heavy crossbows and turned them toward Haarn.

"Leave these lands," Haarn ordered. He stood unafraid before them, certain that he could move even more quickly than the crossbowmen could pull the triggers on their weapons. The trick was to recognize when they were going to fire. "There will be no more wolf hunting."

"Says who?" one of the two big men demanded.

"If you continue hunting," Haarn promised emotionlessly, not thinking of the mother wolf he'd seen killed earlier, "I will hunt you, and I will slay you all before the sun rises again."

"Like hell you will," Tethys said. He pointed the long sword he wielded. "Shoot him!"

CHAPTER TWO

Druz Talimsir stared at the wraith that had stepped from the dark forest around the party of wolf hunters. She gripped her long sword tightly in her fist as the men around her moved, thronging out in a semicircle to confront the man. At least she thought the forest warrior was a man.

An elf, she corrected herself, spotting one pointed ear a moment later.

The elf stood a few inches short of six feet and possessed a slender build. Still, his wide shoulders and deep chest promised strength, though he didn't pack a lot of weight. Most professional sellswords would have looked at the slender figure standing before them with never a qualm about a physical confrontation.

Druz had experienced several combat situations during her years as a mercenary. Though she was only twenty-five, she'd battled orc hordes and bugbears that had tried to take merchant convoys she'd signed on to protect. During the last year, before an injury in Alaghôn had separated her from the mercenary group she'd signed on with for the previous three years, she'd fought in the Serôsian War.

That war was a year past, but employment for mercenaries willing to battle the pirates, the shark-worshiping sahuagin now freed throughout the sea, and the nations that battled each other for shipping lanes, salvage from the battles above and below the sea, and trading rights with the newly re-discovered city of Myth Nantar burgeoned. It was one of those battles between shipping guilds that had drawn Druz to Alaghôn.

Studying the slim elf before her, Druz felt certain that her luck had completely soured. That man, dressed as he was in hide armor, his wild black hair pulled back to lay on his shoulders and festooned with sprigs of wood and blossoms of a half-dozen plants, might look like a vagabond or a madman, but the mercenary felt certain she knew what the man was. Trying to kill him would amount to a death wish.

"Feather the damn dandelion-sipper and be done with it," Tethys growled again. "I won't have any man threatening to kill me."

But that won't stop you from threatening to kill another man, will it? Druz mused.

The crossbowmen stood on either side of Druz. One of them was Ennalt and the other was Kord—brothers who had signed on with the ragtag outfit. Both of them held their weapons pointed at the forest warrior.

"Don't," Druz commanded.

In her days she'd sometimes served as a unit commander. She'd learned how to pitch her voice so that it garnered instant respect and attention. Kord hesitated and raised the crossbow to aim into the star-filled sky.

"To hell with that," Tethys growled. "Feather that bastard, Ennalt."

Ennalt's trigger knuckle whitened as the man took up the crossbow's slack.

Without hesitation, Druz swung around, bringing her arm up in a powerful sweep that knocked the crossbow up. The catgut string slid across the stock with a short hiss, and the stubby quarrel took flight.

Arvis, Kord's younger brother by a year, and more impulsive than his older brother who was known for his steadfast pace and unwavering commitment, closed on the forest warrior. Arvis stood head and shoulders taller than the forest warrior and normally brimmed with over-confidence anyway. Facing the much smaller man, Arvis showed no hesitation at all as he whirled his battle-axe effortlessly before him.

"Don't fret over this one," Arvis boomed in his deep voice. "I have him." He stepped forward, his grin lighted by the flickering lanterns in the hands of the men around him.

The forest warrior's attention never seemed to break from the men in front of him. His dark green eyes, glimmering in the lantern light somewhat like a cat's, regarded Druz curiously. His head cocked slightly, as if he didn't notice the way the bigger man closed on him. The forest warrior's scimitar stayed mostly out of sight beside his back leg.

"Don't kill him," Druz pleaded. "He's little more than a boy."

Arvis, she knew, would resent her deeply for the comment, but if it would help save his life, she didn't care. Arvis and Kord, though both blooded in skirmishes around Alaghôn and some of the cities along the western coast of the Sea of Fallen Stars, hadn't yet seen twenty.

"Don't kill *him*?" Forras repeated, shifting on his bad leg. "Why, Arvis will break this little upstart in half."

Druz watched, feeling a chill like icy cat's paws kneading between her shoulders. She liked Arvis, though his aggressive nature made him somewhat hard to take.

Arvis made his situation even worse by not taking the threat the smaller man offered more seriously. He stepped in and casually feinted with the battle-axe.

Before he could pull back, the smaller man stepped in quickly, going to Arvis's left. Anticipating the big warrior's attempt to block with the battle-axe haft, the small man backhanded his opponent in the nose with his empty fist.

Yelping in pain, Arvis tried to swing around. Instead of keeping his feet planted and merely shifting, Arvis lifted his left foot. The small man kicked the raised foot from under the bigger man as if the feat were nothing.

Off-balance, trying desperately to recover, Arvis fell to the ground, miraculously managing to land on his knee. His opponent walked to his side without apparent haste, but the effort was amazingly quick. Before Arvis could move, the warrior in hide armor kicked the bigger man's back foot, causing the younger man to sprawl out. Arvis toppled onto his outstretched hands, trapping his battle-axe against the ground under his own weight.

In a few seemingly effortless moves, the forest warrior had Arvis stretched out and the scimitar's blade against the young mercenary's throat like he was a pig awaiting the butcher's bloodletting. Coldly, the forest warrior glared at the other members of the wolf-hunting party, letting them all know that Arvis's life was forfeit if they made any sudden moves.

"Don't kill him," Druz repeated.

Kord started forward.

"If you value your brother's life, Kord," Druz said in a low, anxious voice as she glanced at the big man, "you'll stay back."

Kord hesitated.

"If you force him to deal with you," Druz went on, "he'll kill Arvis without blinking an eye. He'll have one less enemy to face."

Kord plucked the heavy quarrel from the crossbow and tossed it to the ground. He dropped the bow next and showed his empty hands.

"That's my brother," he croaked in a voice that broke. "If you'll allow it, I'll have him back in one piece. If you harm him in any way, know that I won't rest until one of us is dead. I swear that by Helm the Vigilant, god of protectors and guardians."

Arvis trembled, evidently trying to figure out a way to rescue himself.

"Stay," the forest warrior commanded. He pressed the scimitar against the younger man's throat meaningfully.

"If he's meaning to kill us," Tethys grated, "then we're better off working together. He can't get us all."

The forest warrior turned his dark green eyes on the mercenary leader. "Count up after the dust has settled."

No one moved.

Tethys swore black oaths, but he stayed where he was.

For all his mercenary experience, Druz knew that Tethys wasn't an overly courageous man. He was smart on a battlefield, and that made him a successful sellsword.

Making a decision, knowing no one else in the party knew for sure what the forest warrior was or whom he represented, Druz sheathed her sword then unbuckled the belt. She dropped it on the ground, then stepped forward with her empty hands held up before her.

The forest warrior watched her approach but said nothing.

"Clear a path to him, girl," Forras said. "You're blocking whatever chance one of us might have to get to him should it come to that."

Druz ignored the command. Part of the reason the forest warrior allowed her to move in was because she would serve as a human shield.

"Who are you?" Druz asked.

The forest warrior regarded her silently.

"What do you want?" Druz tried again.

"No more wolf hunting," the forest warrior replied, "and I want the scalps you've collected so far. Those that died will not be desecrated further."

"No," Tethys disagreed, placing a hand on the bag at his waist where the wolf scalps were stored. "We're keeping the scalps."

Druz spoke to the mercenaries without turning around or taking her eyes from the forest warrior. "You're going to have to give him the scalps."

"Are you insane?" Forras demanded. "Without those scalps we won't be able to collect our bounty."

"If you don't give him the scalps," Druz said in a measured voice, "he'll kill us, and you won't be able to collect your bounty."

"Why would he kill us?" Ennalt demanded, exasperated. "We don't even know this man." He paused. "Do you know him, Druz?"

"No," Druz answered. "I don't know him . . . but I know what he is."

She met the forest warrior's gaze boldly. Despite her fear of him, and the respect she had for what she guessed he was capable of, she wasn't going to flinch away from him. She wouldn't give him that; she gave no man that.

"He's one man," Tethys objected. "Even if he slays Arvis, there are eight of us."

"I don't want my brother killed," Kord said. "If you do something stupid to get him slain, I'll kill you, Tethys."

"Eight of us isn't enough," Druz said, "and he's not alone."

Warily, the men carrying lanterns moved them so the bull's-eye beams swept the trees around the glen. A wolf bayed in the distance, yipping at the moon that was high in the sky.

"I don't see anyone," Tethys replied.

"You won't see anyone until it's too late," Druz said.

She recalled the tales her blacksmith father had told her of men like the one standing so coolly in front of her with his scimitar at Arvis's throat.

"Who are you?" Tethys demanded of the forest warrior.

"This night," the man said quietly, "I'm a protector of the wolves you people would slay to line your palms with gold."

"He's a druid," Druz said. "One of the Emerald Enclave."

Her announcement started a quick chorus of conversation between the other mercenaries. Arvis, eyes straining in their sockets, looked at the man holding him captive with new—and perhaps fear-filled—respect.

Everyone in Turmish knew of the Emerald Enclave and the druids who filled the organization's ranks. Despite the power that the various cities wielded along the Turmish coastline fronting the Sea of Fallen Stars as well as the Vilhon Reach, no one did anything involving the land without the consent of the Emerald Enclave. The druids' first order of business was to preserve nature, and if that meant no civilization could invade pristine, sylvan glens or wooded areas that could be harvested by loggers, that was what it meant.

Tethys spat and growled a curse that offended even Druz, as hardened as she was to the ways of mercenary men and battle.

"Is that right?" he asked the forest warrior. "Are you a druid?"

"I won't allow the killing of any more wolves," the man replied.

"You can't stop us," Forras said.

The forest warrior turned his deep green eyes on the man. The moonlight threw emerald sparks from them.

Druz acted immediately, seeing the druid's left hand twitch. She shoved Forras away. The man stumbled when he had to unexpectedly shift all his weight to his weak leg. He turned to Druz, lifting his sword threateningly.

"You damned fool!" Druz snapped.

"Are you siding with him, then . . . ?" Forras's voice trailed off when he spotted the long, thin wooden dart quivering in the trunk of the tree he'd been standing in front of only a moment before.

"He would have killed you," Druz said, glancing over her shoulder at the forest warrior. "He still might." She studied the elf's hand, looking for a telltale sign that he had another dart ready.

Tethys took affront at the druid's action. "You'd kill a man over a *wolf?*" he demanded in disbelief.

"Yes," the druid replied. "The balance of nature must be kept. Your actions here unsettle that balance."

Forras regained his composure but stayed within reaching distance of Druz. "The wolves are feeding on the herd stock nearby."

"The cattle and sheep being raised here by the stockmen living in these lands have become—by rights—part of the wolves' prey," the elf druid said. "Those creatures, brought in by farmers, unsettle the balance of these lands by grazing. The wolves only make the sharing of the land more equal."

Druz didn't agree, but she didn't offer her opinion either. Since the recent war, many countries and nations around the Sea of Fallen Stars had suffered. With so many ships lost to the sahuagin and pirates, trade had been bad. When countries didn't have goods for sale, they seldom brought in goods either.

What the farmers and shepherds brought in had become increasingly important to the well-being of the area. Now that Myth Nantar had been opened from its hiding place, many things were being rethought considering the Sea of Fallen Stars. Even fishermen struggled to feed their families, and those territories they traded with were constantly redrawn by the nations above water as well as those below.

"The cattle and sheep are more important than the wolves," Forras insisted.

The druid's eyes partially closed in anger then opened again. "You're a fool. Without the wolves to cut down the numbers of deer in the forests and through these lands, there would be little grass for the sheep and cattle. The deer would overpopulate this area in a matter of years."

"There are men who would bring the deer down if they ever reached such plentiful numbers," Tethys said. "They would be glad for the opportunity to fill their larders."

"Are there?" The druid cocked his head and his tone bordered on sarcasm. "I've often noticed that when a city man has to make a choice between hunting, killing, cleaning, and cooking his own meal, he'd rather sit in a tavern and order it already prepared on a plate."

"You've been to many civilized places, then?" Tethys asked.

"More than I care to remember," the druid replied. His blade never wavered from Arvis's throat. "I will give you until morning to get out of this forest. After that, I will track you down and kill you as you have tracked down and killed the wolves."

"The balance you're seeking to protect is false, druid," Druz said. "We seek a wolf that has developed a fondness for human flesh."

The druid shook his head slowly and carefully, without any emotion. "I don't care. A wolf will hunt those that hunt it."

"This wolf attacks children, druid." Druz made her

voice hard and challenging. "Is that the kind of beast you would protect?"

"Children are lost every day. That is part of nature's balance. Only the strong survive."

"The strong," Druz agreed, "and the clever." She paused for the briefest moment, knowing her decision, but not knowing how the druid would respond. "I won't suffer to let that creature live. I saw three of the children who were mauled by the wolf. They are neither strong nor clever. That's why the wolf has singled them out."

At Druz's side, Kord shifted nervously, anticipating the scimitar's stroke that would open his brother's throat.

"Damn it, woman," Kord snarled anxiously.

The druid's eyes remained locked on Druz's, and for a moment she thought he was so cold and intent that her words wouldn't touch him.

Druz placed her hands on her hips, only inches from the hilts of the throwing daggers she had hidden under her leather armor behind her back. If the druid walked away, she intended to try to kill him. Maybe killing the other wolves they'd encountered hadn't been on her agenda, but slaying the one they'd come to find definitely was.

The time passed almost unbearably.

Druz was acutely conscious of the small sounds in the forest around them. She couldn't help wondering what kinds of creatures might be there, and if they were under the druid's thrall. Warriors who lived outside forests and drank in taverns told horrible stories about the vindictive ways and practices of druids in general and the Emerald Enclave in particular.

"One wolf?" The druid spoke softly, his attention riveted on Druz.

"Yes." She held his gaze full measure.

"He has a pack at his heels," Tethys said.

"But there's no evidence that any wolf except for the one has been part of the attacks," Druz said. Tethys was striving to keep the scalps they'd taken, as well as freeing up the way to more. "One wolf."

"Has this wolf harmed any of your kith or kin?" the druid asked.

Druz considered the question, knowing it would be easy to lie, but she felt certain that somehow the druid would know. She'd never been that accomplished at lying.

"No."

"You hunt this wolf for gold," the druid stated.

"That's not the reason," Druz replied. "I saw those children. Their lives will never be the same. No matter what else happens to them, they will live with fear. I believe the wolf needs killing. Perhaps the wolf's death will give them some measure of peace."

The druid cocked his head slightly. "There is more."

"I gave my word to the shepherd when I took his gold," Druz said, not knowing if the druid would even understand the concept of payment for services.

"One wolf?" the druid said.

"Yes."

"Do you know which wolf it is?"

"He's full grown, starting to age. He has an old wound on the side of his muzzle." Druz touched the right side of her face, dragging a finger from the corner of her eye to the corner of her mouth. "It was made by a blade—"

"Or a trap," the druid suggested. "The shepherds and stockmen put out traps. A few years ago, they were successful with them, but wolves are clever and patient. They soon learned how to trip the traps then take the bait."

"Perhaps," Druz agreed, because she didn't know and because agreeing with the theory was the easiest course to pursue. "At any rate, the scars left by the wound still show, and white hair has grown from it."

"I will kill the wolf," the druid stated simply. "All of you can leave the forest."

"The hell we can," Tethys blustered. "The man who hired us expects to see proof that we carried out our assignment."

"I will kill the wolf," the druid repeated. "Not because you say it is necessary, but because the wolf may teach the rest of his pack to start hunting humans."

"You'll protect people?" Forras asked, gazing at the elf druid in open distrust.

"Not people," the druid admitted. "The wolves. If the wolf that has done this teaches his pack to yearn for human blood, they won't live long. Warriors will hunt them out of fear, or if the gold is right. There could be good traits—size, strength—that the wolf leader and his pack could pass on to the next generation if they're allowed to live. I won't have that chance lost if I can prevent it."

Tethys and Forras cursed belligerently.

"Don't act like you're doing us a damn favor," Tethys snarled.

"It would be easier for me," the druid stated, "to kill all of you than to kill the wolf."

The lantern light flickered in the silence that followed the elf's words.

Druz knew the warriors among the group would have a hard time accepting the challenge that the druid's mere presence offered, much less the sting left by the elf's words.

"What will it be?" the druid asked.

The warriors shifted.

Arvis spoke next, his voice hollow and filled with fear. "Kord, I am tiring." His blood seeped slowly down the druid's scimitar. The druid held his position.

"Let him go after the wolf," Kord said.

"You don't speak for all of us," Forras said.

Kord turned to the smaller man, who wasn't small at all. "I will in this matter, or I will stand with the druid."

"Against your own?" Tethys asked. "I've fought with you, Kord—you and your brother. I can't believe that you would—"

"If we live," Kord interrupted, "we'll have the chance to fight together again."

"He won't kill Arvis," Tethys replied, glaring at the druid. "He won't dare. He knows we'll track him down."

"Track a druid?" Druz said. The tone of her voice mocked them. "I've been told that even rangers can't track druids through their homelands." She took a step toward Tethys. "He will kill Arvis."

"You're afraid of his words," Forras accused.

"Only a fool wouldn't be afraid of the promises the druid has made tonight," Druz said. "Kord and I will side with the druid."

"Traitors!" Tethys snarled. "All we have to do is stick together and this dandelion-sipper will back down."

Something large shifted in the forest at the tail of Tethys' words. The men looked behind him, turning slowly.

Though Druz felt relatively safe standing in front of the druid, the skin across the back of her neck tightened and prickled, and it felt like ice water ran down her back.

A huge brown bear followed its nose from the brush at the back of the clearing. The animal looked ponderous and heavy, but Druz knew the mud-splattered brown pelt covered rolling muscle.

Once, when she'd been in Chondath—protecting, under protest, a shipment of exotic wines bound for the Crying Claw—Druz had seen a bear and a bull fight to the death. She'd felt certain the bull would easily disembowel its opponent, but she was amazed by the speed and power of the bear. As it had turned out, the bear had beaten the bull as well as a pride of war dogs that had been loosed on it afterward.

The druid's bear growled, and the barking, howling sound echoed through the forest. It surged to its hind legs effortlessly, standing almost twelve feet tall. Druz guessed that the animal might weigh a ton.

Cocking its head, the bear seemed to glare at Tethys in particular. Its black lips twitched back from fangs white as pearls. Massive claws glinted dully in the lantern light.

Tethys flinched and stepped back involuntarily.

"I already have someone who stands with me," the druid stated quietly.

The bear roared again, and birds settled in the trees for the night took flight around them, daring the darkness rather than stay in the vicinity of the great creature.

"I will go now to kill the wolf," the druid said. "If I find you here in the morning, I will kill you as well." He drew the scimitar from Arvis's throat and slung the blood onto the dirt.

Almost completely exhausted, Arvis collapsed to the ground. Kord started forward, but Druz stopped him, catching his arm with one hand.

"Wait," she urged quietly. "Arvis is still alive. Work to keep him that way."

"How do we know you'll keep your word about killing the wolf, druid?" Forras demanded.

"Because I gave my word." The druid halted at the clearing's edge, almost out of sight in the shadows. "Just as I give my word that I will kill you if you're still in this forest in the morning."

"Your word isn't good enough." It wasn't until after she'd spoken the words that Druz realized how barefaced they sounded.

The forest seemed to grow still around her. The druid stared at her. Druz stayed ready to move, realizing that she was trapped between the elf and the bear. Her throat felt cottony and dry.

"You doubt me," the druid stated flatly.

"The shepherd who retained our services," Druz said quietly, "isn't a man who's going to be easily satisfied. His oldest son was horribly disfigured by the wolf's attack. Even with clerics and healers, it's going to be years before the boy is returned to his full health. The shepherd wants revenge for that."

"This is not about revenge," the druid said.

"That's what I was paid for."

Druz held her head up defiantly. She stepped toward the druid.

Arvis glanced around quickly then pushed himself along the ground as if afraid the druid would punish him first. He stayed down as he moved.

Druz kept walking, closing in on the druid. He flicked his eyes past her warily, looking to see if the others would come to her aid. Druz wasn't surprised when they didn't. The bear was easily the biggest she'd ever seen.

"I'm coming with you," Druz said.

Swift as a bird on a wing, the druid brought his scimitar up to Druz's throat. She steeled herself, stopping her immediate response to draw one of the knives hidden behind her back. She thought she might even have had a chance at blocking the scimitar, but she knew she couldn't allow the confrontation to come to that. If it had, one of them would have been killed.

The blade lay coolly against her neck but didn't bite into her flesh.

"You could kill me," Druz pointed out, knowing she was treading thin ice, "but if you did, perhaps you would rob my species of good traits for the next generation."

Even as she said that, she realized she might have thrown the druid's own beliefs back in his face too hard.

The druid cocked his head. "Perhaps . . . and perhaps there are traits in you that would be better weeded out to increase the longevity of your species."

"I'm coming with you," Druz repeated, though less forcefully than she had the first time.

"For the gold?" the druid asked.

"Because I want the wolf dead. I saw what it did to that child, and I know how I would feel if I was the boy's . . ." Druz swallowed hard. "You don't have a choice other than to let me go. The shepherd who hired us has deep pockets. His stock has done well, and the recent war in the Sea of Fallen Stars has insured that he gets the best prices for his livestock."

The druid waited, his eyes flicking to the other hunters.

"I can tell the shepherd that the wolf has been dealt with," Druz said. She swallowed hard and felt the scimitar's edge bite more deeply. "Otherwise, the shepherd may well fill these forests with hunters."

"It would be bad for the hunters," the druid promised.

Druz glared at him. "Could you kill them all?"

"Perhaps. Patience is its own reward, and I am very patient."

"You couldn't get them all," Druz pointed out. "Not before they did considerable damage to this area's wildlife. Besides hunting and killing wolves, they'd also be living off the land. If we didn't come back, the shepherd will put even more men into the hunt. Those men would wreak havoc in these forests. Is that what you want?"

The druid's eyes locked with hers for a time, and for just a moment, Druz thought her life was forfeit.

The scimitar flashed away from her neck, returning to the druid's side.

"Then come," the elf said. "Keep up, because I'm not going to wait on you."

"I need my gear," Druz protested.

Without another word, the druid turned and vanished into the forest.

Druz cursed, calling on Tyr to guide her and Mystra to watch over her as she foolishly followed her own sense of duty. She sprinted back to the group, snatched up her sword belt, then fisted her personal pack from the ground.

"You're a fool for going with him," Kord said as he helped his brother to his feet. "That man will cut your throat and feed you to the wolves we're hunting."

"He didn't kill your brother," Druz pointed out.

"He knew he would have the rest of us against him if he did." Kord's youthful pride wouldn't let him entirely accept the defeat he'd just been handed.

"From what I've heard about the Emerald Enclave," Druz said, settling the pack across her shoulders, "the druid would probably have made good on his threat to kill us all, even without the bear."

The bear, too, had disappeared back into the forest.

"Don't overlook the druid's generosity." Druz started for the clearing's edge.

"Then why are you going with him?" Kord asked.

"Because I have to."

"That's not it," Tethys put in. "Druz has heard the jingle of the shepherd's money bags. If she goes with the druid and brings back proof of the kill, she'll claim the bounty for herself."

"No," Druz said. "That's not what this is about for me."

Tethys laughed mirthlessly. "We'll see, girl, but if you try to cut us out of what's lawfully ours, I'll slit your throat myself."

26 • The Jewel of Turmish

Druz shrugged off the threat. She'd been around men like Tethys nearly all her life. In the next instant, she plunged into the forest, following the small, wiggling bushes that marked the druid's passage. She lengthened her stride, hoping to catch up.

CHAPTER THREE

Do do you think he has something worth taking, Cerril?"

Angry and paranoid, Cerril turned to the speaker, a small boy of about twelve—a year younger than Cerril. Before the other boy could move, Cerril cuffed his head.

"*Ow!*" the other boy complained, wrapping his fingers and palms around his head in case Cerril decided to try his luck again. He ducked and took a step back. All of them knew to expect violence when Cerril got upset.

"Whyn't you just announce to the world what we're after here?"

"I'm sorry," the younger boy said ruefully.

"If one of these sailors overhears a question like that," Cerril promised in a harsh whisper, "you're going to have to learn to breathe through your ears because he'll cut your throat for you."

"Not if we cut his throat first." The young boy took a handmade knife from his ragged breeches and dragged the ball of his thumb along the uneven blade's edge. Blood dotted his flesh and he licked at it with his pink tongue.

"Oh, yeah, Hekkel," one of the other boys sneered in a harsh whisper, "and how many throats have you cut this tenday? Or any other tenday? You still ain't killed that man your mama's taken up with this last month."

"Shut up!" Hekkel ordered, taking a small, defiant step forward.

Cerril cuffed the small boy on the head again, eliciting a cry of pain this time.

"Gods' blood, Cerril!" Hekkel cried out. "Stop hitting me."

A passing sailor from one of the ships docked in Alaghôn's harbor glanced over at them. He carried his duffel over his shoulder, a jug of wine in one hand, and had his other arm wrapped around the ample waist of a serving wench Cerril recognized from Elkor's Brazen Trumpet.

"Hey," the sailor grunted, coming to a halt and staring into the shadows of the alley where the seven boys took shelter from scrutiny. "What the Nine Hells are ye children doing out here at this time of night?"

"We're not damned children!" Cerril snapped.

He turned to confront the sailor. Anger burned along the back of his neck. His own mother, like Hekkel's, oft times lived with sailing men on leave from one ship or another that put up prolonged anchorage in Alaghôn's port. He'd never known his father.

The sailor laughed, already three sheets to the wind. The serving wench wasn't in much better shape.

"Ye're children," the sailor argued. "Maybe ye're mean, nasty, Cyric-blasted children, but ye're still children."

Cerril's knife leaped to his hand and he started forward. He was big for his age, almost as tall as the sailor and easily as heavy with the broad shoulders and thick chest he'd gotten from the man who'd sired him. He'd also gotten the terrible temper that filled him now. At least, that was what his mother told him when she yelled at him.

"Ye going to come at me with that little tooth, boy?" the sailor taunted. He released the woman and stepped away from her, then drew the cutlass at his side. Moonlight silvered the blade. "If'n ye do, it'll be the last thing ye do this night, I'll warrant ye that."

Cerril stared at the thick blade and felt cold fear twist through his bowels. In stories he told the others in his pack, he'd confronted grown men with weapons before and bested them. Of course, in reality he'd only dealt with men too drunk to defend themselves.

"Oh, leave off these children, Wilf," the serving wench said. "They're just out for a bit of fun. Boys playing at being fierce men, that's all."

The sailor treated Cerril and his mates to another black scowl. He cursed and spat, and the spittle splashed against the cobblestones near enough to Cerril's feet to make him take an involuntary step back.

Cerril bumped into Two-Fingers, who was called that because he'd lost two fingers in a fishing accident. Two-Fingers's sour stench filled Cerril's nose for a moment. Two-Fingers was the only one of them who lived on the streets and truly had no place to go.

"Well, I've got some words for boys playin' at bein' men," the sailor warned. "I've dealt with a few cutpurses an' other assorted rabble in other ports, an' I'm not a man to trouble over trouble for long. An' from the looks of this pack of wild apes, trouble is all they're after."

"Come on," the serving wench urged, pulling at the sailor's arm and setting him to weaving slightly. "Do you really want to spend tonight explaining to the Watch how you came to kill a few of these boys over some unkind words? Or do you want to come up to my room and amuse me for a few hours?"

The sailor grinned. "Since I got me druthers, we'll seek out the amusement, fair flower." He took a faltering step and rejoined the woman, slipping his arm with the wine jug around her. Then he turned a baleful eye on Cerril and the other boys. "But mark me words, ye scurvy lot. If'n ye cause me any more grief this night, why I'll slice ye and dice ye from wind to water, an' I'll use what's left of ye for chum to catch me breakfast."

Cerril swallowed hard, but he made himself put on a brave front. If he ever showed how scared he sometimes got, he knew the other boys would desert him or find a new leader. While he held that position, he'd not always treated them fairly or well.

A young boy with a lamp he'd probably stolen from a

ship or a lax harbor resident called out an offer to guide the sailor and the serving wench through the shadows to their destination. The sailor turned the boy's offer down with a snarling bit of vituperation as the serving wench led him away.

"Good sirs," the boy with the lantern said again, approaching Cerril and his group, "mayhap you'd like a lantern to light your way home this night. For only—"

Then the lantern's cheery glow washed over Cerril and the others, drawing their pale, wan features from the alley's shadows. Cerril grinned and took a threatening step forward, his knife glinting in the lantern light.

"By the pits!" the boy exclaimed, backpedaling a short distance before turning around and running away. The lantern swung wildly at the end of his arm, threading shadows across the two- and three-story buildings fronting the harbor.

"Well," Two-Fingers drawled, "at least you can still scare the local peasants."

Cerril turned to face the other boy. Even large as he was, Two-Fingers still towered over him. Cerril had always disliked that about the other boy, but Two-Fingers's size had allowed him to step into some of the seamier dives around Alaghôn and purchase the occasional bucket of ale the group sometimes shared.

"I can scare more than that," Cerril warned, still holding the knife.

A hint of worry crossed Two-Fingers's face.

"You'd better say it, Two-Fingers," Cerril ordered, the back of his neck burning at the anger that swirled inside him. "You'd better say I can scare more than that. Otherwise I'm going to make sure you only got two fingers on the other hand as well."

That threat of further crippling made Two-Fingers step back into the shadows. After he'd lost the half of his hand while working with his fisherman father, Two-Fingers had been thrown out of the house. There were eight other kids in the household to feed, and having a cripple around wasn't going to improve the family's lot any.

Cerril took a step, going after the other boy. "Say it, Two-Fingers," he ordered again. "Say it or I'll make you sorry."

Two-Fingers backed up against the wall, trapped between a pile of refuse and a nearly full slop bucket from the bathhouse on one side of the alley. He swallowed hard.

"You can," Two-Fingers whispered hoarsely. "You can scare more than that."

His eyes flicked nervously from Cerril's face to the knife in his hand.

Cerril knew the other boys gazed on in naked excitement. Nothing held their interest more than violence, especially when it was directed at someone else.

"Cerril," Kerrin called out in an anxious whisper. "There's your sister."

The other boy's words drew Cerril's attention. He gave Two-Fingers a quick, cold smile.

"Just you mark my words, Two-Fingers. I'm not going to put up with being questioned."

"I won't question you again, Cerril. I swear."

Two-Fingers touched his maimed hand to his chest. Most of his pride and spirit had gone with those missing fingers, and his father kicking him out of the house had robbed the tall boy of whatever hadn't been taken by the accident.

"If you do," Cerril said, unable to leave it alone, "you'll be back to hiring yourself out to them old sailors."

Two-Fingers's face flushed with rage and shame. All that had been a year ago, before Cerril had accepted him into their group. No one ever spoke of that time again. At least, not to Two-Fingers's face. Cerril didn't allow it.

In the beginning, Two-Fingers had been deathly loyal to Cerril for letting him join the gang. It meant he got to eat without selling himself. The other boys stole food from their own homes and brought it to him in the streets. Cerril had established that routine as well. As hard as he was on them, Cerril also took care of them.

"Cerril," Kerrin called again. He waved frantically. "It's your sister."

Blowing out an irritated breath, Cerril turned from Two-Fingers and quickly joined Kerrin at the front of the alley again. He pressed himself against the wall and hid in the shadows.

"So do you think this man has gold?" Hekkel asked again.

Cerril resisted the impulse to cuff the younger boy again. Hekkel's thoughts invariably turned to gold. Before he'd been slain by a thief, Hekkel's father had been a jeweler in Alaghôn's Merchant District. When Hekkel's father was alive, the family lived in a fine house, and members of the Assembly of Stars—the freely elected ruling body of Turmish—had shopped there. That was six years ago, and Hekkel's family had discovered that the city wasn't generous to widows and half-grown children. Hekkel remained convinced that gold could change someone's life. He was living proof that not having it could change lives, too.

As for himself, Cerril knew that having gold only changed a person's life as long as that person had gold and spent it freely. Gold seldom came his way, but he took the coppers and the occasional silver without complaint. Unfortunately, coppers and the occasional silver spent quickly.

"Do you see your sister?" Hekkel asked from behind Cerril.

"Yes," Cerril growled. "Now shut up before I have Two-Fingers bust your nose for you." He said the last because he knew it would give Two-Fingers back some of his self-respect and standing among the group.

"Just let me know when you need it done, Cerril," Two-Fingers offered. "I'll smash the little bastard's nose good and proper."

Cerril ignored them, seeking out Imareen at the back of Elkor's Brazen Trumpet just across the broad cobblestone street leading down to the docks and shipyards. His sister, fathered by another sailor than the one who had fathered Cerril, stood limned in the shadow of the alley behind the tavern.

Imareen's thin, straight figure rarely drew even the drunkest sailor's eye, but she was one of the fastest serving wenches in the city. She'd inherited her lashing tongue from their mother, and her skill with verbal abuse was legendary. Cooks and merchants feared her, and the small bit of power given her by Elkor himself sometimes went to her head.

But Elkor didn't increase her tenday draw at the tavern, and all the other serving wenches at the Brazen Trumpet got large tips. When Cerril had suggested that he and his band would reward her for pointing out potential robbery victims, Imareen had hesitated only momentarily. They'd been working together the last four months.

Imareen had let them know that a man—alone, deeply in his cups, and possessing at least a little in the way of gold or silver—was at one of the tables nearly an hour ago.

An hour, Cerril thought in quick anticipation, is more than enough time for a single drinker to get drunk.

Covering his excitement, Cerril whispered, "Stay here," to the others, then stepped out of the alley and crossed the street.

A dwarven wagon driver rattled across the street from around the nearest corner before Cerril got halfway across. Cerril had to scramble to avoid being hit. The stench of the sweating horses filled his nose.

The dwarf didn't mark his wagon with a lantern or a torch. That, plus the fact that the dwarf whipped the horses and cursed at them, led the young thief to believe the dwarf was about a bit of foul business as well.

The black markets throughout Alaghôn had increased since the Inner Sea War had taken place, and Cerril had occasionally managed to hire his group to hard-knuckled merchants as lookouts. The pay for the work they did was meager, but it also marked targets they considered and sometimes went back to rob.

Cerril's heart beat rapidly with anticipation as he joined Imareen at the back of the tavern. There was nothing better than being a thief in Alaghôn. At least, not to his way of thinking.

"Hurry, you damned child," Imareen chided.

That was their mother's voice, Cerril knew. The tone and the words rankled him, but he managed to ignore them for the moment. He jogged to the back of the tavern and joined his sister.

The fragrant aroma of pipeweed clung to Imareen's hair and clothing. Cerril enjoyed the smell, and when he had coins enough, he often indulged in the habit himself. Of course, if his mother found his small store of pipeweed she kept it for herself, chiding him for experimenting with such a vice—and she said all that with a plume of smoke wreathing her head.

Imareen emptied a slop bucket onto the alley. The splashing noise of the liquid striking the hardpan startled a cat rummaging through a pile of refuse behind the tavern. The feline leaped into the air and dashed up the sagging fence marking the alley's end. Despite her authority with the cooks and the merchants, Elkor still expected her to empty out the privies.

The stench of the slop filled the alley, turning the still air thick and tickling Cerril's nose into a sneeze.

"Listen to you," Imareen groused. "Honking like a goose and making noise enough to wake the dead."

Her foot remained in the back door so it wouldn't close on her. The rumble of men's voices and the ribald strain of dwarven drinking songs echoed out into the alley. Cerril doubted anyone inside the tavern could have heard him sneeze.

"Do you want to talk," he asked, "or do you want to divvy whatever we find in some man's pouch?"

Imareen didn't even hesitate. "Divvy, and you'd better not short me. I'll know if you do."

Cerril nodded. Both times he'd tried to make off with part of his sister's cut, she *had* known. If she could have made merchants realize the power she had to know a lie when she heard it, she could have made a large stipend. However, her unnatural skill seemed only to work with Cerril.

"Who's the man?" he asked.

"A stranger."

He said, "Strangers are good."

"I know, Cerril. I know what I'm doing."

Cerril didn't rise to the old argument that existed between them. Since she was four years older than he was, she'd always told him what to do and not to do, but she knew since he'd taken to making his way in the shadows that the balance between them had shifted. She just didn't want to act like it had.

"Give me some measure of respect in this," Imareen said.

"I do," Cerril said.

He sorely wished that cuffing his sister would work as well as it did with the members of his gang, but Imareen would never stand for it. There was a good likelihood that she'd get up in the middle of the night to stick a knife between his ribs and tell their mother that Malar the Stalker, god of marauding beasts and bloodlust, had taken him in the night.

"He's settling his business with Elkor now," Imareen said. "He'll be out shortly."

"Have you seen his purse?"

Avarice gleamed in Imareen's muddy brown eyes. "It looks small, but it's heavy."

"Small isn't good." Still, Cerril couldn't keep a faint smile from his lips.

"Heavy is good, and this man works to keep his purse well hidden."

"Has anyone else noticed him?" Cerril asked.

"No. No one's noticed him."

"You're sure?"

"Just the same," Cerril said, "keep an eye out. If it looks like someone's following him, wave one of the tavern lanterns in the window."

"I will."

Cerril nodded. "Let's have a look at him."

Imareen opened the tavern door and stepped aside. She followed Cerril inside then led him through the small larder behind the Brazen Trumpet's bar.

The tavern was small and ordinary. Besides the heavy,

scarred bar that ran the breadth of the building, odd-sized tables and unmatched chairs took up the floor space. Nets hanging from the ceiling held colored bottles in bright greens, blues, and dulled browns and rubies. All the liquor had been drained from the bottles, and they'd been re-filled with water. Hundreds of seashells and smooth stones joined the bottles. The nets made for a colorful display. An ensorcelled shark hung above the fireplace. It was nearly as long as a tall man, and the lipless mouth was open in a fearful pose.

Men lounged in the chairs around the tables. Most of them were professional seamen, sprinkled with a few mercenaries. The two groups sat apart from each other. Maybe they'd sailed the same ship across the Sea of Fallen Stars, but each looked down their noses at the other.

"There," Imareen whispered in Cerril's ear.

Cerril studied the man at the bar. Elkor was trying to chat the man up, offering to rent him one of the rooms above the tavern for the night. The man simply shook his head.

He wasn't a local. Cerril knew that from his clothing. While most Turmishan men wore square-cut beards and layered clothing against the humid heat that sweltered the Vilhon Reach, the victim Imareen had marked had a ragged appearance. His clothing was disreputable and he hadn't shaved in days. The man's emaciated form resembled a bag of bones shoved into a burlap bag. He was in his middle years, but his infirmity robbed him of any dregs of youth. Hollow-eyed and pale, he habitually raked his gaze over the tavern crowd.

"What has he been doing since he's been here?" Cerril whispered to Imareen.

"Drinking," his sister answered. "Drinking like a man possessed. And writing."

"Writing?" Cerril pondered that. Writing was usually a merchant's domain, keeping records of things sold and purchased, but writing was something mages also did. "Writing what?"

"I don't know," Imareen admitted. "I read about as well as you do."

Cerril couldn't read at all. Learning that skill had never proven important. He'd had a strong back, and now he had quick hands and an agile mind.

"He was writing in a book," Imareen added.

Elkor fussed over the price he was exacting from the man.

Cerril raked the man with his gaze. He saw no book. "Where's the book?"

"I don't know." Imareen glanced down at him. "Are you afraid?"

Cerril didn't answer.

"People are always claiming to have stolen things from mages," Imareen said. "Why, you could make a name for yourself with just one theft."

"Those are stories," Cerril insisted.

"All of them can't be."

Frowning, Cerril said, "Stealing from mages isn't smart business. I don't plan on living out the rest of my life as a toad. Or worse."

"It might be an improvement."

Cerril shot her a look. "If he is a mage and he questions me, I'll tell him that you pointed him out."

Imareen paled beneath her freckles. "I don't think he's a mage."

"I hope not."

The man settled his bill with Elkor, who looked after the man longingly. Evidently the tavern owner had gotten a good look at the heft of the man's coin as well.

"He's leaving," Imareen said.

"I can see that."

"Well, if you don't hurry you might lose him."

Cerril hesitated for just an instant.

"We don't have anything to show for the night," Imareen pointed out. "If we don't get something, we could be starting a trend of bad luck."

I know, Cerril thought.

Bad luck was a recognized force in a port city. Ships sailed with luck, and any ship branded with ill luck was quickly noticed and just as quickly abandoned by merchants as well as sailors. Cerril believed in luck, always striving for the good and avoiding the bad.

The man walked through the Brazen Trumpet's double doors and out onto the street.

Coming to a decision, Cerril started forward. "Remember about the lantern," he whispered to his sister.

"I will. And don't try to cheat me, Cerril."

Turning, Cerril rushed back through the storeroom and out into the alley. He stayed within the tavern's shadows, stepping out briefly at the corner so that Hekkel and Two-Fingers could see him. He pointed at the man walking up the sloped street leading away from the Brazen Trumpet.

Two-Fingers nodded.

Hekkel immediately stepped into the shadows on the other side of the street and took up the first leg of the pursuit.

Cerril remained on his side of the street. He and Hekkel were the two most skilled at following someone through the city in the shadows. He glanced back at the Brazen Trumpet but didn't see Imareen put in an appearance at one of the windows. Carefully, his breath tight at the back of his throat and in his lungs, Cerril continued following the man.

Their prey seemed content to stay within Alaghôn's dockyards. The man stopped occasionally to stare into the windows of a closed shop that caught his interest. His destination turned out to be Stonebottom's Inn, one of the first structures ever built along the Turmish coastline. Back in those days, the port city had only been an avaricious gleam in a founding father's eye.

Stonebottom's was meager and small, cobbled together from ballast rocks brought over in merchant ships. A lit candle in a glass tube dangled from the sign, revealing the chipped and peeling paint that advertised the name. No candles burned in the two front windows that would have signified a vacancy. Stonebottom's usually stayed full whenever ships were in port.

Knowing they had to take the man before he reached the inn, Cerril increased his pace. Hekkel's shadow flitted along the other side of the street.

Two blocks before Stonebottom's, Cerril signaled Hekkel.

Without hesitation, Hekkel ran out into the street. "Good sir! Good sir! Help me, please!"

The man stopped and turned, putting his back up against the building beside him. His hand darted for his waist sash, and Cerril would have bet anything that he was carrying a blade there. At least the man hadn't turned Hekkel into a toad.

"What do you want, boy?" the man demanded in a thin, worn voice.

"It's my mother!" Hekkel cried, coming to a stop in front of the man. "She fell down! I can't wake her!"

The man remained quiet, his hand out of sight.

"You've got to help me!" Hekkel pleaded.

"I'm no healer."

The man glanced warily around the dark street, but Stonebottom's was located in one of the several old parts of the city. Little foot traffic ever went through that area so early. A few hours before cock's crow, though, the seamen who rented rooms there would come stumbling through.

Cerril stayed within the shadow less than twenty feet away. He breathed shallowly. Thankfully the street was also devoid of lanterns and he remained hidden.

Hekkel was small for his size. Most people not used to children often thought he was a child of seven or eight years. At least, they did until they saw the hardness in his eyes. Still, the man almost hit Hekkel when the boy dropped to his knees and wrapped both arms around the man's legs.

"Please!" Hekkel cried plaintively. "I think she's dying!"

"Here now," the man said. "Get up from there. You need to see someone who can do your mother some good. I'm just a traveler. I've no experience at healing. I'm a scribe."

Carefully, Cerril reached for the window ledge of the cobbler's shop beside him. Hundreds of years of masonry held Alaghôn together. Dozens of styles held sway in the city, and they created a rambling disorder to Alaghôn that provided any number of dead-end streets and orphaned blocks. The mortar of the older buildings was also in a state of disrepair, often crumbling when jostled.

Cerril raked a finger between the stones that made up the window ledge. The mortar broke up easily and he slipped a stone as big as both his fists from the ledge. A half-dozen others were already missing. He threw himself at the man, running quickly.

The man, distracted by Hekkel's caterwauling, didn't hear Cerril's approach until it was too late. Cerril brought the stone around in a hard-knuckled right hand just as the man looked up at him.

The stone caught the man on the side of the head. His eyes turned glassy and he slumped.

Cerril caught the man by his shirt collar and struggled with his slight weight. He stumbled.

"Help me, damn you!" he swore at Hekkel.

"Did you kill him?"

Hekkel released the man's legs and stood, gazing at their victim's slack face.

"No," Cerril said.

He glanced around the street, wanting to make sure no one had seen them. The guards around the docks were pretty lax. For one, the black market paid handsomely, funneled through the Thieves Guild. And for another, men desperate to turn a profit often had no hesitation about killing a guardsman.

"I've got him," Two-Fingers said, joining Cerril.

Two-Fingers caught one of the man's arms and draped it over his broad shoulders. He shifted most of the unconscious man's weight onto him. Cerril grabbed the man's other arm. Together they walked the man into the nearest alley.

The thoroughfare was long and narrow. The scant moonlight didn't even penetrate. They laid the man on the ground. Cerril searched under the man's blouse with practiced fingers and quickly found the small but heavy pouch at the man's waist.

Gold! The thought flooded Cerril's mind when he felt the heft of it. He opened the pouch and poured the coins into his waiting palm.

"Tymora's smile," Hekkel swore softly, voice filled with excitement. "We did all right for ourselves tonight."

Even in the darkness, Cerril could see the dull glint of gold among the coins. His questing fingers found the biggest of them and drew it forth. It was solid, round, and heavy.

"Gold," he whispered.

"I never seen anything like that," Two-Fingers said.

Cerril scowled at him. "Alaghôn gets coins from all around the Sea of Fallen Stars. There's probably lots of coins you haven't seen."

He flipped the coin over. The face held the image of a great, snarling, catlike beast with flattened ears and a mouthful of fangs. The obverse showed a taloned, bestial claw in bold relief. The image caused Cerril's stomach to turn cold.

"Do you recognize it, boy?" a scratchy, weak voice asked.

"Damn it!" one of the other boys swore. "Cerril didn't kill him after all."

"Get a rock," another boy suggested. "Smash his head in! I don't want him identifying us for the guard."

"No." Cerril's voice cut through their fear. He crept closer to the man, feeling something dark and powerful touching him through the cool gold. He held the coin up. "What is this?"

"Do you recognize it?" the man challenged.

Cerril didn't answer. Sometimes it was better to let things go unanswered.

"Of course he does," Hekkel snapped. "That coin represents Malar. The Stalker. Also called the Beastlord. He's one of the Gods of Fury that serve Talos. What of it?"

The man gasped but no sound emerged. Blood trickled down the side of his head onto the ground. He made no move to get up.

The fact that the man didn't try to cry out, and even looked a little relieved, made Cerril yet more uneasy.

"The coin is cursed," the man said. "There's a geas that's been laid on it by Malar."

"You lie!" Cerril exploded.

"Try to throw the coin away, boy," the man challenged.

"That would be stupid," Hekkel said.

Still, Cerril turned his hand upside down. The coin of Malar remained stuck to his flesh, denying the certain fall to the ground. Fearfully, he pulled the coin free of his palm with his other hand, then found it was stuck to that hand.

"Do you feel the power of the geas now, boy?" the man asked, smiling. Blood continued to pump from his wound.

Cerril shook his hand, trying to fling the coin away. His stomach knotted in fear, spilling bile against the back of his throat. Bad luck!

He turned to Hekkel, shoved his hand out, and said, "You want it—take it!"

Hekkel eyed the coin greedily, but fear made him back away. He shook his head slowly.

Totally panicked, Cerril turned back to the man. He found the knife at the man's waist and drew it out. Without hesitation, he pressed it against the man's throat.

"Take it back!"

The man returned his gaze and said, "I can't."

"You can."

"I can't. The coin has to be wanted. I had never even heard of Malar when it came into my position."

Cerril pressed the knife blade harder. "Take the coin."

Slowly, the man reached for the coin in Cerril's hand. The man plucked at the coin but it refused to release Cerril's hand. It lay there in the boy's palm, attached as firmly as a blood leech.

"I can't," the man said, removing his hand. "It knows I don't want it."

Cerril groaned in fear and anger. He almost slit the man's throat, then he realized that doing that might have doomed him.

"What kind of geas is on the coin?"

The man swallowed hard, his eyes narrowing in pain. "I don't know," he said. "The coin drew me here."

"To Alaghôn?" Cerril asked.

"Yes. I've never been here before, but visions of this place came to me in dreams. Nightmares, actually. Gods, but the things I saw during the last few months I've had that thing."

"What are you supposed to do?"

Cerril knew that the nature of any geas, for good or ill—and with Malar the Stalker involved he had no doubt that it would all be for ill—was the need to accomplish something.

"I don't know," the man answered.

"You're here," Cerril pointed out.

"Only because the nightmares ebbed a little when I made the decision to board a ship and come here." The man's eyes fluttered closed for a moment, then reopened. "You'll know what it wants you to do. You'll have nightmares about it."

Cerril glanced up and saw that Two-Fingers, Hekkel, and the others had stepped back from him.

They don't want any of my bad luck rubbing off on them, he thought.

He looked back at the man.

"All I can tell you," the man said, "is that the geas involves a graveyard somewhere in this city. I've seen it in my nightmares, but I haven't had a chance to look for it yet."

Cerril's breath caught at the back of his throat. A graveyard? Alaghôn was filled with graveyards. The last thing he wanted to do—while under the effects of a geas or not—was go to any one of them.

He stared at the fat coin lying in his hand and cursed his own rotten luck.

CHAPTER FOUR

Did you hear that?"

Haarn kept walking through the forest, ignoring the woman trying to keep pace with him. Druz Talimsir's efforts had become so noisy even across level ground that Haarn had finally given up in disgust and paced himself so that she could more easily walk with him. The other wolf hunters were little over an hour behind them.

Druz grabbed his shoulder.

Slipping out of her grasp, reaching for the inner calm that his father had taught him, Haarn stepped to one side. Instinctively, probably because of her training as a mercenary and probably from working in places where she'd had to control others, she tried to grip his shoulder again. She was already twisting sideways and fisting her sword, readying herself for an aggressive response. The druid blocked her grip with an open hand, curling his fingers over her wrist and pushing her hand away.

"What are you doing?" she demanded, drawing back into an automatic defensive posture.

"Don't put your hands on me," Haarn said.

Anger and embarrassment colored the woman's face. "What the hell is wrong with you? I offered you no insult or injury."

"Nothing is wrong with me," Haarn replied. "I don't like to be touched."

The woman's voice bared steel. "I don't like to be ignored."

"I haven't been ignoring you," Haarn replied. "If I had wanted to ignore you, I would have left you in the forest a long time before this. I have allowed you to accompany me as you wished."

"You have *allowed* me?"

Haarn considered his words and found he'd said nothing incorrect. "Yes."

She started to say something but words failed her. Perhaps the woman had a problem with the harsh truth of the matter. He didn't care. What he'd said was true, even if it had been stated in a way that wasn't agreeable with her. He gazed into her eyes until she looked away.

Less than forty feet distant, Haarn heard Broadfoot shifting restively in the brush. The brown bear weighed at least a dozen times as much as the young woman but made even less noise. Still, despite his own feelings about her woodcraft, Druz passed more quietly than the other group making their way through the dark forest no more than a hundred paces away.

A cry of pain echoed through the night.

Druz's head snapped up. "That was a woman's voice."

Haarn made no response. He'd recognized the sound as being from a woman as well.

Without another word, Druz crept through the forest toward the noise of the woman's pained scream as it was repeated. She slid her sword free of its sheath.

Gracefully, more silent than a stirring leaf, Haarn fell into step beside Druz. However, he made certain to give her the personal space she'd dared take from him.

"What are you doing?" he asked.

"I'm going to see what's wrong with that woman."

"There are others with her," Haarn stated.

"I know, but why is she crying out?"

The woman moaned again.

"Because she's in pain," Haarn said.

"That doesn't make you curious?" Druz pushed through saplings and low tree branches.

Haarn gently stilled the quivering saplings and branches as he followed the woman. Where Druz left ripples in the forest, he quieted the wood, making sure, out of habit, that there was little sign of their passage.

The woman cried out again.

"If she's with friends," Druz said, "she wouldn't be moaning like that."

"I've found that city people don't always treat each other well," Haarn said.

"How do you know they're from the city?"

Druz knelt at the edge of the forest. They stood on a small promontory overlooking a shallow valley basin.

Haarn favored this valley and often watched the sun come up over the crest of the high hills around it. The trail worn by hunters and regular traffic cut through the trees. There were some, the druid knew, who would see the trail as a road, a place of civilization and refinement. Haarn saw it as a scar, a place where those who would conquer it rather than learn to live with it had sundered nature.

A tight knot of lanterns wavered in the dark distance. The combined illumination created a hollow space beneath the canopy of the trees and the walls of brush. The nocturnal forest animals watched from discreet distances, all of them giving way to the invaders.

Druz reached into her backpack and took out a device.

Judging from the construction of the backpack and the time that had gone into the making of it, Haarn felt certain that sure-handed gnomes had crafted it. Their talent in the creation of things sometimes put discouraging thoughts into the druid's head. If only the gnomes had learned to live with nature rather than create ways to challenge it. Besides a generous storage space and comfort, the backpack provided a number of pockets of differing sizes.

Moving with accustomed precision, Druz pulled on the thing she'd taken from her backpack. The device elongated in sections, forming a hollow tube. The mercenary placed the tube to her eye and stared through it. She was quiet only for a moment, then she lowered the device and looked back at him.

"They're slavers," she said.

"Yes," Haarn replied.

He didn't tell her that he could smell them from the valley's ridge. The slaves exuded a spicy sweat from the foods they'd eaten and the fragrances they wore. Those unfortunate enough to be caught and held in chains carried a days' old sour, sickly stench. The chain links had been padded so they didn't make much noise.

Slavers occasionally came deep into Turmish from Nimpeth and other lands on the southern coastline of the Vilhon Reach. Nimpeth had long been known as a slave city. The manpower shortages and the damage wrought by the recent war had increased both the demand for and the availability of slaves.

"You knew that?" Druz accused.

"I know it now," Haarn stated.

He returned his gaze to the stumbling progression making its way southeast to the Turmish coastline. They were days away from the Vilhon Reach and whatever vessel might be awaiting them.

"You let slavers raid these lands?" Druz asked, obviously angry. She put her device away.

Haarn didn't even deign to answer the offensive question.

"What are you going to do?" Druz demanded.

"Hunt the wolf," the druid replied, "as we agreed."

"You can't just let those slavers pass. Maybe we can do something."

Haarn looked at her. "Do you know any of those people?"

"I couldn't see them."

"They could be strangers."

"If we don't do something, they're going to be slaves."

Haarn noted the urgency in the woman's voice and knew that her attitude was going to be troublesome.

He said, "Those people could be slaves again in the next tenday."

"You're going to stand by and let that happen?"

"It's none of my affair," the druid said. He nodded

toward the line of slaves and slavers. "What you see there is the work of man, of civilization. Animals don't take slaves."

"Some of those people could be druids."

"No," Haarn said quietly. "No one of my order would allow himself or herself to be taken as a slave." They would die first. He was certain of that.

"If one of your order was down there," Druz persisted, "would you do something then?"

"No one from my order is down there."

A little irritated by Druz's constant talk of things that weren't happening and might never happen, Haarn turned and stepped back toward the sheltering forest.

"Where are you going?" she asked.

"The sooner I kill the wolf we seek, the sooner I can take my leave of you."

"Those people are being taken into slavery."

"It's not my concern."

Haarn kept walking, his thoughts already turning from the slaves and the slavers.

Broadfoot snuffled in the distance, the sound lost amid the night's other myriad noises. Haarn knew no one else would have heard it unless they were standing close to the brown bear. The druid cocked his head slightly, listening for what Broadfoot had sensed.

Furtive footsteps neared their position.

Quietly, Haarn considered the choices before him. The footsteps belonged to men. He'd gotten so caught up in the disagreement with Druz that he hadn't been as attentive as he usually was.

"What?" she challenged. "Don't tell me you suddenly decided that you care about those people down there."

"No," Haarn replied.

The footsteps paused. The druid smelled the spicy meat on the breaths of the men around them and even heard a few garbled and raspy whispers. He marveled at the fact, with the men so near, that the woman didn't know they were there.

"Then why are you—"

Druz reached for her sword as Haarn heard footsteps rush from the forest around them. The sword cleared its leather scabbard and she stepped into a defensive posture.

Knowing the men formed a loose semicircle around them, Haarn lifted his hands slowly from his sides and held them straight out.

"Put down your weapon," Haarn advised.

"No," Druz replied. "I won't be taken as a slave."

"You don't have a choice."

Broadfoot shifted in the trees, edging closer. None of the slavers around them noticed the slight noise the big bear made.

Haarn growled, drawing the rumbling sound from deep in his chest. Broadfoot stopped in his tracks, but snuffled his displeasure at the command. Even with the magic available to him and the years of association he had with the bear, the druid couldn't talk directly to Broadfoot, but he could make his wishes known.

"What the hell was that?" one of the men demanded.

Another man spat. "He's one of those damned druids," he cursed. "We'd be better off killing him now, Brugar. There ain't no easy way we're going to take him with us."

"Lord Vallis is paying by the head," a gruff voice said. "As long as that druid's head stays on his shoulders, it's worth gold."

"The woman's worth more," another man said. "Look at her. See how pretty she is?"

Haarn watched the dark stain of embarrassment touch Druz's features.

"We'll hold her back from Vogalsang's auction block in Nimpeth then sell her to Warryl," the man went on. "Warryl can sell her to one of those fleshpots along the Golden Road down by the Nagawater."

"You'll have to kill me first," Druz promised, lifting her long sword meaningfully. "A quick death now is preferable to a slow death later."

Haarn watched the woman's eyes and felt his respect for her grow. Despite the clumsy way she interacted with the forest and let the men's taunts embarrass her, she knew her own true balance. Most men he'd met, the druid felt from his limited experience with those outside his order, had never been tested enough to reach that. The woman suddenly appeared more intriguing to him.

"Tell her to put the sword down, druid," Brugar commanded.

He was a mountain of a man, standing nearly seven feet tall. His skin was swarthy, almost black. He wore dark leather armor and carried a battle-axe. His shaven head gleamed in the moonlight. Scars littered his arms, shoulders, and face. He glared fiercely at Haarn.

"She won't listen to me," Haarn replied.

"Make her," Brugar ordered, "or I'll kill you both."

Haarn didn't reply. He sensed the greed in the man, knowing that Brugar was already counting the gold he'd be paid for those he captured. The druid also heard the quiet footsteps coming up from behind them. He made himself wait.

At the last moment, a twig snapped under the approaching man's foot. Haarn glanced over his shoulder, already hearing the mercenary in motion as she reacted to the unexpected sound.

Druz spun quickly and moonlight flashed on the naked blade in her hand. She took a step away and almost succeeded in escaping the cruel blow that smashed into her head. Her fleeing step turned into an outright fall as she dropped bonelessly to the ground. The other man Haarn had heard creeping through the forest stood over the mercenary.

The slaver was thin and unkempt, rawboned and ragged. His gaze was feral and fleeting, never looking in any direction too long. He grinned at the druid then spat contemptuously on the ground.

Aware that all the crossbows were now turned on him, Haarn held his position. No emotion touched him as he faced his captors.

"Hyle," Brugar called out, "you better not have crushed her damn skull."

"I ain't crushed her skull." Hyle knelt gingerly and held a palm over Druz's face. "She's breathin' all right. Anyways, any wrong I coulda done her coulda been fixed by the tree-lover over there."

Standing his ground, Haarn glanced down at the mercenary lying helplessly on the ground. Dark blood trickled through her red-gold hair. Anger stirred within the druid.

The fact that the men were slavers had nothing to do with the dark emotion that moved restlessly inside Haarn. This part of the forest had been given over to him for his protection and he had never forsaken that charge. The presence of the slavers was an encroachment upon that territory, but even worse—they knew the group he represented and they had chosen to ignore that. Behavior like that couldn't be tolerated.

Broadfoot huffed and growled out in the forest again, chafing at the restraint Haarn had urged him to.

"Hyle," Brugar commanded, "take that man into custody."

The tattooed man stared deeply into Haarn's eyes for a moment, then broke the contact. "This'n gonna be trouble, Brugar. Be best to just cut him and gut him."

Haarn stood easily, his manner relaxed, but he remained ready.

"Try to kill him," Brugar said, "and I'll slit your throat myself, Hyle. Bind him and gag him. Alive, he's worth a few gold pieces that I'll enjoy spending."

Moving warily, the tattooed man took a leather string from his kit and strode toward Haarn.

"Stick your hands out."

Conscious of the crossbow quarrels pointed in his direction, Haarn held his hands out. Hyle pushed the druid's wrists together and wrapped them tightly with the leather string, then confiscated his weapons. Breathing shallowly through his nose, Haarn distanced himself from the degrading treatment. In all of his years he'd never been taken captive.

He glanced wistfully at the forest. If the woman hadn't been with him, he could have escaped and wreaked vengeance from the protective shelter of the woods. However, he hadn't been in control of his life since he'd started finding the executed and scalped wolves.

Hyle checked the tightness of the leather and seemed satisfied, but the man's mocking, cruel grin faded as he looked into Haarn's face. Suspicion narrowed the tattooed man's eyes.

"What are you doing, druid?"

"Praying," Haarn answered simply.

"You got nothin' to pray for," Hyle said.

"I'm asking Silvanus for the quick deaths of the men who have chosen to become my enemies tonight."

Haarn kept his face impassive.

Scowling, Hyle pulled out a dirty rag, jammed it into Haarn's mouth, and tied a knot behind the druid's mouth to keep it in place.

"If I had my way," the tattooed man promised, "I'd have you sacrificed on an altar to the Beastlord."

A chill threaded up Haarn's spine as he heard the reference to Malar the Stalker. Malar and Silvanus were old enemies, and those who followed each of those gods carried the enmity between them. The druid looked at the other slavers, noticing tattoos upon a couple more of them as they stepped confidently from the forest's darkness. Perhaps all of them followed the Beastlord's teachings. Perhaps everything that was happening followed a grand design Silvanus had put into motion.

Hyle shoved Haarn from behind, pushing the druid down toward the valley floor.

Forcing himself not to resist, Haarn stumbled then began walking ahead of the slaver group. He gathered his power within him, drawing it from the earth, the trees, and the very air around them.

CHAPTER FIVE

The pounding echo trapped inside Druz Talimsir's aching skull woke her. Rough leather bound her hands at the wrists, and she'd lost feeling in most of her fingers. The scent of loamy ground filled her nostrils, threaded through by the thick odor of a cookfire and the stink of meat charred on the outside while grease dripped from the center. Men's voices carried on constant conversations and evidently never-ending arguments.

"There's nothing to fear by letting them know you're awake."

Druz recognized the calm voice as the druid's and opened her eyes. She didn't move. Even if the druid was right, she didn't want him to think she was responding to his voice. He was part of the reason she'd been taken by the slavers. There was no way she was going to believe the slavers had managed to approach him without him knowing, but she had no idea why the elf hadn't warned her.

For one brief moment, she thought that maybe he was working with the slavers. No one knew for certain what the Emerald Enclave's true agenda was in the Vilhon Reach. Most were in agreement that the druids didn't care for cities or further expansion of civilization, but taking up with slavers from Nimpeth was surely something they wouldn't even consider.

"They've settled in for the night," the druid said a moment later.

The cookfires had told Druz that. She opened her eyes and saw the druid sitting next to her. Leather strips bound his hands as they did hers, attached to a padded, heavy chain that lay across the ground. All of the other slaves were bound to the same chain. Druz pulled at the leather with all her strength, but she succeeded only in drawing the attention of one of the guards.

"They caught you, too?" she asked as she pushed herself into a sitting position.

The druid hesitated only a moment. "Yes."

Druz knew at once that the druid was lying. There was no way the slavers would have been able to keep up with him in the forest.

"Why did you stay?" she asked.

He turned toward her and said, "Because I agreed to let you accompany me on the hunt for the rogue wolf."

"Getting captured isn't going to get that done."

Druz struggled to keep the defeat from her voice, but it was hard. She knew what lay in store for all of them—including the druid if he wasn't as good at escaping as he evidently thought he was.

"I didn't want something to . . . happen to you," the druid replied.

"I'm not going to believe you're concerned about my welfare."

His green eyes regarded her dispassionately as he said, "Would you be concerned about mine?"

"No more than anyone else I don't know," Druz replied truthfully. She held up her hands, dragging the heavy chain up after them. "I wouldn't have wished this on you."

The druid nodded. "Nor I you." He paused for a moment, glancing back at the campsite, then said, "However, if something happened to you, there would be no witness to tell the man who hired you that his son had been avenged. Other hunters would be employed, and more wolves would die."

"And that's what worries you?" Druz didn't even try to keep the sarcasm from her voice.

Shifting his dark gaze back to her, the druid said, "Those men would die, too. Would that concern you?"

Druz considered the possibility only for a moment. Images of other hunters getting picked off one by one in the forest filled her head.

"If you killed those men," she said, "they would put a bounty on your head."

"Yes."

Or maybe there already is one. The thought occurred to Druz in a flash. It wouldn't have been the first time a druid from the Emerald Enclave was marked for death by one of the cities of the Vilhon Reach.

She said, "I don't even know your name."

The druid was silent for a time. He shifted against the tree, uncomfortable, and said, "I am called Haarn Brightoak."

Druz shook her head. Knowing his name now, when they were both captives, somehow made the situation worse. She pushed her breath out and tried to relax.

"You should have escaped."

"I couldn't," Haarn replied.

"Because of me?"

The druid gazed at her and said, "Partly, but if I hadn't surrendered myself, these men might have tried to get away."

A chill spread across Druz's shoulders and ran down her spine. She'd heard terrible stories about druids. Some sages maintained that the druids, including members of the Emerald Enclave, were good and honest men and women whose reverence for nature clouded their judgment and made them do things that didn't fit in with civilized thinking. Others proclaimed the druids as savages, capable of torture and brutal killing.

Most of the other people tied to the slaver chain slept. Druz counted twenty-seven men, women, and children other than herself and the druid. One woman held a small child to her breast. All of the slaves looked hard-used, as if they'd been on the chain for days, perhaps even as much as a tenday. Their skin was sunburned and their clothing, common and homespun at best, hung in rags.

"Where did these people come from?" Druz asked.

"A small village somewhere close by," Haarn answered.

"You don't know where?"

"Some of the outlying villages don't have names. They learn to be autonomous, trading only occasionally with passing merchants or each other. Many of them don't see the need to pay the taxes cities like Alaghôn levy on people who only try to survive." The druid turned to her and added, "Living in such conditions, paying faceless tax agents of Lord Herengar and the Assembly of Stars, isn't much better than living in the servitude they're bound for now."

Druz bridled at the comment. Though she didn't know Lord Herengar personally, she knew of him.

"Lord Herengar is a good man," she said, "a fair man."

"Before he was named as ruler of Turmish, acting on behalf of the Assembly of Stars," Haarn said, "he was a leader of a mercenary band called the Call of Arms. He acted in his own interests then, and he continues to do so now."

"Those taxes you speak out against help make the city safe," Druz insisted.

In the back of her mind, she knew she should be more concerned about escaping, but there was something about the druid that challenged her and made her want to make him see cities the way they really were—as homes and havens. Maybe it was the dismissive way he treated her, and maybe it was because she'd never been around a man so arrogant and confident as the druid. Even here in the midst of the slavers he spoke as if he'd trapped them instead of it being the other way around.

Haarn smiled and said, "So Herengar heads up a new mercenary band and demands tribute for his services—one that pays much better."

"Most people in the city wouldn't know how to fight to defend themselves," Druz argued.

"And they lose themselves because they are not taught to do that," Haarn said bluntly. "Take away a person's ability to protect himself, to know enough to survive on his own, and you only have a slave. A privileged slave, perhaps, but a slave nonetheless." He took up the padded chain. "Maybe you can't see the chains on those 'citizens,' Druz Talimsir, but they are there."

"Cities allow people to raise their children in peace." Druz disliked the way the druid seemed to look down on everything about her. "I've fought, defending towns and cities during time of war."

"Against others who felt certain that whatever it was they were after from the places you defended rightly belonged to them," Haarn stated angrily, "because they decided to own one section of a land or another."

"Territorial wars are the most common—" Druz started to go on, but the druid cut her off.

"The land isn't meant to be owned," Haarn said. "It's meant to be treasured and tended. The land will provide sustenance to creatures that understand its needs and its gifts. Cities are spawning grounds for maggots that reap what they will of the land and leave only a decaying husk behind."

The vehemence in the druid's voice surprised Druz enough that she stilled her tongue.

"Loggers fell trees from forests," Haarn continued, "and they never give thought to replenishing those trees. Miners dig in the land and create holes that fill with rainwater that become contaminated and poison other areas. Animal species are hunted nearly to extinction and cause other problems with overpopulation. The sheepherders overgraze the land and render it useless for years. Still other places have been polluted by magical fallout. What happened to the Whamite Isles is a clear example of that." He looked at Druz. "Your cities are toxic in other ways as well. They provide a means and an area for eaters to live and reproduce."

"Eaters?" The term was unfamiliar to Druz.

"Eaters," Haarn repeated. "Civilized man simply eats nature's bounty and puts nothing back into the land. If they had to live off the land, struggle through the four seasons and keep themselves healthy, most of them wouldn't be able to."

"I could live off the land. I've done it before," Druz argued hotly, feeling certain that the druid had lumped her in with the Eaters he spoke of.

"But you've never learned to be happy living with what nature has to offer," the druid accused. "Otherwise you'd never go back to those cities and its laws and its taxes."

"I like the idea of a home," Druz said. The thought occupied her mind a lot. Her parents hadn't had much, but they'd been generous with what they had. For the past nine years, Druz had lived a mercenary's life: traveling from engagement to engagement, praying to the gods that she didn't get killed or maimed, and living in a crude barracks. "I like taverns and eating a meal someone else has prepared. I like the marketplaces, and I like seeing things from other lands."

"We're not intended to have all the world. You should learn to live where you are," Haarn said, raking his dark gaze over the slavers.

A small group of men sitting at a cookfire still talked and drank from a bottle they passed around. They'd arrived back in the camp a while ago. No one else had shown up, nor did any more bands seem expected.

"You've never had a . . . wanderlust?" Druz asked.

"Of course I have," Haarn said, barely paying attention. "I've wandered all over Turmish."

"Did you ever go to a city?"

"No."

Druz couldn't believe that. "How can you talk so badly of Alaghôn and other cities if you've never seen one?"

Haarn looked at her. "Have you ever been bitten by a poisonous viper?"

"Yes."

"You know the poison will kill you if left untreated."

"Of course," Druz agreed as she worked at her own bonds.

She found no looseness in the leather ties. Her aggravation at the druid increased, but she knew it was a byproduct of her own helplessness. Railing at their slaver captors wouldn't be safe or satisfying, and the druid's chain of logic eluded her.

"If you didn't see the viper that bit you," Haarn asked,

"do you believe that the poison would kill you just as certainly?"

"Yes."

"That's how I feel about the people I've met who come from cities. I don't have to see their cities to know that they're unacceptable."

"That isn't fair."

"I don't have to be fair," Haarn said, then he started chanting.

The guttural words sounded incredibly old and harsh to Druz, but she felt the magic in them. During her sojourn as a sellsword she'd had several occasions to work around combat mages. Once at a fair in Westgate a seer had told Druz that she carried a hint of magic about her. Druz had chosen not to pursue that possibility—she didn't much care for magic, and mage schools were expensive—but she'd always known when magic was working around her, if it was close or if it was strong.

She knew the magic Haarn used was powerful just by the way it prickled her skin and tightened the hair at the nape of her neck. He spoke a single word at the end of the chant and a sudden cold feeling stabbed into Druz's stomach.

Haarn's features started to melt, collapsing and flowing like a beeswax candle. Feathers took the place of flesh as the druid dwindled in on himself, becoming smaller and smaller. In a matter of heartbeats, a great horned owl stood on clawed feet where the druid had been sitting only an instant before. The leather fetters lay on the ground.

The owl unfurled its great wings and leaped up. Though the winged predator's weight prevented it from speedily gaining ascent, the owl flew nevertheless. The druid in owl form sped toward the five slavers gathered around the cookfire. Druz heard the wings beat the air as the owl sailed over the sleeping slavers.

One of the slavers noticed the owl's approach and cried out in alarm as he dragged at the sword sheathed at his side. Without hesitation, Haarn raked his owl's claws across the man's face, savaging his features into a bloody ruin and narrowly avoiding the sword blow that cleaved the air for him.

The slaver fell back, squealing in pain and fear. The other slavers grabbed for their weapons and shouted an alarm. Even as the rousing slavers struggled to come to their feet and react, the huge brown bear broke the tree line around the clearing and charged into the camp. The bear roared and the sound was deafening.

The slavers yelled in fear and called on their gods. In the next instant, the bear was among them, flailing and rending with its great claws and fangs. Men dropped away from the bear's attack, and many of them never moved again. The bear was as vicious as it was relentless.

Haarn, in owl form, attacked a man who had fitted a crossbow to his shoulder and was taking aim at the bear.

The slaver dropped his weapon and screamed, "My eyes! My eyes!"

He stumbled back and fell into one of the campfires. Smoldering embers rose into the night air along with the man's renewed screams of pain.

The chain holding Druz's leather restraints jerked. She glanced down the line of slaves and saw that most of them had roused. Three of the men grabbed rocks from the ground and stood ready to defend themselves. Druz pulled at the leather binding her, but there was no way to get free. She watched helplessly, knowing that if the druid wasn't successful in killing the slavers, he might have doomed them all to harsh deaths.

The owl cut the air and glided over a small wagon that sat at a tree on the other side of the camp. A pair of horses neighed loudly and fought against the ropes and hobbles that held them. The owl dropped from treetop level and plummeted with folded wings. The druid touched the ground again in human form.

Haarn raced to the small wagon and went through one of the chests in the back. He located his scimitar and a small kit that Druz assumed he'd worn under his blouse because she hadn't seen it earlier. He also took out her sword belt. Firelight danced across his features and the wild black hair that brushed his shoulders. His face was cold and impassive, and the absence of emotion—fear or anger—made him appear like an alien thing.

The bear roared and growled deep in its huge chest as a crossbow quarrel took it high in one shoulder. The offending sliver of wood and fletching looked incredibly small against the bulk of the ursine. Turning its broad head, the bear snapped at the quarrel and bit part of it off, leaving only a few inches embedded in its flesh.

Haarn threw himself into the attack. Firelight glinted along the scimitar's length as the druid engaged one of the slavers. The fight lasted only a moment. Perhaps the druid had never been to a city to accept proper tutelage, but his bladework was some of the best Druz had ever seen.

Fiery red lightning strobed across the night sky like a hag's withered claws. Druz smelled the change in the weather as the humid heat that had plagued the day suddenly chilled. For a moment she believed the druid might have summoned the weather change, and she knew the slavers probably believed that as well.

Out of over twenty men that Druz had counted, a dozen lay stretched out on the ground. Many of them never moved, and the others wouldn't be getting to their feet soon, nor were they in any kind of shape to resume the fight.

Twisting viciously, the druid avoided a desperate sword cut from his opponent. Still carrying Druz's sword in his other hand, the druid whirled and brought his scimitar around in a flash that was almost too fast for even Druz's eyes to follow in the uncertain light. The scimitar's last few inches slashed through the slaver's throat.

Crimson bubbled down the man's shirtfront as he dropped his blade and reached for his throat. Druz knew from experience that the slaver wasn't going to survive the cut.

Coldly, the druid stepped forward as the dying man dropped to his knees. Haarn's attention was already focused on his next opponent. He stepped forward and took his place at the bear's side with a graceful ease that showed years of experience.

The remaining slavers broke and pulled back.

The slaver leader, Brugar, called the surviving men to him, holding his battle-axe in two hands before him.

"Form up a damn line!" he called. "Do it now or the damned forest elf is gonna gut you all!"

The men scrambled, pulling into a loose formation behind their leader.

Haarn threw Druz's sword belt over to her. Kneeling, the druid plucked a throwing knife from a dead man left stretched out by one of the bear's blows. His eyes never left the slavers as he tore away a piece of the dead man's red shirt.

Standing with the piece of red cloth trapped between his fingers, the druid spoke words in a guttural tongue. The red cloth frayed in the whipping winds that preceded the cannonade of thunder that shook the earth. Lightning threaded across the wine-dark sky again, briefly illuminating the camp and the horror it had become as if in the brightest day.

One of the men tied to the chain darted forward, intent on claiming Druz's sword belt. She turned on the man, catching his eyes with hers.

"No," she commanded.

She felt pity for the people bound to the chain, but she knew from experience that she couldn't do them any good if she wasn't able to take care of herself.

The man backed away resentfully and said, "If they get the chance, they're likely to kill us now that you people have interfered."

Interfered? Druz bridled at the comment, then pushed it out of her mind. During her years of service she'd sometimes found herself cursed by the same people who'd thanked her for her help at first. It had gone the other way too when an engagement played out well.

Druz gripped her sword hilt and slid the weapon free of its scabbard. Holding the sword trapped between her knees, she slid the leather binding her wrists against the sharp edge. The leather parted like a spider's web. Still, her hands had numbed and she knew she couldn't properly wield the weapon, so she made herself wait.

One of the slavers reloaded the crossbow he held while the others screamed at him to hurry.

"Haarn!" Druz called out, seeing that the druid was praying again and might not have seen the threat.

She became aware of a distinct buzzing noise that cut through the silence left after the thunderous cracks. Even as the crossbowman brought his weapon up, a swirling mass of flying beetles slammed into him. The insects cut at the slaver's flesh. Bright drops of blood streamed from his face and arms. The beetles clustered to the man, covering him the way bees swarmed over a honeycomb.

The slaver threw the crossbow down and tried to flee, but the flying beetles pursued him. He didn't go a half dozen steps before he tripped and fell, seemingly weighed down by the heavy mass of beetles clinging to him. The man stopped writhing and fighting in seconds, and chill horror cut through Druz as she realized she didn't know if the man was alive or dead.

The bear growled a challenge and started forward. Almost carelessly, the druid reached out and caught up a handful of fur.

"No, my friend," he said softly, holding onto the massive ursine.

The bear twisted its wedge-shaped head and growled again. It sounded as if the bear was protesting the fate of the slavers.

"Kill them," Brugar snarled, starting forward.

Druz took up her weapon. Though feeling hadn't quite returned, she knew she couldn't leave the druid standing against the slavers on his own.

Haarn raised a hand and uttered a few more words.

Another prickling sensation passed through Druz, almost strong enough to buffet her as much as the storm winds that came howling through the forest. She watched in amazement as the trees around the slavers came to life, twisting and writhing like arthritic snakes.

"Brugar!" one of the men yelped.

Tree branches reached down and caught the man up, curling around him and ripping at his clothing and skin with rough bark.

A jagged flash of lightning sizzled across the black sky, turning the surrounding world harshly white for a heartbeat, then dropping the curtain of night back into place. Only two of the slavers escaped the groping tree branches that lifted them high into the air.

The bear left the druid's side in a diving lunge that took it back to all fours. Before the two slavers could take more than a handful of steps, the bear closed on them. Jaws distended widely, then snapped closed, ripping through the back of one man's neck. A mighty paw slammed against the back of the second man's head, crushing the skull like a grape and spilling a loose-limbed corpse to the ground. The bear shook its first victim then dropped the body and stood up. It growled a challenge, reaching for the men suspended in the trees.

The slavers drew their legs up, barely out of reach of the bear's claws.

The wind picked up in intensity, bringing an almost wintry cold with it. More red and purple lightning darted across the black sky.

The druid stood unmoving in the winds and peered up at the slavers. It was easy to believe, Druz realized, that the man had summoned the storms.

"I am Haarn Brightoak," the druid stated in a loud voice, "charged by the order of the Emerald Enclave to protect and care for the lands you have invaded."

Lightning flashed again, followed immediately by booming thunder that almost drowned out the pleading cries of the men trapped in the trees.

Can he crush them? Druz wondered.

She'd never seen the spell before, but she'd witnessed black tentacles summoned by combat mages that had wielded incredibly destructive force. The men hanging in the trees, she knew, had to be asking themselves the same thing.

The slavers struggled against the grasp of the still-moving tree branches, screaming out in pain as the rough bark tore into their flesh. Even if they got free, the bear and the druid waited below.

There was no escape. Druz realized that even as she knew the slavers had to. She'd seen men kill coldly in battle before, and even some kill coldly afterward. Some of those kills had been merciful, putting injured men out of their misery, but some had been done with a vengeance. She didn't know what emotion moved the druid, and she didn't know if she could stand by while the men were ruthlessly executed.

The trees finally stopped moving and resumed their normal shapes. The bear growled threats at the slavers, who wisely made no attempt to climb down from the trees.

"Leave these lands," the druid commanded in his fierce voice.

"Are you going to guarantee us safe passage?" Brugar called down.

Haarn didn't hesitate. "No."

"Then what are you going to do?"

"Let you go free," Haarn replied. "Whether or not you make it out of these lands is up to you. Animals will hunt you until you are clear of this area, and they will devour you if they catch you."

"That's no kind of bargain," Brugar objected. "You've killed over half of my men. We've got damn little chance of getting clear of here."

"Nature doesn't bargain. It is neither merciful nor merciless and only requires that the strong survive. Whether you're strong enough to survive is up to you."

Haarn turned away and the storm winds whipped his hair across his implacable face.

"Druid . . ." Brugar called.

"In a few moments, I'm going to release these people," Haarn replied without turning around. "I'm sure they'll avail themselves of the weapons that are lying around this campsite. Perhaps they'll even choose to shoot you down from the trees with the crossbows they find . . . if you haven't left. I understand that a crossbow doesn't require much skill."

Brugar snarled oaths. "If those peasants think that I'm going to—"

Haarn looked up at the man. "If you dare attack them in return, I'll hunt you all down and kill you. None of you will ever see home again. I offer my oath to Silvanus on that."

Quietly, after only a little hesitation, the slavers climbed down from the trees. As soon as they reached the ground, they ran for their lives.

The druid turned his attention to the people tied to the heavy slaver's chain. His scimitar flashed, reflecting the lightning as the impending rain started to fall in heavy drops.

Unfettered, the people gathered in small groups and took shelter from the pelting rain, but they were careful to avoid the trees that had captured and held the slavers. A few of them scavenged among the supplies the slavers had left behind, seeking out other garments as well as something to eat.

Druz kept her sword naked in her fist. Even with the power that the druid had shown, she didn't trust the slavers completely to leave the area. They'd left too many things behind. Maybe, she thought, staring at the trees that now just looked like trees again, the slavers had been scared enough.

Glancing back at the druid, she watched as he quietly talked to the wounded bear. The massive animal dropped down to all fours and nuzzled the man. Gently, Haarn put his foot against the bear's shoulder, gripped the broken cross-bow quarrel, and pulled it from the animal's body. Blood leaked out of the wound, matting the bear's fur. Growling, the bear licked the wound with a bright pink tongue.

The druid spoke softly to the bear, then prayed for a moment and placed his hands over the animal's blood-matted shoulder. Blue light gleamed from under the druid's hands, and Druz's skin prickled again in response. When the druid took his hands from the animal, the bear moved its shoulder tentatively, then put its weight on the limb with greater confidence. The bear rumbled again, but this time it sounded almost pleased.

Haarn turned from the bear and walked to the wagon. The released slaves backed away from him fearfully, but a few of them muttered that he was probably coming to claim his choice of whatever gold and silver the slavers might have left behind. Instead, Haarn only recovered the few items of his that were personal belongings. He rigged his weapons once more about him without a word and set off into the forest.

"What are you doing?" Druz asked.

"Leaving," the druid replied.

"You can't—*we* can't just leave these people here like this."

"I don't owe them anything."

"You freed them."

"I came after the slavers," the druid said, "not to free those people. They're responsible for themselves. If they're meant to live, they'll find a way."

He stepped into the brush without hesitation or a backward look. Caught off-guard, Druz quickly went to reclaim her own kit from one of the men, who had taken it from the wagon.

"That's mine," she said.

"I found it," the man said, clutching the leather kit to him.

Druz showed the man the sword in her fist. "I'm not leaving here without that kit," she stated in a calm voice.

Even though she'd felt sorry for them a moment before, she also knew she'd take what was rightfully hers. She'd been in cities before that had been attacked by invading forces. Even after the invaders were routed, looting had gone on in the shops and homes that had been damaged. The citizens had taken whatever was left by the invading forces.

"Let her have the bag, Larz," a thin woman with a bruised face said.

"I found it," the man said.

"It's probably hers."

"Maybe she's lying."

Angry and frustrated, Druz stripped the bag from the man's hands. She'd liked the man better when she'd believed he was a victim. Stepping back from him, she tucked the kit under her arm and opened it. She took a few small packages from the kit and handed them to the woman.

"Food," Druz said. "It's not much, but maybe it will help see you back to your homes."

"The slavers burned our homes," the woman said. "They burned us out when they took us."

"I'm sorry," Druz said.

"What we've got here," the woman said, "is all we have."

"At least you're still alive and free," Druz said.

"Free to starve to death in this forest or to fall to one of the vicious beasts that live here," a man muttered. "If we don't catch our death in this rain."

"We need someone to guide us out of here," the woman told Druz. "We have small children with us. Maybe we can't pay you for your services now, but there will come a time when we can."

"No," Druz said softly, forcing herself to be hard. "I'm sorry. I can't." She glanced at the forest in the direction Haarn and the large bear had gone. There was nothing to mark their passage. "I've got to go."

"If you leave us here, we may die," the woman said.

Druz sheathed her sword. "Maybe you won't," she replied. "Head east. Alaghôn lies in that direction. Perhaps you'll encounter a merchant caravan. Stay together and you should be all right."

The ex-slaves' faces showed the doubts they had.

Haunted by feelings of guilt but knowing she'd already undertaken an allegiance, Druz jogged in the direction Haarn had taken, hoping the druid had not gotten too far ahead of her and wasn't going to try to leave her behind. She didn't allow herself to look back at them because she didn't think she'd be strong enough to keep going.

She knew it wasn't strength that had allowed the druid to leave the slaves. The man simply didn't care for any of the people they'd freed. The realization chilled Druz as much as the rain that soaked her clothing because, for a time, she'd tied her future to the druid's.

CHAPTER SIX

"You're sure this is the place?"

Eyes burning from only occasional restless sleep over the last three days, Cerril glanced up at Two-Fingers's hoarse, whispered question. He stood on trembling legs only from sheer force of will and a desire to survive. Leaden-gray fog rolled in from the Sea of Fallen Stars and carried a cold mist that had already dampened Cerril's hair and skin. The young thief pulled the thin blanket more tightly around his shoulders and shivered again.

Another of the small cemeteries that pockmarked Alaghôn's surrounded them. Headstones and markers, tumbled and disheveled, offered visual proof that most—if not all—of the families that had left dead there in the past had long since died out or moved away. Rampant weeds and untrimmed trees formed living walls that subdivided the land of the dead.

"Is this the place?" Two-Fingers asked again. "Is this the cemetery you dreamed about?"

Cerril peered out at the piles of broken markers and shattered crypts. Nightmares—vibrant and bloodcurdling—had haunted what couldn't have been more than a handful of hours of sleep during the past three days.

"Perhaps," Cerril said.

"*Perhaps?*" Hekkel sounded restless and angry.

Before he realized it, Cerril took a step toward the smaller boy and gripped the haft of his knife.

Hekkel stepped back, tripping over a toppled headstone and sprawling in the greasy loam that had been left from the rain earlier in the day.

"Don't touch me!" the smaller boy yelled.

Two-Fingers gripped Cerril's shoulder. "He's not who you're here to be mad at, Cerril." Two-Fingers spoke gently, and there was a trace of fear in his voice.

For a moment, the blanket flying around him and rage boiling inside him, Cerril considered shrugging Two-Fingers's grip off and leaping down on Hekkel, except he knew he wouldn't be satisfied until he'd cut the boy's heart from his chest. Instead, Cerril made himself turn away.

Two-Fingers drew away quickly. Wan starlight blunted by the thick cloud cover formed a dulled sheen on his round face.

"I'm sorry, Cerril," the bigger boy mumbled.

Hekkel slowly, warily, got to his feet. "Maybe we should forget this," he suggested.

Drawing the sodden blanket back around him, grateful for even the small amount of warmth he drew from the cover, Cerril shook his head. His hair was so damp it stuck to his face, but that wasn't entirely due to the weather. A fever had plagued him, along with the nightmares.

"No," Cerril said, turning to look out over the time-ravaged cemetery. Rats scurried among the stones, their red eyes gleaming in the darkness. "We finish this tonight."

During the course of the two previous nights, Cerril had led them through over a dozen cemeteries. They'd been chased from three of them by the city watch and by a couple of gravediggers preparing a plot for a burial the next morning.

Until the dreams had sent him into the cemeteries of Alaghôn, he hadn't known how many graveyards there were in the city. He still didn't know an exact number, but he had garnered a better sense of the city's long history from his endeavors.

Even before Turmish had become a nation, Alaghôn had existed as a trade port to the Sea of Fallen Stars. Nomadic tribes traveled from the Shining Plains to trade with sea-faring merchants who stopped over during their journey to the southern lands. Even the dwarves of the Orsraun Mountains came down from their digs and cities to barter gold they'd clawed from the clutches of the earth.

As the trade port became a city, growing by leaps and bounds as successful trade ventures encouraged new business, death followed. Besides war and robbery, plagues claimed the lives of the settlers. The Year of the Clinging Death took nearly half the populations of the entire Vilhon Reach. War with pirates and other nations followed, lasting hundreds of years. Alaghôn stood as a city despite the worst of it, but citizens fell and were buried, sometimes in mass graves. The Plague of Dragons in 1317 began in Alaghôn and spread throughout the Vilhon Reach.

The Time of Troubles had followed forty years after that, and none of Faerûn remained untouched. Gods had walked the lands, and death and destruction had followed. The building of more gravesites had followed as well.

Knowing that the other boys in the group were on the verge of deserting him, Cerril plucked Malar's coin from his belt pouch. The gold coin glinted dully under the overcast night sky.

Effortlessly sliding the gold coin on top of his thumb, Cerril sent it flipping through the air with a practiced toss. Even heavy as it was, the gold coin twisted and twinkled, making the most of the available light.

At the apex of its flight, the coin seemed to catch a brilliant streak of light. The gold burned reddish-yellow for a moment, like it had suddenly caught fire or was freshly hammered from a dwarven forge. Noticing the effect, Cerril feared for his hand as the coin plummeted. Over the last three days, he'd felt nothing but evil from the coin.

The fire died out in the coin as suddenly as it had come. It fell heavily into Cerril's palm. Even if he'd deliberately tried to miss the coin, the cursed thing would have landed in his hand. Despite trying to lose the coin over the past few days, even to the point of luring pickpockets to snatch it from him, Cerril had been unable to get rid of the thing.

Cerril gazed at the coin lying against his palm. The heavy heat of the coin weighed against his palm. Breathlessly, he curled his fingers over it.

"That was a sign," Hekkel whispered.

"We're in the right place," someone else added.

"Where, Cerril?" another boy asked. "Which way do we head?"

For a moment, Cerril was afraid to answer, certain that the coin was only fooling with him. He felt a burning grip seize his heart and tug him forward, and he took a stumbling, protesting step. For a moment, the pressure around Cerril's heart eased, but it immediately tightened again, drawing him forward.

"This way," Cerril said in a squeaking voice that surprised him.

He raised his hand with the coin in it, as if the coin was now leading him. The others couldn't feel the pressure around his heart, but they couldn't miss the raised arm.

"It's pulling him!" one of the boys crowed excitedly. "The damn thing is leading him."

Cerril stumbled through the graveyard, feeling the pressure inside his chest increase even as he fought against it. He grew more afraid. Malar was a dark god, given to vengeance and bloodlust. During the Time of Troubles, Malar had tried to invade Gulthmere Forest and destroy the Emerald Enclave druids there. Nobanion, the Lion God of Gulthmere, also known as the guardian of the Reach, had turned the Stalker away from the forest.

The viselike grip tightened around Cerril's heart, urging him on. Drums sounded in the boy's ears, and for a moment he thought someone was beating them in the graveyard, then he realized that the sound came from the panicked rush of blood pounding through his own head.

Cerril's pace quickened from a halting stride to an uncertain-footed trot. He listened to his own footfalls smack against the rain-drenched loam. Weeds rustled as they pulled at the blanket he wore around his shoulders. Dead branches scraped through his hair and against his skin like a beast's claws.

High-pitched squeaks erupted from the dozens of rats that ran in front of Cerril. Several narrowly escaped getting trampled beneath the boys' feet as they pursued Cerril. Their excited whispers echoed in his ears.

Propelled by the anxiety that filled him and pressed against his heart, Cerril ran through the thickets of brush and fallen trees. Cheaply-made grave markers shattered beneath his feet. Here and there a few graves stood partially open, their denizens strewn across the ground. Grave robbers plied their craft in Alaghôn, but most stayed away from the burial grounds of the wealthy due to the wards that guarded them. None of them were brave enough to attempt robbing the grave of a wizard.

Perspiration poured from Cerril, forced out by the fever that filled him onto his chilled skin. Black spots swam in his vision as he rounded a freestanding tomb that had its roof partially caved in by a lightning-blasted oak.

A dozen crypts stood against the cemetery's back wall. Vines covered the wall. Flowers and leaves along the vines shivered as the cool wind raked its talons through them. Most of the crypts were in various stages of disrepair. Some of them were only a framework that had folded down onto the stone coffins.

Cerril's eyes lit on the largest of the crypts.

There, he told himself, and he knew he was right. Malar's coin pulsed strongly within his closed fist.

Cerril glanced across the rear section of the graveyard. His eyes focused on the squat, broad building that tucked into the graveyard's back wall. The roof was angled just enough to keep rainwater from collecting on it. Despite the building's obvious age, the roof remained intact, covered in wooden shingles that had to have only been replaced a few years before. None of the other crypts had a roof in such good repair.

"Is that it?" Two-Fingers asked.

"Yes," Cerril said, unable to stay back any longer.

The grip on his heart was too firm, too sure. He followed an overgrown path between rows of graves littered with rubble. No ornate markers or statuary occupied the grave-yard's rearmost section.

The crypt was less than ten feet tall and was easily forty feet across. Though he couldn't accurately judge how far back the crypt went, Cerril felt certain it had to have been as deep as it was wide, if not deeper. Cracks tracked several of the layers of stone used in the building's construction. Weeds and saplings jutted from the cracks, seemingly growing from the building's corpse. A short flight of steep steps led up to a wide entrance where splintered wooden doors sagged from broken hinges. The thin veneer of stain and lacquer had worn away in places.

"Do you know what this building is?" Hekkel asked in a hushed voice.

"What is it?" Two-Fingers asked.

"See?" Hekkel pointed, just barely visible from the corner of Cerril's eye. "If you look hard under those creepers and vines, you can see a symbol there."

"It looks like the head of a goose," Two-Fingers said.

"Not a goose," Hekkel said. "That's a picture of a stream or a river pouring down into a lake."

"You think this is a well house?" Two-Fingers asked. "Or a bathhouse where the dead are cleaned?"

A couple of the boys cursed as they considered that possibility.

Cerril knew he almost lost part of his group then, and he didn't want to face alone whatever lurked inside. "It's not a bathhouse for the dead. That sign belongs to Eldath."

"Who is Eldath?" one of the younger boys asked. His name was Aran, and he'd only arrived in Alaghôn a few months before, an immigrant from the Whamite Isles that had been nearly destroyed during the Serôsian War. Legend had it that the Taker, Iakhovas, had caused the destruction of the Whamite Isles. Now, according to reports, only the undead remnants of the island populations lived there.

Steadily feeling the pull from inside the building, Cerril reached the top of the short flight of stairs and walked into the crypt. Shadows cloistered in all the corners and it was hard to keep from imagining them moving.

"Eldath is a goddess," Hekkel whispered as the group followed. "They call her the Quiet One. She's a healer, and she serves Silvanus and helps the druids of the Emerald Enclave."

One of the boys cursed and spat. "My brother works as a logger. He hates the damned druids because they keep interfering with his work and making things hard for everybody."

"So this house belongs to Eldath?" Aran asked.

"No," Cerril answered. "It belongs to the Temple of the Trembling Flower. They represent Eldath in Alaghôn."

"I've never heard of it."

"The temple is small," Two-Fingers answered, surprising Cerril by even knowing of it. "Not many people are interested in worshiping a goddess who preaches that peaceful intentions can overcome a sword blow."

"So why would a coin bearing Malar's symbol call us here?" Aran asked.

The question, Cerril knew, was a good one—one that Cerril had been entertaining since he'd recognized the structure for what it was.

"Malar directs his believers to destroy the followers of Eldath as a show of faith to him."

"Bet that would make Eldath's priests take up a mace or a cudgel," Aran said.

"No," Cerril replied as he brushed away the cobwebs that blocked the entrance to the building, "it only makes for fewer worshipers for Eldath."

He peered inside the structure and saw cheaply made caskets crumbling on iron-studded shelves. Several of the caskets had broken and moldered away, revealing bits of skeletons wearing scraps of clothing.

"Damn!" Hekkel swore. "Skeletons! Those Cyric-blasted things could be enchanted to come alive and attack anyone who enters this place."

Cerril turned when he heard the footsteps of the group halt behind him. The fever burned within him again, pulsing at his temples.

"Those skeletons aren't going to rise," he said.

"There's no reason for us to be here, Cerril. You can go the rest of the way yourself. Malar's geas was laid on you, not us."

"Then I'll go myself," Cerril said, and his words echoed throughout the building.

"You just want us along because you're scared," Hekkel said.

Cerril was scared, but he struggled not to show it and to keep his voice normal as he said, "Gold and gems divide much easier when there's only one person."

Hekkel took a step forward, baited as surely as one of the rats they caught for the blood games in some of the sailors' taverns.

"What gold and gems?"

Flipping Malar's coin again, Cerril deftly caught it from the air. The gold slapped against his palm.

"Malar called me here," said Cerril, "to this place of Eldath. I've already told you how the Stalker sets his believers onto those who worship the Quiet One." He paused, knowing he was about to tell his biggest lie ever. "Do you think that Malar would call me here, to this place claimed by Eldath, and not reward me?"

Hekkel's response died on his lips as the possibility locked into his brain.

"I'm sure," Cerril said, turning back to continue through the rooms of broken caskets and dismembered skeletons dressed in rags, "that there's enough here to take care of us all, at least for those among you brave enough to see this thing through."

"Cerril's right," Two-Fingers agreed in a stronger voice. "Whatever Malar's giving him for this service, he's being generous enough to share it with us."

"Cerril's not a generous person," Hekkel objected.

But no one was listening to what Hekkel had to say anymore, Cerril noticed. The lure of gold and treasure was too much for the other boys. Alaghôn was a city filled with small treasures that had been hidden away and found many years later, and it was filled with still more stories of those forgotten treasures left by wealthy merchants, pirates, thieves, and nobility that had visited the Jewel of Turmish. Inventing the possibility of another such treasure was no stretch at all.

"What was this place?" Two-Fingers asked, following Cerril through the doorway into another room.

Cerril followed the pounding in his chest, going straight back and avoiding the other rooms that lay off the first one. He brushed more cobwebs from another open doorway.

"This was a charity crypt," he said. "People who die without kith or kin to bury them, or those who wander into Alaghôn and get killed but go unclaimed, end up here."

"The priests say they care about these people?" Hekkel sounded doubtful.

"No," Cerril replied, stepping through another doorway and across a broken skeleton that was sprawled on the floor, "the Assembly of Stars pays the temples. Other rulers paid them in the past."

"Why?" Two-Fingers asked.

"Because," Aran put in, "corpses that don't have a proper burial sometimes rise and walk again. I heard stories about that."

"You should be real familiar with that," Hekkel said, "after what happened to the Whamite Isles. Heard there's a lot of dead up walking around over there."

"Take that back," Aran said angrily. "Take that back or you'll be sorry!"

"Oh yeah?" Hekkel said. "And why will I be sorry?"

"Because I'll catch you sleeping," Aran said. "I'll catch you sleeping and I'll cut off your ears. You'll never pass a mirror again without realizing how sorry you were for saying that."

"You little runt," Hekkel said.

Cerril considered turning around and slapping them both down—their strident voices whipped the pounding between his temples into a renewed frenzy—then the closed door at the back of the charity crypt caught his eye. He stared at the wooden marker embossed with the flowing river of Eldath on it.

"Quiet," Two-Fingers ordered. "Cerril's found some-thing."

Instantly, all other noise inside the charity crypt stopped.

Cerril could almost hear the group stop breathing behind him. He stepped forward and tried the door. The handle refused to turn, and the door wouldn't budge. Cerril stepped back and raised his voice.

"Two-Fingers."

"Yeah."

"Open the door."

Two-Fingers moved forward, almost big enough to fill the front of the door.

"Do you want it all in one piece?" he asked.

"I don't care."

Bracing himself, Two-Fingers slammed a shoulder against the door. The old, rotted wood shattered. Instead of the door breaking open, though, a hole appeared and Two-Fingers accidentally staggered through.

The bigger boy turned around, shocked by his own suc-cess, and said, "It's open."

The door opened onto a small room that once must have housed a record keeper's office. A scribe's inkpot lay shattered on the stone floor, and moldering books lined shelves built into the walls.

"Light a candle," Cerril said as he stared around the room.

Someone took one of the candle stubs from a mounting on the wall and lit it. The wavering yellow flame filled the small room with light and hard-carved shadows that danced on the walls.

"I don't see any treasure," Hekkel commented.

Cerril went through the books, not knowing exactly what it was that he hoped to find. There was nothing in the book stacks, and equally nothing in the small desk against the wall. He knelt down, checking under the draw-ers because he'd learned that people often stuck secreted items there. None of the drawers had anything stuck under them.

He noticed a shattered inkpot on the floor. The small, fragmented glass pieces reflected light from the candle. The ink had been spilled dozens of years before and had dried to a solid black spot. However, the pool of dried liquid inscribed two fairly straight lines that ran perpendicular to one another.

Cerril knee-walked over to the lines. Seeing the way the ink seemed to have suddenly stopped in both places, he drew his dagger and traced the blade's sharp point along the edges.

"Two-Fingers," he said, "there's a hidden entrance here. Can you open it?"

Two-Fingers removed two L-shaped shims from his clothing. Holding them tightly, he hooked the shims into the floor, getting in behind the concealed trapdoor. Growling with effort, he lifted a section of the floor away.

Hekkel pushed forward the lighted candle he held. The flickering flame chewed down through the darkness that filled the opening.

"It's a passageway," Two-Fingers said.

"I know," Cerril said, then eased down into the opening, following the spiral staircase down into the bowels of the graveyard.

CHAPTER SEVEN

The wolf gazed down from a rocky promontory forty feet above Haarn.

Druz Talimsir, unaware of the wolf's vigilance, threaded through the forest only a little ahead of the druid. She'd grown quiet in her anger and had become competitive. Two days had passed since the confrontation with the slavers.

Drawing back into the shadows of a gnarled oak tree whose growth had split a boulder as tall as a man on the mountainside, Haarn studied the wolf. The animal was huge, standing half again as tall as the bitch wolf that stood at his right.

A jagged streak of lightning cut through the night, spearing through several clouds. In the night's usual darkness the clouds hadn't been visible, but with the lightning passing through them, they had length and width and breadth that faded away between blinks. The superheated air prickled Haarn's nose. The druid knew rain was going to come at any moment. He could feel the air laden with moisture as it wrapped around his body.

Haarn knew his and the woman's scents hadn't alerted the wolf because he'd been careful to keep them downwind of the pack. Broadfoot had roamed a lot while Haarn had kept his pace down to something Druz could handle, and the bear had never gotten upwind of the wolf pack that they followed. Something else had set the wolf onto them.

A chill storm wind whipped the wolf's thick gray and black fur. A narrow thatch of fur stood up along the wolf's backbone, running from his hindquarters to the top of his skull. Jagged lightning scored the sky again, striking bright light with the sudden intensity of a blacksmith's hammer.

Druz fought her way up the precarious incline Haarn's tracking skills had led them to. The spoor left by the wolves had been hidden and spread out. The delays had led Druz to accuse Haarn of delaying the confrontation with the wolf. Haarn had made no response to the accusation, and Druz had remained with him. Both of them knew she had no real choice.

The mercenary's anger showed in every line of her body and in the forced movements during her struggle to gain ground up the hill. Her foot slipped on the muddy loam and Haarn knew it was from fatigue. The woman had pushed herself too hard and too far. The druid had done the best he could to pace her, but she wasn't one to hold back. It was an admirable quality, but one that was misplaced in their current venture.

Guilt touched Haarn. Druz Talimsir was worn out and near exhaustion. The druid knew it was his fault; he'd gotten caught up in the hunt, torn between his own convictions as they'd neared their goal, and hadn't noticed her struggles.

Rock and mud clods tumbled down the mountainside as Druz pushed up another half-dozen steps. She came to a stop along the ledge. Frustration showed in the hard lines of her back. The trail they followed was little more than a game run, too narrow and too ill defined for easy passage.

Lightning seared the sky again, bleaching the charcoal gray rock into the color of white bone. The wolf's eyes blazed orange like chunks of coal as it peered down from the ledge. Silver saliva gleamed on the black muzzle. The wolf's nose wrinkled, then the lips pulled back and revealed sharp teeth.

He's hunting, Haarn realized. Anxious.

Ill ease shifted in the druid's stomach. Animals killed to eat. That was something he understood. That was natural, but an animal that killed for sport was sickening. That trait made them almost human.

Broadfoot coughed, revealing his presence in the shadows a few yards away. The bear grew impatient, and Haarn sensed a little confusion as well. Broadfoot didn't maintain a large attention span, and bears never made a practice of hunting red meat, keeping their tastes limited to nuts, fruits, tubers, and honey.

After the past two days, Broadfoot knew they were searching for the wolf, though he wasn't clear on why. Even after spending years with the bear, Haarn knew that each of them had concepts that the other couldn't understand. Broadfoot followed not out of duty or curiosity, but because Haarn led. The bond between them had lasted for years and ran bone deep.

On the precipice above, the wolf's lean haunches trembled. Excitement thrilled through the creature's thick chest. He swayed, shifting his weight from paw to paw. The bitch at his side eased forward. She held her ears flattened and tight to her head, her tail tucked between her legs.

He's taught them to hunt humans, Haarn realized.

The sickness in his stomach soured. Bile bubbled and burned at the back of his throat. He scanned the promontory, looking for the other wolves in the pack.

The bitch got too close to the edge for the lead wolf's liking. He snapped at her, white fangs flashing, grazing flesh beneath her pelt at her shoulder. Red blood flecked on the wolf's teeth. The bitch jerked back as if scalded. More blood matted her fur as the wound continued to dribble.

As she turned, Haarn saw that the bitch was heavy with unborn pups. She looked scrawny, almost used up by the coming birth. Her eyes rolled white as she continued backing away, and her muzzle dipped low to the ground.

Druz cursed, and her words seemed to crash through even the storm sounds echoing throughout the forest. The rolling thunder was a natural sound in the forest, but a human voice wasn't.

Haarn glanced up at the wolf.

Impatient, the wolf paced on silent pads along the promontory.

"Are you coming?"

Haarn glanced toward the mercenary and found her staring at him. Her accusation stood out from her body. Mud streaked her face and matted her hair. Her clothing was damp and hung heavy with sweat and soil.

Above them, on the promontory, the wolf shifted. He stepped backward, all but disappearing in the brush that topped the ledge.

Haarn didn't know if the wolf would run or try to stand his ground. It was evident that the wolf had understood that Druz wasn't alone. Remaining silent, Haarn stepped from concealment and crossed the ledge to join the mercenary.

"I thought you'd given up," Druz said.

"No," Haarn replied. He glanced up at the promontory, but the angle he was at denied him sight of the wolf.

"What are you looking at?"

Haarn shook his head. Though Druz seemed incapable of seeing most things that took place in the lands around her, she read people well. Perhaps she hadn't spotted the wolf above her, but she knew that his attitude about the night and the things in it had changed.

"What?" Druz stepped in front of him, preventing him from attempting the climb she'd tried to make.

"I'm going to climb up," Haarn said. Claws clicked against stone above, but the sound was too slight for Druz to notice.

Druz's eyes held his. "Something's up there."

Haarn held an answer back from her for only a heart-beat. "Yes."

"The wolf?"

"Yes."

Druz's face tightened. "Why didn't you tell me?"

"Because I wanted to watch the wolf as he watched you."

The hard look on Druz's face softened. "The wolf is watching me?"

"He was," Haarn said.

The mercenary looked up. "And now?"

"I don't know. We'll have to climb up and see."

"What if he's gone?"

Haarn surveyed the muddy mountainside, seeking small places, secure places, that his hands and feet could work with. Druz was good. If they could have waited till morning, when the light was better and she was more rested, she could have made the climb.

"If he's gone, we track him some more," the druid replied. "One of the bitches is heavy with pups. That's why they've been traveling so slowly."

"Slowly?" Druz shook her head. "The pack hasn't been traveling slowly. We've only now caught up with them."

Haarn reached up and flattened himself against the mountainside. His fingers traced the hold he'd spotted—a small piece of jutting rock—and he tested it. When the rock held his weight, he pulled himself up. Mud slid along the front of his clothes. He knew the wolf could hear them coming.

"I don't think he's planning to go any farther tonight," Haarn said.

"He's stopping?"

Haarn reached above and found another hold. Now that he had the rhythm, scaling the mountainside got easier. He eased himself up, fitting his fingers and moccasins into place.

"Yes," he said.

"Why?"

"Because they haven't eaten in the last two days."

"How do you know that?"

"Because we've been trailing them," Haarn replied. The muscles in his arms, legs, and back warmed against the storm's chill. "If they'd eaten much, there would have been sign."

"They're planning to eat us?"

"Yes," Haarn said. "If they weren't interested in that, they'd have been gone as soon as they'd seen you."

"What are we going to do?" Druz asked.

Haarn smiled and said, "Try to not get eaten."

He kept climbing.

Cerril followed the flickering glow of the candle he'd taken from Hekkel down into the bowels of the secret crypt beneath the burial house. The spiral staircase had either been crooked when it had been installed, or it had shifted during the decades or perhaps hundreds of years it had been there. Cerril had to lean away from the central pole at times and against it at others.

Still, the spiral staircase was a short trip to the rooms below.

Once he gained the ground, Cerril discovered that the floor there had been hewn from bedrock then covered over with stone. Dank, bare earth walls drank down the candle's glow. In a half-dozen places, though, small streams of water trickled along the walls and ran through cracks between the stone flooring. The thick, cloying smell of damp earth and rancid water tickled his nose as he stared around the chamber.

The other boys gathered around Cerril. They stayed behind him and well within the fragile safety of the candle.

"We shouldn't be here," one of the boys said. "This is a bad place. I can feel it."

"Damn," Two-Fingers said. "This is a cemetery. It's a bad place for anybody."

"Grave robbers steal from them that are fresh dead," Hekkel said. "Only reason they don't steal from them that are old-dead is because somebody done got to them."

Cerril raised the flickering candle and said, "Nobody's been here since this place was sealed."

"You don't know that," Hekkel said.

Feeling Malar's coin warm and heavy in his hand, Cerril said, "Yes, I do."

He moved forward, drawn by the coin's pull. The

candlelight slid across the ceiling. For a moment he thought none of the others were going to follow him, then he heard the rustle of their clothing.

The trickle of water running down the walls echoed throughout the room. Boots and bare feet slapped against the wet floor.

"It's raining outside," Hekkel said. "Coming harder now."

Cerril knew that. The sound of the storm rumbled in the distance, and the sibilant rush of rain threaded through the burial house.

"Who built this place?" Two-Fingers asked.

"Eldath's priests," Cerril answered.

Cerril followed a curving, narrow passageway from the chamber the ladder had led down into. The candlelight had no problem illuminating the height or the width of the passageway, but it didn't penetrate the depth.

"Why?" Two-Fingers asked.

"To keep people away from whatever is being kept in here," Hekkel said. "Any half-brained lummox could have figured that out."

"Probably got all kinds of gold and treasures down here," someone said. "We'll fill up our pockets and get out of here before anyone can stop us."

"Yeah," another boy said. "Alaghôn is a city filled with secrets. It could be somebody stuck a corpse down here and then forgot all about it. Whatever they left on it will be our gain."

"I'll bet they didn't leave anything on the corpse," Hekkel griped. "I don't see how anything could be left as long as this thing must have been left here. Chances are that rats have been at whatever was left. I'll bet you can't even strip the clothes from the body, wash them, and sell them to a ragman."

"We're not here for rags," Cerril said.

He wanted the other boys to stay brave, to stay behind him.

"Then what are we here for?" Hekkel demanded.

"Something more. Otherwise Malar's coin wouldn't be

pulling me."

Cerril stepped with more care, following the downward slope of the uneven floor. He wondered if the whole underground area had somehow been wrenched out of kilter at some time in the past.

"Should have let that man keep it," a boy farther back in the crowd muttered.

Cerril started to turn around and curse the boy, if he could find him, but his attention was riveted to the end of the passageway. The candlelight caught the walls surrounding them, twisting shadows as the flame danced, but only revealed the tilted rectangle of darkness at the passageway's end.

Blood boomed in Cerril's ears as he raised the candle to get a better look.

"There's something in there," someone said.

"I thought I saw someone moving," another boy said.

"That's just your imagination," Two-Fingers growled, but a quaver of fear rang in his voice. "Whatever's in there has been dead a long time."

"Just because it's dead don't mean it can't hurt you."

"We should leave," Hekkel whispered. "Just turn around and walk back out of this place and forget it ever existed."

Cerril wished they could do that too, but the coin wouldn't let him turn or take a backward step. It drew him on like a moth to flame. His hand trembled as he stepped toward the waiting darkness, but the shifting shadows of the underground crypt disguised that.

"You leave," Two-Fingers said. "I'll be glad to take your share."

With his heart thundering in his chest and feeling as though it was going to explode at any instant, Cerril stepped through the darkened doorway. Two steps later, the candlelight revealed an elaborate coffin that occupied the center of the room.

"Rats!" Hekkel exclaimed.

"They ain't going to hurt you," Two-Fingers said. "They're . . . they're all dead."

Cerril gazed down at the floor in front of the mysterious coffin. Dozens of rats, most of them reaching from the tips of his fingers to his elbow in length, lay stretched out on the floor. Only a few of the creatures had come to their deaths in recent times. Most of them were skeletons. Spiders, once industrious enough to make elaborate webs, hung dead in the center of their creations or on the floor. One of the arachnids struggled in its web. The legs twitched, but the spider gave no indication that it would ever get free.

"Tymora's blessing," someone breathed into the stillness of the room. "Goddess look over us."

"Cerril," Two-Fingers called. "We shouldn't be here. Whatever killed them rats and spiders is like to do for us as well."

"No." Cerril took a step forward, drawn toward the coffin in spite of the overwhelming fear that filled him. "I can't leave."

"Well, I can," someone said.

"If you leave," another said, "you don't share in what we find down here."

"What we find?" Hekkel repeated. "We're gonna find whatever killed them rats and spiders. That's all. Me, I don't want none of that."

"Cerril," Two-Fingers called. "Is that what we're gonna find here? Just death?"

Cerril took another step forward. His fear made his legs weak. He hoped they'd collapse beneath him, thinking that way he'd never have to take those final few steps to the coffin, but his knees held. Only three short strides later he stood at the coffin's side.

Candlelight danced along the icy surface. Dozens of facets caught the gleaming reflections of the burning candle. A wet sheen clung to the coffin, but Cerril knew the coffin wasn't melting.

Two-Fingers called for him again, but Cerril couldn't answer. All of his attention was riveted on the strange coffin.

Despite the muggy heat trapped inside the small room, a preternatural chill ate into Cerril's bones, chewing through his flesh without pause. Over the last few minutes, the candle had burned down to little more than a stub that leaked melted tallow over the thief's fingers and hand. Earlier the heat from the tallow had been almost hot enough to burn and had caused some discomfort. Now the melted tallow hardened almost at once, adding layers of thickness that created a shell over his hand.

"Cerril," Two-Fingers whispered. "C'mon. We shouldn't be here."

Cerril gazed at the diamond-bright coffin and saw the reflection of the boys behind him. All of them had moved back and filled the small passageway that led into the crypt.

The coffin had been crafted from chunks of ice. All the pieces had been shaved so the fit was precise despite the angles that were required to encase whatever lay within.

"Cerril," Two-Fingers pleaded.

Hypnotized by the icy beauty of the coffin, Cerril knelt. Malar's coin pulsed heat in his hand. His breath fogged the coffin's gleaming exterior for a moment then cleared away as he took his next breath. Hesitant, fear strong within him now, he touched the coffin with his free hand.

Cold fire burned into Cerril's fingers. When he tried to move them, he found they'd frozen to the coffin. Panicked, he yanked his fingers back. Imprints of his fingers—and a few bits of skin—showed against the icy surface, then they froze over and returned to smooth blue ice.

Cerril wasn't certain if the imprints and skin had sloughed away or been absorbed into the coffin. He tried to draw back from the coffin but found he couldn't. Before he knew it, his hand bearing the Stalker's coin rose. Despite his best efforts, he followed his possessed hand up.

"What are you doing?" Hekkel asked.

Cerril tried to speak but couldn't. Even if he'd been able, he knew he'd only scream in terror. His gaze locked on a design that had been etched into the icy surface of the coffin, scored deep, but almost covered up by the gleaming layers of frost. The design showed a flowing stream, the mark of Eldath.

The frost retreated from Malar's coin in Cerril's shaking fist. Eldath's mark grew brighter and turned red with heat. Steam poured from the mark.

Trembling, Cerril placed Malar's coin on top of Eldath's mark. Even before Cerril could withdraw his hand, the coin turned blistering hot, scorching his fingertips. He drew his fingers back, sticking them in his mouth to cool them, not wanting to use the icy surface of the coffin for any kind of relief. He didn't trust it.

Steam poured from the coffin around Malar's coin. The gold glowed red as it sank into the ice and obliterated Eldath's device.

Cerril stared at the sinking coin then staggered back as the ice shattered and exploded outward. Dozens of flying ice chips struck his face and arms. Several of them drew blood as a great steam cloud obscured the coffin.

Some of the boys behind Cerril screamed in fear. Feet slapped against the stone floor.

The candle dropped from Cerril's nerveless fingers. His breath caught in the back of his throat as he spotted the crimson threads covering his arms. Even as he realized he was looking at his own blood, the falling candle flame died.

Darkness filled the crypt area.

Screams and curses filled the room behind Cerril. He made himself start breathing again even though he felt like his lungs had frozen fast inside his chest. A lambent blue haze dawned inside the room.

A figure rose from the shattered remnants of the coffin. It was man-shaped, dressed in dark funeral clothing. Ivory colored bone showed at the figure's breast. Horrified, Cerril couldn't help looking at the figure's hands. Skeletal fingers flexed slowly. The hooded figure's head turned toward his hands, surveying the fleshless bones with casual interest. The hood turned toward Cerril, shadows masking the face within.

"Who are you, boy?" a cold, harsh voice demanded.

Steam roiled around the figure.

"N-no-nobody," Cerril replied.

He managed to get his legs working under him again. Bracing himself, he took two quick steps backward.

The figure surveyed him in silence for a moment, then said, "Are you one of Eldath's followers?"

Cerril shook his head. "No." His voice cracked and echoed within the crypt.

"Why?" the hooded figure asked.

"I was forced," Cerril responded.

"By whom?"

"I don't know. The coin brought me here."

The hooded figure cocked his head. "What coin?"

"Malar's coin," Cerril answered.

He tried another step back but his legs felt weak and he didn't trust them.

The figure nodded. "Malar."

"Yes," Cerril replied, cursing the god beneath his breath.

"I had thought Malar had forsaken me."

"Malar—Malar," Cerril said, stumbling over the words, "told me there would be a reward."

Even though the hood shrouded the figure's face, Cerril could tell that the figure within grew more interested at his declaration.

"A reward?" the figure asked.

Cerril tried to speak but couldn't. He nodded instead.

Insane laughter pealed through the crypt. The noise sounded as if it came from the bottom of a well, growing stronger as it caromed off the walls.

"Cerril!" Two-Fingers yelled from the other room. *"Cerril!"*

Despite the terror in Two-Fingers's voice, Cerril couldn't tear his eyes from the figure as it approached him.

The figure glided across the stone floor. Shattered pieces of the ice coffin darted away from the hem of its funeral garb. Whatever spell had bound the coffin together no longer had any power over the figure.

"Cerril!" Two-Fingers yelled. "The damn stone has replaced itself at the top of the stairs. We're locked in!"

The fact didn't surprise Cerril. Whatever he had helped free was powerful. The young thief had no doubt about that.

"Do you know who I am, boy?" the figure asked in its thundering voice.

Cerril shook his head.

"Answer me!" the figure roared.

"No," Cerril said. "No, I don't know who you are."

"You should, boy," the figure said. "You should have known. No one should ever forget me."

It reached up, skeletal hands closing on the hood's sides. It tugged the hood back as a gust of swirling fog obscured it for a moment, then in the next heartbeat a corpse's face showed through.

Patches of blue-black skin clung to the dingy ivory skull. Wisps of beard as thick and as unkempt as a horse's tail jutted along the jawbone. Dull red, the color of fresh-spilled blood under bright moonlight, glowed at the back of the cavernous eye sockets. High cheekbones stood out above the crooked-toothed rictus.

"No one will be allowed to forget me, boy," the figure rasped.

Breath tight in the back of his throat, Cerril watched as the figure's jaws unhinged. Somehow it had spoken to him without opening its mouth. He saw the abnormal sharpness of the teeth, knowing they'd been filed to points.

"Borran Klosk has returned," the figure declared, "and all of the Vilhon Reach will tremble to learn that."

Numb with fear, Cerril stumbled backward. Two-Fingers and Hekkel yelled in the other room at the end of the long passageway. Cerril turned to flee and smashed his face into the side of a wall. The pain put an edge on his wits again, allowing him to get control of his body. He ran, fleeing back up the passageway. He pushed his hands against the walls to control his flight. Fast as he was though, he was certain he could hear the figure's clothing flap as it pursued him. There was no escape. Cerril knew that, but he had to run.

Only a little farther on, he caught sight of Two-Fingers standing at the top of the spiral staircase. The bigger boy was slamming his hands against the stone that had covered the opening and locked them in. The hollow thumps of his efforts echoed throughout the chamber. Several of the other boys shrieked and cried out.

Cerril opened his mouth to yell a warning, but incredible pain filled his head. He lost control over his legs and fell to the ground, landing on his knees. Something moved, twisted with horrible pain inside his head, then his vision blurred and went out of focus. The pain felt like a rat eating through his head.

Paralysis held Cerril. He couldn't move, couldn't breathe, couldn't scream out in pain. A terrifying sucking sound echoed within his head. He gazed at the fear-filled faces of the boys on the other side of the room. All efforts he made to cry out to them to help him failed.

Pain wracked through his head again. Something broke with a liquid crunch. There was a brief moment of relief as the pressure inside his skull faded. Then cold horror filled him as he spotted the snake-like thing that lashed the air two feet in front of his face.

The snake-like thing was as thick as a broom handle and dark purple. Blood clung to it but was absorbed almost at once. Somehow the figure had thrown the snake-thing *through* his head. Coiling on itself, the snake-like thing came back at Cerril's face. Three hooked claws clacked together at the thing's end.

Still paralyzed, unable to defend himself, Cerril watched in terror as the clawed appendage bit into his face. Unable to fight back, he felt himself pulled around, falling into a helpless pile of loose limbs on his side. He stared up in revulsion, realizing that the purple snake-thing was the dead man's tongue, expelled over those sharp, bright teeth.

The thick purple tongue lashed out again, leeching onto Cerril's face. Despite the lethargic numbness overlying his need to escape, the boy felt the tongue suckling at his cheek, feeding on the blood that welled into the wounds it had caused. Cerril couldn't move to defend himself, couldn't even scream.

The tongue pulled free after a moment and slid under his chin, the dark purple flesh hard and cold against his skin. Then the tongue bit deep, sinking into the fevered blood that hammered against his throat. Even as the renewed assault of pain hit him, darkness quick and feathery as a raven's wing swooped down and blotted out Cerril's senses.

CHAPTER EIGHT

The wind howled along the mountainside, coming in from the east in great swirling gusts that hammered Haarn and whipped his hair. A chill hung in the air, but warm layers mixed in with it, letting the druid know the storm wasn't going to be an easy one, and that it was almost upon them now.

He climbed with steady grace, managing the thinnest of grips with practiced fingers and toes. Straining, he forced his body up the sheer side of the mountain. Pausing to regain his breath for a moment, he gazed down at Druz Talimsir.

The woman climbed the rope he'd set for her, but he still moved upward with more alacrity than she did. Her hair hung in sweaty clumps around her shoulders.

Stubborn, Haarn told himself as he watched her, and proud.

Both of those were good traits, if exercised with proper restraint. His mother would have been pleased with her spirit, but Haarn knew his father would have faulted Druz for her self-aggrandizement.

Druz gazed up at him in defiance.

"You're not waiting on me."

Haarn nodded and turned back to his attack on the mountainside, knowing the wolf pack waited for them. He could smell the stink of them, and he'd heard them growling among themselves, stoking up their courage to attack him and the woman. They were hungry, and a storm was blowing in. Wherever they holed up to wait out the storm, the wolves wanted to do it on full stomachs.

He reached up and caught another hold, shifting his head a little to avoid the mud that slapped under his left eye.

"Are they still there?" Druz asked.

"Yes."

Haarn estimated that less than three feet remained to the top.

"What makes you so sure?"

"I can hear them."

She was silent for a moment then said, "Then they can hear us."

"Yes."

"They'll be waiting."

"They already are," he said.

The rope slid against the rough stone fronting the mountainside as Druz pushed up.

"They think they can kill us," Druz said.

"Yes," Haarn replied.

He pulled the other end of the rope she'd climbed up to him. As she'd climbed, he'd held onto the other end, managing a rope loop, and took it up higher to find a new place to tie on.

Small trees and brush spotted the mountainside's edge. Haarn chose a thick-boled fir tree and tied the rope fast. Below, Druz swapped ends of the rope again and began climbing the final ten-foot stretch. Breathing out, knowing that their climb up the mountain had given Broadfoot plenty of time to come up the other side and provided a distraction for the wolves, Haarn pulled himself up onto the ledge. The bear traveled faster than Druz could have.

The wolf pack remained hidden in the shadows of the brush crowning the mountaintop. Despite their silence, Haarn smelled them even over the howling winds. Their anticipation and hunger colored their odor.

Druz threw an arm over the top of the ledge and began

hauling herself up. Wariness tightened her features as she glanced around the promontory.

Haarn kept his voice soft and low. "They're biding their time."

He opened his senses to the forest world around him, searching for Broadfoot.

Ah, he thought, there you are.

The bear's scent threaded the air and Haarn didn't think the wolves had noticed it or considered its presence important.

Druz started to draw her sword.

"No," Haarn said when he heard the rasp of steel against leather. He turned to face her.

She cut her eyes toward his, her sword half out of its sheath. "If they rush us there's no place to go."

"No, there isn't," Haarn said, stepping forward. "We know that already, and so do they."

He walked beyond the shelter of the trees and out into one of the clearings atop the mountain where the rocky strata had proven impossible to dislodge. Standing in the center of the huge rock shelf half-buried in loam, trees, and brush, the druid spoke a few words of a prayer then inscribed a series of arcane characters in the air before him.

The characters glowed an eerie blue for a moment then dissipated as if torn apart by the winds.

Haarn felt the power of the spell invade his mind, opening corners of understanding to him that he could never quite remember afterward. The spell was an old one to him, but it had never quite become too familiar. A quiet filled his thoughts, then it was invaded by an angry series of throaty growls.

"What are you doing?" Druz asked.

Haarn ignored her. If his spell was going to work, he had to stay focused. He concentrated on the growling noise, knowing that it came from the wolves. As his enhanced senses sharpened, he recognized that there were eleven distinct voices among the pack. Three of them were male.

What is man doing? a soft voice asked.

Watch, a strong male voice answered. *Wait.*

When will we eat? My cubs are hungry.

Soon. We all eat soon. Rush now, we may have to chase their bodies to bottom of mountain.

Druz Talimsir stepped up beside Haarn. Her fist still wrapped around her sword hilt.

"What's going on?" she asked.

"I'm going to talk to the wolf," Haarn replied.

The mercenary looked at him. "We're not here to talk to the wolf. We're here to kill it. We had an agreement."

"Yes," Haarn agreed, "but I don't want to kill them all if we don't have to."

"They hunt as a pack. All of these animals are man-killers."

Even caught up in his spell as he was, Haarn couldn't miss the vehemence in her voice when she called the wolves *animals.*

"The wolves follow a leader," he told her. "Take the leader away and you can change the pack."

"We may not have a choice about how many of them we kill."

"I'm working so that we will," Haarn said, but he didn't know if it would work.

The lead wolf strode from the darkness. As he moved into the opening, a fierce blaze of lightning lit the heavens. The wolf growled. Dark fur stood up in a spiky ridge along his back. The wolf's gait was the crooked movement Haarn was familiar with, the hindquarters following the forelegs at an angle.

With the spell in place, Haarn understood the wolf's growl.

Human, the lead wolf snarled, twisting his head sideways and flashing his fangs in open threat.

Food, a female voice said. She emerged from the shadows and flickering lightning reflected in her eyes. *Kill humans, Stonefur. We eat.*

Quiet, the lead wolf ordered.

Stonefur moved with rolling precision that seemed too

loose to stay together, as if he were a puppeteer's device and the strings had become worn and frayed.

Haarn maintained eye contact with the wolf and turned his body to keep the creature before him. The druid's throat worked, but growls came forth instead of words.

You are called Stonefur?

The wolf closed his jaws and took a step back. Muscles coiled and quivered beneath the sleek fur.

You speak, the wolf said.

Yes.

Excited confusion rippled through the growls of the other wolves. They strode forward from the shadows, five on either side of Stonefur.

Are you wolf-man? Stonefur asked.

No.

Haarn wondered if the wolves had encountered a lycanthrope at some point. It would have been the only way Stonefur would have known about the existence of werecreatures.

You know me, Haarn continued. *Open your nose. Breathe me.*

The druid spread his empty hands at his sides and the wolf approached with caution but stayed well out of arm's reach. Feral gleams ignited in the yellow-green eyes as they flicked back and forth between Haarn and Druz.

Not wolf-man, Stonefur said. *Know you. You lifekeeper. Protector of lands.*

Yes. Haarn remained still.

Not afraid of Stonefur?

No.

The wolf snapped his jaws, and for a heartbeat, a lightning flash made the fangs look blue while the wolf's eyes turned orange.

Stupid human.

I respect Stonefur's pack, Haarn growled.

The wolf preened, drawing his wedge-shaped head high and unfurling his tail like a flag in the wind.

Stonefur great killer, said the wolf. *Stonefur kill many humans. Eat humans. Feed pack good.*

I know.

The wolf paced in a semicircle before Haarn.

Why you here, lifekeeper? You search for Stonefur?

Haarn didn't break eye contact. *Yes.*

What want?

You can't keep killing humans.

Haarn noted the crafty set to the wolf's eyes as he paced. Stonefur knew how the meeting was going to go. Perhaps conversation with prospective prey wasn't the wolf's usual method of operation, but Stonefur was intelligent.

The other wolves milled around, their attention shifting from Haarn to Druz.

Stonefur kill humans if want, the wolf declared. *Humans more challenging than other food. Fun to kill. Human young feed many wolves. Only one kill.*

Killing humans stops, Haarn said.

Not stop. The wolf stood still. *Stonefur say when stop. Not lifekeeper. Lifekeeper be friends with humans if want. Not Stonefur. Not Stonefur's pack.*

I will stop you.

Stonefur growled and even the druid's spell couldn't translate. The wolf's teeth flashed and snapped as the first raindrops swirled into the mix of whipping winds.

The rain stung Haarn where it struck him, and spread an icy chill over his exposed skin. The stones in the clearing would become slick with the precipitation.

How lifekeeper stop? Stonefur challenged.

Without hesitation, Haarn drew the long-bladed dagger at his hip.

You kill Stonefur?

Yes. Haarn kept his voice as cold and unflinching as the storm rain.

The other wolves moved in closer, growling threats and baring their fangs.

Stonefur snapped at the other wolves, then ran at them and smashed against them to halt them. The female bearing pups fought with Stonefur, but the bigger wolf snapped his jaws and bit into the bitch's ear. Blood streaked the fur as the wolf bitch turned and trotted back.

The lead wolf slunk back toward Haarn and growled, *Stonefur save lifekeeper.*

No, Haarn said. *You saved your pack.*

Lifekeeper not kill all pack. Not strong enough.

I didn't come alone, Haarn said.

Haarn whistled between his teeth. Broadfoot shambled through the forest line farther down the mountain. The bear pushed up from all fours and stood on his two back feet, towering even amid the trees that surrounded him. The bear growled and the sound rolled in with the thunder.

Stonefur resumed pacing, changing his course so that his new path crossed between the druid and the bear, holding both of them back.

You can't stop me, said the wolf.

I will, Haarn promised. *You have a choice to make.*

What choice? The wolf glared with baleful eyes.

Whether you die or whether your whole pack dies.

Stonefur turned his muzzle toward the pack. They shifted in nervous anticipation.

Lifekeepers powerful, a male wolf said.

Haarn knew the males would probably be no problem. Their whole lives had been about following the male. If they saw Haarn as more powerful than Stonefur, they wouldn't take part in the coming battle. The wolf bitches would be different.

Lifekeepers don't kill furfolk, a wolf bitch said. *Humans kill furfolk.*

Stonefur has taught you to kill humans, Haarn said. *This can't be allowed.*

Humans kill furfolk, the wolf bitch repeated. *Lifekeepers battle humans.*

Killing humans will bring more humans, Haarn said. *Hunters have already gathered to track you down.*

Let them come, Stonefur said. *Humans not hunt as good as Stonefur. Stonefur kill humans better.*

Many wolves have already been killed while the hunters have been searching for you, Haarn said.

Stonefur tossed his head. The wolf bitches spread out and crept closer to the druid and the woman.

You do humans' work, lifekeeper? Stonefur challenged. *You come to slay furfolk as well?*

Haarn returned the wolf's gaze full measure. *I came to kill you.*

Why? Stonefur's tongue lolled out in disdain.

To keep the humans from hunting wolves. If I give them your head, they will stop hunting.

Maybe they only tell you that.

If the humans continue to hunt, Haarn said, *then I will kill them.*

Tossing his muzzle into the sky, Stonefur said, *These our lands, lifekeeper. Our place here before humans. Before elves and dwarves.*

No, Haarn disagreed. *The gods made all.*

Some places were made for furfolk. Some places made for scalefolk. Some places made for featherfolk. I take places back that belong to me. I hunt where I want, what I want, just like humans.

The humans will grow afraid of you and your pack, Haarn replied. *More wolves will die. I can't allow that.*

You side with the humans, lifekeeper? The wolf's voice held a taunting lilt.

Anger touched Haarn then. *I side with the balance that Silvanus struck when Toril was made. A druid of the Emerald Enclave can do nothing else.*

You choose to kill furfolk, Stonefur accused. *Your god not choose that path. That humans' way.*

Haarn called to mind words that his father had told him when he first started teaching Haarn the druidic ways: *Sometimes a tree must be sacrificed so that the forest may prosper.*

The wolf threw back his great head and howled at the storm clouds above. *Stonefur not your sacrifice, lifekeeper.*

Not my sacrifice, Stonefur. I serve Silvanus, and if my path is true, I will be made triumphant.

Strength brings triumphs, lifekeeper. The wolf stood erect and expanded his chest, making himself look larger and more threatening. *I will suck the marrow from your bones.*

"What's going on?" Druz asked above the storm.

Thunder split the air around them, and the lightning came so close to the mountaintop that Haarn felt the heat. For an instant, everything was rendered in two-dimensional black and white.

"I'm trying to save the others," Haarn said.

Druz turned on him, raising her voice. "You can't save them all."

Haarn met her gaze. "I won't kill any more here than I have to. Neither will you."

She started to reply, but the wolf interrupted them with his growls.

Leave, lifekeeper. Take your bitch with you and live.

Haarn didn't bother to correct the wolf's assumption. He faced the great animal and said, *No.*

Stonefur growled, *Then you die!*

This is between you and me, Haarn said. *The others need not die.* He prayed that would not happen.

They will not die, Stonefur growled.

If they stand with you, Haarn swept the other wolves with his gaze, *they will die tonight, or on another night. I will finish what I start, and—Silvanus guide me—I will not falter once I have begun.*

Thunder cascaded through the night, and the druid felt the tremendous noise vibrate through his moccasins. The pack shifted its attention to Stonefur.

Decide for us, the she-bitch heavy with pups said. *We follow where you lead.*

Broadfoot growled.

Stonefur glanced at the big bear. The wolf licked his chops in consideration. Rain dripped from his wet muzzle. Even the wolves knew they couldn't all escape Broadfoot's wrath.

You fight me, Stonefur said.

Yes, Haarn agreed.

When I beat you, the bear no longer take part against me.

No.

A sinking feeling dawned in Haarn's stomach. He felt a

moment of vertigo shiver through him. There was no turning back from where he stood and he knew it.

Stonefur flashed his teeth and said, *Then we fight.*

Without a word, Haarn started slipping off his gear and hide armor.

"What are you doing?" Druz asked.

"Preparing."

Haarn folded his hides and his clothing so that they turned in to themselves. There was a chance they could stay drier that way.

"For what?" the woman demanded.

"To fight."

"You're going to fight the wolf?"

"Yes." Haarn was irritated with her, not believing that she needed this explained.

"Why did you remove your armor?"

"To make the confrontation more fair."

"That's stupid."

Haarn let out his breath, watching the wolf prowl and build up his own confidence, and fought back an angry retort.

"No," he said, "it's the only way I can do this."

"You have powers, Haarn," Druz said. "Use them."

"No. This must be balanced." Haarn glanced at his companion. "However this should turn out, you're going to stay out of it."

"The hell I will!" Druz's eyes flashed beneath the hood of her traveling leathers. "I'll not be left up here on this mountain to be slaughtered by those wolves."

"You won't be harmed."

"You can't know that."

"Broadfoot will protect you should it come to that," Haarn said. He stood bare-chested in the near-freezing rain, clad only in his moccasins and breeches, which were damp and heavy. "Broadfoot will also keep you from interfering with this fight. He won't be gentle."

"I didn't come here to—"

"*Woman!*" The tone in Haarn's voice caused Druz to stop speaking and step back. "You came here to get that wolf's head. I'm going to give it to you. Don't argue with me."

Fire flashed in Druz's eyes.

"I have bound us all with this agreement," Haarn said. "I'll not suffer it broken."

"A warrior doesn't give away his strength," Druz argued.

"I'm not a warrior."

Haarn transferred his knife to his left hand. In his mind, he knew his declaration, defensive as it was, wasn't true. During his years, he had fought at his father's side as well as on his own, but those fights had been against men for the most part, not animals who lived in the forests and plains.

Druz said, "You're setting yourself up to fail."

"I won't fail," Haarn told her. "Not as long as I've got a breath left within me."

The clouds burst without warning, unleashing the torrent of rain that had been threatening. He pushed away all thoughts of the cold and concentrated on staying alive.

Your long tooth won't be enough to save you, Stonefur said, flicking his tail.

Easing down, eyes on the wolf, Haarn reached into his discarded gear and retrieved a small fighting club. The weapon was short-hafted and was run through by a leather wrist thong. It was shaped by a knife blade, hardened by druidic spellcraft, and capped in bone.

It's fair enough, said Haarn.

"You're not going to use your scimitar?" Druz asked.

"No," Haarn answered.

"You can't take that monster on with only a knife and a club. That's suicide."

"It's as balanced as I can make it." Haarn popped his arm and caused the weighted club to snap into his hand. "The scimitar would give me too much of an advantage."

"You didn't seem to mind taking the advantage where you could against the slavers."

"No," Haarn said, "I didn't." He nodded toward Stonefur. "Let it begin."

The wolf turned to his pack. His fierce growls drove them back into the shelter of the brush and trees. Stone-fur came toward his opponent at an oblique angle.

Gathering his courage and his sense of purpose, Haarn circled as well. His attention was torn between the wolf and Druz Talimsir. He didn't know if the mercenary would be able to restrain herself. And if she didn't, Haarn knew it would cost them all.

Stonefur rushed in, catching Haarn in mid-stride as he circled. Quick, white fangs flashed for the druid's crotch, drawing his hands down to protect himself. Haarn's hands only met empty air, though. Stonefur shifted directions without effort, gliding by, then sinking his fangs into the druid's right ankle. The wolf remained on the run, using his weight and his grip to yank Haarn off-balance.

CHAPTER NINE

"Eldath's mercy, Brother Tohl, awake!"

Tohl stared at the grinning visage of Borran Klosk standing before him. The battlefield on which they stood—near Morningstar Hollows, a small village northwest of Alaghôn—was one Tohl had seen many times, but never during the time of the epic battle between forces of the living and hordes of undead. During his career as a priest of Eldath in Alaghôn, he'd made the pilgrimage to the battlefield several times. Acquainting the acolytes with Alaghôn's history in regards to Borran Klosk had been part of his responsibilities for decades.

Mist swirled up from the battlefield spattered bright with the blood of men, elves, and even a few dwarves. Men and elves had lived in Turmish then, as well as other cities along the Vilhon Reach. The dwarves had traveled down out of Irongfang, their city in the Alaoreum Mountains, when they'd heard about the menace Borran Klosk and his undead minions had presented.

Brother Tohl knew it was a dream as he surveyed the carnage—he'd had similar nightmares over the years. Borran Klosk had never shown up in any of those earlier dreams.

The mohrg stood amid the death and devastation. A torn and tattered purple cloak hung from his shoulders and fluttered in the breeze laden with flies and the stink of death. Though Tohl had never before seen the commander of the undead armies that had threatened to overrun Turmish, he had no doubt about the creature's identity.

Klosk strode among the dead. Besides the humans, dwarves, elves, and a few scattered gnomes and halflings, there were also corpses of men and women of all races that had been dead long before the battle had taken place. As the mohrg moved among them, he touched a few with the crooked bone staff he carried. After he passed, the touched corpses jerked and pushed themselves to their feet and started shambling after their master.

"Follow me," Borran Klosk entreated.

The undead lurched after the mohrg, stepping toward the deepening sunset.

"Brother Tohl!"

Tohl knew the words came from some other place than the dream. For a brief moment he considered following the words out of the horror that surrounded him.

Wait, a soft voice bade.

Mistress? Tohl stood his ground. During all his years he had prayed to Eldath and felt certain that the Quiet One had worked in his life in small ways, but he'd never before heard her voice. Even so, the old priest was certain he heard it now.

Patience. Something can be learned here.

Tohl's heart beat faster and threatened to rouse him from the dream. He had a vague sensation of being shaken, of someone's hand on his shoulder. He ignored the intrusions and stayed within the dream.

Marshalling his courage, girded by the certainty that he was doing Eldath's work, he crept around the fringes of the battlefield. He stayed within the trees outside the clearing that Borran Klosk and his undead army followed. Branches whipped at Tohl's face and tore at his skin

Despite the fact that he knew he was in a dream, he didn't doubt that Borran Klosk had the power to hurt him. A stray thought that perhaps he wouldn't wake from the dream if the mohrg discovered him chilled his spine.

Courage, the quiet, calm voice said.

I've never been long on courage, Lady, Tohl admitted.

I will be with you, Tohl Farmarck, as I have stood with others against Borran Klosk in the past.

Before he could stop himself, Tohl remembered all the priests, warriors, and helpless victims who had died warring against Borran Klosk. He felt guilty, then he wondered how much of his thoughts Eldath was aware of. He continued up the steep rise, drawing within sight of Borran Klosk again.

The mohrg topped the crest and started down the other side.

Scrambling, panting for breath and trying to ignore the burning in his lungs, Tohl forced himself to the top of the crest. He peered down as the mohrg continued down the other side.

The brush and trees grew denser at the bottom of the crest. During the decline, the dozen or more sluggish streams of water that drained the mountains farther south and east became white-water rapids no more than two or three feet across. Once they reached the flatlands below, the streams blended to become a small creek that snaked through the swamplands below.

We are near Morningstar Hollows, Tohl realized.

Yes, the quiet, still voice whispered in his head.

But everything is different.

The Morningstar Hollows that Tohl remembered was marshland, filled with knobby-kneed roots anchoring huge river pine, oak, elm, walnut, and pecan trees.

This is the way it was, the quiet voice said, *before the Alaoreum River roared free of its banks the first time, consuming Borran Klosk and his army. Pay attention, Brother Tohl. There is something to be learned here, and the tapestry of magic that has rent the night there and to which you are linked has opened this window of opportunity.*

Yes, Lady.

Excitement thrilled through Tohl, but dread kept pace with it. Borran Klosk had always been recognized as Malar's tool. The Stalker possessed particular hatred for Eldath's followers as well as the druids who followed the ways of Silvanus.

Borran Klosk walked into the marshlands.

Heart beating at the back of his throat, Tohl followed. His courage came from his belief in Eldath and the powers of the Quiet One, for he had little confidence in his own abilities. He could think of no reason why he had been singled out for this experience, but he couldn't forego it.

Only moments later, Borran Klosk stopped. The undead army gathered around him.

For the first time Tohl realized that the battle had been devastating for Borran Klosk's minions as well. Several of them were missing limbs. At least two dozen zombies trailed the pack by dragging themselves through the muck with their arms, their lower bodies or legs missing.

Borran Klosk spoke in an arcane tongue Tohl couldn't understand.

Listen, the quiet voice urged.

I can't understand, Lady.

The harsh words and rolling consonants gave Tohl a headache that he knew owed part to the magic the mohrg commanded.

Listen, the quiet voice insisted.

An abrupt change occurred inside Tohl's head. He felt a sickening lurch, then Borran Klosk's horrid voice came as if from a long distance away.

"—now find ourselves hunted by every city or nation along the Vilhon Reach," the mohrg told the undead grouped around him.

Tohl knew that the words he heard didn't come from the undead creature's mouth, not with the thick, obscene tongue writhing in there.

"Perhaps," Borran Klosk went on, "our efforts to secure these lands for ourselves and for Malar will fail."

There was no response from the crowd.

They were mindless, the quiet voice whispered into Tohl's mind.

Tohl took the goddess's word for it, for he had never seen an undead for himself.

Borran Klosk, the quiet voice said, *was—and remains—jealous of all those who live. That hatred drives him to destroy life.*

Remains?

Patience, Brother Tohl, all will be made clear to you, then you must take action.

Of course, Lady.

Tohl pushed aside his curiosity as much as he was able and concentrated on the scene before him.

"The thrice-cursed Emerald Enclave is choosing to involve themselves in my affairs," Borran Klosk declared, "but I am prepared for them."

He reached into the tattered cloak he wore and drew out a small leather bag. Improbable though it was, the mohrg opened the bag and shoved his whole arm inside. There was a momentary pause, then Borran Klosk pulled his arm back out. His hand gripped a small, shiny, red jewel that glowed even in the dim light provided under the leafy canopies.

"I have found a means to defeat the druids," said Borran Klosk, "as well as to bring the whole of the Vilhon Reach to its knees."

His hands worked with surprising speed, dismantling the jewel into several pieces.

I don't know what that is, the quiet voice replied to Tohl's unspoken question, *but I can feel even from here, through you and across the years separating this place, that whatever Borran Klosk has contains great power.*

Trembling in ill-contained fear, Tohl felt trapped as he gazed at the mohrg. Even with his limited ability to sense the magical nature of the world through his ties to his chosen goddess, he could feel something . . . wrong . . . about Borran Klosk's prize.

"I cannot yet bring forth the powers held in these devices, but the time will come. Malar has given me his blessings, and I know I will be made triumphant."

Borran Klosk took a step forward, sinking knee-deep in the muck and the mire of the marshlands. The pieces of the jewel glittered in his hands in the dank shadows.

"I have carried this for years, assembling it over that time. Now, with the Emerald Enclave abandoning their neutral position regarding the fate of the civilizations of the Vilhon Reach, I am in danger. So I call upon you, my lieutenants, to carry what I no longer dare to possess."

Five shambling mockeries of human beings stepped forward from the undead army around the mohrg. Four of them were men, one was a young woman with long, dark hair. She could not have been dead for long because she was intact and unblemished. The four men had been dead much longer and showed the worse for wear.

"The druids pride themselves on their knowledge of the cycle of life," Borran Klosk said. "They untangle the webs of life and seek to address a balance that only they can see." The mohrg approached the first of the men. "But Malar has given me the seeds to disrupt the work of the druids. I can tear apart the fabric of their existence, and I will, as soon as the power I need grows larger."

"Malar has been kind to you," the woman said in a clear voice that carried across the watery land.

"Malar has been kind to us all," Borran Klosk agreed, "but he is a most demanding god. We will succeed in this endeavor on his behalf or he will see to our eternal destruction."

"What would Malar have us do?" another zombie lieutenant asked.

"Guard that which I am about to give you," Borran Klosk said. "Guard it until my return. I have one final battle which needs to be fought."

"We will go with you," the zombie woman said.

"No." Borran Klosk shook his head. "We can't afford to lose that which I am about to give you. You must stay here."

"Then give us what you will, Borran Klosk."

Borran Klosk turned to the zombie that had spoken. "Prepare yourself."

The zombie stood before the mohrg with its arms loose.

Without hesitation, Borran Klosk held one of the jewel pieces in his fist. He mouthed words that couldn't be translated by whatever spell Tohl was under. A lavender glow surrounded Borran Klosk's hand. When the brightness leveled off, the mohrg rammed his fist into the zombie's chest.

Tohl quavered and grew sick at the sucking, oozing sound Borran Klosk's fist made inside the zombie. He controlled his stomach with effort.

A moment more and Borran Klosk withdrew his hand. The jewel piece glinted within the obscene recesses of the zombie's chest.

"What I have given," Borran Klosk said, "you will defend."

The zombie bowed its head. "What you have given, I will defend."

The undead creature pulled its broken chest back together, then it tore the ragged breeches it wore into strips and used them to bind its chest.

In quick succession, Borran Klosk implanted the jewel pieces into the other zombies, including the female one. All of them repeated the litany the mohrg spouted, and Brother Tohl knew it had to be part of a binding spell.

Lady, I thought all of Borran Klosk's minions weren't capable of thinking.

As did I, the quiet voice agreed. *It's apparent there were things about Borran Klosk that we didn't know, but they are known now.*

If this has all happened before, why didn't you know about it then?

Brother Tohl, there are mysteries even unto the gods.

The declaration was unnerving, made more so because the quiet voice said it with such calm. All of his life, Tohl had believed in the virtuous strength of Eldath. To hear that the Quiet One didn't know everything was almost sacrilegious.

Lady, what are we to do here?

We will watch, Brother Tohl, and learn. Then I shall decide how we are to act.

Tohl puzzled over the events unfolding before them.

If these things happened hundreds of years ago, said the priest, *as they must have, why do we have to know them?*

Malar is making a bid to gain more power in the Vilhon Reach. The events of the undersea war waged by the sahuagin and the being called the Taker has unbalanced many things within the Sea of Fallen Stars. Beliefs change as blame is sought.

Tohl knew that was true. Eldath's following was gaining ground. Even a number of followers in the depths of the Sea of Fallen Stars had stood to recognize the Quiet One as their chosen goddess.

In the marshlands, Borran Klosk returned his attention to his first lieutenant. The mohrg said words that Tohl felt certain were never intended for human or living tongues. The wet muck at the zombie's feet yawned open, sucking down water, mud, and the undead creature. An instant later, the yawning chasm closed as if it had never existed.

Continuing to chant, Borran Klosk buried the remaining zombies. The earth sucked and shifted, and water gurgled.

Are the jewel pieces still there, then? Tohl watched as Borran Klosk chanted prayers and spread his hands out across the foaming water.

I don't know, the quiet voice admitted.

Later, Tohl pointed out, *the Alaoreum River was caused to flood. The forces that were unleashed would have changed all of this land.*

I know. Still, there must be a reason Borran Klosk has risen again.

Fear shivered through Brother Tohl anew. Memory of the tombs of Eldath filled his mind.

Borran Klosk is buried away, said the priest. *No one has been down to his tomb in hundreds of years.*

We locked him away, the quiet voice said. *We never destroyed Borran Klosk. For all that we tried, the Stalker prevented us.*

Because Borran Klosk was Malar's own. Tohl watched the mohrg start to move his army on through the marshlands. *Some say that Borran Klosk was bent and twisted by the Stalker's own hand.*

Yes.

How can Borran Klosk be returned?

Through Malar's design.

When?

Tonight, the quiet voice said. *While you were sleeping.*

We have to do something.

Be at peace, Brother Tohl. We are doing something. I followed my own designs to you, to the thing that binds you to Borran Klosk.

But there is nothing.

You have made the tales of Borran Klosk your life's work, Brother Tohl, the quiet voice said. *I have made you a watchdog of sorts over the mohrg's uncertain captivity. Malar found a way to reach through the protection I wove through my priests. Borran Klosk has been roused, and he is feeding on the life's blood of children even now.*

"No!" Tohl couldn't hold back the startled cry that burst through his lips. Sour bile burned in his throat.

Borran Klosk turned in the marshlands, looking back across the marshlands and up the hill that led to the lower regions of the area. The horrible face grimaced as if the ragged nose that clung to the mohrg's features could scent an unwelcome stench.

"Human," he snarled. "Find him and kill him."

Tohl hunkered in the brush. Desperation flooded the priest as he searched for a way out.

It's all a dream, he told himself. *Nothing but a dream.* But he knew that wasn't true.

It's time to wake, Brother Tohl, the quiet voice told him. *Staying here is dangerous for you.*

The zombie army spread out then began making their relentless way toward the priest's hiding place. Brother Tohl held his position a moment, then had to flee as the first of the army pushed through the brush to get at him. He turned, slipping on the mud, then caught himself on his hands and shoved himself forward. Even after he broke cover, there was no clamor or cry that broke out behind him. The pursuit by the undead remained silent, and they made better time than he did over the broken terrain.

Let go of the dream, the quiet voice urged.

I'm trying, Lady.

Tohl clawed through brush and pushed himself up a number of times when he stumbled over the knobby tree knees that projected up from the water-soaked ground or the ones that lay covered by the dark water.

You must. It is the only way you will live.

Brother Tohl ran uphill, thinking that the high ground might offer him some kind of advantage. He avoided part of one of the streams that he thought looked deep, and stepped through another just to plunge into the water up to his waist. He kept falling, submerging for a moment and getting a mouthful of foul water before he pushed his head back up above the surface. He tried to step out of the water but discovered that a submerged tree or rock caught his foot.

Help me, Eldath!

I can't, the quiet voice replied. *This place is beyond my reach, Brother Tohl. Time here is unfolded somehow, the past accessible through you. I can't extract you from the powers that have drawn you there.*

Please!

Frantic, Tohl watched as the zombies came closer. They had trouble with the uphill grade and the mud, but they never stopped coming. The priest closed his eyes and tried to awaken. In the dim recesses of his mind, he heard the excited cries from someone in his sleeping chambers within Eldath's temple in Alaghôn. He focused on the cries, trying to draw himself back along the sound of the voice.

Let go, the quiet voice said.

I'm trying, Lady! I swear to you that I am trying!

Brother Tohl's breath came in ragged gasps. Tears wet his cheeks. He was more afraid than he'd ever been in his life. He watched in frozen horror as the shambling zombies descended upon him, thick as a murder of crows.

One of the zombies grabbed Brother Tohl's arm. The priest felt like a vise had gripped him. He screamed.

"Brother Tohl, you must wake!"

Tohl felt someone shaking him. His breath caught at the back of his throat. Unable to keep his eyes closed any longer, he opened them and stared into the eyes of the young priest shaking him awake.

"Brother Tohl," the young priest said. He looked bleary and disconcerted.

Tohl peered around his bedchamber, discovering he was back within Eldath's temple in Alaghôn. No zombies had followed him.

"Brother Tohl," the young priest said.

"Yes?" Tohl responded.

"You talked of zombies, of Borran Klosk."

Brother Tohl thought of the graveyard at Alaghôn's heart. He gazed up at the younger priest, recognizing him in the weak candlelight the other must have carried into the room.

"Yes," said Tohl. "Yes, I did, Effrim."

The candlelight glinted against Effrim's golden locks. The younger priest's pale blue and dark green robe hung over his tall, lanky frame.

"You can release me now, Effrim," Tohl said.

A dank cold clung to the bedchamber, and in some ways it smelled of the marshlands where Borran Klosk had been.

"Of course, Brother Tohl."

Effrim stepped back. He pressed his hands against each other, twining the fingers together in a nervous habit that was familiar to Tohl.

"Send someone to wake Father Albern," Tohl said as he sat up.

"Father Albern isn't here."

Tohl started to object in irritation. Father Albern was seldom anywhere else but the temple.

"Remember?" Effrim asked. "Father Albern left a tenday ago to attend a meeting in Myth Nantar."

Tohl remembered. "How many priests are here at the temple?" he asked.

"Counting you and myself, five."

Eldath, it is too few, Tohl told himself.

He hesitated for a moment, thinking maybe the goddess would answer him or offer some direction, but she was gone, as distant from him now as the marshlands in

Morningstar Hollows.

"Brother Tohl?" Effrim gazed at him, waiting.

What would Eldath have me do? Tohl thought.

He chose to believe the goddess was working even now on the problem of Borran Klosk's rising. Still, he couldn't sit idle.

"Gather the other priests, Effrim."

The younger priest hesitated. "They will wonder why."

"Tell them we are going to investigate the possibility that Borran Klosk has broken free of his grave." Tohl didn't blame the younger man for gazing at him in slack-jawed surprise. To many of the younger priests, the mohrg was just one of the stories they'd grown up with. "Effrim?"

The younger priest blinked.

"Get moving," Brother Tohl said, stripping off his own bedclothes and reaching into the small trunk at the foot of his bed for fresh robes. "If Borran Klosk is free, we may already be too late."

CHAPTER TEN

Haarn threw himself around as he felt the wolf's jaws tighten on his ankle. Stonefur sought to sever the druid's hamstring, leaving him crippled. Haarn's effort to escape helped the wolf's fangs cut deep furrows around his ankle, but it also kept Stonefur from gaining a decent grip. Haarn reversed his hold on the fighting club, holding it instead by its thicker end. He rammed the club's narrow end down, managing to aim it between Stonefur's jaws.

The club's wooden haft clacked against the wolf's teeth. Haarn shoved the club forward, jamming it into Stonefur's jaws, widening the distance between them.

Stonefur howled in pain and frustration, still struggling to maintain a grip on the druid.

Ignoring the pain in his ankle, Haarn took a fresh hold on the knife in his other hand. He gazed at the wolf's exposed throat, knowing his opponent wouldn't have time to move before he was able to slide the blade into his neck. Still, even knowing the wolf would kill him in a moment if the chance presented itself, Haarn hesitated. A druid was trained to kill out of mercy, whether to ease an animal's suffering or to control overpopulation, and sometimes to eat, though feeding oneself at the unnecessary expense of an animal was frowned upon.

Haarn's own father had killed for food several

times that he could remember. Since going out on his own, from under his father's wing and tutelage, Haarn had seldom killed any animal, even those bearing dreadful and grievous wounds. Many druids would have killed an afflicted animal outright, but Haarn had worked to save them. Over the years, he'd challenged and killed more poachers than animals.

"Haarn, strike!"

Galvanized by Druz Talimsir's command, still reticent, Haarn struck with the knife.

An instant before the blade slid home, the wolf shied backward. The knife missed Stonefur's throat by less than the thickness of a finger.

Off-balance from the lunge, Haarn was ill prepared for the wolf's follow-up attack. He ducked, collapsing toward the muddy ground and wrapping his left arm over his head.

Stonefur's leap carried him too high. The slavering jaws didn't close on the druid's head as intended, but they grazed Haarn's arm. The trickle of blood along the druid's limb felt warm and welcome against the freezing rain.

Still in motion, Haarn threw himself to one side, falling over into a roll before the wolf could claw him. Stonefur hurtled overhead but landed on the ground. The wolf's callused pads and claws dug into the stony earth, stopping him short and bringing him back around.

You will die, lifekeeper, Stonefur promised.

The other wolves in his pack howled their approval.

Haarn tested his injured ankle as he got to his feet, wanting to make sure it would stay strong enough to support him.

Kill! the wolf bitch carrying pups snarled. *Kill, and let's eat, Stonefur.*

The wolf came again.

Haarn dodged to one side, but his foot slipped on a rain-slick stone and he almost fell. Before he could get clear of the wolf's headlong rush, Stonefur's fang gashed him again, ripping along his ribs. Fire burned the length of the druid's wounds. Before Haarn recovered, the wolf returned.

Ragged fur tore across Haarn's mouth as the wolf slammed his shoulder into the druid's face. Stonefur's jaws snapped closed on the juncture of Haarn's left shoulder and neck, seeking the jugular.

Bowing his back, Haarn fell forward in an effort to dislodge the wolf. He felt the flesh on the top of his shoulder tear. Warm blood cascaded down his body. Desperate, the druid swept the club around, swinging it from his knees.

Stonefur had expected the blow, though, and made sure he wasn't there when it arrived. Before he could recover from the neck wound and from being off-balance, Haarn looked up just in time to see the wolf's paw streak toward his face. The claws bit into his cheek, tearing down to the bone with ease.

Blood spurted up into Haarn's left eye, blinding him. He swept his knife up, keeping it along his arm. His hand touched the wolf's fur, but the animal wasn't there when the blade followed his hand. He knuckled his right hand around the club's handle then pushed himself erect.

Stonefur galloped in wide circles around the druid and growled, *You tire, lifekeeper. Men no match for wolf clan.*

Haarn exhaled, saying a small, silent prayer to Silvanus to gather his attention and make his heart cold toward his opponent.

I kill you, lifekeeper, Stonefur taunted, *then we take time with woman. Chase her, bite pieces off and eat them, and let her run till she can't run anymore. Her death will be slow, painful.*

Haarn had no doubt that Stonefur would make good on his promise, and the druid knew that no matter how skilled a warrior Druz Talimsir might be, she was no match for the wolf pack.

Stonefur raced by, cut back toward Haarn, and hoped to score another blow with his claws. Haarn chose to avoid the attack, stepping back and giving ground. Seeing the reaction as a weakness, Stonefur pressed his conceived advantage, racing forward again.

Haarn brought the club up and managed to jam it across the wolf's open jaws, fending his attacker off and keeping the saliva-covered fangs from his face and throat.

The druid teetered backward, off-balance. Before he could recover, the wolf dug his claws into the muddy ground and lunged forward.

The druid fell backward, trapped under the wolf's massive weight. The cold, greasy mud slapped against Haarn's bare back with chilling intensity. His breath left his lungs in a rush. When he breathed in again, he smelled the wolf's fetid breath and the stench of wet fur. He struggled to keep the club in place in his opponent's jaws and stay out of reach of Stonefur's fangs. Sharp rocks dug into Haarn's back, bruising and tearing the exposed flesh.

Broadfoot growled, sounding angry and fearful.

Stonefur turned his head, biting down on the club and seeking to tear it from Haarn's grip. Lightning flashed and was reflected in the pitiless depths of the wolf's wide eyes.

"Haarn!" Druz called.

Drawing part of a breath, Haarn yelled, "Stay back!"

If she didn't, she would bring the rest of the pack down on them. Even with Broadfoot and the spells Silvanus had placed at his disposal, the druid didn't know if they could escape the whole pack alive. He didn't trust the wolf's word either. Stonefur had learned to kill and lived for the bloody carnage he could cause. Haarn saw that, and his heart hardened. He remembered Druz's story about the boy who had been attacked.

You're a killer, Stonefur, Haarn accused.

Yes, the wolf replied, excitement in his voice. *Human flesh taste good.*

You hunt children.

Easy prey, the wolf countered.

He braced himself and butted Haarn in the face with his broad head. Haarn felt the wolf's teeth rattle along the club. He shifted his weapon with the wolf's movements, desperate to keep his opponent's jaws from his flesh.

You harder to kill, Stonefur said, *but more fun. I kill you, too. Soon.*

Haarn didn't have the breath to make a reply. Hot saliva dripped from the wolf's muzzle onto his exposed neck, feeling like freshly spilled blood. The stink of the wolf filled the druid's nostrils. With his throat exposed the way it was, Haarn knew all the wolf had to do was bite the veins on either side and let him bleed out.

Gathering his strength, Haarn shoved up against the wolf, trying to throw Stonefur from him. The wolf growled in triumph and bowed his back, using his hold on the club to stay on top of the druid.

Kill lifekeeper, Stonefur, the female called.

"Haarn!" Druz yelled.

Stonefur's orange eyes locked with Haarn's and the wolf said, *Your female calls out for you.*

Haarn said nothing, desperate to find the leverage that would allow him to break the wolf's hold. He kicked, trying to find a foothold in the mud. The rain beat down on him, blinding him as he gazed up against it.

Maybe I only wound you, Stonefur said. *I cripple you so that you can watch as we kill your female.*

You promised you wouldn't do that.

Haarn heaved his weight to one side, trying to slide from under the wolf.

I lied, howled the wolf.

Stonefur lunged at the druid's face again.

Haarn jerked his head to one side. The wolf's wet fur grated against his wounded cheek, tracing liquid fire against his face. He stifled a groan of pain.

The wolf regrouped at once and attacked again.

Using the club to block the brunt of the animal's fierce attack, Haarn drove his knife toward Stonefur's chest. The blade caught a flash of lightning an instant before it struck the wolf's body. Instead of penetrating Stonefur's ribcage as Haarn had hoped, the knife skidded along the wolf's shoulder bone and ripped through flesh to grate against the animal's spine.

Stonefur growled in pain and rage. Jerking his head, he turned and seized the offending hand before Haarn could withdraw it. The movement left the club free, and Haarn wasted no time in smashing his weapon into the wolf's side. As close as he was, the club did little more than bruise the wolf.

Haarn distanced himself from the pain in his savaged arm. He knew Stonefur worried at his wrist with the deliberate intent to sever the tendons. A wolf's attack, like that of feline predators, was designed to break down its prey piece by piece until it was helpless.

Levering himself over, Haarn used his opponent's displaced weight and the lock on his wrist against him. Before Stonefur could fight back, Haarn was on top of him. Struggling to straddle the great beast, Haarn drew the club back and bashed the wolf in the side of the neck.

Stonefur gave a painful howl and released his hold on Haarn's wrist. Blood matted the lighter colored fur under the wolf's muzzle.

Haarn felt light-headed from blood loss and exertion. He'd given too much away to the battle. Perhaps if he'd kept the scimitar they'd have been better matched, but he wasn't sure, and the balance had to be maintained. He drew the fighting club back and prepared to smash it against Stonefur's skull.

Lightning rent the air, and cracking thunder followed on its heels.

Haarn's breath came in ragged gasps. His chest heaved, causing his wounds to echo with dulled pain. Gazing down into the wolf's eyes, he hesitated.

To kill an opponent, his mother had told him, you must be willing to look him in the eyes, know that you will have his blood on your hands and maybe in your mouth, and accept that there is no other way. If you hesitate, you are lost.

She had been a warrior, a Harper, and had often been called away for unknown missions. Her views and those of Haarn's father had often clashed, causing for great arguments. Even though his father and mother cared about many of the same things, the paths they took to arrive at the same destination were always different.

The wolf struck as the memories tumbled through Haarn's mind, as the druid was torn between giving life and taking life. Stonefur bowed his back, bringing his hind legs up and clawing with frantic effort.

Cold fire burned through Haarn's stomach and thighs. The claws ripped through his flesh and clothing. Knowing he was exposed in his present position, he abandoned it, throwing himself to the side. He felt blood coursing down his body and hammering at his temples as his heart thudded in his chest. He pushed his hands against the ground in an effort to get to his feet. The mud gave way, though, and he fell, bumping his face against a sharp-edged stone. When he lifted his head, he saw blood on the stone, then Stonefur's body blotted out a jagged fork of lightning that cut through the night sky. Before Haarn could shift, the wolf was on him.

Stonefur snarled and howled, throwing his weight across Haarn's body. His fangs snapped at the back of the druid's head, gouging deep cuts in his skull. Releasing the club, Haarn reached up with flagging strength and hooked his fingers into the wolf's fur.

I kill you, lifekeeper, the wolf snarled. *I drink your blood. I eat of your flesh. I continue to hunt where I want— what I want.*

Haarn levered his arm, trapping the wolf, then he used the animal's attempt to pull away and gain another attack to shift his own weight. The druid rolled, dizziness spinning in his head, feeling like he was trapped in a waking dream and moving in slow motion. He struck with the knife, grazing the huge wolf's flanks. On his knees now, he braced to meet Stonefur's attack. His fingers knotted in the wolf's fur felt the shift of muscles and weight that let him know the animal was coming again.

Stonefur's head slammed into Haarn's blood-streaked chest. For a moment, the druid thought the wolf's great strength and weight had broken his ribs. The air rushed from his lungs at the contact. Black spots swam in his vision, threatening blindness. His consciousness teetered on the edge of slipping away.

Broadfoot roared a thunderous challenge.

Haarn fought his own body. If he was lost, so were the bear and the woman. He drew another breath, staving off the waiting blackness, and focused on the wolf. His grip wasn't strong enough to control Stonefur. The wolf lunged at his throat. Haarn pulled the wolf to him then, catching the creature off-guard.

Clasping the wolf to him, Haarn fell backward. He hooked his knife hand behind the wolf's back, afraid that if he didn't hold the wolf close that Stonefur would rip his throat out. The ground came up hard against his back, ripping into his flesh despite the mud. Keeping his fingers hooked into the wolf's thick coat, Haarn rammed his forearm into the animal's side again and again, seeking to drive the breath from his attacker.

Close-in fighting had to be quick and vicious, no quarter given or asked. Haarn's mother had taught him that despite his father's protests. According to his father, druids were never to get that close. Haarn's mother had taken part in a number of battles, though she never talked of them, and was of a different opinion. Sometimes the only way to kill an enemy was to look him in the eye and slip a blade home.

Haarn panted, striving to even his breath out and ease the harsh burning in his lungs. The wolf's dander, though muted by the wet coat, filled Haarn's mouth and nose. Fear touched the druid, but the immediacy of the situation kept it at bay. Still, despite Haarn's best efforts, Stonefur bit into his back.

Blinded by pain and fury, blood still seeping into his eye, Haarn tightened his grip around the wolf's neck, hoping to shut the animal's breath off. One of Stonefur's leathery ears raked against Haarn's face. Seized by impulse and the desire to live, the druid opened his mouth and took the ear in as the wolf began to rake his midsection with his claws again.

Haarn bit down, plunging his teeth through the wolf's ear.

Stonefur squalled in pain and changed his tactics. No longer interested in attacking, the wolf sought escape. Instead of raking Haarn with his claws, he pushed against the druid.

Unable to hold his opponent with his flagging strength,

Haarn felt the wolf squirm from his grip. Stonefur shook his head, helping Haarn finish sawing the ear off. The leathery piece of flesh remained in Haarn's mouth, which was filled with blood.

Panting, eyes only half open and threatening to close out of exhaustion, Haarn swallowed the wolf's blood and forced himself to his feet. He swayed in the storm winds, searching the muddy ground for the club. His breath puffed out in gray patches before him, burning as it entered and as it left his body.

Druz stood where he'd left her, but her sword was naked in her fist. Concern marked her features beneath rain-matted hair. Broadfoot roared again, filling the night with his challenge.

Stonefur trotted back and forth only a few feet away. The bloody stump of his shorn ear thrust up from his head, no longer cocked at an angle the way the other ear was. The wolf shook his head several times, slinging blood over himself and the ground.

You will die, lifekeeper.

Then come slay me, Haarn said. *You already know I'm no boy to be stalked without fear of injury. I've marked you, and even if I let you live after this, everyone will know you.*

You were lucky.

Haarn spotted the club only a few feet away. He strode toward it, watching the haunted lights in the wolf's eyes. Hunger showed in those orange eyes and hate as well, something Haarn had seldom seen in the eyes of an animal. He'd only found it in the eyes of those beasts that had spent time in the company of humans, and he wondered at Stonefur's background.

Standing in the cascading rain as the storm raged around them, Haarn prayed to Silvanus. Steeped in two schools of thought, Haarn had often found himself conflicted. He didn't know what he might have chosen had his mother not stopped coming to the forest years before, but that conflict was fading. The outcome of the battle before him resided in the sphere of his mother's teachings, not his father's. His father's skills had brought him to the wolf, but they couldn't save him.

The druid gripped the club and knife as the driving rain sluiced blood down his body. His stomach, back, and thighs bled profusely, but the muscle walls holding his internal organs remained intact. Liquid fire ran through his shoulder and neck where Stonefur's fangs had torn into him. He kept his feet apart in the manner his mother had taught him, left foot forward and right foot back, perpendicular to his forward foot. He kept his knees slightly bent, weight balanced. It was the most basic martial arts stance, the position everything else evolved from.

Haarn breathed out in slow deliberation, focusing his thoughts and quelling his fears. In doing that, he lost some of the perspective his father would have wanted him to keep. The wolf was no longer a part of the forest or of the world Haarn had sworn to protect as a druid.

The wolf was an enemy.

Perhaps, Stonefur said, *I should let you live.*

No, Haarn said, standing his ground and no longer mirroring the wolf's movements. He became the center of the world—as his mother had taught him. As the center, all things would come to him. That kind of thinking was foreign to druids, who believed they wove through the cycles of nature without creating ripples of their own. *If it doesn't end here, Stonefur, I will track you down, and I won't hold back the powers that are mine to command.*

You might not see me coming.

I'll see you. Haarn raised his voice so that the other wolves could hear over the din of crashing thunder tearing through the heavens so hard it seemed to shake the ground. *I swear to you by Silvanus's blessed eyes that I will kill all that run with you.*

Cunning and vicious, the wolf kept trotting, waiting for the moment he judged proper to strike. Lightning seared the sky, whiting out the world, and Stonefur chose that moment to attack.

Haarn had only a momentary glimpse of movement, then the lightning blinded him as the ensuing thunder deafened him. The whirling winds and the cold rain deadened his skin. His heart thudded in his chest.

Stonefur launched at him, jaws wide, blood leaking into his mouth from the stub of his ear.

Moving with a grace that surprised him in the condition that he was in, Haarn slammed his club into the side of the wolf's head. The shock rolled along the druid's arm, but he kept his stance tight, following up with the knife still held along the side of his arm. The blade sliced into Stonefur's flank.

Blood poured down the wolf's side as he landed in a rolling heap.

No mercy in his heart, Haarn went after the wolf.

Stonefur rolled to his feet and pushed up only a step ahead of the druid's arrival. The wolf raced away, muscles bunching under bloody fur.

Haarn stood his ground as the wolf cut in a semicircle, as he knew it would. He'd observed the movements of too many wolves over the years to be taken by surprise by the feint. By the time Stonefur reached him again, Haarn was set.

The wolf tried for Haarn's wounded ankle again. The druid swung the club into Stonefur's head, connecting with the animal's bloody ear.

The impact of the wolf's body crashing against him knocked Haarn from his feet. Haarn rolled, controlling his body and coming to his knees. There was no hesitation within him as he struck, no more confusion over what he was supposed to do. His knife blade flicked across the wolf's withers, opening a long cut over his hipbone.

Coughing, fatigued, and hurting, Stonefur yelped in anger and rolled to his feet while Haarn was still on the ground.

Haarn focused on the wolf's great body, knowing Stonefur outweighed him. The druid poised, on one knee and the other foot beneath him, watching as the wolf recognized the opportunity.

Muscles rippled under the wolf's bloodied fur. Claws dug for traction on the muddy ground. Clods flew behind Stonefur as the wolf hurtled toward the druid.

Haarn waited then shifted to the right and ducked. Still moving, he ripped the blade across the wolf's exposed abdomen. Thick, salty blood poured down onto Haarn.

Graceful in spite of the mortal wound, Stonefur landed. His ribs flexed, and the gaping wound in his abdomen showed. The wolf's entrails started to spill from within.

You've killed me, Stonefur snarled.

He lapped at his wound but gave up the effort. His muzzle came away stained and dripping crimson that washed away in the stormy downpour.

"Yes," Haarn said in his own voice, knowing the wolf would understand just the same. At this moment of death, there could be no lies between them. "You disrupted the balance. There was no other way to end this."

Weakened and hurting, Stonefur came at the druid again. His clawed feet dug into the earth.

Haarn tried to dodge out of the way, knowing he only had to stay alive a little while longer before the wolf's life played out, but in his weakened condition he couldn't move as fast. He shifted, intending to throw himself to the side, but his right foot slipped in the mud and went skittering away beneath him. Instinct made him drop the club and try to catch himself. When he made a frantic grab for the fallen weapon, he realized it was too late.

Stonefur crashed into Haarn, knocking the druid back, slavering jaws reaching for his throat. The foul stench of the wolf's breath invaded Haarn's senses and seared his cheek. The rough, raspy tongue raked along Haarn's jaw.

Shifting to protect his wounded midsection, Haarn brought the knife up in a short, tight arc. He felt the tip glide along the wolf's ribs, then sink home.

Pain froze Stonefur as he lay atop Haarn. The druid felt the blood-slick and rain-matted fur against his hand where he'd driven the knife to the hilt. At least two or more inches of steel had pierced the wolf's heart.

Blood leaked from Stonefur's flaring nostrils and mouth. A choking sound rumbled in his throat. Lightning strobed the heavens again, but there was little left in the wolf's eyes to light. Rattling sounded in his lungs and the great beast grew heavier.

I die, Stonefur gasped.

Yes.

Sorrow and pain ached in Haarn's chest. He no longer tried to hold the wolf from him, and knotted his fingers in the bloodied fur to hold him close.

No! the wolf bitch roared. *Not kill Stonefur! Not let!*

Knowing the wolf was coming from the slick spatter of paws against the stones and mud, Haarn tried to push Stonefur's great weight from him. The wolf's ribs trapped Haarn's knife, leaving him unarmed as he shoved to his feet.

The wolf bitch leaped the last six feet, aiming herself at the druid.

Haarn reached out and caught her muzzle, trapping it in his hands.

She has life within her, he thought. They are Stonefur's get, and they hold the promise of greatness.

The wolf bitch's weight pushed him back into the mud. She snarled and growled, but the effort came out strangely through her trapped muzzle.

Wounded and battered as he was, Haarn wasn't certain he could survive her attack. Her grief and hunger, and the protective urges that filled her from the pups being so close to being born, made her overpowering. She squirmed and struggled to get her jaws free. Her claws raked at his chest, then a shudder passed through her and she stopped.

Staring into the feral eyes only inches from his own, feeling the strength drain from the wolf bitch, Haarn felt a new fear dawn in him.

"No!"

The wolf bitch slumped to the side, propelled by a booted foot. A long sword jutted from the wolf bitch's side.

"No," Haarn repeated through a dry throat. He stared up at Druz Talimsir. "Do you know what you've done, woman?"

She frowned, leaning on the long sword and twisting it to widen the wound that had killed the wolf bitch.

"I saved your life," said Druz.

"Get away from her. Now!"

Confusion darkened Druz's rain-soaked features. She withdrew her sword but remained close by.

"By Tymora's skirts, but you are a hard one to understand. She had you. She would have killed you."

"No, she wouldn't have. I could have handled her." Haarn took in a deep breath as he forced himself into a kneeling position.

Dazed and bleeding, Haarn stared at the dead wolf as he rolled to his knees. He stretched his hands out, calling on the power that Silvanus had entrusted in him. Many druids had the power to heal wounds. As he laid his hands on the wolf, he felt and heard the last breath go out of her. The convulsive shudder that shook her shivered through him.

"What are you doing?" Druz sounded incredulous.

"I would heal her if I could," Haarn said, "but she's beyond anything I can do."

"That's stupid," Druz said. "Tymora's blessing on fools and children. Even if you did heal her, she'd only go for your throat again."

Haarn ignored Druz's words. Saving the wolf bitch was beyond him, at least in his present condition. He stared at her sides, seeing the movement caused by the pups struggling in her womb. Making his decision, he forced himself to stand, placed a boot on Stonefur's body, and yanked his knife free. Turning, he crouched, struggled with his balance and unfocused vision, and plunged the knife into the wolf bitch's body.

CHAPTER ELEVEN

Brother Tohl held fast to the side of the small wagon he and Effrim had liberated from the meager resources the Temple of the Trembling Flower had at their disposal. The wagon, though serviceable, had seen better days. The rudimentary spring struts had long since given out, making for a rough ride through the pitted back roads Tohl directed the younger priest to follow. A lantern mounted at the side of the wagon swayed as the ironbound wheels crashed over the rain-filled potholes, and still more rain came down in solid sheets.

Over the sound of the rain and the cart Effrim said, "Maybe it would be better if we alerted the city guard."

"No," Brother Tohl responded, already drenched even though he wore his best traveling leathers.

"We are only six priests," Effrim said.

"I pray to Eldath that we are enough," Tohl said through chattering teeth.

The horses' iron-shod hooves struck fire from the ill-fitted paving stones. Rarely more than a few people were out on the streets so late at night, and the storm had driven most of them indoors. Only a few sailors just now come up from the docks braved the fierce rain. None of them gave more than a moment's notice to the racing wagon.

In the back of the wagon, the other priests prayed in low voices that scarcely rose above the clattering horses' hooves. All of them were old, in their last years of service to Eldath. Sadly, Tohl knew the Quiet One's influence had ebbed. Few on dry land were drawn to Eldath, though worship of the goddess flourished among the sea elves and others deep within the Sea of Fallen Stars. After the dream, though, and the revelations it had brought, Tohl knew Eldath had not abandoned them. He blinked water from his eyes and squinted through the rain.

"There," he said, spotting the entrance to the graveyard where Borran Klosk had been entombed all those years ago.

He pulled his traveling leathers tighter around him as he saw the gloom and bleakness that clung to the place.

Effrim pulled on the reins, guiding the horses toward the path overgrown with weeds and brush. The horses stumbled at the graveyard's entrance. Effrim laid the lash across their backs and talked to them. Showing flat-eared reluctance and snorting in fury, the horses paused a moment more at the entrance then raced forward again as if dashing into a clearing.

The wagon jumped and bucked as it careened across the broken ground. Many of the graves had sunken over the long years, creating coffin-sized pits that held water inches deep. Effrim was hard pressed to keep the horses under control.

Lightning stabbed down from the sky and touched a grave ornament ahead of them. The iron rod shaped like a budding flower encircled by a sunburst symbolized Chauntea, the Great Mother. The lightning shone white-hot for a moment then faded away, leaving the super-heated metal glowing cherry red and smoking in the rain.

"That was close," Effrim said.

The glowing metal dimmed a little as they passed. Effrim brought the wagon to a halt in front of the tomb. The horses stamped and surged against the traces.

Tohl hoped it was the cold and rain that made the horses restless, but as he gazed up at the tomb, he knew it was likely something else that scared them. Steeling himself, the old priest stepped over the wagon's side and dropped to the muddy ground.

"Brother Tohl," Brother Micahan whispered as he joined Tohl. "There is the possibility that if Borran Klosk did rise from his coffin, he might already be gone."

Tohl studied Micahan's cowled visage. Micahan was old and thin from lean years and hard work. His hands had started shaking these past few years and grew worse with each passing season.

"If Borran Klosk is gone," Micahan continued as rainwater dripped from his hooked nose, "what will we do then?"

"We will try to follow his trail, Brother Micahan, to the best of our abilities." Tohl replied, whispering as well, not wanting his voice to carry too far into the tomb. It was a childish fear, he knew, but it was also one he couldn't escape.

Micahan nodded and whispered, "As Eldath wills in her wise generosity."

"Praise be those days that I can continue to give to those less fortunate," Tohl quoted.

He turned from the elder priest and hefted the mace he'd brought from the temple. It had been years since he'd taken up a weapon. The weapon felt clumsy and crude in his hands.

Effrim handled his own warhammer with certain skill. He practiced most mornings, but even he, the youngest and most physically able among them, didn't display too much confidence in his combat skills.

All of them gathered around Tohl as another lightning streak seemed to set the sky on fire. As the white brilliance flickered above them, Tohl studied the men gathered before him. They had believed in him enough to rise from their beds, endure the cold, whipping rains, and lay their lives on the line to fight a monster.

Tohl had never experienced anything like that moment with them, and he was disappointed when words failed him. With all the blessings and prayers and counseling he'd done over the years, something should have come to him.

"Eldath willing," he said finally.

"Eldath willing," the priests whispered around him.

Holding his mace in one hand, Tohl lifted the lantern from the wagon and turned toward the tomb. The others followed, none of them speaking.

At the top of the stairs, about to enter the building, Tohl turned when he heard the wagon surge into motion behind him. He watched in disbelief as the horses tore through the graveyard back in the direction they'd come. Before they'd covered half the distance, one of the horses stepped in a deep hole and went down. Tohl heard the snap of breaking bone even over the distant echo of thunder. The falling horse took down the other animal as well, causing the wagon to slam into both of them and overturn. When the wagon settled against the ground, neither of the horses moved.

"Effrim," Tohl said.

At once, the younger man peeled away from the group and raced across the graveyard. Tohl watched Effrim check both animals then run back to the tomb steps.

"Dead," Effrim said when he returned. His breath was tight in his throat. "Both animals."

"It's an omen," Bowdiek whispered, then stopped himself.

"Or a sacrifice Malar himself arranged," Vhoror commented.

Tohl forced doubt from his mind and said, "It's nothing more than bad luck. Come on."

He stepped into the tomb and held the lantern high, leaning on the certainty that Eldath watched over him. The dream had tied him to Borran Klosk and brought about personal attention from the Quiet One. He tried to keep that in mind.

The lantern light bathed the outer chambers, highlighting the disuse and neglect of the tomb. A slithering noise echoed through the darkness. The sound made Tohl's skin prickle.

"What was that?" Vhoror asked.

Tohl stopped when the sound reached his ears, and the others had stopped with him. Holding the lantern high, the mace gripped in his hand, Tohl examined the rooms that lay before them. Only the flickering shadows moved there, but he couldn't help thinking how evil often chose to cloak itself in the raiment of night.

"It's nothing," Tohl said a couple of breaths later, when the sound wasn't repeated.

He continued forward and discovered the broken door that led to the record keeper's room.

"Someone has been here," Effrim said.

Studying the rotted wood, Tohl said, "That could have been done days, even tendays ago."

Effrim squatted and touched a clump of matter on the floor. His finger came away stained. "Mud. It's fresh, and from the shape it looks like someone tracked it in from outside."

Despite his growing fear, Tohl stepped through the broken doorway, letting the lantern guide his way. He said a silent prayer to Eldath, asking the goddess to watch over him. The lantern light filled the small room.

No one was there.

Tohl gazed at the section of floor that hid the passageway to the secret tomb. A feeling of relief washed over him when he saw that the stone was still in place.

"The tomb hasn't been disturbed," Vhoror whispered. "We can go."

"No." Tohl's throat felt phlegmy and thick, making him force the word out.

"Brother Tohl." Vhoror spoke in that precise way of his that grated on the nerves. Over the years, he'd shown his skill in the way of an argument. "We have seen that the tomb has not been disturbed. Our work here is done."

"No," said Tohl, "we have seen that the entrance to the hidden tomb is closed, but we don't know that Borran Klosk's tomb is likewise undisturbed."

As soon as Tohl spoke the mohrg's name, a cold, wet wind whipped through the front of the tomb and wound through the room until it reached the priests. Even protected as it was behind glass panes, the lantern flame danced in wild abandon, and the priests' shadows performed mad capers on the walls.

"We should leave this place," Micahan whispered, drawing in on himself.

"After," Tohl said, "I have talked with the Quiet One."

"You were dreaming," Vhoror accused.

Stifling the anger that rushed to mix with the fear that filled him, Tohl said, "If I dreamed I spoke with Eldath, then I also dreamed the mohrg has been released from his prison. You have nothing to fear from such a dream, Brother Vhoror."

Vhoror showed no shame at the rebuke. His eyes flickered with anger, and Tohl knew no matter how this night turned out that Vhoror would exact some price for the affront.

"As you wish, Brother Tohl," Vhoror said. "It appears you've gotten us all up from needed sleep and seen us soaked to the skin without need."

Tohl turned from the other priest and crossed the room to the section of false floor. He tapped the floor with his mace and it made hollow echoes on the other side. Nothing else sounded. Feeling a little better, he went to the record keeper's desk and shoved it to one side so that he could get at a hidden place in the wall. When he had the small compartment open, he hung the mace from a strap around his wrist and removed the two hooks from within.

Returning to the false floor, Tohl handed the lantern to Effrim, laid the mace beside the stone section, and slid the hooks into place. The floor section was heavier than he remembered, but he stayed at the task until the stone lifted from the opening.

The stench of death wafted from the secret tomb, made thicker by the storm's humid air. Thunder cracked outside and the noise drummed into the building, echoing once again below. The noise made the secret tomb sound cavernous.

"I smell blood," Vhoror said.

Tohl took the lantern from Effrim. Both of them trembled. Tohl guided the lantern toward the yawning opening and the complete blackness beyond.

"Did you not hear me?" Vhoror demanded. "I said I smell blood."

"Yes, brother," Tohl said, "the monster's tomb has ever been steeped in the stink of blood."

"It's fresh blood," Vhoror insisted.

Tohl thrust his arm into the hole and felt a wet coil of wind slither up his sleeve.

"At the very least," Vhoror continued, "that scent will draw other undead to this crypt. Those foul things that cling to the remnants of the Whamite Isles at times get caught in currents and are washed up here. If they scent this, they will come."

Tohl scanned the spiral staircase that led to the rooms below. Nothing moved on it.

"We're priests, Brother Vhoror," said Tohl. "If the undead come, Eldath, in her infinite wisdom, has seen fit to give us the power to turn such creatures. Perhaps we will save others who would fall prey to their untender mercies."

"You're being foolish."

"I'm following my belief," Tohl responded.

He gathered himself then stepped down into the opening. Keeping the lantern high, he followed the spiral staircase down. Effrim followed him next, and the other priests trailed after with obvious reluctance. Vhoror brought up the rear.

The spiral staircase shifted with a sudden groan and a shriek that felt like fingernails along Tohl's spine. He stopped and wondered if the staircase was going to collapse.

"Here," Effrim said, pointing at a section of the wall.

Tohl redirected the lantern. The beam shone on one of the support posts that had been driven into the wall. Light glanced off bright metal. The staircase had slid sideways enough to clear the bolt and reveal that it was no longer attached.

Effrim touched the bolt sticking out from the wall. He drew his finger back with a jerk, then turned it over to examine it. A thick drop of blood oozed from his fingertip. He put it in his mouth and sucked at it.

The response was a normal one, Tohl knew, but standing there in Borran Klosk's tomb and prison, knowing what Borran Klosk was and what he had done, the innocent gesture seemed obscene.

"It's sheared," Effrim said. "Something snapped it off, and recently, or it would not be so shiny."

The words hung heavily on all of them.

"Perhaps," Micahan said, "with all the rains tonight there was a shifting in the earth. The rainy season makes coffins sink into the ground."

"It's been hundreds of years," Vhoror protested.

"It may have been as much as a tenday ago," Micahan said. His face looked hollow and pasty as it was lifted from the recesses of his cowl by the lantern light. "Metal takes time to rust, just as Eldath in her mercies takes time to convert." He nodded at Tohl. "If we're to do this, Brother, we'd be better served by getting it done. Morning will come all too early."

"Of course," Tohl said and took up the march down the staircase again. It quivered and quaked the whole way.

Once at the bottom of the staircase, Tohl kept the lead and guided them through the twisting passageways.

When they reached the final room, lantern light reflected from the pools of water that remained of the ice coffin. The light also reflected from the dead eyes of the boys who sat arranged against the far wall. At least, the light reflected from the eyes of those who still had them.

Astonished fear froze Tohl in the entrance to the room. Borran Klosk was nowhere in sight.

"Eldath's mercy be upon them," Micahan said. He glanced up at Tohl. "We can't leave those children here. You know what will happen to them if we leave them."

Tohl nodded without speaking or returning the older priest's gaze.

"They will rise," Micahan said. "They will rise in a day or two."

Tohl gazed at the horror before him. He remembered the stories of Borran Klosk's undead army and how the mohrg had raised it.

"We can't let that happen to these children," he said.

"They're thieves," Vhoror complained. "They came here and broke open this tomb. I say they got what they deserve."

Tohl whirled on the man, his fear and anger getting the best of him. "Still your tongue, Vhoror. The mohrg has been released. Whatever these boys were before this night, they are victims now, and they will be cared for as best as Eldath has taught us to do. In my presence and in theirs, you will speak with respect."

"Of course," the old priest said.

"We've got to get the other priests," Tohl said, gathering his splintered thoughts, gazing with helpless horror at the dead children. "We must lay these . . ." Words failed him. ". . . to rest. We must find—" He found he didn't want to say the mohrg's name. "We must find the creature that escaped from here."

He gave the children a final look, said a quick prayer, and led the way back to the spiral staircase.

They made their way up, and Tohl shuddered every time the metal construction hammered against the stone wall. The sound echoed throughout the tomb. Tohl clambered through the opening. His exertions and fear wore on him, leaving his breath ragged and harsh.

He offered his hand to Micahan. The old priest struggled with the ascent. His hand felt cold and clawlike in Tohl's grip.

Bowdiek came through next, followed by the other priests until all six of them stood in the room.

Turning, Tohl shone the lantern light on the wall with the door. The light fell over a pile of at least a dozen skulls that had been left in a haphazard stack in the doorway.

"Those weren't there before," Effrim said.

Tohl gazed at the skulls, unable to speak, swallowed by a sense of impending dread.

"You fools!" Vhoror exploded. "It was Borran Klosk! He's not gone; he's still here!"

Something plopped into a thin pool of water in front of Tohl. The light made the dark liquid stand out against the water. Another drop joined the first, and they looked like squids spreading out their tentacles.

"The ceiling," Effrim whispered. "Eldath have mercy on us. It's coming from the ceiling."

In slow motion, feeling the fear hammering away inside him, Tohl angled the lantern up.

CHAPTER TWELVE

Haarn's knife sliced through the wolf bitch's flanks, but he took care to cut through only the outer layer of hide and muscle. Cutting deeper would have released poisons from her body and killed what he strove to save.

"What are you doing?" Druz asked.

"I can save the wolf cubs." Haarn placed his knife back in its boot sheath. "You killed the mother, but you didn't kill her cubs."

Haarn probed at the wound and prayed to Silvanus to guide his efforts. He hoped he had the knowledge to stave off death for Stonefur's line.

"She would have killed you," Druz said.

Unwilling to argue, Haarn concentrated on the bloody task at hand. He slipped his fingers into the wolf bitch's body and felt for the cubs. He let his fingers rest for just an instant against the straining womb and he could feel the squirming bodies inside. He hoped they were strong enough.

Broadfoot padded closer, his shadow covering a pool of water. He stood on his hind legs, tall against the night, and watched the wolves that remained of Stonefur's pack. Anxious and distrustful, the wolves shifted in the protection of the tree line.

Lightning shivered through the sky again, and for a moment Haarn saw the silver rain flash against the dark tan of his hands streaked with bright crimson blood.

He took a small blade he had sewn into his clothes. It was little more than a knuckle joint long, and he hoped it was up to the task.

Shoving his hand back inside the wolf corpse, Haarn traced the womb with his little finger while holding onto the little blade with his thumb and forefinger. He pressed against the tiny body with his little finger, moving it out of harm's way as best he could.

With deft precision, Haarn slit the womb. Hot liquid spilled out over his hand, mixing with the blood already there. A moment later it gushed from the wolf bitch's body. Druz sucked her breath in and took an involuntary step back.

The slit he'd made in the womb remained too tight to allow him to withdraw one of the cubs. Knowing time was running out, that the pups were already suffocating, he pushed his other hand into the wolf bitch's corpse and tore the womb.

One of the small, furry bodies slid out into Haarn's waiting hands. He felt it squirm in his grasp, strong and limp as it flexed. Breath tight in his throat, pain pounding his temples, he pulled the pup from its dead mother. He hunkered over to shield the infant from the rain and the bitter cold.

"Get my clothing," he told Druz. "I've got to keep them dry."

The warrior hesitated for a moment, as though she was going to argue, then she rose and got her own pack.

"I've got some blankets in here," she said, taking one of them out.

Haarn used the tiny knife he held to slit the umbilical cord, then nicked the placenta. He tore the hole in the placenta larger and removed the pup.

"Here," he said, and Druz took the pup without complaint and wrapped it in the blanket.

Haarn threw the placenta toward the other wolves. The membrane plopped on the ground only a few feet in front of them. One of the females dashed from the shadows, plucked the placenta from the mud with her sharp teeth, and returned to the pack.

"What was that?" Druz asked.

"Birth sac," Haarn said. "The females will eat it, as the birth mother usually does."

He removed another pup and began tearing the next placenta open.

"How are you going to feed the pups?" Druz asked.

Pain hit him again so hard he thought he was going to black out. He fought his way back to consciousness, then reached for the next pup.

"The pack always cares for the young," Haarn said as he handed over another pup and reached in for the next. "When one of the females starts carrying a litter, all of the bitches in the pack start producing milk. The pups nurse from all of them, just as all the males share in taking care of the young."

Druz leaned in closer to Haarn, shielding the pup from the storm winds, then adding it to those already in her blanket. Haarn kept working despite the exhaustion that ate at him.

There were five cubs in all. All of them were healthy except for the last one. Somehow its umbilical cord had gotten wrapped around its neck and almost strangled it.

As he held the young wolf pup, Haarn knew he was going to lose it if he didn't do something. Summoning his remaining energy, he prayed to Silvanus. The words of the prayer filled him, dulling the pain for a moment. He looked into the newborn wolf's face, memorizing the blunted length of the pup's muzzle.

"What's wrong?" Druz asked.

"It's dying," Haarn said, never losing the thread of the spell.

A golden glow filled Haarn's cupped hands as he shielded the pup. The glow reflected against his chest, showing the blood that streaked his body. His bare skin was pebbled in goosebumps from the cold and aches dawned deep within his bones as the spell took the last of his strength.

The golden glow from the druid's hands seeped into

the small, still form he protected. Just before the glow died away, the wolf pup stirred. A moment later, as the cold ate into Haarn with redoubled fury, the pup opened its mouth and whined with hunger. Haarn turned to Druz, feeling the sickness seething in his own head, and offered her the wolf pup.

Showing care and concern, Druz plucked the pup from Haarn's hands.

Without another word, knowing he couldn't have moved even if he'd tried, the druid pitched over. He had a brief impression of cold mud over his face and body then felt nothing at all.

The oval yellow beam of Tohl's lantern raked the tomb's ceiling then froze on the bizarre figure of Borran Klosk clinging to the uneven stones there. The claws of his fingers and toes wedged into the space between the stones. A horrific grin split the mohrg's cadaverous face. Blood covered Borran Klosk's body and spattered his cloak.

"Welcome," the mohrg whispered in his thin, cold voice. "Welcome, and prepare to die."

Effrim lunged forward with his warhammer, singing the praises of Eldath in his strong, clear voice.

Borran Klosk scuttled away and the warhammer missed by inches. The long, grotesque purple tongue uncoiled from his obscene mouth and lanced at the young priest.

Tohl watched in numb horror as the tongue smashed through Effrim's forehead and out the back of his skull. Chunks of white bone and bloody matter flew over Micahan, who stood as if dazed. Then the old priest slumped to the floor, his eyes locked wide and staring at nothing. Effrim's corpse dropped only a moment later.

With a jerk of his head, Borran Klosk tore his tongue free of Effrim's body. Blood smeared his face and ran down his chin as the tongue recoiled. He smiled again, cocking his head.

"The Vilhon Reach will die, dragged to its doom by those who have died already."

Praying, Tohl raised Eldath's symbol before him. The disk showed the graven image of a stream. He invoked his spell, one of the earliest he'd been taught to use against the undead. He felt the energy leave his body and saw Borran Klosk wince.

"Foolish priest," the monster crowed in triumph, "you cannot turn me with your piety and your faith. I am death incarnate, made whole by Malar's strong hand. I will slake my thirst with your blood."

Vhoror slammed into Tohl, causing him to stumble and struggle to stay on his feet. Borran Klosk's tongue missed its mark, slapping against the wall behind Tohl and shattering through stone.

"Move, you damned fool!" Vhoror roared.

He continued shoving against Tohl, striving to reach the doorway.

Knocked forward by Vhoror's greater girth, Tohl staggered through the skulls, sending them flying in all directions. Tohl caught himself, his mind flying through the spells available to him.

"Move! Move!" Vhoror shouted, continuing to push him.

Tohl turned to the other priest, wanting to tell him that they'd stay alive if only they kept their heads. Before Tohl could speak, Vhoror's head broke and came apart in crimson ruin, his features leaking down from his shattered skull. Borran Klosk's tongue emerged from the priest's head like a caterpillar seeking escape from a too-tight cocoon.

A last, surprised gasp puffed from Vhoror's lips as life left him. As quickly as it had thrust through the priest's head, the tongue withdrew, leaving a gaping hole in its place.

Tohl's stomach lurched as he realized how much of Vhoror's blood was on him, and how it felt blazing hot against the chill of the wind and rain. Tohl stood his ground and prayed as he'd been taught, holding fast to his faith. He dropped his mace to the stone floor, knowing it would do him little good against the mohrg. Raising the symbol of his goddess before him, he sat the lantern at his feet, and gestured with his free hand.

For a moment, Tohl thought the spell had failed, then the buzzing and chirping of insects filled his ears.

Borran Klosk dropped from the ceiling, intent on the two priests remaining in the room, but the mohrg's baleful glare took in Tohl as well, letting him know he hadn't been forgotten. The monstrous tongue cleaved Daraghin's chest, tearing like a blade through cloth.

Thousands of flying insects filled the tomb. They flew toward Borran Klosk and clustered upon him.

To Tohl, it was like watching moss grow on a rock, only measured in the space of heartbeats. In less time than it took to draw a panicked breath, the insects covered Borran Klosk like a layer of wriggling skin. Other insects formed a cloud around him, but even more continued to pile onto his body.

Borran Klosk screamed, but the sound wasn't filled with pain as Tohl had hoped. Rage fueled the inarticulate roars. Still, the mohrg seemed trapped as the clusters of insects filled the room.

An arm thrust through the flying cloud, and it took Tohl a moment to realize that it was human.

"Brother Tohl!" Bowdiek called. "Eldath's mercy, help me!"

Seizing the lantern again, Tohl ran forward and yanked the other priest from the embrace of the flying insects. Tohl felt something crunch beneath his feet. When he looked down, he saw that the stone floor was covered with beetles and other crawling insects.

Bowdiek coughed and wheezed, and Tohl guessed that the man had swallowed some of the insects. Glowbugs, locusts, and flying beetles littered his hair and body, but when Bowdiek was out of the room where Borran Klosk was, they left him and streaked for the mohrg.

"Come on," Tohl said. "The spell won't last for long."

He tugged Bowdiek's arm and got them both moving toward the next door. Bowdiek slammed against the wall near the doorway. Thinking for a moment that the priest had misjudged his step, Tohl turned to Bowdiek and grabbed his shoulder, prepared to pull him onto the correct path.

Bowdiek's face pressed against the tomb wall, blanched white in pain and fright. His mouth worked but no words came out, then a gout of blood covered his lower face.

Lifting the lantern, Tohl saw that Borran Klosk's obscene tongue had ripped through Bowdiek's lower back so hard that it had penetrated the tomb's stone wall. Bowdiek couldn't move—he was pinned. Pain flared through Bowdiek's eyes, then they turned up until only the whites showed.

Tohl felt Bowdiek's corpse shiver as Borran Klosk's tongue tensed and shifted. Glancing over his shoulder, Tohl spotted the mohrg tearing free of the insect-infested room, pulled by his tongue, which was still anchored to the wall, and to Bowdiek.

Borran Klosk gibbered and raked insects from his eye hollows. Other insects crusted his mouth and the remains of his nose.

"Still here, priest?" Borran Klosk mocked as he drew himself toward Bowdiek's twitching corpse. "Your friend is still hanging around."

The mohrg stood only a few feet away. He yanked his head back and his tongue popped free of both the wall and the corpse then snapped back into his blood-drenched jaws.

Bowdiek dropped to the floor.

Tohl turned and ran. He fled through the hallways, listening to the bony slap of Borran Klosk's skeletal feet against the stone floor.

The doorway to the graveyard appeared ahead. Tohl pushed off the last passageway wall with his free hand, still carrying the bobbing lantern with his other, struggling to keep his bearings even though the wick's flame flickered. In a dozen more strides, he was through the final door and out into the graveyard.

Eldath's blessing, but he was old. Tohl knew that, but the wheezing breaths that seared like hot irons through his lungs branded that truth into him. His knees felt like they were coming apart, but he kept them moving. Before he could stop himself, he glanced over his shoulder.

The mohrg ran with surprising speed, and the cloud of insects pursued him, though they were beginning to thin. The spell should have lasted longer, but it was fading. Tohl wondered if the magical nature of the mohrg had altered the spell in some way.

Tohl wished he was in another dream, but just as he had known he was dreaming before, he knew he wasn't now.

He tripped. Something caught his foot and he went sprawling. The wet ground coated him and he smacked up against a leaning headstone whose letters had long since worn away.

The splat of bony feet cleaving the graveyard mud drew Tohl's attention, sounding almost as fast and as loud as his heart hammering in his chest. He clawed his way to his knees and looked back the way he'd come.

Borran Klosk ran through the rain showing no sign of exertion. The hideous creature moved with the fluid grace of a great cat.

Fear deluged Tohl in one final wave. Galvanized into action, he reared back and threw the lantern as hard as he could.

The lantern flipped end over end then smashed against the mohrg. The glass fuel reservoir shattered against the undead creature's chest. Oil ran over the bared bone and remnants of flesh. Despite the downpour, the fluid ran over Borran Klosk's body and the fiery wick stuck to his chest. The oil caught fire and blue and yellow flames raced over the mohrg.

Tohl watched in horror as Borran Klosk never broke stride. The horrid, fleshless face and the death's-head grin was the last thing he saw. He had a brief impression of the grinning jaws splitting open and the purple tongue exploding outward, then it felt like a dwarven warhammer slammed into his head, and he was dead before he could draw a last breath.

"Merciful Tymora," Druz Talimsir called as she looked at Haarn lying naked and unconscious in the mud, "give me the strength to endure."

The newborn wolf pups squirmed in the blanket. Their mewling cries reached her ears and sparked a tenderness that confused her and made her angry.

Lightning sizzled across the sky, followed almost at once by the hollow boom of thunder that rolled across the mountaintop. The sound made Druz realize again how far she was from anything familiar, and she had to do something about the unconscious man lying in the mud.

The wolves still lounging in the tree line continued watching her. Druz couldn't help but wonder how long it would take before they rushed her. Even armed and as skilled as she was, she knew she wouldn't last long before they overcame her. Her only chance was to run or climb a tree before they dragged her down, but she knew she couldn't leave the druid unguarded. The wolves would kill him for executing their leader, and they probably had no love for Druz, who had killed the pregnant bitch.

Beneath her breath, she damned the druid. He had to have known he wasn't going to be strong enough to climb down the mountain. Instead of healing a motherless wolf pup, he should have healed himself.

She started to put the blanket-wrapped wolf pups aside. Plaintive yips sounded from the struggling newborns. She stopped and pulled the blanket back in close to her, feeling the warmth of the pups and the way they moved against her.

Druz couldn't abandon them. If she had known for sure that the wolf pack would take care of them she might have left them there, but she didn't know that. All she knew was that Haarn had risked his life to save them.

She felt trapped as she eyed the restless wolves and cuddled the blanket to her. Glancing around the mountaintop, she tried to find some place she could use as shelter, thinking she could put the wolf pups there and return for the druid.

The bear yawned as it towered above her. Druz feared the bear might grow bored and wander away, leaving them defenseless against the wolves. Reaching to her side, she took hold of her sword hilt.

The bear swayed for a moment then dropped to all fours. The bear nudged the unconscious druid with his muzzle. Haarn didn't respond. Growing more restless, fur dripping from the downpour, the bear pushed at Haarn with a paw.

Druz watched with growing concern. The bear's shiny black claws could slice a man to ribbons.

Moving with gentle care, the bear shoved one of his front legs under the unconscious druid and lifted him with no apparent effort. The bear stood to his full height again, cradling the man as if he were a babe. When he had his burden secure, the bear gazed at Druz, gave a low growl, and started walking away.

Not wanting to be left alone with the waiting wolves, Druz got to her feet, surprised at how her muscles ached from the climb up the mountain. She gathered Haarn's gear, carried the wolf pups in the blanket in one hand and Haarn's gear in the other, and stepped through the mud after the bear.

Halfway down the mountain, battling with treacherous footing, Druz followed the bear as it turned to the right of the narrow game trail. She didn't see the cave beside the trail until the bear hunkered down and walked through it.

Hesitant, Druz stood outside for a moment. The bear growled to her from inside, and the resulting short-lived echo around the beast's voice let her know how small the cave was. Despite her best efforts, the blanket containing the wolf pups had grown wetter and the newborn litter was in danger of getting soaked. Holding onto the blanket of pups and Haarn's gear, she strode into the cave.

Lightning flashed outside, giving Druz a momentary glimpse of the bear and the druid against the back wall of the cave. The animal sat down next to the man, pressing his bulk against Haarn to share his warmth. The bear turned his broad head and ministered to Haarn's wounds with his tongue.

Druz dropped Haarn's gear and slid her own sword free of its sheath as another streak of lightning ripped through the sky and revealed the wolf pack outside the cave. They waited in the tree line opposite the game trail.

After placing the blanket of wolf pups on the uneven cave floor, Druz shrugged out of her backpack and sat it on the floor as well. Keeping an eye on the cave mouth, working in the darkness of the cave, she rummaged through her pack until she found her flint and tinder.

She opened the metal case, drew out her flint and steel, and a small amount of tinder. She piled the tinder on a small cloth from the metal case, then struck sparks and got the tinder going. A thin trail of smoke rose from the pile of tinder. She took a beeswax candle from her pack and lit it.

Shielding the fragile flame with her hand, Druz studied the cave. The fetid smell of animals clung to the stone surfaces. Piles of animal spoor, old and new, lay scattered around the cave, but there were signs that men had sheltered there as well. A ring of stones occupied a section of the floor in front of the bear. In the back, out of the sweeping winds that carried part of the rain into the cave, someone had left a small pile of dry wood.

Druz soon had a small fire burning in the ring of stones. Taking bandages and mendicants from her pack, she approached Haarn with caution. The bear rumbled and watched her through winking eyes as she began to tend to the druid's wounds.

When she finished, she returned to the fire. She sat

near the flames, letting the welcome heat bask into her. Painful twinges poked at her body as she pulled her knees up and rested her chin on her knees. Her eyes burned from the smoke, the storm, and fatigue. Hunger pangs made her stomach feel hollow.

She kept her sword at her side and took the time to re-string her bow. It was doubtful that the wolves or any other creature would try to gain entrance into the cave with the fire and the bear, but she wanted to be prepared.

After a time, despite the anxiety that filled her, Druz's eyelids grew heavy. With the warmth from the fire filling the cave, she retreated to a wall and placed her back against it, resting her sword across her thighs and her bow near to hand.

Just as her eyes were about to close again, a reflection from the campfire flashed out in the woods. Awake at once, Druz gripped her long sword and rose to her feet. Tired as she was, she made the mistake of stepping between the fire and the movement. Shifting to one side, heart pounding faster even though her head didn't feel very clear, she gazed at the woods opposite the cave.

The wolves had noticed the movement as well. The pack closed in on it with menacing growls.

Druz thought at first that it was a traveler, stranded by the storm, who knew about the cave. The possibility of sharing the cave with a stranger wasn't welcome, but she wasn't going to leave someone to the mercy of the wolves. She started to return for her bow, then noticed that the pack had clustered around a section of ground beneath an aging sycamore tree.

Rainwater washing down from the mountain had eroded the earth from the sycamore's roots, baring the woody knees. Something glittered on the ground, reflecting more light than even the wolves' eyes.

Judging from the pure ruby glint that captured the gleam from the campfire, Druz guessed that it was a piece of glass or a jewel. Curiosity stilled her, and she was surprised to feel the hair lifting on her arms.

The wolves backed away. Their whines echoed under the trees as the muddy ground pushed up and broke open like an egg white bubbling in a frying pan. An arm shoved through the mud, followed by a hollow-eyed skull and bony shoulders.

CHAPTER THIRTEEN

Fear dried Druz's throat and locked her breath in her lungs as she watched the skeleton continue to force its way from its unmarked grave. Instinct made her reach for Tymora's coin tied at her neck.

The skeleton lay still for a moment after it had crawled from the ground. One of the wolves, emboldened by the skeleton's apparent helplessness, crept closer. Snarling black lips twitched back from white teeth. With a growl, the wolf launched itself at its intended prey. The wolf's teeth grated against the mud-slick bones.

Orange light flared in the hollows of the skeleton's eyes. It moved, snapping like a trap. The bony hand curled into a fist and jerked around like a mallet, cutting through the air. Almost too quick for the eye to follow, the skeletal fist crashed into the wolf's skull.

The animal collapsed, its skull destroyed.

Lurching, the skeleton forced itself to its feet and swayed in the storm winds. Ignoring the rest of the wolves, the skeleton turned its attention to the cave.

Druz drew herself farther back into the cave, aware that it wouldn't do any good. The fire was all the skeleton needed to see to know that the cave was occupied. She tightened her grip on her sword and asked Tymora's blessing.

Glancing over her shoulder, she said to the bear, "We've got trouble."

The bear shook himself then rose from the floor. Hunkered below the cave's low ceiling, the bear crept forward, snuffling for a moment, then cocking his head and loosing a fierce growl.

The skeleton strode from the tree line without hesitation. Clods of mud mixed with grass and tree roots dropped out of the skeleton's ribcage.

Taking a two-handed grip on her sword, Druz glanced at the bear and said, "Go get it."

The bear growled again and dropped to all four feet, and retreated to Haarn's side.

"Damn it," Druz swore, stepping up to block the way.

The cave that had offered them shelter from the rain had become a deathtrap.

Lightning flashed again, setting the jeweled shape in the skeleton's ribcage blazing with ruby light. The skeleton spread its arms as it neared.

Druz made herself breathe and thought, What is it about this damned druid that seems to draw so much bad luck?

She was certain that had Haarn been awake he'd doubtless wonder the same thing about her. She set herself and got ready to swing, but just before she committed herself, the skeleton stopped.

The grim jaws closed and resumed their mirthless grin. Relaxing, the raised arms clacked against the mud-smeared ivory thighs. Orange glow dimming in the eye hollows, the skeleton turned and walked away.

Druz released a sigh of relief, but she didn't relax until the skeleton abandoned the washed-out game trail and vanished into the forest. Even then, she stood at her post for several more long minutes until the stinging rain propelled by the cold storm winds drove her inside to the deeper shelter of the cave.

Frightened and near exhaustion, she sat with her back to the cave wall and kept watch over the entrance. The campfire flickered at the corner of her vision as she fought to keep her eyelids open. When she closed them, intending to rest for only a moment, sleep claimed her.

Wrapped in bloody priest's robes and shrouded in the night, Borran Klosk walked Alaghôn's streets once more. Hunger and madness warred within him as what he saw conflicted with what he remembered.

Eldath's priests had trapped him for years. He had the sense of that from the changes in the city around him. Once familiar, Alaghôn had grown yet imploded as well. New buildings, taller and grander, stood where claptrap buildings once teetered. In other parts of the city, once grand buildings had been left to decay like bad teeth.

The storm continued to crackle and spit around him. Water sluiced through the uneven cobblestones and poured down the pitted iron grates to the sewers that ran beneath the city and out into the Sea of Fallen Stars.

Borran Klosk walked with purpose. His skeletal feet clacked against the stones and splashed through the water. A passing wagon, laden with workers fresh up from the dockyards where men still labored to unload a ship, splashed muddy water over him. He kept walking, ignoring the dull, distant cold.

The deep, abiding hatred Borran Klosk had for living men—and elves and dwarves and the rest—squirmed through the empty space where his stomach had once been. Even though he'd been without a stomach for years, he'd never lost the sense of it.

As he walked, the hate festering inside him, he gazed in at taverns and inns still open to the late-night trade from the docks. Even over the rumble of thunder and the crash of waves, he heard the laughter and conversations of the living. Their simpleminded joy, their very ignorance of his passage, angered him more.

He gave in to that anger, turning his steps toward a small tavern. The tavern was on the second floor, squeezed between storage space for the two shops on either side of it.

A fat dwarf with a dark beard guarded an iron-barred doorway. As Borran Klosk neared, the dwarf came to attention. He kicked the big head of the double-bitted battle-axe at his feet, causing the heavy weapon to revolve in his palms and come to a natural grip in both his hands. The dwarf tried a grin, but his eyes remained hooded and wary.

"Hail and well met, traveler. Judgin' from the cut o' yer robes, ye've been up that well-known crick an' back down again, ye have."

Borran Klosk said nothing. The wind slapped at the hood of his robe, but left it in place.

"Gonna cost ye a silver or two to get in," the dwarf warned. He shifted the battle-axe, his callused fingers rasping against the hand-tooled wood. "An' I'm gonna have to see the color of it afore I let ye in."

Without breaking stride, Borran Klosk opened wide his jaws and spat out the long purple tongue. At that distance there was a chance the dwarf could have evaded the attack, but Borran Klosk's tongue caught the dwarf flat-footed. The hard cartilage smashed through the dwarf's throat, tearing through the flesh with ease. Knocked backward, the dwarf slammed up against the iron-barred door blocking access to the stairs. The dwarf's face flexed as he tried to scream, but the sound died unborn in his mangled throat.

Borran Klosk withdrew his tongue and caught the dwarf's falling body with one hand. The salty sweetness of the dwarf's blood filled the mohrg, taking the edge off his hunger. Borran Klosk tossed the dwarf's corpse away. He tried the iron-barred door but found it locked. Bracing himself, the mohrg gripped the iron bars and yanked.

Metal screeched as the iron bars pulled free of their moorings. Ignoring the possibility that anyone had heard the door rip loose, Borran Klosk flung the door aside and strode into the darkened chamber. From above, the sound of revelry continued unabated. The mohrg followed the steps up, lusting after the life that filled those voices.

At the top of the stairs, he gazed through a wide doorway into the tavern proper. Dim light glowed through dingy lantern glass and scarcely made a dent in the shadows that filled the room.

Scarred and dark, the bar ran the room's length against the opposite wall. A fat human with a curly wheat-colored beard leaned on the bar and talked with a dwarf woman showing considerable years. Three men dressed in the torn clothing of sailors talked at one of the half-dozen tables scattered across the middle of the room. An elf dressed all in black sat at a table by himself, fingers twining around a glittering silver dagger resting point-down on the table top. Two women, both showing signs of a hard night's work, sat listless and uncaring, not interested in attracting the attention of potential customers.

It was, Borran Klosk reflected, the dregs of night. Creatures of flesh and blood slowed during these hours, but the mohrg felt stronger than ever.

The bartender glanced at the new arrival. His head was a massive boulder set atop the broad mountains of his shoulders.

"Something I can do you for, friend?"

Pulling himself up in disdain, feeling the thick purple tongue moving with anticipation in his body, Borran Klosk stepped into the room. The dead priest's robes whirled around him and dripped scarlet-tinted water onto the hardwood floor.

"Maybe you should have stayed in the hallway a little longer," the bartender growled, "instead of coming into my place and making a mess of it."

He reached for a mop leaning against the wall behind him and came around the bar. The dwarf woman said something too low for Borran Klosk to hear, but she laughed at her own wit and reached for the schooner of ale before her.

"Aye, Serrim," the bartender said, "an' I'll thank ye to keep such comments to yerself." He glanced back at Borran Klosk. "An' if ye've come to sup here, friend, ye're a mite too late, ye see. The victuals has all been put away for the e'ening."

"What there was of it," the dwarf woman agreed.

The bartender stopped in front of Borran Klosk and unlimbered his mop.

Borran Klosk stood his ground. Though his emotions

weren't the same as they had been before his transformation, he still felt a twinge of anticipation.

"Mayhap ye'd care to move them big feet of yers," the bartender suggested as he mopped toward the mohrg.

"No," Borran Klosk said.

Stooping, the bartender peered toward the mohrg's concealed face. "What did ye say, little man?"

With brazen boldness, Borran Klosk reached up and swept the hood back from his head.

"No," Borran Klosk repeated.

He knew even the dim lighting would reveal his fleshless face and hollow-socketed skull. He didn't care what he looked liked. That such a sight caused fear in those who still had blood coursing through their veins served him well.

"What the hell are ye?" the bartender asked in a hoarse voice. His eyes rounded in fear as he stumbled back a step.

"Klosk!" the dwarf woman croaked, spewing ale. "Borran Klosk! He's returned!" She hefted a battle-axe from the floor beside her.

If Klosk had possessed lips, he would have smiled. Though he was certain he'd been gone a long time, his name and deeds had been remembered.

"Yes," the mohrg spat, "I am Borran Klosk. Fear me."

The bartender lashed out with the mop, trying to push Borran Klosk away. The mohrg reacted with blinding speed. Before his transformation he'd been a warrior as well as a mage, and though the men he raised from the dead did not retain their memories, he had.

The rain-drenched robes whirled as Borran Klosk spun. He knotted a hand into a hammer-like fist, caught the broom in his other hand, and snapped the end of the mop off. Before the collection of dirty rags fell to the floor, he stepped in, pulled the mop across his body, and brought his fist back up. The mop handle snapped again, leaving the bartender with only a precious few inches jutting from his hands.

Stuttering a surprised oath, the bartender stumbled

back, but Borran Klosk was on the man like a hawk taking a dove. Whirling, noticing the other men and women in motion around the room, the mohrg drove the splintered end of the mop handle through the bartender's chest. Flesh and bone gave way to the unforgiving blow, and the wooden shaft split the man's heart in two.

"Die, darkspawn!" the dwarf woman yelled as she raced across the room with her battle-axe raised.

With superhuman speed, Borran Klosk evaded the dwarf's blow. The axe sliced through the air, dragging the woman forward a half step. Before she could recover her balance, Borran Klosk seized the back of her head in one hand and her chin in the other. He wrenched her head and felt her skull separate from her spine with a sudden snap.

The dwarf's eyes widened in disbelief as she died.

Gleeful, Borran Klosk savored the woman's death for a moment, holding her sagging body upright by her head without effort. He watched the life drain from her eyes and rejoiced in the savage jealousy that had filled him since he'd clawed his way free of the first grave to hold him captive.

Movement to the left alerted Borran Klosk and gave him only a moment's warning. Spinning, the mohrg watched as the black-clad elf rose to his feet. His voice rang out with words in a tongue Borran Klosk didn't recognize. As the words tumbled from his lips, the elf pointed.

Something blurred through the air before Borran Klosk, and he felt an incredible agony rip into him. His knees weakened and even his supernatural vision wavered and filled with whirling black comets. Screaming, the mohrg forced himself to remain standing.

The elf murmured again, and the other men in the tavern stood back and watched, holding their weapons before them. When the elf gestured again, a flaming arrow leaped from his fingers.

Twisting with uncanny speed and grace, Borran Klosk dodged the spell. The flaming arrow struck the wall behind him, scorching the impact area and leaving smoldering ruin in its wake. Concentrating on the elf, wondering if he was part of the damned Emerald Enclave, Borran Klosk spoke his own spell and pointed toward the elf.

The magical energy spewed through Borran Klosk's palm and became a windstorm in front of him. Another gesture sent the windstorm toward the elf. Howling winds tore through the tavern's interior, extinguishing candle flames and knocking over chairs and tables.

The howling windstorm struck the elf before he could move or defend himself. When the winds slammed into the elf, they lifted him from his feet and hurled him back through the window overlooking the street. Glass shattered and the thin panes crumpled and tore loose. Arms flailing, the elf screamed and tried to catch the sides of the windows. Before he could get a strong grip, he was blown through the window and vanished.

Still in motion, Borran Klosk scooped the battle-axe from the floor. The wall where the elf's spell had struck burst into flame. Light and smoke filled the small tavern. A crossbow bolt tore into the priest's robes and slammed against the mohrg's pelvic bone. Setting himself, Borran Klosk unleashed his tongue.

The thick, purple appendage sped across the room and ripped through the guts of the woman who'd fired the crossbow. Once his barbed tongue had penetrated its target, Borran Klosk whipped his head back. His tongue opened the woman's midsection like an overripe tomato and spilled her entrails before her.

Screaming, dying, the woman dropped.

Borran Klosk pulled his tongue back into his skull. He listened in satisfaction to the dying woman's pain-filled screams and pleas for help. It had been so long since he'd heard someone beg for her life . . . he'd missed the sound.

"Run!" one of the sailors cried, shoving the man in front of him toward the door.

Borran Klosk leaped in front of the door. The mohrg drew the battle-axe back, fitting both hands around the handle. He swung, slicing the axe in a transverse sweep across the sailor's body.

The sailor fell in halves, a horrified look frozen on his

features. Before the next sailor could pull back, Borran Klosk raised his captured battle-axe dripping with gore and brought it down again, cleaving the sailor's head from crown to chin. He lashed out with the tongue again, spearing the remaining sailor through his open mouth and tearing his brain out the back of his skull.

Sadistic glee filled Borran Klosk as he turned on the last living person in the tavern. The woman cowered against the back wall, trapped by another wall on one side and the fire from the elf's spell on the other.

She sobbed and wailed, and the shrieks were a joyful noise to Borran Klosk. Walking toward her, he dragged out the enjoyment. Torture, if there were time yet remaining before the city watch arrived, would be a welcome diversion.

"Stay away!" the woman shrilled. She held her empty hands up before her.

Borran Klosk cocked his head, surveying her.

"No! Please don't kill me!" She shrank down, dwindling to a kneeling position with her arms wrapped around her head. She kept her eyes averted from his skull, but looked at his skeletal feet covered in blood.

Stopping just out of the woman's reach, Borran Klosk gazed down at her and said, "Do you know who I am, woman?"

"Yes."

"What is my name?"

The woman shook her head, gasping in painful fear.

Borran Klosk opened his jaws and let his tongue spill out. The dripping purple appendage coiled like a restless snake as it approached her. The mohrg relished the taste of the woman's fear, so palpable through the tongue. Some of his other senses, and the pleasures of the flesh, had been taken from him or dulled by the magic that brought him back to unlife, but they had been replaced by the ability to taste another's fear. For Borran Klosk there was no finer elixir.

"If you know my name," the mohrg said, "say it. Spare your life a little longer."

He caressed her cheek with the bloody tongue, leaving smears in its wake.

The woman trembled, gasped, and cried. Tears tracked her face, and the mohrg tasted the sweet salt of them.

"Your death," Borran Klosk promised her, "is a certainty. It can be the most horrible thing you've ever been through, or it can come so fast you're not even aware of it. The choice is yours."

"I don't want to die."

Grabbing the woman's hair, Borran Klosk yanked her head back up at him.

"Please. Please don't hurt me."

"My name," Borran Klosk commanded, shaking her head.

Coughing and hacking, eyes blurred with drink and tears, the woman said, "Borran Klosk."

"And you remember me?"

"I've heard tales of you since I was a little girl," the woman said. "I never thought you were real—only something made up to frighten children." She wailed, "Gods help us if you are real."

"I am real," Borran Klosk declared, pressing his fleshless face close to hers. "I am real and I am come back from the icy pits where the priests of Eldath kept me. I am come back for my vengeance."

Holding a hand up before her face, the woman wept and trembled.

Borran Klosk laved the tears from her cheeks with his bloody tongue, tracking her face and marking her features with grotesque patterns.

"Do you want to live, woman?"

She hesitated, and he knew she thought he was trying to torture her further by giving her false hope. Light from the flames clinging to the wall danced over her face and sparked highlights from her hair.

"Answer me," Borran Klosk said. "Would you live if you could?"

"Yes. Gods help me for being so weak."

Borran Klosk touched the woman's face with his hand and said, "Then I shall let you live."

An uncontrollable shiver ran through the woman. "Thank you! Gods bless you for that!"

"Only one god has blessed me," Borran Klosk said. "I will do Malar's work to bring this city to its knees. Aye, and even the whole of the Vilhon Reach if the Beastlord should choose to put that within my grasp."

The fire clinging to the wall crept closer to them, and Borran Klosk could feel it soaking into his bones.

"You will let me go?" the woman asked.

"Yes," Borran Klosk said, turning his grim visage on her, "but your life comes with a price."

"Anything, Lord Klosk."

The woman bowed her head, flinching from the flames that licked too close. Outside, through the open window, thunder echoed along the street as a man's voice took up a harsh cry of warning. The dead elf had not gone undiscovered long.

"Tell them," Borran Klosk said, "that I am coming for them. Do you understand?"

The woman nodded.

"Tell them that I will not rest this time until all of Alaghôn is within my power." Releasing the woman, Borran Klosk took a step away and said, "Now go."

Fear held the woman in place, and she only trembled.

Borran Klosk grabbed the woman by the arm and yanked her to her feet. He shoved her toward the door near the dead sailors.

She stumbled and almost fell, but she kept her balance and ran toward the door. Her hands wrapped around the back of her head, as if afraid he would strike her with his tongue. She disappeared through the door and her footsteps rang on the stairs.

"Help!" she screamed. "Someone help me! He's killed everyone!"

Satisfaction filled Borran Klosk as he surveyed the burning and bloodied ruin of the tavern. Even before he'd been reborn as a mohrg he'd burned with hatred. As a living man he'd stalked and killed dozens of men, women, and children of all races. He'd been careful, but in the end the city watch had gotten him. After he'd been humiliated in court, then executed in public and buried, he'd risen, undead and vengeful. Whatever had compelled him to kill while he'd still been human had only grown in power since his rebirth.

Going to each of those he had slain, Borran Klosk put his hands upon them and spoke the words that would bind them to him should they rise again—and they would rise, he knew, as long as the townsfolk didn't destroy the bodies.

He gazed at the corpses, wondering if enough people would believe the woman he'd spared to make the families of the dead let the bodies be destroyed. He thought perhaps they might, but it didn't matter. If these and the dead priests weren't to be the first of his new army, then there would be others.

He crossed to the smashed window and looked down. Rain swirled in, riding the harsh storm winds and drenching him anew. He braced himself on the broken sill, gazing down at the body of the elf clad in black.

"A monster!" the woman screamed out in the street.

A man had seized her, thinking maybe that she was too drunk to know what she was doing.

" 'Ere now," the man said, folding the woman into his large arms and keeping her from striking him. "An' tell ol' Kafeer some'at's the matter."

"Borran Klosk," the woman yelled. "He's back. He told me to tell everyone."

She turned and pointed back up at the tavern.

Knowing he was backlit by the flames claiming the tavern, Borran Klosk raised his hand and revealed his skeletal arm beneath the stolen priest's robes. Lightning flared, and his arm burned brilliant white from the reflected glare.

A group of soldiers dressed in the colors of Alaghôn's city watch rounded the corner. A commander astride a war-horse led them, matching his mount's speed to the men slogging through the water-covered street.

"Where away?" the commander demanded. He carried his sword naked in his fist, the polished steel catching flickers from the lightning and the colored lanterns of the businesses still open at the late hour.

"There!" the woman screamed again, pointing at the tavern window where Borran Klosk stood.

Heeling his restless mount, the iron-shod hooves ringing against the cobblestones, the commander glanced up at the tavern. He pointed with his sword and shouted, "Get that man down from there!"

The guardsmen hastened to do as the commander ordered, falling into a two-by-two column.

Borran Klosk's tongue writhed in hungry glee as he watched the warriors start across the street.

"Are you that confident, Borran Klosk?"

Wheeling, the mohrg turned to face the speaker. His tongue flexed before him, ready to spring and pierce.

CHAPTER FOURTEEN

Framed by the doorway leading to the stairs, glistening from the rain that clung to his skin in the firelight, a small woman watched Borran Klosk. Her simple brown breeches and green shirt showed no insignia nor gave any indication of her station. Beneath her hood, unbound black hair surrounded her gaunt, pinched face, emphasizing her deep-set white opal eyes.

If Borran Klosk had not felt the woman's eyes on him, he would have sworn she was blind. He considered killing her outright but held himself at the last moment, giving in to curiosity. Whatever she was, alive though she may be, the scent around her didn't taste as human as it should have.

Turning his attention back to the approaching city guard, Borran Klosk spoke words of power then pointed toward the street. A wall of violet flames sprang up from the cobblestones and darted around the larger puddles. Water hissed, spreading clouds of steam, and the heat drove the guardsmen back.

"Send for a watch wizard!" the commander roared, taking a firm hand with his nervous mount.

One of the guardsmen took off at once.

"Is this what you think you should do, Borran Klosk?" the woman asked amid the harsh yells of the guardsmen and gawkers below. "Squander the second chance Malar has given you to wreak havoc among your enemies?"

"Have a care, woman," Borran Klosk replied.

He sensed the woman walking closer to him, and he was amazed at her lack of fear. Gathering his energies, the mohrg gestured again. He watched as a shadow blurred the area in front of the watch commander.

The man screamed and swung at the air with his sword. His hoarse voice scared the men in his group, dividing their attention between him and the wall of twisting violet flames that gave off searing heat.

"What does he battle?" the woman asked, peering over Borran Klosk's shoulder.

"His own fear," Borran Klosk replied. "The spell I employed gave form to his private aberrations."

The watch commander screamed himself hoarse, startling his mount. Two of the guardsmen ran to him and attempted to help. One of them got a sword slash across his face for his trouble. The other backed away. The commander stiffened and fell from his saddle. His limp body smacked onto the cobblestones.

"He's dead?" the woman asked.

"Yes," Borran Klosk said, watching the blurred shadow fade away as the commander died. "Touched by whatever he most feared in this life."

"Perhaps he envisioned himself fighting you."

A faint smile touched the woman's shadowed face.

Borran Klosk faced her, intrigued anew. "I am," the mohrg said, "a frightful thing to behold."

The woman's opal eyes met his gaze without flinching. "I've never seen anything more horrid."

Standing close to the woman, Borran Klosk found himself aware of her simple beauty. Her face was almost triangular, holding the wide-spaced opal eyes and coming down to a firm chin beneath a full-lipped mouth. Even though he was dead and the flesh and most of its natural calls had left him, he found himself drawn to the woman on a level he'd never experienced even while alive.

"Who are you?" he asked again.

"You may call me Allis," she answered.

"May?" Borran Klosk mocked her with his tone. "You are impudent, child."

"I've seen worse things than you, Borran Klosk."

Her demeanor was calm and easy. Before he could restrain the anger that burst within him, Borran Klosk swung a mallet-hard, bony fist that would have broken her skull if it had connected.

The blow never landed. With incredible speed and poise, the woman dodged to one side and said, "You're making a mistake."

Borran Klosk flailed at her again, but she dodged his next blow with even more ease.

"You're wasting time," Allis said. "Even with your power, do you think you can stand against a watch wizard? Surely after your demonstration of power one is already on his way."

Borran Klosk spat his thick, purple tongue at her. She threw herself to one side and the vulgar appendage missed her by inches. Steadying himself, the mohrg lunged for the woman with his tongue again and again. His disbelief grew stronger as she continued to evade his attacks. He prepared another spell then pointed at her. Blurred energy sped from his outstretched hand and her shirt seemed to explode. Strange appendages sprang out of her. She leaped for the ceiling, and clung there by four hairy, jointed legs.

Staring at the woman in awe, Borran Klosk noted that her features had undergone drastic changes as well. Instead of two wide, opal eyes, there were now several orbs, each of the same peculiar hue. The long hair had become short, stiff bristles. The triangular face rounded, and became an almost featureless ovoid. Only a lipless slash remained of her mouth.

"A werespider," Borran Klosk said, staring up at the fantastic creature on the ceiling.

Allis clung to the ceiling and gazed down. Her new face betrayed no emotion.

"I've never seen a werespider before."

"I was sent here to find you," Allis said.

"Who sent you?"

"Those who follow the Beastlord's ways." Allis tilted her malformed head. "Your first sacrifice was not in vain, Borran Klosk. Nor was your resurrection intended to be wasted by railing at the city watch and inciting a battle."

"Malar still has interests in Alaghôn?" Borran Klosk asked.

"In all the Vilhon Reach," she said. "I was sent to guide you."

"Guide me where?"

"To a place," Allis said, "where you can raise an army of undead."

Allis's body shimmered again. She dropped from the ceiling, her legs shrinking back into her body. By the time she landed on her two feet, she resembled a human woman again.

"The Beastlord doesn't want you to wait to strike," she said. "The time is now."

More shouts came from the street. Allis peered through the window.

"The flames are dying," she said, "and it won't be long before reinforcements arrive. We need to go."

"Where?"

"Into hiding for now," Allis said. "Tonight, Malar willing, we'll take a ship."

"We?"

"You have allies here, Borran Klosk, and you have more coming. Malar also caused the five you buried all those years ago in the swamplands around Morningstar Hollows to rise from their graves."

The name surprised Borran Klosk. One of his final battles had been fought there, but no one living had known of the preparation he'd made with the five pieces of Taraketh's Hive. In fact, few had even known of the magical gem's existence before the mohrg had discovered it.

"The five have been raised?" he asked.

"They are on their way here now."

Borran Klosk's thoughts spun.

"You crave vengeance," Allis stated. "Malar has guided

you to Taraketh's Hive, and he has returned your freedom. Don't be so prideful that you have cause to regret the Beastlord's generosity."

Glaring at the woman with harsh intensity, Borran Klosk said, "You have eluded me so far, woman, but rest assured that I can kill you, and I will should I deem that necessary."

"My life has been spent in the service of Malar," Allis said. "Kill me and another will take my place to guide you, unless the Beastlord withdraws his favorable consideration of you and has you destroyed."

Though Borran Klosk wasn't too afraid of that instance, the possibility did give him pause. Only Malar's blessing had returned him to life as a mohrg after he'd been executed.

"Malar's benediction doesn't come without price," Allis said. More shouting sounded out in the street. "We need to go."

Leading him to the back of the tavern, Allis changed into her werespider shape again and leaped up to the ceiling. She used a knife from a sheath at her belt and cut through the ceiling. In less than a minute she was through to the rafters.

With some reluctance, feeling that such an exit from a fight was beneath him, Borran Klosk climbed up after her.

Borran Klosk stepped out through the opening and followed her across the rooftops. His mind whirled in fascination at all that had been set before him. As his gaze roamed over the storm-blasted city, taking in the new shape of the skyline and the much bigger harbor out toward the Sea of Fallen Stars, he felt the old hunger for vengeance against the living return to him.

Alaghôn Watch Sergeant Faholian Tahrass walked through the graveyard and gazed at the dead bodies that had been taken from the crypt by men in his command. One of the corpses lay naked under the misting rain.

"Who are these people?" Tahrass asked.

He'd been a member of the watch for seventeen years and not much surprised him. He'd been privy to murder and every kind of sadistic abuse a thinking creature could do to another.

Dorric Chansin, Tahrass's young aide de camp, knelt beside the stripped man. Chansin wore rain leathers but they did little to mask the lean hardness of his body. A tracker, his hands roamed the area around the bodies.

"Priests," Chansin answered.

"Priests?" Tahrass shook his head, hoping Dorric was wrong. "What makes you think that?"

Chansin took up one of the corpse's hands. "They're dressed in robes. Their hands are soft. The men don't have much coin between them, but they don't look poor." He held up an object that dangled by a string from his fingers. "And they all carried these."

"Symbols of Eldath."

Chansin closed his fist over the symbol and gazed up, eyes slitted against the rain. "You follow Eldath's teachings?"

"It is my wife's faith," Tahrass said, "and my two daughters'. I have my own. Eldath's ways of peace are not for someone like me."

Chansin gave a short nod and turned his attention back to the bodies. "There are some who say Eldath is taking a more active hand in the affairs of the lands around the Sea of Fallen Stars, in light of the return of Myth Nantar to the knowledge of men."

"Even so," Tahrass said, "why would these men come to this place in the dead of night?"

"I don't know." Chansin took a slim-bladed dagger from his boot and used the point to examine the gaping wound in the naked priest's head. "I would like to know what made this. I've never seen the like."

"Magic, mayhap," Tahrass suggested.

He glanced up from the body, feeling uncomfortable gazing at a fresh corpse in a place where so many old ones were kept.

"Maybe they were already dead," he added.

"And climbed up out of their graves?" Chansin smiled despite the harsh circumstances.

"Could be," Tahrass replied, taking no offense. "During the years I've stood watch over Alaghôn, I've heard several tales of the dead walking out of graveyards or ambushing people when they come into them."

"How many have you seen yourself?"

"None."

"There you go," Chansin said. "With mages poking into everything, and necromancers tinkering with things best left alone, I know it's possible that such a thing could happen, but I've never seen it."

"You're too young to remember," a creaky, hoarse voice said.

Turning, Tahrass spotted a thin old man approaching them. Chansin stood, showing respect.

"Mage Vorahl, I meant no disrespect."

Vorahl was ancient even by standards set by mages. His skin, even though his health and life had been prolonged by spells, clung to his bones like coarse parchment. Age had pulled the man in on himself, collapsing him a lot over the twenty years that Tahrass had known him.

Rain had turned Vorahl's gray hair dark, but silver highlights glinted from the lantern light. His dark purple robes held the badges of his office in the watch, and the intricate sigils of his craft. His staff, once just a tool, now supported his infirm steps. He glanced at the assembled bodies.

With pain showing on his face from the effort involved, Vorahl bent over to look at the corpse. His sticklike fingers clung to the staff for support. He shook with palsy and perhaps from the cold.

"You shouldn't be out here," Tahrass said. "We can take care of this."

The soaking cold was almost too much for him, and his rain leathers offered more proof against the elements than the mage's robes.

Vorahl waved the watch commander's words away and

said, "When I heard about this, I knew I had to come."

Tahrass waited, watching the agony the old mage put himself through to examine all the priests' bodies.

"Six of them?" Vorahl asked as he gazed at the yawning mouth of the violated crypt.

"Yes," Chansin answered.

"And you got them all?"

"We think so."

Anger clouded Vorahl's crumpled face as he turned back to the two guardsmen.

"You think so?"

"We took out all we found," Tahrass said.

In all the years he'd known the old mage, he'd never seen Vorahl so close to losing control. The wind whipped through the graveyard, raking wet whispers through the trees.

"We must find them all," Vorahl stated. "Every man who was murdered here this night must be found."

"We will," Tahrass promised. He waved toward the lanterns bobbing through the graveyard. "I've got men out looking for any more bodies and whoever did this."

"You won't find him here," Vorahl commented, straightening and looking around the ivy-infested stone walls surrounding the graveyard. "He'll be long gone from this place."

"Who?" Chansin asked.

"Borran Klosk," Vorahl answered. "These men were priests from the Temple of the Trembling Flower."

"How do you know?"

"Because," Vorahl said with an air of impatience, "all those years ago the Emerald Enclave, at the behest of Silvanus, entrusted the priests of Eldath here in Alaghôn to lock the creature away."

"Borran Klosk is a myth," Chansin said.

"Then a myth killed these men," Vorahl snapped, "and escaped into the night."

He turned from the younger man and hobbled around the bodies, taking care to keep even the hem of his robes from touching them.

"We need to identify these men," Vorahl said.

"I've already sent a man to fetch a priest from the temple," Chansin said.

"As soon as these men are identified by the other priests," Vorahl said, "their bodies will have to be destroyed."

"Why?" Chansin asked.

"If they are not, they will rise again." Vorahl's voice lowered. "All killed by Borran Klosk stand a good chance of rising once more as a mindless beast bent on the savaging of all living things. If they don't follow Borran Klosk's leadership, they will kill on their own. A roaring fire is the only way to insure that they don't return—a fire to burn them first then a sledge to shatter their charred bones. Even burned skeletons have been known to walk."

A sudden light flared south of the graveyard, climbing over the top of the stone wall. The nimbus of yellow light warred against the night and the storm.

"That's a fire," Chansin said.

"It has begun," Vorahl said in a solemn voice. "May the gods preserve us."

CHAPTER FIFTEEN

Morning light woke Druz Talimsir. She rose with slow deliberation, keeping her back to the cave wall.

The druid and the bear were gone.

Though she knew that neither Haarn nor his animal companion would have thought twice before abandoning her, the druid shouldn't have been able to move so quickly.

Her legs tingled with weakness from all the climbing the day before, and the smell of cooking meat filled her nostrils and caused hunger pangs to erupt in her stomach. She turned to the mouth of the cave and started out. Pausing at the entrance, she took up a defensive position and lifted her sword in front of her, ready to strike. Straining her ears for any noises outside the cave, she peered around the entrance.

A campfire nestled in a ring of stones on the ground in front of the cave. A brace of coneys hung from a spit over the fire. The slender rabbits' bodies dripped grease, sending flames leaping up at them. Haarn knelt at the disturbed grave, a curious look on his face.

"What made this?" he asked without lifting his eyes from the hole in the ground.

Druz didn't answer, her irritation growing at the druid's uncanny ability to know she was up and about. She'd made no noise.

"Did you hear me?" he asked, facing her.

"Yes," she replied. "I heard you."

"Do you know what made this?"

"A skeleton."

Druz sheathed her sword, wondering if the druid intended to eat all the coneys or if there would be any left over. Her stomach rumbled again.

"Did you summon it?"

"How would I do that?" Druz said. "I wouldn't even have known it was down there."

Haarn turned his gaze back to the deep hole.

"Where's the bear?" Druz asked.

"Foraging."

Haarn examined the muddy ground around the hole, but Druz was sure he'd done that once before at least. For the first time she also noticed he was still nude save for herbal poultices that clung to his wounds.

"How are you?" she asked.

"I'm fine," replied the druid.

"Your wounds—"

"Are only inconveniences."

Haarn stood and gazed down the mountainside into the forest. He peeled the poultices from his body to reveal wounds that had already knitted together and were well on their way to healing.

"The skeleton left a good set of tracks," he added.

Following Haarn's gaze in the direction of the rising sun, Druz said, "It's headed east."

"For now," Haarn agreed.

"I was surprised when it didn't try to kill us," Druz said. "Why would it just leave?"

"That's something I'd like to know too."

Haarn glanced at her then walked to where his clothing hung on a branch.

"You'd have been better off getting out of those clothes before sleeping last night," he said. "They would have been dry by now."

Druz didn't say anything. As a mercenary, she was used to nudity. Living in the field was a hardship that didn't differentiate between genders. The druid was different, though, but she didn't know why.

She looked at the coneys steaming on the spit and said, "I thought you didn't like to kill animals."

Haarn dressed, showing only a little stiffness in his movements.

"The rabbit population is rising too quickly here," Haarn said, settling his scimitar around his lean hips. "We need the meat after the way we've been pushing ourselves."

He padded barefoot through the mud, hardly leaving an impression despite the looseness of the ground. Druz watched him in wonder. The wolf had savaged him the night before, but Haarn hardly showed any sign of injury.

Haarn took one of the spitted coneys and handed it to Druz.

"Thank you," she said.

She sat, a dull headache throbbing at the base of her skull and spreading up through her temples. She pinched meat from the coney and dropped it into her mouth. The meat was almost too hot, but the flavor was amazing.

"It's very good."

Haarn nodded, but he seemed a little uncomfortable with the compliment. His eyes kept drifting to the hole in the earth.

"Where are the wolf pups?" Druz asked, remembering them for the first time that morning.

"I gave them to the pack," Haarn answered. "They made it through the night and seemed strong enough to survive."

Druz looked around and asked, "What of the pack?"

"They've gone."

"With no more trouble?"

Haarn shrugged. "They tried to hide Stonefur's body," he said, "but I found it."

He pointed at a hide-covered lump back by the mouth of the cave.

"I took Stonefur's head so you would have it as proof."

Druz pulled more strips of meat from the coney and continued eating.

"Are we heading back today?" she asked.

A hot bath followed by a night in a feather bed seemed too good to be true. She promised to treat herself to both those things when she got back to Alaghôn.

"I'm not," Haarn said, making a neat pile of bones in front of him, each one broken where he had sucked the marrow from it.

"What are you going to do?"

Haarn looked east and said, "I'm going to follow the skeleton."

Terror filled Alaghôn as news of Borran Klosk's return spread through the community. During the night, the stories had circulated through the sailors' bars and been taken with them back to their ships. By morning, the stories flowed to the townspeople buying bread and meat for their tables, washing back from the merchant ships to land like the tide, by way of cargo handlers and merchants. In each telling the stories of the watch's encounter with the mohrg and the violent deaths of the priests of Eldath grew fiercer and uglier.

High in one of the older buildings on the west side of Alaghôn, not far removed from the gate that allowed entrance in from the western trade routes, Borran Klosk gazed down from between the slats of a boarded-over window. From there the mohrg watched people gather fearfully in the streets and along the docks.

"You take pride in your accomplishment," Allis said.

For a moment, Borran Klosk did not answer. After whisking him away to this hiding place, traveling swiftly across the rooftops of the city for a time, then dropping down to the street level and managing all the twists and turns there, the werespider woman had disappeared. No longer of the flesh, the mohrg needed no sleep. He'd passed the long, slow night aching for revenge against the living who still called Alaghôn home. It had been everything he could do to stay hidden, and only his fear of Malar's retribution had stayed his hand.

Sails lifted on one of the ships in the harbor. Slowly, the great Sembian merchant ship turned and headed east, bound for other ports.

They escaped, Borran Klosk couldn't help thinking.

The idea rankled him, but he consoled himself with the thought that though the ship's crew had escaped his physical wrath, his arrival had given them stories they would never forget and never forget to pass on.

Borran Klosk turned toward his visitor, momentarily putting aside his anger at her for not having come earlier. His great purple tongue slid through his jaws and tasted the air, licking the woman's scent from it.

"Yes," he said, "I do take pride in the fear they have of me. I have expended great effort to acquire that fear."

Allis regarded him from the doorway at the other end of the room. She was holding a woven basket that was covered by a dingy scrap of cloth. She looked like she was just returned from washing laundry.

She said, "You are everything I was told to expect."

"Who told you what to expect?" Borran Klosk asked.

Ignoring him, she crossed the room and deposited the basket on a slanted, three-legged table.

The rooms had been vacant for years. Spider webs filled the corners and created fragile latticework bridges between piles of rubbish. Judging from the amount of refuse in the building, for a time after being vacated it had become a dumping ground for the businesses and homes around it.

Unleashing the rage that filled him, Borran Klosk reached for Allis, closing his skeletal hand around her upper arm and pulling her around.

The woman turned easily, coming around almost like a lover acknowledging the favored attentions of her suitor, but even as that thought filled Borran Klosk, he saw her change. She wasn't afraid of his grim, fleshless face as he'd thought she would be.

Her head erupted, becoming bigger and rounder, sprouting eyes and fangs. Venom dripped from the slash of mouth that no longer fit a human face. The arm Borran

Klosk held turned rough and covered over with spiky hair. Her simple green dress dropped to the floor, pooling around misshapen spider feet as she soared above him in height.

"No!" she said, her voice filling the enclosed space. "Don't you dare put your hands on me!"

As a spider standing on six of her eight legs, the woman was taller than Borran Klosk, almost to the point of bumping her head on the ceiling rafters, and she was almost four times as large. She struck with her other forward leg, slamming into the mohrg's chest and head with incredible strength.

The impact lifted Borran Klosk from his feet, though if Borran Klosk chose not to be moved, not much could move him.

He flew across the room, mind working with lightning speed, and slammed against the far wall. He broke through the thin boards that covered the bare bones of the wall and stopped against the inside of the outer wall without breaking through. The impact fractured his left femur in two places, the breaks quite apparent.

Borran Klosk threw a hand out, a spell already on its way. He watched the giant spider bob and weave at the other end of the room. The realization that she was afraid of him soothed the mohrg's nerves like a healer's balm. He was more in control of the situation than he'd expected.

His anger vanished, replaced by triumphant humor. In the past, his peers had pointed to those quicksilver mood changes as proof of his madness, but he knew he only looked on the world in a manner different from most. He closed his hand, stilling the destructive magical energies he'd almost unleashed.

Borran Klosk grabbed the edges of the wall and extracted himself. Debris from the shattered wall rained around him, but he ignored it. His left leg moved awkwardly as the broken ends of the femur grated against each other. He reached down then spat his tongue out.

Wrapping the broken bones in the thick purple tongue, he used the magic that was an inherent part of what he'd become. Pain flared through his leg for a moment, then was gone. When he removed his tongue, the femur had been healed and nothing remained of the breaks.

Borran Klosk raised his fierce gaze to the werespider and said, "You're afraid of me."

The huge spider shifted back and forth, scuttling on the tips of all eight legs, the fat body hanging ponderously between them.

"You are evil," Allis accused.

"And what are you?" Borran Klosk advanced on her.

"I am a servant of Malar."

"Then why fear me?" Borran Klosk asked, continuing to walk toward her. "I, too, walk in the Beastlord's shadow and serve his wishes."

"I don't fear you."

"You lie," Borron Klosk said, letting his tongue whip through the air. "I can taste it."

The spider retreated, pressing up against the wall behind her. She was too large to attempt to go through the door or any of the windows, and returning to human size would weaken her.

She said, "You live only to kill."

"As does Malar," Borran Klosk said.

"That is but one aspect of his nature," Allis objected.

"A very important aspect."

The spider reared up on her four back legs, flattening against the wall. She held her four front legs before her, raised to defend herself if necessary.

"Malar called me here to help you," she said.

"Malar doesn't speak directly to someone like you."

Borran Klosk stopped in front of her. He shook broken pieces of boards and splinters from his bloody priest's cloak.

"Who?" he asked.

The spider didn't hesitate. "I can't tell you," she said. "If I did, they would kill me."

Summoning a fireball, Borran Klosk held it dancing in his fleshless palm. The heat was intense. He heard leftover cartilage in his hand pop and crackle, surrendering to the heat. The fire couldn't actually harm him, but the effect of the crackling sounds on Allis was immediate.

The spider shivered and drew back, the flames of the fireball reflected in all of her eight eyes.

"What do you think I will do?" Borran Klosk whispered.

The cold, dispassionate words hung in the emptiness of the room. The spider shifted, and for a moment Borran Klosk thought she might try to escape from the building. The thought of a gigantic spider suddenly scuttling across the rooftops of Alaghôn amused him. Everyone in town would assume it was his handiwork, and in a way it would be.

"It is a group of wizards," Allis said. "They serve Malar, follow his bidding, and work to strike against the Emerald Enclave."

"Wizards?" The thought excited Borran Klosk. "Compatriots, then?"

The promise of allies held a certain allure, but it might also mean having shackles. Since his return from the grave, Borran Klosk had known no master and recognized no peer save for Malar. Meeting other wizards who served the Beastlord was not something Borran Klosk looked forward to with any relish.

"No," the spider answered. "You'll find no friends among them. The wizards serve Malar for their own desires, and the only company they want is their own."

Starting to feel pain from the magic flame, Borran Klosk put his other hand over the fireball, extinguishing it. He was certain the werespider didn't know extinguishing the fireball showed greater power than creating it. Unleashing destruction was always much simpler than harnessing the same energies.

"Return to your human form," he commanded.

Allis hesitated for a moment, then she quivered and slowly dwindled into herself. In only a short time, she stood naked before the mohrg.

Even though much of the way of the flesh had deserted him, Borran Klosk still felt a hint of desire stir within him. The werespider was a beautiful woman, and standing before him as she did while totally defenseless made her even more desirable.

"How did you come to be part of this group?" Borran Klosk asked.

"They recruited me," she answered.

"How?"

"By blackmailing me. And they made sure the Emerald Enclave knew of me."

"Knew what?"

"That I am dual-natured," she answered.

"Why should the Emerald Enclave care?"

"They think that lycanthropes who were turned rather than born are an abomination against nature and should be forced into one nature or the other or killed outright. Those born into the life naturally are tolerated as long as they remain true to themselves."

"The wizards are lycanthropes?"

"No." Allis kept her gaze directed over Borran Klosk's shoulder, as if she were staring through him. "They all practice necromancy."

Borran Klosk laughed, and the harsh, bitter sound echoed in the room.

He asked, "A league of undead wizards?"

"They aren't undead," Allis said. "At least, not the wizards I've seen, but they are all evil. The Beastlord offers them power, just as Malar offered you power all those years ago."

"The power didn't come soon enough," Borran Klosk said. "I was unable to assemble the jewel in time to use it against the druids of the Emerald Enclave."

"Your task remains to assemble the jewel," Allis said, and the sparkle in her eyes told Borran Klosk that she delighted in telling him that. Attempting it would surely draw the wrath of the Emerald Enclave down on him, though the fear never quite left her.

"You are to call down the destruction," Allis said, "that Taraketh's Hive will open for you. Once you have done that, the druids will be driven from Turmish—perhaps even farther beyond before they are able to gain mastery over the jewel's power."

Anger twisted inside Borran Klosk. He spat out the

thick purple tongue, tired of tasting the bile that seemed to hang in the air. "I do not do their bidding."

Allis lifted her chin and rebellion fired anew in her eyes. "You will."

Unleashing his tongue, Borran Klosk splintered the wall to the side of her head.

She flinched, but only little, and swallowed hard again. Her gaze met his boldly for a moment before sliding away.

"The people who control you have no control over me," Borran Klosk announced.

"They control whomever they wish," she told him. "You wanted Taraketh's Hive, didn't you?"

Borran Klosk glared at her.

"They can take that from you," Allis said softly. "They raised the dead that you buried so long ago. They can just as easily return those cadaverous minions back into the ground somewhere short of Alaghôn, only this time the wizards will stop your minions in places that you won't know of."

"Don't threaten me, woman," Borran Klosk warned.

"I'm not," Allis said. "I'm just stating a fact. Perhaps they'll even see to it that the priests of Eldath lock you away once again."

"They want something from me," Borran Klosk said, and he found himself needing to hear that statement as much as he needed to tell the woman. "They won't let me fall so easily."

"If you prove difficult," Allis said, "they will."

Borran Klosk turned from the woman, not wanting to believe her, but he did believe her. She was too calm, too complacent in her words, and she took a certain measured delight in passing them on.

"If your damned wizards come for me," he said, "they'll do so at the peril of their own lives."

"They won't come for you," Allis told him. "They won't have to. You'll be hunted all over Alaghôn after last night, and though it might take them time to bring you down, they will. They will withhold the gifts they offer you today, and they'll keep Taraketh's Hive from you."

"Gifts?" Interested, Borran Klosk looked at the basket the werespider had placed on the slanted table.

Allis picked up her dress, which had been ripped considerably as she'd changed forms. Still, she pulled herself into it as best as she could. Her eyes never met his while she dressed.

Crossing to the table, Allis lifted the cloth from the basket and revealed the items inside. She took a small oval mirror from inside a black wooden chest that was filled with padding to protect the mirror. She waved a hand over the mirror, spoke words that Borran Klosk almost recognized, and placed the looking glass on the tabletop.

"First," she said, "I bring you proof that the five you buried with the pieces of Taraketh's Hive have risen."

Borran Klosk didn't need her mystic bauble to tell him that, but he remained silent. Even now he could feel them drawing steadily closer.

Allis pointed to the mirror.

Drawn by the sight of a figure moving within the glass, Borran Klosk came closer. He peered into the mirror and saw a scene as though through a hazy fog.

A skeleton marched through swamplands with a long stride. Murky water came up to the skeleton's shins. In the hollows of its chest, lodged behind the breastbone, a jeweled cube burned bright and hard. The skeleton carried a short sword in one fist, and divots of mud still filled its cavernous eyes.

Allis waved her hand again, and the other four skeletons bearing pieces of Taraketh's Hive came into view, each in turn.

"You see," she said, "all is as I have promised. They have no will of their own but to serve Malar—and you—in the best way they know how."

"And what of the other gifts you said you bore?"

Reaching into the basket again, Allis took out a section of gray and pink coral almost as long as her forearm.

She held it out and asked, "Do you sense the death on this?"

"It's coral," Borran Klosk said. He tasted the salty scent of it with a flicking caress of his tongue. "It reeks of death."

Intrigue filled him. Even after everything he'd done, all the foul murders he'd committed, nothing had tasted so exquisite.

"Where did you get this?" he asked.

"From the Whamite Isles."

Borran Klosk's tongue leaped out again, drawing closer to the coral. "I've never tasted death like this. Not even that wrought by my own hand."

"There has never been death like this before," Allis said. "The islands are encircled by drowned ones and other undead. This was taken from the reefs that surround the Whamite Isles and was magically altered."

Borran Klosk's tongue flicked out again, and he could sense the magic energies bound within the coral. It was the most powerful thing outside of Taraketh's Hive that he'd ever encountered.

Allis extended the coral to him and with some trepidation, Borran Klosk accepted it. As soon as his bony fingers touched the coral, it grew, shimmering as it changed. In a heartbeat, the coral had formed an elbow-length glove of white and pink streaks that perfectly encased his hand. A buzz of power filled the mohrg.

"What is this?" Borran Klosk asked.

"Power," Allis answered. "The power to wake the dead of the Whamite Isles and call them to you."

Borran Klosk held the glove up before him, admiring it. For a moment, he worried that the mystic thing had ensorcelled him in some way, but he had safeguards—spells and magical items about him—that guaranteed such things could not easily affect him.

The power was real. He felt it surging within the glove and within him.

"Use it," Allis urged, "and you will raise an army to follow you back here to Alaghôn. No one will be able to stand before them. All of Turmish, and perhaps even the Vilhon Reach, will fall under your power."

Borran Klosk flexed the glove upon his hand. It moved as supple as leather, far easier than even the flesh he could remember wearing all those years before.

"And these wizards that you serve," he said, "they want me to have such power?"

"Serve your own dark desires, Borran Klosk," Allis said, "and you will serve theirs."

CHAPTER SIXTEEN

Haarn ran, cutting through the overgrown grass that sprouted from the low valley's marshy ground. Despite the speed at which he'd been moving for hours, he knew he could run for hours more. From the wheezing gasps of his companion, he likewise knew that Druz Talimsir could not.

He grew irritated again at his own inability to leave the woman, as he knew he should have.

I gave her Stonefur's head, he thought in disgust. That's all I owed her.

Druz gasped for breath but in a controlled manner, showing training and stamina, but her abilities were nothing when compared to the druid's. Her passage through the marshlands, punctuated with discordant splats of her boots slapping mud, echoed around them.

Ahead, the valley sloped up again, leaving a thin trickle of stained brown water running through the heart of it. The long rain of the preceding day and night still wound through the land, and a tenday or more would pass before the sun burned away what the ground couldn't absorb.

Haarn started up the slope, then stopped under a copse of trees. Scanning the ground for the trail he was certain he'd find, he waited for Druz.

"Tymora's blessing," Druz gasped. "I thought we were never going to stop running. Have you lost the trail?"

"No," Haarn said, only just keeping the scorn from his voice.

The skeleton's trail was there for anyone to see. Over the last three miles, the stink of moldy, dead flesh had carried more strongly on the air. They were much closer than they had been, practically on the undead abomination's heels.

"Wait here," he told her.

"What are you going to do?"

Haarn didn't pause to answer her. It was surprising how many questions she asked, but he supposed it was because she was used to being in control.

"Haarn," she called after him, irritating him further because she must have known how far her voice would carry.

"Wait," he growled over his shoulder.

He raced up the side of the valley, finding the firmest spots and rocky shelves at a glance. Running in zigzag fashion, he spotted the trail he was looking for.

A dolodrium plant, one of those that sprang up when the rainy season started and turned the drylands to verdant marsh, lay broken and twisted on the ground. An imprint beneath it, the one that had broken the frail plant, showed three toes and the ball of a skeletal foot. The thing he pursued had come this way.

Despite his pressing need to eradicate the undead thing, Haarn took a moment to harvest the dolodrium blossoms. The plant was hard to find even when someone was looking for it. When harvested properly—from within the third morning sun to the moon of the fourth night, only a small window of time—the dolodrium plant yielded medicinal flowers that could be crushed and boiled into a weak tea that helped cure infections and headaches.

Broadfoot snuffled only a few feet away and stepped out of the trees. The bear stood on his rear legs and scented the air, snuffling again. The prey was near, and Broadfoot knew it.

Silently agreeing, Haarn followed the trail across the uncertain foundation of too-wet ground. In three other places he spotted evidence of the skeleton's passing, all of them marked by bare spots where the yellowed grass had been torn away.

Haarn continued up the hill, catching Broadfoot from the corner of his eye as the bear lumbered uphill as well. Reaching the crest, he flattened and stayed within the cover offered by the scraggly brush and tall grasses.

Gazing down the hillside on the other side of the valley, aware of the hot afternoon sun burning down on the back of his neck, Haarn spotted deer, rabbits, ground squirrels, and nearly three dozen different kinds of sparrows, finches, and songbirds. There were no paths, save for game trails. "Civilized" men from Turmish and other places around the Vilhon Reach had not yet found the valley.

Blowing his breath out, controlling the anger that filled him, Haarn stared down at the yellowed ivory form that forced its way through the brush and tall grasses covering the eastern side of the short mountain range. Revulsion filled the druid.

The skeleton showed no affinity for the living world around it, merely bulling its way through whatever obstacles it encountered. Already, the skeleton was a quarter of a mile away and moving at a steady pace, unhampered by the fatigue of flesh, running on the mystical energies that had called it forth.

Broadfoot snuffled again, sounding angry this time.

Wanting to take advantage of surprise, Haarn lifted his arms and spoke a shapeshifting spell. Magic flowed throughout his body, molding it along the lines of the great horned owl. Pain, only a little discomforting because it was so small, echoed throughout his body as he changed. His father had told him that not every druid with the ability to shapechange suffered through any pain at all, but that some agonized during the spell.

In his owl shape, Haarn leaped from the mountain's crest and caught the north, northeasterly winds. The druid lifted from the mountain, tilting his wings.

Broadfoot grumbled in displeasure. The bear had never cared for Haarn's abilities to alter his shape and leave him behind.

An owl's sight was far keener than Haarn's own half-elf eyes. The terrain revealed itself to him in intimate detail, and he seemed able to track every motion. He whipped his wings, gaining altitude to get a better view of the countryside.

He saw Druz Talimsir stumble up the mountainside, stubbornly not giving up the pursuit. Broadfoot took to the foliage, racing down the mountain to intercept the skeleton, which so far had given no notice that it even knew anyone was around. Marsh hares and brightly colored birds scattered ahead of the skeleton. Screams from the angry birds that had been feasting on floating eggs and drowned lizards and rats filled the sky.

Haarn winged toward the skeleton. Flying came naturally to the druid in his owl form, and he'd had years of experience. Sunlight glinted from his claws as he sped toward the skeleton.

Something warned the creature before Haarn arrived. The druid knew he made no sound gliding on the owl's wings. He thought perhaps his shadow had fallen over the ground in front of the skeleton, then he realized he'd flown into the sun, which still hung slightly to the east. He reached the skeleton only a heartbeat before his shadow did.

Still, the undead thing whirled and drew up an ivory arm to ward off Haarn's attack.

Haarn raked at the creature with his owl's claws. The hard black nails tried to rip the ivory bone of the skeleton's uplifted arm, but left only scratches as Haarn passed.

Wheeling high in the sky, shutting his eyes tight against the sun, Haarn gloried in the rush of air sweeping by him. Part of his owl's mind wanted nothing more than to follow the wind and leave anything earthbound far behind him, but he controlled the impulse and stretched out his wings, gliding around in a tight circle to his left. Glancing down, he spotted his prey.

The skeleton ran, ducking under scraggly trees and brush, disappearing at times, but the cover didn't last for long. Though the ground was marsh at the moment, it was normally dry and baked hard. Only the hardiest grasses and less demanding of trees thrived there.

Haarn flew, speeding through the air and judging from the brief glimpses of ivory when the skeleton would come into view again. When it did, he struck the foul creature in the back of the head, knocking it off balance.

Flapping his wings and dropping the right one so he could see the skeleton, Haarn watched the undead thing tumble to the ground. Ruby lights glinted from the skeleton's rib cage.

Haarn tried to identify the thing inside the skeleton but couldn't. Turning his attention back to the attack, he swooped again, hoping that the force with which he struck the skeleton would knock its skull from its shoulders. He knew that action sometimes destroyed the spell that animated a skeleton.

The creature had only succeeded in pushing itself to its knees when Haarn struck again. His blow toppled the skeleton over on its side, but not before the creature managed to fling an arm out and strike Haarn.

In his owl form, Haarn was weaker and more vulnerable. If the skeleton's blow had connected more solidly, Haarn's wing, and possibly his back, would have been broken. Off-kilter, paralyzed a little from the impact and knowing that he could no longer stay aloft, the druid spoke the spell again and struck the marshlands as a half-elf instead of an owl.

Buried facedown in the muck and slime, Haarn heard the skeleton's feet slapping through the mud toward him. The druid threw himself to one side, feeling the weight of the mud clinging to his body. Even as fast as he was, the skeleton managed to catch him with part of a blow that set Haarn's ears to ringing.

The thing was frightfully quick, quicker than it had any right to be. Its jaws opened, and even in the daylight Haarn could see the unnatural fire in the skull's hollows. The thing's mouth snapped open, revealing broken, jagged fangs. An odor, the musk of the grave acerbated by the dank marsh water running slowly around them, clung to the skeleton.

Haarn had barely set himself to face the thing, his hand on the hilt of his scimitar, when it lunged at him.

"Are you having any luck, lady?"

Shinthala Deepcrest looked up from the smooth river surface she'd been studying. She shaded her eyes against the late morning sun to glance at her unexpected visitor.

"Ashenford Torinbow," she greeted, rising from where she sat beside the Calling River.

Despite the fear that thundered in her heart and the fatigue that gripped her from maintaining the scrying spell she'd been using, she summoned a smile for the man who stepped down from the rocky shelves toward her.

"Lady," the half-elf said, taking Shinthala's offered hands in his own and kissing them gently. "You are as beauteous as ever. A sunrise full of her own glory."

Torinbow's greeting embarrassed Shinthala. Despite her position as one of the Elder Circle of the Emerald Enclave, she wasn't used to such pretty words.

"You came all this way to turn my head with your flattery?" she asked.

Torinbow squeezed her hands and released them. "Lady, I came here to Ilighôn only to visit with you, and perhaps to sup of good Kate's table while we talk of my travels along the Vilhon Reach."

Shinthala took her hands from Torinbow's. He was a half-elf with pale blue eyes and golden skin. At five eight he was still inches below Shinthala's own six feet plus in height. His light brown hair was neatly coifed and hung in curls to his shoulders.

"How long have you been on Ilighôn?" she asked.

"Only long enough to disembark the ship that brought me to Sapra then begin the long march here to the Elder Spires."

"I suppose you've heard the news."

"About the beast being freed from Eldath's prison?" Torinbow nodded. "I didn't sleep since I heard of it this morning, and the trip over by ship wasn't restful with the storm playing hob as it was."

Remembering her manners, Shinthala asked, "Have you supped?"

Torinbow shrugged. "A bit of crust and some hard cheese along the trip up the Hierophant Trail, Lady. There wasn't much time for taking on provisions. I insisted upon leaving the city at once when I heard about Borran Klosk. Thankfully the horses we were able to procure in Sapra were fleet of foot and strong of heart."

"You learned of Borran Klosk's freedom in Sapra?"

Torinbow nodded. "Only this morning."

Shinthala grimaced and said, "Then the news has spread as far as the city."

"All of Sapra was talking about it while I was there, which I assure you wasn't long. Perhaps I was misled, but I think much of the news of Borran Klosk's attacks on Alaghôn got carried over on the ships that left there last night and arrived at Sapra only this morning. Some captains chose a hasty departure. The mohrg's reputation is still strong there."

Anger touched Shinthala, and she knew she wasn't much good at hiding her displeasure. Besides being a member of the Elder Circle of the Emerald Enclave—one of the three druids who were the leaders of that organization—she'd also led battles against Malar's forces as a hierophant druid.

"Tongues wag too easily these days," she said.

"It's the war, Lady, and the changes that have taken place within the Sea of Fallen Stars. Much of what the citizens of Sapra knew about their sea has changed. They fear what happened to the Whamite Isles might someday happen to them."

"There is no chance of that," Shinthala declared, then gestured up the plateau above them at the open structure of wood and granite that provided only meager shelter from the elements. "Not as long as the Emerald Enclave chooses to maintain the House of Silvanus here."

"May Silvanus forever bless this place." Torinbow touched his chest over his heart respectfully.

Shinthala echoed the blessing then turned her gaze higher up the plateau. Other druids were there in the House of Silvanus. Some of them were deep in prayer and meditation, while others had returned to the Emerald Enclave's stronghold to heal and exchange knowledge.

The Calling River at Shinthala's feet started out as one of the three waterfalls that spilled from the plateau that was the House of Silvanus. While the Calling River ran south from the Elder Spires, the Springbrook and the Elder Rivers ran to the east and the north. All of the waterfalls plunged into the waiting rivers below and created a misty skirt that surrounded the House of Silvanus.

The Hierophant Trail was the only overland trail allowed on the island, and it was barely visible through the thick forest laden with heavy boughs. The rest of the island was protected and sanctioned by the druids who dwelled there. No one traveled throughout the rest of Ilighôn who wasn't a druid or ranger or someone who knew woodcraft and respected nature. Sapra was ten miles away. Torinbow and his group had made good time.

"Come," she said. "I fear I'm growing lax in my duties as a hostess. I've some journeycake put away. Kate will prepare the midday meal soon, and the journeycake will break your fast till then."

"Thank you, lady."

Shinthala led the way toward the House of Silvanus. Even after years of service as an Elder of the Emerald Enclave, she drew a lot of attention from the younger druids encamped among them. She knew the attention was due to her height. Many expected humans to be tall but had not seen many women over six feet. Gray had started to touch her long, dark brown hair at the temples, but her green eyes were as bright and clear as ever.

The only sounds around them were the rivers burbling and the wild things that filled the forest and the sky. Only occasional wisps of conversation came Shinthala's way, but she heard the name of Borran Klosk repeated several times. She led the way up the plateau, leaning into her ascent.

"Have the other druids around Alaghôn and the coastal cities been warned of Borran Klosk's return?" Torinbow asked.

He trailed along closely behind her, as sure-footed as a mountain goat.

"Birds were sent out early this morning," Shinthala said.

"Have you talked to any of them?"

"Two," Shinthala said. "I contacted Mornis and Chackery through the crystals we share." Only a few of the druids had the enchanted crystals. They were the same blue-white quartz that wizards often used in making crystal balls. "Neither of them had any news of Borran Klosk's return."

"Do you think that's odd?"

"Not really," Shinthala said. "After all, the exodus from Alaghôn appears to be headed eastward, out to sea, rather than south into the Vilhon Reach or north or west into the marshland and desert."

"The druids who faced Borran Klosk all those years ago left an army of undead buried in that marshland and desert," Torinbow said. "The citizens of Alaghôn surely remember that. They're probably fearful that they'll run into that same army again, once more raised from the earth."

"The undead things that stood with Borran Klosk in Morningstar Hollows will never rise again," Shinthala said. "Those who served the Emerald Enclave then made certain of that."

"No one thought Borran Klosk would rise again, either."

Despite her calm nature, Shinthala almost lost her temper. Since learning of Borran Klosk's return, she'd spent all morning with her scrying spells and the effort had nearly exhausted her.

She said, "It's still not been proven that he has."

"You've not been able to find him?"

At the top of the plateau, Shinthala stepped through a forest of sensual delight. Vibrant growth showed everywhere. Trees and flowering bushes caught the eye only for a moment as woodland creatures scampered through them and birds glided through the air. Songbird music and flower fragrances rode the gentle wind. Shinthala knew every song and every scent.

"No," she told Torinbow as she gazed at the House of Silvanus.

No matter how many times she had seen the sacred place, she never lost her wonder of it. The druids who'd built the House of Silvanus had constructed it from the natural materials at hand. They took advantage of the shapes of trees and enhanced the rocky shelves that provided some respite from the elements. During part of the day, light filtered into the inner courtyards, then was shaded as the sun tracked across the sky. At night, guests in the House of Silvanus could gaze upon the stars.

Water burbled and ran around the island that housed the main body of the structure. Fed from an underground spring, the small lake was thirty feet deep in some places and had steep sides. The central core of the spring ran down through the plateau and into the mountains. Over the years, druids had sought the source of the spring, trying to discover what pushed the water up to such incredible heights. None had been able to fathom its true depth, but there was speculation that the spring was fed from a source deep below even the sea bottom that surrounded them.

"If Borran Klosk is once more at large," Shinthala continued, "I can't find him. Perhaps someone more gifted than me will be able to."

"If you can't find the mohrg, dear lady," Torinbow said gently, "I dare say no one could."

Shinthala stopped, stretched out her hand, and tracked her fingers through an open blossom. Golden pollen stuck to her fingertips. The sweet powder glistened in the swath of sunlight just within her reach. The heavy buzzing sound of a bumblebee reached her ears only a moment before she saw the fat-bodied creature. She remained still as the bumblebee flew to her fingers. The insect drew the pollen from her fingertips then flew off in its zigzag manner.

"What do you think, Ashenford?" Shinthala asked. "Do you think the monster once more walks the coast of the Vilhon Reach?"

Torinbow hesitated then said, "I don't want to assume that these are just stories spreading from a few drunken men with nothing else to do . . . and there is the tale of the slaughtered priests of Eldath."

"That story is true," Shinthala said. "I received a message myself from a senior priest of Eldath's temple in Alaghôn. The priests were murdered by an unknown hand in the graveyard where Borran Klosk was imprisoned."

"The possibility exists that someone else could have murdered them there to encourage that conclusion," Torinbow said.

Shinthala gazed out at the children of the druids who summered on Ilighôn. Toddlers of both sexes played in the water with leaf boats they'd made, or chased butterflies under the supervision of their parents and their animal companions.

Shinthala said, "I didn't defend Gulthmere Forest against Malar's forces by assuming every rumor I heard was only that."

"Perhaps your tie to the mohrg just isn't strong enough," the half-elf suggested.

Reaching into the leather pouch at her waist, Shinthala took out an object and showed it to the half-elf. Torinbow nudged the cylindrical object with a forefinger.

"A sliver of bone?" he asked. "From Borron Klosk?"

"Retrieved from Adrius Glistenmoon, one of the Great Druids who served during the war against Borran Klosk."

Warily, Torinbow drew back his hand from the bone sliver.

"My tie to Borran Klosk was tight enough," Shinthala said. "Even though he still slept in the crypt the priests of Eldath had prepared for him, I should have seen him there."

"But you did not?"

Shinthala closed her fist cautiously over the bone splinter. So far she'd seen no indication that it was still animate, still undead.

Returning the sliver to her pouch, she said, "Perhaps this piece of Borran Klosk was gone too long from the rest of him."

"Or perhaps someone of considerable power is hiding the mohrg."

"That thought had occurred to me, but why would someone do that?"

"Borran Klosk was one of Malar's favorite playthings," Torinbow said. "If the Beastlord resurrected him, it may well be that he has hidden the mohrg as well." The half-elf scowled. "Borran Klosk can't remain hidden. He will attempt to raise another army of undead to overtake the Vilhon Reach, as he has done before."

"That will never happen again." The thought shivered through Shinthala despite the warm sunlight around her. "Back then, when the Vilhon Reach was younger and the Emerald Enclave had yet to come into its power, no one was there to watch something like Borran Klosk manifest itself. He pulled together his army of undead because no one saw."

Unwilling to stand there and talk of such things, she started on for the main section of the House of Silvanus. She walked to the water's edge then followed the marble and granite stepping stones that were magically set on the surface. The stones didn't move beneath her.

On the banks, druids, rangers, and those called into the service of Silvanus sat wrapped in prayers. Flower petals, meager offerings from the bounty Silvanus provided, floated on the water.

As Shinthala walked, she noticed the water roil beneath the stepping stones. The first time she'd seen it, she'd been wary. A water elemental prowled the small lake and the spring that fed it. The elemental was a guardian put there by Silvanus to watch over his charges.

"Lady," Torinbow said. "There is one thing I feel I must bring to your attention."

The hesitation in his voice conveyed grave discomfort.

"Speak your mind, Ashenford," she told him. "We've long been friends, and in this time—if Borran Klosk is truly risen—then we must definitely remain so."

"We speak of the army the mohrg must raise," Torinbow said, keeping his voice low so it didn't carry to the other druids and rangers gathered around them, "and we know that Borran Klosk has the power to do so."

"If the townspeople of Alaghôn feel that Borran Klosk is among them again, they will surely keep watch over the cemeteries. The mohrg will not find a following so easily."

"Not from the cemeteries of civilization," Torinbow agreed, "but there may be another source."

"The only way Borran Klosk can raise an army is by killing living beings and animating their corpses."

"What if the corpses are already animate?" Torinbow asked. "What if they're already undead?"

"Borran Klosk won't find an undead army already in Alaghôn, or even all of Turmish and beyond," Shinthala said.

"I'm not talking about Alaghôn or even Turmish," Torinbow said. "The Whamite Isles . . ."

The cruel horror of that possibility had not presented itself to Shinthala until that moment.

"Since the Taker's War," Torinbow continued, "the Whamite Isles have been ringed by hundreds, possibly thousands, of drowned ones."

"Borran Klosk would have no reason to go there," she said, though she knew the hope was a desperate one at best.

"If the mohrg wants to raise an army," Torinbow said, "he will go there. We have reports, though none of them confirmed, that Iakhovas was behind the massacre on the Whamite Isles, but what if Malar had a hand in it as well?"

Shinthala shook her head. "You're starting at shadows, Ashenford, and I mean no disrespect in the saying of that."

"None taken, Lady, I assure you. Were you not here to question me, I'd have to take that on myself." Torinbow hesitated, closed his mouth, then opened it again and said,

"I believe we would be remiss if we did not investigate the possibility. The Whamite Isles are close enough to Turmish that Borran Klosk could try for them."

Shinthala sighed. Seeing the wisdom in the half-elf's words, she said, "I'll travel to Sapra and arrange for—"

Torinbow cleared his throat. "Lady, if you'll forgive my meddling, I've already seen to it."

"You're not meddling. I appreciate your efforts, and you were well within your rights as an Elder to assign such a task."

"Thank you, Lady."

Shinthala's mind flew quickly. "If Borran Klosk should decide to undertake a voyage to the Whamite Isles, he'll need a ship, and he'll have to come from Turmish or he'll spend tendays, even months at sea."

"Borran Klosk, from what I remember of the stories, was not known for patience." Torinbow said. "The mohrg won't wait to strike."

"Someone freed Borran Klosk from his crypt," Shinthala said. "This has been planned. I'll gather another flock of doves to carry the message and instruct druids everywhere to go to Alaghôn. Perhaps it's not too late to stop the monster there."

She prayed to Silvanus that it was so, but even as much as she believed in her god, she had her doubts.

CHAPTER SEVENTEEN

Whipping his scimitar in front of him, Haarn barely managed to block the skeleton's claws from his throat. The clang of metal against bone echoed over the marshlands as Broadfoot roared a challenge.

The druid moved slowly. With moccasins caked in mud, his feet felt heavy, awkward, and his reflexes were slowed as a result. The skeleton gave him no time to use spells, and Haarn was forced to simply defend himself.

Turning, setting himself in the mud, the druid blocked the skeleton's attacks. As he parried just to keep himself alive, Haarn caught glimpses of Broadfoot closing in. Above, on the ridgeline, Druz began her descent, sliding down the steep, mud-encrusted mountainside. Haarn knew with grim certainty that the fighting would be over long before Druz could reach him. Only Broadfoot stood a chance of reaching him in time to help.

He parried the skeleton's strikes again and again, giving up step after step of the muddy ground, leaving a ragged battlefield in his wake.

Despite the ravaged ground and the thick mud, the skeleton had no problem pursuing Haarn. It lunged after him, taking long, slapping strides through the mud. Without a true mouth and only a leathery husk for a tongue, the undead thing's voice came out as a barely audible, growling hiss.

There was no finesse to the skeleton's attack. It swung its arms like bludgeons, depending on its sharp talons to flay him.

The skeleton was far stronger than Haarn had at first realized. The creature was an inhuman dreadnought that kept on coming. As it struck, the ruby jewel inside its chest rattled against its rib cage. Sunlight splintered from it in a cascade of crimson colors so bright they almost hurt the druid's eyes.

Haarn dodged behind a tree, and the skeleton lashed out again. Narrowly avoiding the blow, Haarn narrowed his eyes as the heavy claws ripped through bark. A cloud of splinters flew into the air, and the sound of the impact was like nothing Haarn had ever heard before. A shiny patch of white marred the tree where a patch of bark nearly the size of Haarn's head had been.

Haarn brought the scimitar up in both hands, driving it toward the skeleton's skull. The undead thing managed to get a hand up first, though, and the clang of bone against metal rang across the marshlands. Mud sucked at Haarn's feet as he shifted. He struck again, but the skeleton managed to block him once more, though this time a finger bone flew from one of its hands. They were moving so fast that the druid couldn't tell which finger had been lost.

Abandoning all hesitation, the skeleton threw itself at Haarn.

Knowing his undead opponent's weight would drive him into the mud and trap him, Haarn jumped to one side, trying for as much distance as he could. He knew Broadfoot was almost on them now, and he trusted the great bear to help guard his back.

Before the skeleton could reach Haarn, who struggled to extricate himself from the mud, Broadfoot's shoulder hit the skeleton so hard that bone shattered and broke. Knocked off its feet by the terrific force, the skeleton flew through the air, scattering pieces of itself as it flipped and cartwheeled.

Haarn shoved himself to his feet and spat mud. Slimy

muck caked his face and blurred the edges of his vision. He started forward as the skeleton struggled to draw itself to its feet once again. It stood on unstable legs in the splintered shadows that tracked the ground beneath the trees shivering gently in the breeze.

The skeleton's jaw moved, and it leaned down to seize a broken tree limb that floated on the water. As the skeleton turned, drawing back the limb in a threatening manner, the jewel inside its rib cage twisted and gleamed like a coal that had just been hit by a blast from a smith's bellows.

As if surprised, the skeleton glanced down at its broken rib cage. Within its ivory prison, the jewel glimmered and spun, rattling in wild abandon. The skeleton loosed an ululating wail as if in pain, sinking to its knees and holding its arms across its rib cage. The ruby light squeezed between its arms and lanced at the ground.

An invisible force scooped up a load of muck-encrusted earth. Water and young toads spilled off the sides of the earthen burden, plopping down into the hole that rapidly drained the nearby marshlands.

Taking cover behind a young elderberry tree, inhaling the sweet scent of the blossoms and aware of the bees working the flowers around him with no concern at all, Haarn prepared a spell, sheathing his scimitar. He touched the symbol of Silvanus at his throat and threw out his hand.

The trees around the skeleton bent and snaked their branches down toward the undead creature.

The beam of red light leaping from the jewel slashed through the tree branches. The smoldering limbs dropped into the shallow water of the marshlands, hissed, and sank beneath the dirty surface.

The clump of mud writhed and jerked into motion. The mud flew into the air and came down in a sprawling mass.

Not believing what he was seeing, Haarn watched as a creature forced itself to an erect position.

Shamblers, also called shambling mounds, lived in warm wetlands and underground caverns. Carnivores, they hunted animals even as big as they were. Haarn generally left them alone unless they unduly threatened a local animal population.

Like the other shamblers Haarn had seen, this one resembled a huge mass of rotting vegetation until it stood and revealed its humanoid shape. Two massive tree trunk legs, each sprouting root-like appendages as thick as Haarn's forearms, supported the creature. While the body of the shambler was yellowish brown, the same as the mud and muck of the marshlands, the two arms showed green as if freshly grown. The arms stretched out over twice the shambler's height, and moved like whips. Only a short distance from the shoulder, the arms each flared out into two pieces that looked like vines.

The shambler snapped out one of its vinelike arms. The arm sailed through the air with uncanny accuracy for a creature that seemed to have no eyes, and struck Broadfoot's shoulder. The attack ripped through the bear's fur and opened a crimson gash nearly a foot long.

Blood wept from the bear's terrible wound and matted fur. Angry and in pain, Broadfoot reared to his full height and started for the shambler. The shambler reacted at once, flailing the bear with the lashlike appendages that made up its arms. More bloody welts opened up on Broadfoot's body, but the bear didn't give ground.

"No!" Haarn yelled, yanking his scimitar free again.

He pushed away from the tree and ran at the shambler, certain Broadfoot would be slain before he could get away. Behind the shambler, the skeleton turned and started into the forest, making its way east again. Before Haarn covered the distance to the shambler, the skeleton had disappeared.

The shambler drew back its right arm again and whipped it forward. The smack of tentacles against the bear's flesh was interrupted by a sucking sound. As Haarn braced himself in the mud, he saw the blue-dyed fletching of an arrow jutting from the lump atop the shambler's shoulders. As he chopped at the tentacle that wrapped around one of the bear's legs, Haarn saw another arrow pierce the shambler not two inches from the first.

Haarn hacked at the arm holding Broadfoot. He brought the scimitar down in a two-handed swing. The blade cleaved deeply into the creature's muck and vegetation flesh and left gaping wounds that would have killed anything mortal. Even the shamblers Haarn had encountered before would have been seriously injured and probably withdrawn from the fight.

The creature released its hold on Broadfoot.

"Back," Haarn told the bear, grabbing a handful of fur and urging Broadfoot away from the shambler.

Haarn stayed with the bear, glancing back the way he'd come. Haarn spotted Druz already fitting a third arrow to her string.

"Aim for its chest," he called. "There's an organ that serves as its mind. That's the only way you can kill it."

Readjusting her position and stepping around a clump of brush, Druz steadied, then fired again.

The arrow flashed by Haarn less than a foot to his left. There was no warning from the shambler as it raced forward again, pursuing Haarn and Broadfoot even while Druz's arrow was in flight. The third arrow took the shambler in the shoulder, and if it hurt the big creature at all, it didn't show in the way it moved.

The threat drew an immediate response from Broadfoot. The bear shrugged off Haarn's tugging hand and gave in to instinct.

Haarn stepped away, setting himself in the mud, and watched helplessly as the bear met the shambler's lunge. Though Broadfoot was the taller of the two, even the great bear didn't have the shambler's bulk. When the shambler slammed into Broadfoot, the force of the impact carried the bear backward. Broadfoot tried to stand his ground, but the mud gave way beneath his clawed feet.

Another arrow feathered the shambler's chest, and Haarn silently acknowledged Druz's skill with the bow. Even with four arrows in it, the dread creature wasn't slowed at all. Two of the shafts snapped off as it fought Broadfoot.

The bear stood his ground, leaning on the shambler's

greater bulk and managing through sheer strength and rage to hold the monster back. The shambler's vinelike arms whipped again, leaving furrows of torn and bloody flesh. During the next attack, the shambler wrapped the two appendages at the end of its left arm around the bear's broad upper body and tightened its grip. The shambler's rootlike feet plunged into the ground and took hold.

Locked down as it was and holding Broadfoot, Haarn knew that the shambler was at its most vulnerable—and most deadly. The constricting power of even a normal shambler could break a man in half. The bear would only take longer.

Haarn prayed to Silvanus for his next spell, then unleashed the power within him as Broadfoot's growls of rage tightened to shrill agony. With the constricting coils around him, Broadfoot couldn't take another breath. If the bear's ribs didn't shatter and pierce his heart, then he was doomed to a slow death by suffocation.

Gripping the scimitar, Haarn hurled himself at the creature. He knew it was aware of him by the way it moved its body, but it had already chosen its victim and the only way it could engage Haarn was to release the bear.

Haarn stepped behind the shambler, praying that his spell would work in time. Holding the scimitar in both hands, he drove it deeply into the creature's broad back. Nearly a foot of steel penetrated the shambler's body before the scimitar stuck. A frantic buzz reached the druid's ears, and he knew at once it was the horde of flying carrion beetles his spell had summoned. He just didn't know if they were arriving in time.

The shambler shifted slightly as Broadfoot's wailing blows finally died away and the bear slumped in the creature's vine-arms.

Fearing the bear was dead, hoping his companion was only unconscious, Haarn shoved the scimitar harder. The wound gaped more obscenely and made sucking noises like a man pulling his boot from mud, then the flying beetles arrived.

Sunlight and shadow alternately dappled the insects' hard carapaces as they streaked toward the shambler. Haarn held the wound open. Some of the beetles flew into the gaping hole, but others clustered over the shambler's back, forming a hard crust of chitin-covered bodies.

Haarn ripped the scimitar free of the wound, satisfied the gorging mass of beetles would keep it open, and sprinted around the shambler. If the creature felt the invasion of its body, it gave no indication.

At the shambler's side, still gripping the muddied scimitar, Haarn brought the blade crashing down into the vinelike arm that was wrapped around Broadfoot. The bear's legs twitched and his eyes were closed, but the druid knew his companion was alive.

Druz stepped into place on the other side of the shambler. She'd dropped her bow somewhere behind her, but she wielded her long sword with grim intensity.

The shambler released its hold on Broadfoot. Weak and helpless, the bear dropped into the mud, but Haarn heard the whoosh of air sucked into Broadfoot's lungs.

Crouching again, pulling the massive tree trunk legs free of the ground, the shambler faced Haarn in eerie silence.

The druid's senses, so finely tuned to everything in nature, registered nothing from the shambler. During his years serving the balance, Haarn had seldom encountered such a thing. Even corpses, those left to rot and decompose as a natural progression, never resonated such a vacuum.

The shambler drew back an arm, getting ready to whip it forward.

Haarn gave ground, slipping in the nearly knee-deep muddy water. He took a fresh grip on his scimitar and glanced at Druz, who had also backed away.

"The skeleton!" the druid gasped. "Don't let it get away."

"You can't face this thing alone," Druz objected.

"Go! We can't afford to lose the skeleton!"

"I'm not going to leave you!" Druz argued.

Haarn had no more time to argue. The shambler focused on him, whipping its arm forward.

"We both need to get out of here," Druz said.

Haarn leaped to the side, hurling himself from the path of the shambler's strike. The vine appendages cut deeply into the wet ground.

Shoving himself up, Haarn glanced at Broadfoot. The bear still hadn't regained enough strength to rejoin the battle. He didn't have enough strength to escape either, but Haarn knew escape wasn't an option. The shambler had to be destroyed.

Shifting again, the shambler focused on Haarn, whipping its arms at him so rapidly it seemed the air was full of them. The druid turned some of the attacks away with the scimitar, and others he managed to avoid, but his skill and speed wasn't going to save him forever. Already his breath rasped in his throat and the taste of the sour mud made him want to retch. His arm and leg muscles burned.

The shambler ignored Druz's attacks, concentrating on Haarn, who leaped and dived through the water and across the muddy ground as quickly as he could. Nothing human could have moved as fast as he was moving, but then, nothing human pursued him. He leaped again, arcing high over the vines that streaked for him, flipped easily by tucking his knees into his chest, and came down—then what had been inevitable on the uncertain terrain finally happened. His moccasins came down, thudding into the mud, and the loose earth gave way beneath him. Haarn flailed, trying desperately to gain his feet again, but there was no time.

The shambler flung an arm forward. The vinelike appendages wrapped around Haarn's ankles and lower leg with bone-breaking force. Freeing one hand from the scimitar, he grabbed for an exposed root revealed by the sloshing water. His strength held against the monster's but only for a moment. Renewed agony flared through his legs as the shambler reset itself and yanked upward. Haarn's vision blurred, and he almost passed out from the pain as his knees and hips seemed to come apart. He shot into the air.

With astonishing ease, the shambler held the druid upside down by his legs. Haarn spun crazily, still managing to grip the scimitar. Blood rushed to his head in a thunderous roar and caused black spots in his vision, but he clung to his senses.

The shambler stumbled, one massive tree-rooted foot coming up from the ground. The huge body writhed, back arching as it strove to remain erect.

Haarn saw movement in the center of the shambler's chest only a moment before it burst open and revealed the carrion beetles still gorging. Foaming yellow sap filled the wound, and several of the beetles were dead.

Looking at the damage the swarm of insects had done, Haarn knew that even as fast as they worked they wouldn't be able to destroy enough of the creature to save him. As the druid spun again, he saw Broadfoot shifting, striving to get to his feet, but not enough strength remained in the bear. Druz would only serve to get herself killed if she stayed and tried to help.

Haarn prayed to Silvanus as he accepted his fate. The Keeper of the Balance remained neutral in the laws of nature, between predator and prey, but Haarn couldn't believe Silvanus was going to stand by and allow him to be killed by the undead shambling mound summoned by the blasphemous skeleton.

Still, he knew he had to struggle. The fight for life was innate within him no matter how futile that fight appeared. He gripped the scimitar in both hands and tried to summon the remaining strength from his body. He doubled up, curling in on himself, then swiped at the appendage that dangled him so easily.

The heavy blade cleaved into the thing's arm, and Haarn felt it shiver all through his dangling body. A fine mist of yellow sap sprayed out, soaking into the druid's clothing.

Before Haarn could strike again, the shambler whipped him around and slammed him into the ground like a wildcat shaking a rat. For an instant, the druid was submerged in one of the deep pools. He clawed at the mud with his free hand, slapping cold handfuls over his legs, hoping the lubrication would break the shambler's grip.

Effortlessly, the shambler pulled him into the air again. Roaring blood filled Haarn's head, and he stared down at the large rocks that studded the marshlands. If he landed on one of those, his head would split open or his shoulder would be crushed.

The shambler shivered again, and Haarn dared hope that the rampage of the carrion beetles had had more of an effect than he had at first supposed. Instead, the druid noticed that he could see through the shambler. The hole was almost large enough for a full-grown man to crawl through. None of the carrion beetles remained alive.

There was no hope, but Haarn steeled himself to grip the scimitar again with both hands. He could not die, not without fighting.

Frightened birds cried out from the treetops, creating a mad cacophony of screeches and whistles, then a voice Haarn knew—and sometimes feared—rang out from somewhere below.

Clad in fine robes that bore a hood to hide his features, which were further masked by an illusion spell to help him pass as human, Borran Klosk strode the dockyards of Alaghôn with impunity. No one recognized him, but all assumed he was a rich merchant or perhaps even a lord come down out of Alaghôn or elsewhere in Turmish.

The mohrg gazed out from under his cowl and smelled the blood of the living around him. He could almost taste their flesh. His thick purple tongue moved restlessly. One quick flick was all it would take, then the captains, crew, cargo handlers, and merchants would know he was among them. They would all run, fearing for their lives. The image was delicious.

"No," Allis whispered.

Borran Klosk growled. They walked, arms touching,

down the dockyards alongside a merchanter frigate called *Mistress Talia* that flew the colors of Sespech.

"If you reveal yourself here," the werespider said, "you will only get us both killed."

"Perhaps not," Borran Klosk challenged.

"You will earn Malar's wrath. Better to earn his appreciation."

The threat grew thin on Borran Klosk. He gazed along the docks. Even in late afternoon, Alaghôn labored to shift cargo and carry on trade. The harbor was filled with ships of all sizes, flying flags from lands all around the Sea of Fallen Stars.

The ships lining the docks were unloaded first. Other ships at anchor in the harbor waited to be unloaded, but some of the smaller vessels—cogs and caravels that serviced coastal waters—off-loaded onto small boats that brought the cargo ashore. Boom arms brought cargo off in huge nets, and the sounds of boatswains' yells and curses to direct the teams pierced the conversations going on around them. Turmishan merchants, their heads covered in turbans and their beards cut square, dickered with ships' captains on the docks or led them to the dockyard taverns and inns where they could ply them with wine, women, and song. Fishermen still hawked their wares from carts, though not many were buying. The clatter of humanity, who were always moving and always noisy, rolled around Borran Klosk.

It was almost too much to bear.

"Take it up!" a man yelled from *Mistress Talia*'s upper deck. "She's all together now, she is!"

A boom arm near Borran Klosk shifted as sweaty, grunting men bore down on it. The freighter bobbed in the harbor as the load came off her deck. Water shifted and slapped against the freighter's barnacle-encrusted hull.

"She's clear!" the man above called out.

A young bard sat on a stack of crates near the boardwalk and strummed her yarting. From the hesitant starts she made, Borran Klosk surmised that the bard was composing. A smile that the mohrg couldn't show, since he lacked a face, dawned inside him as he heard the words.

> "Borran Klosk,
>   Still reeking fresh from the grave,
>   Faced down the Alaghôn Watch
>   —At least, those who were brave.
>   Heroes died that night,
>   Eaten by the . . . by the flames
>   Of the mohrg's evil wizardry.
>   Borran Klosk, just another of death's names."

Borran Klosk looked at Allis and said, "They sing of me."

Allis nodded, but her gaze was on the merchanter.

"We are taking this ship?" Borran Klosk asked, divining her interest.

He hadn't sailed much, hadn't been aboard a ship since he'd been brought back from the grave, and only a few times when he'd worn flesh and blood.

Nodding, the werespider said, "I booked passage for us to Sespech."

"I don't want to go to Sespech," Borran Klosk said, and he had no intention of doing so.

"We're not," Allis said. "That's where the ship is bound. The destination will change when we take over the ship." She looked at him with her opal gaze and added, "You have the power to turn men to you, to kill them and raise them again from the dead, and you have more power than that. The ship will be ours."

Borran Klosk looked at the frigate with clearer understanding and some humor. Turning to face her, Borran Klosk leaned in closely, so closely that she wouldn't be able to miss the fires that burned in his hollow eyes.

"Not ours," he told her. "Mine. They will be mine."

Nostrils flaring and color showing on her cheeks, Allis hesitated a moment, pride warred with fear. Fear won, he could see it in her eyes, and she nodded.

"As you say," she said.

Allis turned from him, giving her attention to the sailor standing at the boarding ramp.

"We have passage," she said.

"Aye, ma'am," the sailor replied. He was short and lean, his clothing heavily tarred against the elements. "I'll be after havin' yer names, I will. To check against the ship's manifests the quartermaster keeps, ye see. Cap'n Ralant runs a tight ship, he does." He looked up, placed his fingers in his teeth, and whistled. "Hey! Vonnis!"

One of the men aboard *Mistress Talia* turned and looked down. "What do ye want, Durgel?"

"Two to ship aboard, sir," Durgel responded.

"Awfully damned early, if you ask me," the older man said, taking a stylus and ship's log from under his arm.

"We didn't ask you," Allis said.

Bristling, the sailor said, "Don't go getting airs with me, woman."

Unleashing the anger that filled him, Borran Klosk spoke and gestured. The sailor at the top of the gangplank grabbed his neck and dropped to his knees. His face reddened, and he couldn't breathe.

"Vonnis!" Durgel cried, racing up the gangplank.

Allis turned to Borran Klosk with an angry look. "What are you doing?" the werespider asked.

"Getting us aboard," Borran Klosk replied, "in a manner that will be more . . . tolerable."

He started up the gangplank as the first sailor tried to tend to the second.

"You will alert them," Allis whispered, hesitating for an instant before she followed him up the gangplank.

Borran Klosk swept the ship's deck with his gaze. Durgel tried valiantly to help Vonnis, but the sailor wasn't even aware of the magical constriction the mohrg used. The other men around the dockyards kept to their work, and only a few curious stares came from *Mistress Talia*'s crew.

Drawing even with the two sailors as Durgel fought to hold Vonnis down while crying out for help, Borran Klosk gazed down at the man he'd afflicted.

"Someone get a healer!" Durgel told one of the nearby crewmen. "Ol' Vonnis is havin' himself an attack of some kind, he is!"

Borran Klosk spoke again, removing the constriction from around the quartermaster's neck.

Vonnis gasped like a dog on a too-hot day. His eyes filled with fear as he gazed at Borran Klosk.

"Ye did this?" Durgel demanded, rising and reaching for the skinning knife that hung at his hip.

Before he could pull his knife, Allis had one of her own only an inch from his eye. Sunlight glinted on the razor-sharp edge.

"No," she said.

CHAPTER EIGHTEEN

Durgel's hand froze, then the sailor slowly released the knife and took his hand way.

"I don't want no more trouble," Durgel said. "Don't want it at all."

"Good," Allis said.

Borran Klosk stared at the quartermaster, who had yet to draw a full breath.

"Don't ever treat me or the woman with me with such disrespect again," the mohrg said.

"I . . . won't," Vonnis gasped.

The fear the quartermaster exuded was almost enough to make Borran Klosk drunk with it. Killing the priests had been good, but they'd been schooled to control their emotions. The victims in the tavern had passed too quickly, and the men of the watch had been too far away. Everything the quartermaster felt radiated into the mohrg without filter.

"What's the meaning of this?"

Borran Klosk looked up from the frightened quartermaster to the old man standing on the upper deck. He wore dark robes and had a fierce gray beard that still held smudged traces of red. The sun and harsh elements of the sea had browned and wrinkled his face. Shaggy hair wafted in the breeze.

"We have paid for passage," Allis said.

Durgel helped Vonnis to his feet. The quartermaster continued to gasp and hack as he struggled to get his wind back.

"What does that have to do with your treatment of Vonnis?" the old man asked.

Borran Klosk felt the old man's magic. Tendrils of the unseen force pried and lifted at the spell of illusion the mohrg had woven over his own fleshless features.

"He was rude," Allis said.

"He did not lay hands upon you," the old man said.

Borran Klosk felt the unseen tendrils wither and die as his own spell rendered them useless.

"I would have killed him for that," the mohrg said. "I punished him for his rudeness."

"Punishment such as that is better left to his captain," the old man said.

"You come close to rudeness yourself," Borran Klosk warned.

The old man's lips closed tight and his dark eyes glittered.

"Have a care how you carry yourself, good sir," the man said. "I'm Hildemon, ship's mage aboard *Mistress Talia*, and I'll brook no threat from any man."

"You've got the gold I've paid for passage," Borran Klosk said. "If you want a little extra gold for my rashness in dealing with your man, so be it. Name your price."

After all, whatever gold he paid would be reclaimed when he overtook the ship.

"They wanted onto the ship early," Durgel said. "An' ever'body knows ain't nothin' to do aboard. It's gonna be hours before we haul anchor and set sail, even with all the crew working."

Hildemon's face wrinkled and he asked, "Why would you want to come aboard so early?"

"I've done everything in port that I care to," Borran Klosk said. "I stayed up all night, and I wanted to see this ship, perhaps even place a few investments of my own after I see what cargo you're carrying." That would be excuse enough for him to learn the run of the ship.

The old mage was silent for a time.

Borran Klosk knew that *Mistress Talia* was a ship

down on her luck. Remnants of the Taker's War still existed throughout the Sea of Fallen Stars, and the waters were rife with pirates. *Mistress Talia* had battled a ship on her last journey, and the scars of that fight still showed on her deck and sections of missing railing. The gold Allis had paid for passage had been welcomed with no questions asked.

"Quartermaster Vonnis!" the old ship's mage called out.

"Aye?" Vonnis croaked through his bruised throat.

"We've got a cabin for these people?"

❂

"Hold, you foul beast!"

Druz Talimsir glanced quickly to her left, thinking that the voice had come out of thin air. She brought her sword up, ready to defend herself.

An elf dressed in hide armor, with a helm of deer horns and falcon feathers, seemed to step out of the tree beside her. His black hair was knotted through the deer horns and ran down his back, leaving his smooth, unblemished face in full view. A dark green cloak hung from his shoulders. Like all elves, he didn't show any indication of age. His dark emerald eyes flashed with angry fire.

His presence filled the marsh.

"Beware this thing," Haarn said, still dangling upside down. "A skeleton called it up from the earth."

The shambler turned. Though it had no eyes, it seemed to sense the elf in some manner. The elf was smaller than Haarn, smaller even than Druz, and more slender. Still, when he started toward the shambler, Druz moved to follow him into battle. The elf threw up a hand without glancing in her direction.

"You can't face that thing by yourself," Druz protested.

"Stay," the elf said. He closed on the shambler, stepping gracefully through the uneven terrain masked by the water.

The shambler loosened its squeeze on Haarn and

pulled its feet out of the ground. It turned, and as if toying with the new arrival, the shambler dangled its captured prize in front of the elf.

The elf spoke, but Druz couldn't understand the language, though she got the impression it was an old tongue.

As the elf's words died away, he raised his right arm. A blazing blade formed entirely of twisting red and yellow flames nearly four feet long sprouted from his hand. The flames danced and shivered, and Druz expected the elf to yank his hand back in pain. Instead, the elf lashed out with the fire sword.

The move caught the shambler unprepared and the flame blade cut through the shambler's vinelike arm. Haarn dropped from the shambler's grip like a fresh-harvested fruit.

For the first time, Druz saw the shambler hesitate before attacking. She thought the thing might have recognized something even more fearsome than itself.

The elf stood there with his blazing sword and the wind blowing through his hair. He spoke again as the shambler attacked with its other arm. Moving only enough to avoid the whipping lengths of the vinelike appendages, the elf lashed out with the flame sword again. Smoke puffed from the amputated end of the shambler's arm as the first half of it dropped, sizzling, into the mud.

Nearby, working in spite of the pain that still racked him, Haarn stripped the dead length of the shambler's arm from him. He tried to get to his feet, but his legs kept going out from under him.

Stepping back, opening his arms wide, the elf shouted to the heavens, his face upturned. Dark clouds formed above the shambler. Sparks flitted like fireflies inside the clouds. The shambler started forward then, like an avalanche of mud. Before it had taken three steps, the swirling dark clouds above it unleashed a column of white-hot flames that descended on the shambler.

Holding her empty hand up to shield her face from the heat, Druz peered through her fingers. Almost between heartbeats, the shambler dried out, hardened, then flaked to pieces. When the column of fire died away, a pile of gray ash—all that remained of the shambler—spread out over the water.

Druz sucked in a breath, only then aware that she'd been holding it. Wicked and acrid, the stench of the dying creature filled her nose.

"The skeleton," Haarn said.

"What skeleton?" the elf asked.

"I was trailing a skeleton."

Haarn pushed himself up from the ground with some difficulty, but Druz was still amazed at the druid's resilience.

"Who is the woman?" the elf asked.

Seizing his scimitar from the muddy ground, Haarn glanced at Druz, then quickly looked away. He looked self-conscious.

"She's . . ." he said. "She's a . . . friend."

Despite the tension of the moment and the unexplained appearance of the elf, Druz almost smiled in disbelief. She couldn't understand Haarn's deference to the strange elf. Since she'd known him she'd never seen him defer to anyone, but with the elf he acted like a student facing a harsh taskmaster.

"She shouldn't be here," the elf said. "She has the stink of city upon her."

Druz's ears burned in embarrassment and anger, but it was hard to be rancorous with someone who had just saved her life.

"I know," Haarn agreed. "Other business brought us together, business that I had no say in."

"You always have a say in the things you do, Haarn," the elf said. "I've always taught you that."

Blood tracked Haarn's face. He squatted and checked on Broadfoot then glanced over his shoulder as he tended the bear.

"If I could have gotten rid of her," he said, "I would have."

He rummaged on the ground and found a hunk of green and white moss. Praying over it, he closed his hands, hiding the moss from view, then opened them again to reveal that the moss had become more vibrant and healthy. Working quickly, he packed the moss into the bear's wounds.

"I didn't give him a choice," Druz said, giving in to the anger that overrode her fear.

The elf shot her a look and said, "If he'd chosen to leave you, woman, you wouldn't be here."

The elf squatted and ran his fingers through the gray-white ash. He felt the consistency, smelled it, then put a pinch of the ash on his tongue. His face turned lemony tight and he spat the ash out.

"Dead things," muttered the elf.

Finished with the bear, Haarn pushed himself erect again and said, "The skeleton remains free."

"Which way?" the elf asked.

He stood with easy grace and Haarn pointed.

"How did you come to follow it?"

"The business I had with the woman put me close to where it dug up itself from the ground," Haarn said.

The elf frowned at the pile of gray-white powder and asked, "The skeleton had the power to create this shambler?"

"Yes."

"You've fought skeletons before?"

"Of course I have," Haarn said. "I faced my first skeletons with you."

"So you did. Have you ever seen one then or since that can handle magic like this?"

Haarn shook his head and started forward in the direction the skeleton had taken. Broadfoot lifted his big head and whined a little. The bear put his front paws out and tried to rise but couldn't get up the strength.

"There's a jewel in its chest," Haarn said as he pushed himself into a jog, slogging through the water. The elf followed.

"What kind of jewel?"

"I don't know," Haarn admitted. "I didn't get a good look at it, but I know it created that false shambler."

"That creature was very strong," the elf said. "If it had

been any more powerful, I might not have been able to destroy it."

Staggering forward, Druz felt her body screaming as she took up their rapid pace. They plunged seemingly without effort through the uneven land and brush that constantly threw Druz's own gait off and slapped at her eyes. She didn't know what reserves Haarn must have been drawing from after the frantic pace they'd been traveling at since morning and the beating he'd taken from the shambler.

Just as black spots started swimming in Druz's vision and her breathing was beginning to burn the back of her throat, she saw the druids—the elf was surely another druid—slip through the wall of brush and scraggly trees. The land sloped down and water that had been lazy and stagnant on the marsh gathered speed as it tumbled down the long, steep descent ahead.

Gazing at the broken ground, shading her eyes with one hand, Druz saw where several streams had formed and bled off into a small river that roiled between two irregular banks. Nearly a quarter-mile away, the skeleton kept up its steady pace. It pumped its arms, running hard and throwing out clods of mud from its skeletal feet.

"There," Haarn said, pointing.

The elf glanced at him and asked, "Can you shift?"

"Not now," Haarn said.

Nodding, the elf lifted his arms.

"The skeleton is very powerful," Haarn warned.

He turned and jogged along the edge of the steep dropoff, looking down.

"So am I," the elf said.

He held his hands straight up, and as she watched, Druz saw the elf shrink and sprout feathers at the same time. In seconds, he was a great horned owl, almost identical to the one she'd seen Haarn turn into.

The owl took to the skies, leaning forward and falling over the edge. Spreading his wings, the great bird caught the wind and leveled off in a steep glide that took him straight toward the skeleton.

Haarn found a less steep section of the incline and

started down. Druz followed him, nearly falling half a dozen times in the first three steps.

"You know this elf?" she asked, watching the owl bear down on his quarry.

"Ettrian," Haarn said.

He released his hold on the incline and slid twenty feet down. A cascade of falling mud and rock followed after him, breaking like a wave over his head and shoulders.

Druz sheathed her long sword and removed the scabbard and belt from her waist. She gripped the weapon in both hands as she stepped off the incline and slid after Haarn. The passage was rough and bruising, but she caught herself at the end of it, not surprised that the druid was already in motion. As they slid down the next section, Druz saw the great horned owl fold his wings and drop.

When Ettrian reached the ground, he stood on human legs again.

"He . . ." Druz hesitated. "He walked out of a tree."

Haarn slid again, making his way to the level land. "I haven't yet learned that spell," he replied.

Ettrian reached into his cloak and drew out a quarterstaff as he faced the skeleton. Druz had heard of magical cloaks with pockets like bags of holding, though she'd never seen one before.

She gathered herself at the end of the final slide, drew her long sword from its scabbard, and kept the scabbard in her left hand. She ran, pushing herself to match Haarn's pace.

Seeing the elf druid square off against the skeleton, Druz worried that they might arrive too late to aid Ettrian against the skeleton. She pushed herself harder, feeling muddy clumps in her hair bang against her head and shoulders, feeling the burn through her fatigued muscles, hearing the rasp of her own breath as she tried in vain to fill her lungs again. If they arrived in time, what was there to say that the skeleton wouldn't summon yet another shambler to act as its guardian?

The skeleton lashed out at Ettrian. Using the quarterstaff, the druid knocked the blows aside and returned a few of his own, succeeding in driving the skeleton back. A familiar, somber look played on the druid's face, and Druz recognized it as a look Haarn often wore.

Whirling, Ettrian dodged a blow meant to take off his head, took a quick step to the side, then rammed the quarterstaff between the skeleton's ribs and twisted violently. Bone snapped off, and the sound reached Druz's ears over the slapping noise of Haarn's feet and hers meeting the muddy ground.

When Ettrian stepped away, tearing free several of the skeleton's ribs, Druz saw the crimson flash of the ruby falling from the thing's rib cage. The elf increased the level and speed of his attacks, aiming his quarterstaff at the skeleton's head.

Druz didn't know if smashing the skeleton's skull would stop it.

Kneeling, the skeleton grabbed a fistful of mud and slung it toward the druid's face. Ettrian dodged and darted for the gem lying in the mud. Before he could reach it, the jewel blazed with unholy crimson light and a bolt of power crackled through the air. When the bolt touched Ettrian, the force lifted him from his feet and threw him backward more than two dozen paces.

"*No!*" The word ripped from Haarn's lips in full-throated agony.

Stumbling, obviously wracked with debilitations of its own, the skeleton reached down and picked up the jewel.

Ettrian used his quarterstaff to push himself up. His hide armor had protected him from part of the magic attack, but it was charred and torn, showing raw, red meat underneath. Spotting the horrendous burns covering the druid's flesh, Druz didn't understand how he was still conscious, much less able to move.

Balancing on his quarterstaff, Ettrian reached back into his cloak. Pulling his hand out, he flung it at the skeleton. Druz was close enough that she saw the small objects released from the druid's hand.

Despite his wounds, Ettrian had thrown with accuracy. The four small pellets all landed within the vicinity of the skeleton, and Druz was sure that at least two of them had struck the undead creature.

The four objects exploded, throwing out huge gouts of fire. The concussion blasted hot air over Druz and knocked her from her feet. She rolled to her side, her head spinning from the exertion and the lack of air as her lungs ached and burned from the acrid smoke.

Staring through the smoke, she saw Haarn pushing himself back to his feet only a few feet away. Soot stained the half-elf's face and arms, broken by splashes of yellow and orange mud.

"Silvanus' mercy," Haarn whispered, "will this dead thing not return to the grave?"

Looking through the billowing smoke, Druz stared in disbelief at the skeleton. One of its arms had been blown off by the series of explosions and one foot was missing, but still it stood on the stump and reached out again for the jewel.

"Haarn," Ettrian called, "don't let it take the jewel."

The elf hobbled toward the skeleton, a look of dark intent on his soot-stained face.

The skeleton hobbled away from him, stumbling on one good foot through the craters that had been left by the explosive spell. It folded the jewel up under its remaining arm and bared its fangs, showing spaces where even more teeth had been knocked out. As it continued moving, the skeleton's lower jaw dropped away, giving a clearer view of the fragile spine holding the cracked skull in place.

Haarn, still limping, rushed forward, his scimitar bared in his fists. Closing on the skeleton, the half-elf raised his blade and drew back to swing. Instead of slicing through the spine as he'd obviously intended, Haarn swung through open air. The jewel glowed fiercely, and the ground opened up and sucked the skeleton down. Only a small mound remained to mark the skeleton's passage.

Reversing his blade, Haarn drove it deeply into the ground. It stopped when only half the length of the blade had sunk into the mud, but Druz knew the skeleton wasn't there. Whatever magic had flared from the jewel had taken it away.

"Haarn?" the elf asked.

Looking up, his eyes looking haunted in his scorched and soot-stained face, Haarn shook his head.

"We've let it escape," the elf said. "We had our hands on it and could have prevented some of this madness, but we let it escape. There's only one place that thing would be headed."

Ettrian swayed drunkenly as he balanced on his quarter-staff. Glancing to the east, he pointed with his chin.

"It could only have been called forth by Borran Klosk," Ettrian said, his voice growing weaker.

The name stirred more fear inside Druz. Even before the horror stories of the Taker spread over the Vilhon Reach there were stories of Borran Klosk. The legend of the evil mohrg rang through every alehouse and tavern. When men gathered to tell stories of what might have been and what might be, Borran Klosk's name was never far from their lips.

"Borran Klosk is dead," Druz said.

"Yes," Ettrian agreed, "and returned yet again. I was given word from the Elder Circle only this morning. Every druid who can answer has been called to Alaghôn to stand against the evil." He paused. "It looks like you might yet live to see a city as you've desired, Haarn."

Druz listened to the exchange, noting the resentment in the elf druid's words despite his weakness and pain.

"No," Haarn said. "I told you I never wanted to see a city, never wanted to be—"

"There's a part of you that belongs to your mother, isn't there?" Ettrian challenged, then his eyes rolled up into his head and he fell.

Haarn raced to the elf druid's side.

Druz joined him and watched as Haarn pried at the burned armor covering Ettrian's mid-section. She was surprised at the anxiety flashing in Haarn's eyes.

Fresh blood spilled from the cracked and open blisters that had mottled the elf's lean frame. The stink of burned meat clogged Druz's nostrils. She put a hand over her mouth and nose.

Gently, Haarn moved the elf aside and reached for the cloak. The garment's magical nature was further revealed by the fact that it had taken little damage from the mystic bolt. Haarn reached into one of the pockets sewn into the inside of the cloak.

Even though she knew the cloak was magical, it still amazed Druz at the way the druid sank his arm into it up to his elbow. He searched frantically, and pulled a potion from the pocket. He held the glass bottle up and surveyed the pale blue liquid contained within.

"A healing potion?" Druz asked.

She marveled at the bottle. Had it been kept in a regular pouch, it would surely have been shattered.

Haarn broke the seal then reached down and cradled the elf. Tilting Ettrian's head back, Haarn struggled to pour the liquid into him.

"Open his mouth."

Grimly, Druz placed her hands on the wounded elf's face. Skin and flesh tore under even the slight pressure she put on him. She almost drew her hands back.

"I'm afraid I'm going to hurt him."

Haarn looked up at her and said, "He's dying."

Druz had held men who'd died on battlefields, but none of them had been cooked the way the elf had. The exposed flesh on his arms cracked open in places. She couldn't help thinking that if she pulled at the meat it would fall off the bone. Steeling herself, she took shallow breaths and held the elf's head.

Working cautiously and tenderly, Haarn pushed a finger against the elf's lower lip. The flesh split and bright red blood beaded over Ettrian's mouth and chin.

"Do it," Druz said.

Haarn pulled the lip farther down, causing flesh to tear at the corner and reveal the elf's crimson-stained teeth. Uncorking the potion bottle with his teeth, Haarn poured the blue-tinged liquid slowly into the elf's throat.

For a moment, the healing potion only pooled in the elf's mouth. Then, with a convulsive swallow, Ettrian drank the liquid. Haarn waited patiently then poured more liquid into the elf's mouth. This time, the elf swallowed more quickly, showing signs of regaining strength. Though Druz hadn't believed it was possible, Ettrian drained the contents of the bottle.

"What now?" Druz asked.

"We wait," Haarn answered in a hoarse voice. His eyes never left the unconscious elf.

"Is he a friend?

Haarn hesitated then shook his head slowly and said, "Ettrian is my father."

CHAPTER NINETEEN

In the shadows of *Mistress Talia*'s cargo hold, Barnaby waited to die. At least, he wanted to die a quicker death than the monsters that prowled the merchanter promised. The huge spider-shaped woman was the most terrifying thing he'd ever seen, but it was the dead man with the purple tongue that was the most lethal. Never in his twelve years of life had Barnaby ever given much thought to dying.

Another scream echoed through the hold and Barnaby cringed even tighter into the narrow space. He was small for his age, and often the butt of jokes for it, but this night he was glad of his small stature. If he hadn't been so small he would never have been able to fit between the crates.

The screaming man stopped with an abruptness that left no doubt in Barnaby's mind that he was dead.

The merchanter was only a day out from Alaghôn, headed south across the mouth of the Vilhon Reach. At least four men, two of whom had been on watch, had been lost during the first night. The captain had blamed the uncommonly rough seas and the storm winds that still racked the coast of Turmish.

"Hand me that damn lantern, I tell you!"

Barnaby recognized Ridnow's voice, but not the fear that echoed within it. Ridnow was a seasoned sailor, a man who'd sailed the length and breadth of the Sea of Fallen Stars dozens of times, and he didn't scare easily.

"I said, give me that gods' damned lantern, boy, and ye had damn well best be quick about it."

"Ye're gonna set fire to the ship," a younger voice shrilled.

"Ain't ye got it through that thick knob of yers, boy? That there's Borran Klosk an' he ain't here to take none of us back alive. It's yer choice whether ye dies like a man or ye end up spitted on that foul tongue of his."

Gathering his courage, knowing Ridnow and the younger man were close by, Barnaby peered around the corner of the crate. He stayed so close to the crate that the effort earned him a new splinter in his cheek.

Lantern light threw dancing shadows against the walls of the cargo hold. Ridnow stood near a stand of wine barrels. He was a man of normal height but deep-chested and broad-shouldered. Clutching the lantern in one fist, Ridnow held a bloody, double-bitted dwarven battle-axe in the other. The younger man was Deich, a sailor Barnaby knew but not well.

To see the fear so clearly etched on the sailor's face was disheartening. Tears came to Barnaby's eyes and he wiped them away with the back of one arm.

"There's going to be more of them, you know," the young man said. "Every one of us he slays rises up against the rest."

A crooked grin twisted Ridnow's lips. "Well, that damned corpse ain't killed us yet, Deich. Ye an' me, we still got a chance to be heroes."

"I don't want to be a hero," Deich said. "I just want to get off this ship alive."

Thunder rumbled outside the ship and *Mistress Talia* heeled over hard to port. Deich stumbled and almost fell but caught himself against the line of crates that Barnaby hid behind.

Another man screamed, this one closer.

"They're coming for us now," Deich said.

He shifted, taking up a position to the left and behind Ridnow. The younger sailor's only weapon was a skinning knife.

"Aye," Ridnow growled, "won't be long now an' we'll see if them damned monsters bleed, too."

As Deich tried to stand firm and Ridnow made his preparations, Barnaby realized that an unaccustomed silence had descended inside the ship's hold. The roaring noise of the storm hadn't quieted, of course, nor the creaking protests of the merchanter as she still managed to dive and glide between the hills and valleys of the raging sea.

There were no more screams.

"C'mon then, ye great gout o' black air an' pestilence!" Ridnow challenged. "C'mon an' see if'n ye got the guts what's needed to take the life of a true fightin' man!"

Barnaby glanced around the crate. There, at the other end of the cargo hold, stood Borron Klosk. The light from Ridnow's waving lantern illuminated the skeletal figure, highlighting the naked bone.

"I killed your captain, your ship's mage, and the rest of your crew," Borran Klosk said.

The purple tongue flipped out of the grinning jaws and flicked the air.

Tears leaked down Barnaby's face, but he didn't know how he could be crying without knowing it. Pain knotted his guts.

"Mayhap ye have," Ridnow acknowledged, "but ye ain't finished with ol' *Talia* yet, an' she ain't proper finished with ye."

Borran Klosk started forward. Barnaby saw no undue haste in the monster's movements, but his thoughts were immediately drawn to the unseen spider-woman. Where was she?

Borran Klosk came on as if unconcerned about the dwarven battle-axe the sailor held.

Movement high above the cargo, trapped for a moment in the dulled glow of the lantern Ridnow held, captured Barnaby's attention. He glanced up just in time to spot the spider-woman scuttling across the beams above. She had an insect's head with only vaguely human features. He didn't know how he'd ever thought her beautiful when he'd first laid eyes on her.

He thought only briefly of calling out a warning to Ridnow and Deich, but he knew it wouldn't be enough to save them. Ridnow and Deich were going to die. It was better not to die with them.

The spider-woman dropped, sliding along a length of gossamer. Her fat body fell over Deich and her eight legs wrapped tight around him. Deich screamed but only once.

Horrified, Barnaby watched as the spider-woman bent down and seemed to kiss Deich's neck. When she brought her ugly head away, crimson stained her mouth and dribbled down her misshapen chin. Barnaby clapped both hands over his mouth and tried not to scream. He hoped the muffled noise that escaped him would be lost in the sounds of the storm and the creaking ship.

"Deich!" Ridnow called helplessly.

"You lost him," Borran Klosk said. "Now you stand nearly alone." His purple tongue flicked the air. "Only one more remains after you."

He knows! He knows! The panicked thought filled Barnaby's mind.

He was scarcely able to restrain himself from hurling out of the hiding place he'd found and—and—

Only the fact that he had nowhere to go stopped him.

"Aye, monster," Ridnow said fiercely. "Mayhap I have lost me captain and me crew, but I ain't a-gonna let ye have leave o' this ship. In case ye ain't been proper piped aboard, welcome to yer own death!"

Whirling, he turned and smashed his axe through the end of a barrel. The astringent smell of alcohol laced the cargo hold and burned Barnaby's nose.

Ridnow swung the battle-axe again, completely destroying the keg. Amber liquid spilled out across the cargo hold deck, running first in one direction, then another as the ship shifted.

Watching the reflection of the lantern in the pale amber liquid soaking into the wood, Barnaby realized what Ridnow intended to do. The alcohol would burn hotter and faster than whale oil.

Something sloshed against Barnaby's thin shoes, soaking them. At first he thought it was brine, that *Mistress Talia* had sprung a leak somewhere and the sea was getting in, but the liquid reeked of alcohol. He cursed, drawing the attention of the spider-woman. Her opal eyes shone as she smiled at him.

Barnaby was chilled to the bone.

The spider-woman dropped Deich's lifeless body, but her middle legs still worked busily weaving a web around her prey.

Without another word, Ridnow slammed the lantern against the deck. The wick inside the lantern dimmed and nearly went out, then the flames licked across the spilling alcohol, filling the cargo hold with blue and gold light as they ignited the amber liquid with a rushing *whoosh!*

Knowing he would be dead if the flames caught up to him, Barnaby sprinted out of hiding. He ran past the spider-woman, keeping a line of crates between himself and her. Wide-bodied as she was, she couldn't get through the hold nearly as fast as he could. He streaked for the back of the hold, toward the small ladder.

He slipped under another stack of crates, feeling the heated air catching up to him as the flaming alcohol poured across the shifting deck, then vaulted over a line of barrels. The spider-woman jostled and bumped cargo in her wake as she tried to catch him.

Blood thundered in Barnaby's ears as he caught hold of the ladder and started up. Permitting himself one frightened glance over his shoulder, he saw Ridnow wreathed in the yellow and blue flames. Even as he was burned alive, the sailor screamed out in defiant song and ran at Borran Klosk.

The mohrg's long purple tongue leaped free of its housing and smacked into Ridnow's head. Barnaby saw the old sailor's brain's break through the back of his skull, propelled by the monstrous tongue.

The ladder shivered. Glancing down, Barnaby saw that the spider-woman had made her way to it and was even now shifting her terrible body again, changing to something more womanlike but maintaining the horrible head.

Barnaby climbed, hands and feet moving so rapidly it seemed as though he was swimming up the ladder. At the top, he flung back the hatch then pulled himself up and out into the lashing rain sluicing the merchanter's decks.

He slipped on the wet deck, going deaf from the howling winds of the storm, and pulled himself back to the hatch and peered down. Flames spread throughout the cargo hold, filling it with reddish-orange light. He only had a moment to think about how very far away from shore he was, and how many sharks might be in these waters—or sahuagin that had been released in the Taker's War— before a wild gale rose up from below.

As fierce as the winds were above deck, they were dwarfed by the cyclone that filled the hold. Barnaby squinted against it, his face burning from the blast of heat that rushed out at him. He watched as Ridnow's flaming corpse flew through the air and thudded against the back wall of the cargo hold. Even as the big sailor's body started to fall, the winds blew out all the flames and darkness filled the hold.

From within that darkness that reeked of smoke and death, the mocking tone of insane laughter cascaded out. The obscene noise warred with the thunder that shook the black heavens above the soaked white sails of the merchanter.

Gathering his courage, feeding on fear, Barnaby slammed the hatch closed. He turned and thought he was going to be sick when he saw the undead sailors crewing the ship. A wall of black water rose off starboard bow and rushed for the ship. Silver-white lightning split the sky in a startling blast of incandescence that turned the foam riding the curler of the wave silver-white as well.

The undead crew moved slowly, as if they'd forgotten that a ship in a storm had to be waited on hand and foot. The wave of black water slammed into the ship, breaking over the side and washing across the deck. Some of the ship's crew washed overboard, and it was terrifying to watch the men go without screaming. Normal men who knew they were about to die always screamed, and a man falling into the black sea so many miles from shore was surely going to die.

The massive cold that came from the brine surprised Barnaby and took his breath away. He clung to the closed hatch while the ship rode out the worst of it then pushed himself away, pausing only to latch down the hatch. He slipped and slid across the wet deck, bumping into one of the undead sailors.

The thing had half of its face torn away and was no longer recognizable. Barnaby didn't know if he'd known the man or not. The boy ducked as the dead man reached for him, its torn, ragged mouth open hungrily. They ate flesh. At least, one of the sailors who'd talked about the undead crewmen among them said they ate flesh.

Barnaby pushed off the port railing as *Mistress Talia* caught another bad wave. He caught the rigging just as the ship got caught in the next trough, wallowing and corkscrewing like a fat pig settling into a favorite mud pit. The rope ate at his calloused hands as he clung there, breath rasping between clenched teeth.

Lightning flared again, ripping most of the shadows away from the ship's pitching deck. The hatch shattered and exploded outward. The spider-woman's gruesome head and shoulders appeared. The opal eyes reflected the lightning haze as they gazed around at the deck. They rested squarely on Barnaby.

Heart hammering in his chest, Barnaby started up the rigging. There was nowhere else to go. Even if he could get to one of the freighter's three longboats and manage to get it cast off the ship, he could never hope to keep it afloat without more crew. He climbed, hands and feet moving rapidly, not minding that the rigging and ratlines were dripping water and the rain falling into his eyes was blinding.

Fear made him glance back over his shoulder, and things only got worse when he did. He made himself look back up at the lightning-laced heavens and into the teeth of the blinding rain. On and on he climbed, daring to think that the spider-woman wouldn't climb after him.

But she did. He felt her moving in the rigging below him even though he didn't look to make sure she was there. At the very top of the rigging, Barnaby stopped.

There was nowhere else to go. The sails billowed and cracked around him, and at times they obscured sight of the spider-woman easily climbing the rigging.

He looked up from her and at the storm above and the black walls of rolling water around him. *Mistress Talia* rode deep in a trough and if the undead crew didn't get control of her, she'd founder and possibly break and go down.

Barnaby gazed around at the threatening expanse of the Sea of Fallen Stars. The spider-woman was only a few feet below him and closing fast. A great sadness filled the boy, overcoming even the fear that had trembled within him for the last handful of hours as the crew was hunted down and killed.

Gathering the last of his courage, aided in his decision by his own flagging strength, Barnaby timed the pitch and yaw of the ship, waiting until it gave him the greatest motion, then he released his hold on the rigging, letting the arc of the ship throw him far out to sea. He spun in the air, watching *Mistress Talia*, dangerously close to becoming lost herself, and he plummeted into the Sea of Fallen Stars.

The cold, black brine closed over Barnaby, and it seemed he could still hear Borran Klosk's mocking laughter in his ears.

CHAPTER TWENTY

Haarn came awake with a start, knowing a night-mare had roused him but not able to make any sense whatsoever of what the dream had been about. His body ached all over. Sleeping on the ground under a meager shelter hadn't been as good to his injured body as he'd hoped.

Wood smoke tainted the air. The smell would make a few animals curious, but it would scare the majority of them away. Fire generally meant humans, and the animals had learned to be afraid of men. Some would come in the hopes of getting table leavings, and some would come only to watch from afar.

He lay silent for a moment and prayed, then he meditated and made sure his body was loose and ready to deal with whatever the day offered. The rain that streamed down outside the over-hang where he'd fashioned a serviceable lean-to spattered against the ground, creating a lull of background noise. The overhang was on slightly higher ground, so there was no worry about water soaking their sleeping area.

Haarn rose, feeling twinges and aches that bit bone-deep. He'd used his healing powers to aid his father and had tended to his own wounds as best he could with what herbs he had or could find.

His father lay at the back of the overhang near the fire, draped in his own cloak and Haarn's.

Druz had volunteered the blanket from her own kit, recovered after the battle in the marshy glade, but Haarn had known she wouldn't be comfortable in the night without it. The storm had brought considerable chill to the evening hours.

"You're awake," Druz said from her place sitting beside his father.

She had her strung bow across her knees and her long sword standing against the back of the overhang beside her.

Haarn crossed the shelter to his father's side.

"He's slept well," Druz said.

Tenderly, Haarn lifted the poultices from his father's wounds and examined them. Blackened, crusty scabs covered all of the burned areas, and with the extra healing Haarn provided through his magic there probably wouldn't even be any scars left. The healing potion had done remarkable work on Ettrian, possibly even saving his life, though Haarn believed Silvanus was more responsible for that.

After getting Ettrian settled as comfortably as possible a day and a half before, satisfied that his father's life wasn't in any immediate danger, Haarn had seen to arranging the shelter. Druz had helped, and she'd tried to get him to rest, but he couldn't. Borran Klosk's name kept echoing through his head.

Satisfied with the progress Ettrian was making, Haarn sat down beside him. He gazed at his father's stern face and felt the old confusion gnaw his empty stomach. There were pleasant memories from when he'd been small, from those times his mother had stayed with them deep in the forest, but those had quickly passed when his mother rode away. Haarn had been no older than four or five. After that, his mother's visits had come less and less frequently, lasting only days instead of tendays, then finally—the last time nearly fifteen years past—only hours. His father had grown sadder and angrier, and with his mother's absence Haarn had grown aware of his father's turning away from him as well, as if he was to blame for her leaving.

Haarn reached out and slapped Broadfoot on the haunch. Covered in herbal poultices that made the animal stench even stronger in the lean-to's enclosed space, the bear snuffled irritably, raised his wide head for a moment, then put his head back down and slept.

Sleep would be best, Haarn knew, but nervous energy and the need to be up and moving around filled him. He'd always felt that way around his father as a young man, and even more so since he'd become increasingly independent.

"Borran Klosk is a fable," Druz said. "Why is your father here really?"

Haarn looked at her and said, "After you saw that skeleton claw up from the ground, after you saw that red jewel in its chest and the damage it did to all of us, you want to believe that Borran Klosk is some kind of old wives' tale?"

A thoughtful expression filled Druz's face. She sucked in one cheek as she regarded him.

"My father," Haarn said, glancing at him, "is not a man to pass on gossip. He sought me out to bring me the news the Emerald Enclave had sent him."

"From Ilighôn? That's a long way to send a message."

"My father is an important man," Haarn said. "He's not one of the Elder Circle but his voice carries weight in the Enclave."

"Is . . . is he going to be all right?"

The pounding rain outside the lean-to echoed in the silence that hung between them. Ettrian chose that moment to take a sonorous breath that lifted his chest beneath the traveling cloaks that served as blankets.

"In time," Haarn answered, feeling proud of his father, proud of the way he fought to get better in spite of the injuries that plagued him. There had always, in spite of the other confusing feelings, been a respect between them. "I've seen my father recover from far worse than this."

A moment of silence passed between them, broken only by the crackling sputter of the campfire.

"There's a sadness in your voice when you speak of him," Druz said.

Haarn said nothing, wanting his private feelings to be his own. People who dwelt in cities, especially humans, seemed to think it a crime for a person to possess a private thought. Still, he'd gotten to know her at least a little over the few days they'd been traveling together. He looked at her, feeling the hot smoke sting his eyes, and wondered what his father must think about him traveling with a human woman obviously of mating age. It had to have reminded him of the woman who'd left them.

"I don't mean to pry," Druz said.

He knew that was false. Whatever other shortcomings she had in the wilderness, Druz Talimsir had certain gifts regarding the paths and trails men's minds took.

Ettrian stirred within the pile of cloaks.

"Haarn," he whispered.

The elf turned his head and gazed about with fevered eyes.

"I'm here, Father," Haarn said.

Stretching out his hand, Ettrian said, "I'm cold and . . . I'm thirsty."

With the rain falling in great abundance, acquiring fresh water was no problem. Haarn started to push himself up.

"I'll get it," Druz offered. She got to her feet and went to the lean-to's edge to retrieve a waterskin. "I just filled this."

She handed the waterskin to Haarn.

Cupping his father's head, Haarn lifted him up and helped him drink, taking his time and not quitting until his father had slaked his thirst.

Ettrian glared up at him with his fevered eyes and said, "I've been dreaming of your mother again, Haarn, remembering how she left us."

Maybe, Haarn thought, they'd been sharing nightmares.

"Do you remember how she left us, Haarn?"

"Yes, Father."

"She was wrong, and she was selfish," Ettrian croaked, trying to make his voice fierce.

Looking at his father, Haarn remembered how strong he'd thought the man had been. He was a skilled druid, master of the quarterstaff and learned in his spells. The Elder Circle of the Emerald Enclave respected his opinion and sometimes sought his advice regarding events going on in lands under or near his custodianship, but there was a weakness in him. Haarn had seen that, too.

"Yes, Father," Haarn whispered, feeling the hot flash of tears claw at the back of his eyes.

He wished he thought better of the woman who'd birthed him. If she had only betrayed him, Haarn didn't think he'd have held her actions so much against her—if it hadn't been for the way it all but robbed him of a father as well.

"She was so pretty," the elf whispered.

Haarn took his father's hot hand and squeezed gently. He wished Druz wasn't there to see his father in this moment of weakness.

Ettrian held his hand weakly, but the grip was still there, stronger than the day before. A moment passed, and the rhythm of Ettrian's breathing told Haarn that his father slept. He released his father's hand then used the waterskin to make a poultice for Ettrian's forehead.

Haarn prayed to Silvanus, put his hands on his father's body, and released the magic. The power flowed from his heart, through his arms, and out his palms. An incandescent blue light flowed along his father's body, though Haarn was sure no one else could see it. His magic was for his eyes alone, and so the experience had been but for things that affected the physical world, but anyone could see how Ettrian's wounds healed so much in just that brief contact, how the scabs dried and started to turn loose of their moorings in his father's flesh.

Haarn sat back against the rock wall and took deep breaths. His body shook, but he gave thanks to Silvanus for providing him the power to heal. When he opened his eyes, Druz was looking at him.

"Are you all right?" she asked.

Haarn resented the question. She always seemed to be prying, trying to find the weak and uncertain parts of him.

"Why would I not be all right?"

A hard look flashed through her eyes and she said, "Gods, but you're a stubborn man, Haarn Brightoak. I was only asking because I'm worried about you. You were injured as well, and you've spent every waking moment taking care of us—your father, Broadfoot, and me—though I can take care of myself."

Anger flickered in Haarn's stomach and he considered reminding her how he'd had to show her where to find nuts, berries, and edible mushrooms. He refrained through a supreme effort of will.

"There's no reason to worry about me," he said.

She wanted to object—he saw that in her face—but she didn't. Instead, she drew her knees up higher and wrapped her arms around them.

"I know that," she said. "I guess what bothers me most is that I feel like a burden."

The sudden change in her thinking caught Haarn off-balance. He didn't know what to say.

"I'm not used to feeling like that," Druz went on. "I'm a good sellsword. No one has ever said they didn't get what they paid for."

She stopped herself and shrugged.

"Well, hardly anyone," she continued, "and that was through no fault of my own. I fought for those people and bled for those people, but winning what they wanted wasn't possible."

Haarn leaned forward and fed the campfire from a small pile of sticks and broken branches they'd gathered the day before.

"You're not a burden."

She looked up at him. Haarn felt uncomfortable.

"If it weren't for you," he explained, "I wouldn't have been able to rest while tending to my father."

"You've rested very little."

"I wouldn't have rested at all if you hadn't been here."

Druz nodded and said, "Thank you."

Haarn watched her for a while, expecting more questions. Broadfoot's and Ettrian's breathing filled the overhang over the snap and crackle of the campfire. After a time, the sound lulled Haarn. He leaned his head back and closed his eyes. He couldn't have had them closed for very long at all before the woman spoke again.

"What happened to your mother?" she asked.

Slowly, Haarn opened his eyes and looked at her. An uncomfortable expression filled her face.

"I mean, if you don't mind saying. It's just that your conversation with your father made me curious. Staying quiet all the time . . . I'm used to having someplace to go, people to talk with, but I've just been sitting here for the last day and a half."

Haarn tried to think of what to say, whether to answer her question or to tell her it was none of her business.

"I'm sorry," Druz said. "Obviously I've stepped over a line here. You go on back to sleep and I'll watch the fire."

Irritation filled Haarn. He wanted nothing more than for the woman to be quiet. Problems already danced in his head regarding his father's health and what the return of Borran Klosk might herald. He didn't need to rake over the coals of past hurts, but he didn't like the fact that she sat there feeling alone. He knew how to keep the peace within himself, but she was out of her element and not necessarily among friends.

"My mother," Haarn said, "deserted us."

"Why?"

Haarn hesitated.

"Maybe that wasn't a good question," she said quickly.

Haarn knew she wanted to know, and he wanted her to know. He looked at her, realizing she was more like his mother than he wanted to admit.

"I don't know," he said.

Druz nodded.

Haarn drew in a deep breath and assembled his thoughts. He'd never talked to anyone about his feelings regarding his mother, and he'd never had the opportunity to talk to someone so like her.

"My mother was a warrior. I don't even know where she hailed from."

His father never told him and he couldn't remember his mother ever saying. A twinge of guilt shot through him, but he walled it away with other thoughts and feelings of her that he couldn't bear to think of.

"When she left us, she said only that she had to return to where she'd come from, that there were things she'd left undone."

"And she never returned?"

"A few times," Haarn said. "She stayed away longer and longer each time, until finally one day she didn't come back at all."

"How did your father and mother meet?"

"She was pursued into the forest by a band of men. My father chose to aid her."

"Why?"

Haarn shrugged. "He never said. I never asked. What was done was done. Silvanus teaches acceptance of things past and a knowledge of things to do now with hopes for a balanced future."

"She might have been an outlaw."

Haarn nodded, frowning.

"I apologize. I shouldn't have said that."

"It may well have been true. It's not as though I haven't thought that myself. Most civilized people who end up here come because they've been chased from the cities by their own kind or because they're searching for gold or treasure."

"Your mother might not have been able to return after her last visit," Druz said. "Her absence might not have been totally by choice."

"I thought she might have been killed, perhaps jailed."

Haarn was surprised at how much the old pain and confusion returned to him.

"If she was a warrior," Druz said, "she may have signed on to fight somewhere. There've been any number of disputes that have drawn mercenaries to Turmish or the Reach."

Some, Haarn knew, had pitted mercenaries against the druids of the Emerald Enclave. The possibilities twisted his guts. For his mother to have loved Ettrian and fallen to another druid in battle would have been the cruelest of fates.

"She might have come from some place on the far side of the sea," Druz said, as if guessing the twisted tangle of his thoughts. "Maybe she intends to return one day."

"It's been years."

That stopped her only for a moment. "Maybe she has returned and was unable to find you or your father."

"There are ways for her to get in touch with my father," Haarn replied, "places she could have left messages. She never has." He blew out his breath. "There is no excuse for her behavior."

Druz eyed him. "Is that you speaking, Haarn, or your father?"

Anger ran deeply in him then, and he had trouble containing it.

"Grant me Silvanus's patience, woman, but you are arrogant."

"Not arrogant, Haarn. It doesn't take a sage to see you're conflicted in this. Gods' blood, but you'd have to be if you had any kind of heart—and I know you do—but I also heard your father's accusation about you finally getting to see a city. I have nothing against your father, but you didn't deserve that."

"You know nothing about what comes between my father and me."

"I know enough to make some assumptions. Your father is bitter about loving and losing your mother, but he was brave enough and strong enough to raise you by himself." Druz eyed him. "Do you want to see a city?"

Haarn hesitated, wondering if she knew him well enough after the past few days to know a lie from him if she heard it. He started to speak, caught himself, then said, "I don't know."

"You don't know if you want to see one, or you don't know if you want to deal with your father's feelings when he finds out you want to see one?"

Haarn didn't answer.

Druz sighed and wrapped her arms more tightly around her legs.

"I grew up in Suzail," she said.

The name meant nothing to Haarn. He didn't suppose he'd ever met anyone from there before, or perhaps they hadn't cared for anyone to know.

"It's the capital city of Cormyr on the Lake of Dragons," she explained.

"I've heard of Cormyr." Actually, Haarn had heard very little.

"I grew up in a small house," Druz said. "My father was a blacksmith, a man good with armor and arms, which is a craft that will keep a man hale and hearty in Cormyr, but there are enough skilled craftsmen there that he was never going to get rich. Still, he provided for all nine children and his wife."

She gazed into the fire, and Haarn sensed that she had hurts of her own.

"I was the fourth in the line of children," she continued, "and the first girl. My three older brothers all worked with my father. My mother thought I would provide help in caring for the children and keeping house, but I had my own interests."

Haarn sat and listened to her, amazed at how soothing her voice could be after thinking for days only about how she could drone on and on.

"When it became apparent that I wasn't going to be the housekeeper my mother wanted and that Josile, the girl next to me, absolutely loved those things, she was given the chores and I got the opportunity to work with my father in the smithy."

"You found that work preferable?" Haarn asked.

"For a time," Druz admitted. "I was a fair hand at repairing armor and hammering out horseshoes, but I came in contact with men and women who'd traveled around all of Faerûn. Suzail, as large as it had seemed to me, was only a stopping place for them, a waystation while they rested to continue their travels to far-away destinations. One day, after I was grown, or at least thought I was, I decided I wanted to travel. Over the years, I'd been learning swordcraft from anyone who'd teach me. I learned well, and some said I had a talent for it."

Haarn agreed, but he kept his thoughts to himself.

"One night I left Cormyr, caught the first ship that would hire me on as a sellsword," Druz said, "and I began making my way as a mercenary."

"Have you been back to see your family?" Haarn asked.

"Several times."

"What did your mother and father think about the life you'd chosen?"

"They didn't like it," Druz said. "They still don't, but they know I'm happy. I'm getting to travel, and the things I fight for—" She wrinkled her nose. "—usually, the things I fight for are of my own choosing and causes I believe in. It's not a life for everyone, but it's the life I chose. That's why I'm telling you this, Haarn.

"Maybe the cities aren't to your father's liking, and maybe they won't be to yours, but you shouldn't have to feel guilty about wanting to see them and explore those ties to your mother. I mean no disrespect for your father. Please understand that."

Some of Haarn's anger and resistance went away, and he thought perhaps he did understand, though he wasn't certain why Druz would be so adamant about telling him.

"If you ever did get curious about cities and wanted to see one," Druz said, "and if I were available to show you one, I . . . I think I'd like that very much."

She glanced away from him, as if unable to any longer hold his gaze.

Haarn looked at his father's sleeping form. Normally elves didn't sleep, just went into a meditative trance for four hours or so every day. He could never recall his father sleeping.

"He loved her very much, didn't he?" Druz asked some time later.

"Yes," Haarn whispered. "Losing her almost killed him."

"He'd never known that kind of love before? I know elves are long-lived."

"If he has, he's never mentioned it."

"And he's never loved like that again?"

"No."

Haarn fed more wood to the fire, basking in the warm radiance.

"Not many people are fortunate to know a love like that," Druz said.

"Love like that," Haarn said, meaning it, "is a terrible thing."

"Do you really think so?"

He gazed at her, surprised by the intensity in her eyes.

"I've seen what it can do to people."

"You've only seen what it did to your father. Love like that is special, not something easily found."

The tone in her voice suggested that she'd had more than a passing interest in the subject.

"Love like that is a death trap. Better to find someone you like, share time together, then be on about your business."

"And you practice that, Haarn?"

Druz's voice carried a biting chill to it that was worse than anything outside the protection of the lean-to.

Haarn looked at her, seeing the challenge there and not totally understanding it. He let his breath out when his lungs started to ache, not even knowing he'd been holding his breath.

"No," he answered. "That's not what I practice."

A smile, partly coy and partly relieved, played on Druz's lips and she asked, "Have you ever been with a woman, Haarn?"

Haarn's face burned and he couldn't believe his concern for his father and their forced encampment in the lean-to had led them to this subject.

"Now you're stepping over boundaries."

A triumphant gleam showed in Druz's eyes and Haarn couldn't understand it at all.

"I withdraw the question," she said, "and offer my apologies."

Haarn nodded, feeling only a little relieved.

"Love like your father and mother had isn't necessarily a bad thing," Druz said. "Wolves mate for life."

"Stonefur mated for life," Haarn said coldly, "and his mate attacked you. You killed her without a second's thought."

His words visibly stung Druz. Her face pinched shut. Glancing down, she pulled her blanket up and turned away from him.

"Since you're awake," she said, "I'm going to sleep now."

Haarn watched her do exactly that, and he was irritated at her for raising so many questions in his mind and leaving him with them. He glanced at his father, knowing Ettrian's presence had triggered some of those questions as well.

Haarn settled back against the stone wall of the overhang. Never in the past two days had he been so aware of how uncomfortable it was. He gazed at Druz, sleeping so childlike beneath her blanket—except for the naked dagger in her fist—and tried not to think about any of the questions she'd raised within him. It didn't work, not even when he directed his mind to prayers to Silvanus.

CHAPTER TWENTY-ONE

Borran Klosk stood on *Mistress Talia*'s flying deck, scanning the dark ruins of the Whamite Isles. Lightning seared the sky as light rain continued to fall. At least the sea had quieted.

The ship had been taken over days before, perhaps even as much as a tenday—Borran Klosk was not sure. Only corpses revived by the mohrg's magic crewed the ship.

The change from living to dead had not been without problems. Alive, the crew had been adept at manning *Mistress Talia,* but rising from the dead had cost them something of their skill. Only every now and again was Borran Klosk able to raise one of his kills nearly whole in ability.

The five he'd created to carry the pieces of Taraketh's Hive had been very special. One of them, Borran Klosk knew, had almost been destroyed by druids. He'd managed the skeleton's escape only with the help of the league of wizards Allis served.

Lightning burned the heavens again, but nothing disturbed the surface of the sea. Footsteps sounded on the deck behind him. There was only one person who moved freely about the ship.

Without looking around at Allis, Borran Klosk asked, "Where are the drowned ones?"

"Under the sea," she replied. "They're probably on their way here now. They hunt anything. From what I'm told, even the fish no longer come here."

"We need to go in closer."

"If we do," she said, coming up to the railing where he stood, "we run the risk of being overrun by their numbers before you're able to control them."

Borran Klosk raised his arm and regarded the pink and white coral shell that encased his arm. It looked so simple, so powerless. If he hadn't felt the magic in it, he wouldn't have believed it could do what she promised. He looked back out to sea, trying to discern some movement in the rolling troughs of water, but there was none.

Allis stared at the rolling sea as well. Her hair lay plastered against her skull and her clothes, like Borran Klosk's own cloak, were sodden. Her opal eyes glowed in the darkness.

The gale winds swept *Mistress Talia*'s decks and yet another bolt of lightning pierced the dark clouds.

"Sails!" a man shouted from above.

Borran Klosk looked up at the corpse manning the crow's nest. He had stationed one of the dead men still able to speak up there to act as lookout.

"Where?"

"Off the starboard bow, cap'n," the dead man cackled gleefully.

Unfortunately, though some of the dead men yet maintained enough experience to do their jobs, not all of them kept their sanity.

Even after days at sea, Borran Klosk could not keep straight which was port and which was starboard. None of that mattered in his plans. All he wanted was to get the ship back to Alaghôn with his promised undead army in tow.

"Where?" he growled to Allis, who understood such things.

"To the right," she answered.

Borran Klosk walked in that direction, crossing the narrow flying bridge. Lightning flared again, and this time it reflected from sails.

"No fishermen come out here," Allis said, "and they wouldn't be here at this time of night anyway. They must be looking for someone. Occasionally, treasure hunters come out here, looking to lay claim to cargo lost by ships that were sunk in these waters, and to raid the drowned city itself."

"They see us, cap'n," the dead man occupying the crow's nest said. "They're turning and coming toward us."

Borran Klosk saw that the ship had altered its direction and was now approaching them. Lights moved hurriedly along the ship's deck, and more of them were lit.

"Someone is looking for us," Borran Klosk said.

"No one knows we're here," Allis said.

Borran Klosk fisted the ratline running down to the flying deck and said, "Coming here wasn't as clever as you thought it was."

"There's an army waiting here to be claimed," Allis said.

"I can't hide as easily on the open sea as I could have in the city," Borran Klosk replied. "I know the warrens and alleys there. I could have stayed away from them."

"They would have hunted you down. You didn't stand a chance . . . especially not after the way you announced yourself to them."

Rage filled Borran Klosk and he almost backhanded the werespider.

"I will not be taken again," he said. "I will not be locked away, nor will I allow myself to be destroyed."

"We can hold them off," Allis said.

Borran Klosk wanted to scream and shout, to rail against Malar who had undoubtedly abandoned him yet again. Lightning flared and thunder pealed, sending highlights and a jagged reflection skittering across the sea's surface.

The other ship sailed alongside *Mistress Talia* and matched her speed. Men stood along the other ship's deck. Many of them held lanterns and the lights showed the bows, javelins, and swords the sailors wielded. Among the crew, though, were a number of men Borran Klosk recognized from their dress as druids. Some of them had animal companions with them, and an owl skimmed through the sky, shining silver-gray in a lightning flash.

"Ahoy the ship!" someone yelled from the other vessel. "Identify yourselves!"

None of the undead crew aboard *Mistress Talia* moved. All of them waited for orders from the mohrg. Borran Klosk flicked his tongue out. Even with the storm continuing unabated around them, he tasted the scent of human flesh and blood staining the winds. It was delicious.

"Ahoy the ship!" the same voice repeated, growing angry this time. "Answer up or you'll be paying dearly for your reticence!"

The other ship sailed closer, and Borran Klosk knew that they were well within bowshot. The lanternlight played over *Mistress Talia*'s deck. His undead crewman stared at the flesh and blood crew of the other ship.

"Blessed Lady," a man swore aboard the newly arrived ship, "all them there men are dead! That's a crew of dead men aboard her, it is!"

The owl circled *Mistress Talia*, coming in closer.

Borran Klosk pointed at the owl. A green beam lanced from his finger and transfixed the bird. In less than a heartbeat, the owl roiled into a fluff of feathers that blew away on the storm winds.

The crew aboard the second ship drew back. Several holy symbols appeared and as many curses as prayers came from their lips.

The mohrg leaned on the flying deck's railing and showed the men a confident pose.

"I am Borran Klosk!" he roared above the keening winds that whipped through the sails and rigging. "You know me."

Instantly, several beams from bull's-eye lanterns turned in his direction. They stripped the shadows away from him and revealed him for what he was.

"It *is* Borran Klosk!" someone yelled.

"Kill him!" another cried. "Get the wizards out here!"

Immediately afterward, dozens of arrows sprang from the bows of men on the second ship. The missiles leaped across the space between the ships and tore into *Mistress Talia*'s deck and sailcloth. Several of the arrows found homes in the undead crew as well. Some of the walking corpses stumbled back a pace or two, but none of them went down.

"Get oil up here!" a big warrior yelled. "Get oil up here and we'll burn that damned ship to the waterline! Those undead bastards will go down with it!"

Borran Klosk unleashed a spell, sending an arc of fire streaming from his hand. The fireball deflected off course and shot up into the sky, warring with another brilliant flash of lightning for preeminence in the dark heavens.

A tall, gangly man in elegant robes covered in runes strode onto the second ship's deck. He thrust out a hand. In response, the winds picked up strength and smashed into *Mistress Talia*. Several of the undead crew were blown down, and a handful of others were blown off the deck into the ocean. Overhead, a sail ripped free of its moorings and went fluttering away, disappearing into the darkness.

Borran Klosk clung defiantly to the railing.

"No matter what ill fate awaits me," he told Allis, "I will not be taken. I will not be humbled. My vengeance, my bloodlust, will be slaked in the lives of these men and those alive in Alaghôn and all of Turmish. I will survive this."

"You'll do more than that," the werespider said, touching his arm. "Look."

Borran Klosk turned and looked in the direction she pointed. At first he saw only a few gleams amid the wall of water approaching them from the ruins of the Whamite Isles, and he assumed they were jellyfishes reflecting the lightning or perhaps debris, wood pieces with nails or other bits of metal driven into them, then he saw them change direction.

"It's the drowned ones," Allis said.

Doubt lingered in Borran Klosk, then he felt a fresh infusion of power through the coral glove.

"This is your moment, Borran Klosk," Allis said. "Seize control of the power blessed Malar has put at your disposal."

"Borran Klosk," the wizard aboard the other ship yelled. "Surrender your vessel!"

Ignoring the challenge, Borran Klosk turned to Allis and asked, "Why did this league of wizards you say you work for choose to give this power to me?"

Allis hesitated. She glanced toward the other ship and the light from the blazing fire arrows reflected in her eyes.

"Kill the monster!" someone from the other ship shouted. "Kill him and be quick about it!"

"Why?" Borran Klosk asked again, moving closer to the werespider.

She looked back at Borran Klosk, defeat in her gaze.

"Because they can't use it," she said. "The glove was created by their magic, but only an undead can wear it. They chose you because of your hatred for Turmish, and because Malar instructed them to."

"What is your answer, Borran Klosk?" the wizard on the other ship demanded.

Allis glanced past the mohrg, toward the prow of the ship.

"You must act quickly, Borran Klosk," she said, "else the drowned ones will take us down as well."

Looking over his shoulder, Borran Klosk saw the gleam of white bone swimming beneath the black water now. He recognized the bodies of men, women, and children swimming in the sea. They were less than fifty yards from the ships. So intent was the focus of the men aboard the other ship that none of them noticed the arrival of the drowned ones.

Something butted into *Mistress Talia*.

Borran Klosk felt the echo of the impact through the ship's deck. Gazing down into the water, he saw the heads of the drowned ones clustered by the ship. There must have been fifty or sixty of them, with more coming. Lightning seared the sky, and reflections dawned in the dead eyes or in the empty eye holes that gazed up at him. He felt the hunger that drove them, as insistent as his own.

"Borran Klosk!" the wizard on the other ship called out. "This is your last warning. I won't hold these men back any longer."

The drowned ones at the waterline began forming a pyramid of bodies. The ones on the bottom stayed motionless while the others started piling on, floating higher and higher as the waves rocked them. Already they were halfway up the side of the merchanter and no one had noticed them.

Looking across the water, Borran Klosk discovered that other drowned ones had started their assault on the other ship as well. The mohrg began the incantation as Allis had instructed. Power surged along the coral glove and Borran Klosk felt it down to the very center of his being.

The drowned ones continued clambering aboard each other, climbing still higher.

Men aboard the other ship began yelling. Someone had spotted the drowned ones. Others took up the hue and cry of warning.

"Hurry," Allis pleaded.

The other ship tried to get underway, but the drowned ones had somehow trapped their anchor in the shallows. Before the sailors could cut or release the anchor chain, drowned ones formed a web of bodies and started clambering over the sides.

Borran Klosk listened to the screams and yells of panic and pain from the other ship's crew as the drowned ones climbed aboard. The sea zombies took incredible punishment at the hands of the crew, but they kept on coming. A number of them advanced on the crew while bearing flaming arrows stuck in their blue-gray torsos.

In the light of the lanterns on the other ships, Borran Klosk got a better view of his proposed subjects. Most of them had been drowned and underwater for a year. All of them showed the blue-gray pallor of death, wore only tatters of clothing if they wore any at all, and had innumerable bloodless wounds that left craters in their dead flesh.

When he finished the spell, the shrieks aboard the other ship had reached a crescendo. The ship bucked at the end of its anchor chain like a fish at the end of a line. Lightning flashed across the sky, and in the bright light the blood staining the ship's deck reflected indigo.

The head of a drowned one appeared over the railing of *Mistress Talia*'s flying deck. Water dripped from the torn flesh only halfway covering the ivory bone beneath. It opened its jaws just as Borran Klosk finished the incantation.

Allis screamed and backed away as the drowned ones started for her.

Borran Klosk felt the surge of power that filled the glove and himself. He gazed at the drowned ones before him, feeling the link that bound his mind to the animalistic impulses that still survived in them.

It was as though Borran Klosk's mind had suddenly grown larger, expanding tens, hundreds, maybe a thousandfold. If he chose, he could see through their eyes. He joined some of the minds onboard the other ship and saw the frightened faces of men who went down before him. He almost felt their flesh tear as the teeth bit into them, as if those teeth were his own.

"Lord Klosk!"

Allis's strained, frightened voice drew him back to his own body. He saw the ravaged features of the drowned one before him, mouth open as it prepared to bite him. A shrimp coiled inside one of its vacant eye sockets.

Other drowned ones closed on Allis, gripping her arms as they bore her down to the deck. She was already shifting, turning into a giant spider.

As if he'd been doing it for years instead of only having just learned it, Borran Klosk reached into the minds of the drowned ones that had boarded their ship.

"Stop," he commanded.

And the drowned ones stopped.

Allis shrugged free of those that held her and stood by the mohrg.

"You have them," she said, and there was a flicker of disbelief in her opal eyes.

Borran Klosk peered at the drowned one standing dripping in front of him. The mohrg reached out and caressed the dead blue-gray flesh.

"Not all of them," he said, "but enough to destroy Alaghôn."

He pushed the drowned one aside gently. The creature stepped out of the way and waited there.

Back at the railing, intimately aware of all the drowned ones floating in the water around *Mistress Talia*, Borran Klosk watched the unmerciful execution of the other ship's crew. Some of the drowned ones were destroyed in the assault, but not nearly enough of them. In a short time, the drowned ones would have eliminated every living thing from the ship. The mohrg only hoped that something remained of the vessel when they finished.

He felt filled with wonder as he gazed out over the sea and the ship under attack. He wanted to scream with joy.

"They're mine, Allis. I can feel them. I have an army."

"As you were promised, Lord Klosk."

Borran Klosk listened to the screams of the dying men. They sounded good, almost as if he was causing them himself. His bloodlust was fed, but it was nowhere near full.

"Alaghôn will be the first to fall, Allis," Borran Klosk told the woman, "then all of Turmish. And when I have together again the five jewels that make up Taraketh's Hive, I will destroy all the lands that the Emerald Enclave holds precious. I will be unmerciful in my vengeance for all they have done to me."

He paused, watching as men died aboard the other ship.

"I will kill them all."

CHAPTER TWENTY-TWO

As soon as Haarn entered Alaghôn, nearly a tenday after leaving the lean-to where they'd weathered out the storm and rested while Ettrian healed, he felt closed in. Even in the densest brush he'd never experienced the kind of claustrophobia that assailed him in the city. Broadfoot, fully recovered from the shambler's attack, lumbered at his side, and thankfully, most of the townspeople stayed well away from Haarn because of him.

Druids assigned to identify them to the Alaghôn Watch met them at the gate, directing them to the docks where the Emerald Enclave had set up camp. Borran Klosk, the druids said, was expected at any time. The Elder Circle had scried the mohrg and knew he was headed back to Alaghôn, though few other details were available. Ettrian was passed through immediately, though a few of the druids knew Haarn as well.

Haarn mistrusted the feel of the cobblestone street beneath his moccasins. The hard surface of the street didn't have the springy feel of true land. He felt tied down to it, held back instead of uplifted.

He looked up at the tall buildings until his neck hurt. Some of them were several stories tall, crafted from stone shaped by hammer and chisel, and many windows held stained glass in dozens of different colors.

Twilight deepened over the city, and the setting

sun struck blazing colors from the stained glass. Windows fronting shops—something Haarn had never seen before though he'd heard merchants talk of such places—drew his attention time and again. On the other side of the glass were objects laid out for sale. Vast treasures of clothing, weapons, and food lay spread on sheets and colored blankets. Though he would never take things without paying for them, Haarn couldn't believe others wouldn't be tempted.

"Do you see something you like?" Druz asked.

Haarn came back to his senses, only then aware that he was standing with his nose almost pressed to the window of a shop that sold herbs. He'd admired the pots and cups of leaves, branches, and powders that occupied the display window, and he wondered what the merchant might have that he would want. With the battle surely coming with Borran Klosk, he was aware that his own kit was sorely lacking.

"No," Haarn answered, embarrassed at his own naiveté. "I don't have anything to trade for those things."

"You have the bounty offered for Stonefur's head," Druz replied. "I could advance you some against that, provided you repaid me."

Haarn shook his head. "No. I'll accept no bounty for killing the wolf."

He stepped away from the window, aware that his father had turned and was waiting on him. Ettrian's face showed displeasure, and every line in his body screamed impatience. Since his recovery, which had left him unscarred and in full health once more, he'd gone back to old habits and rarely spoke to Haarn. Most of their conversation had concerned Druz and whether or not they should have gotten rid of her.

Haarn gripped Broadfoot's coat and urged the bear on again. Lamplighters climbed ladders they carried with them and lit the wicks of the street lamps as the night deepened and filled Alaghôn with shadows. The faces of townspeople peered out the windows of taverns and pubs, all of them watching the gathering of druids.

"They don't care for the Emerald Enclave here much," Druz said quietly as she looked around. Her hand never left the hilt of her long sword.

"No," Haarn agreed. "They call us 'Caretakers' when we aid them during times of pestilence or crop failure. When we protect the forests, they call us 'Nature's Chosen,' meant in a derogatory manner."

"What does your father call me?"

Haarn, taken aback, briefly considered lying. "I think you remind him too much of what was lost," he said.

"Do I remind you of your mother, Haarn?" Her voice was soft and her intensity surprising.

Since that day in the lean-to, they hadn't talked of such things. He hadn't dared bring it up and had prayed that she wouldn't. The whole ordeal had been trying, and he didn't know what he wanted to say or what he wanted to hear from her.

"Perhaps," he answered finally.

Druz looked away and took a small breath. "I'm sorry for that."

"You remind me," Haarn went on, though he couldn't imagine why he chose to speak other than the fact that the town must have been more unsettling than he'd at first believed, "of some of the best things about her."

Druz turned back to him and smiled.

"Haarn!"

Looking forward, Haarn saw that his father's face had grown even more impatient.

"The Elder Circle won't wait forever, boy," Ettrian said.

Haarn lengthened his stride, leaving Druz behind. If they talked any more, he wanted to have more of his wits about him. Out in the forest, things between them had been different. He was very conscious that this was her territory.

Even as he hurried, though, he glanced over his shoulder to make certain that she followed. She did, but she maintained a distance. Haarn was unsure which of them the distance was meant for.

Even more overpowering than the sights of the city

were the stench and the noise. Never, not even in bat-infested caves filled with centuries of excrement, had he smelled a stench like that which filled Alaghôn. He pinched his nostrils together as best as he could and breathed shallowly. Some of the scents in the miasma that assaulted him were food scents and probably would have made him hungry had it not been for the sickening odors mixed with them.

The noise was another matter. Where it seemed at times that nature was incredibly raucous, there was no comparison to the noise a city generated. He already had a pounding headache from the din of voices, wheels clattering along the cobblestones, the constant pounding of iron-shod hooves, and tools used by professionals at their craft. Steel rang upon steel at a smithy just down the street from the public stables.

Ettrian followed the twists and the turns of the curving streets as if he was following a clearly blazed trail. Haarn read the signs posted over the streets, recognizing the names of trees and herbs, but not how any of them went together. It was as if someone had written down all the names of plants, animals, and stones that they had known, tossed them in a hat, and drawn them back out. Several other street names were completely unknown to him.

The street they were following took a final turn and headed straight down a steep grade, down toward the black ocean that lapped at the feet of the city. It wasn't the ocean that took Haarn's breath away and froze him in mid-step. He'd seen the ocean before, and he'd seen ships before, though he'd never been on any so huge as the freighters, cogs, and caravels that filled the harbor. The sheer immensity of the harbor slammed into him like a dwarf smith's hammer.

"Are you all right?" Druz stepped in front of him, taking him by the arm and shaking him slightly.

"I didn't know," Haarn said, gazing in rapt wonder at all the ships, all the men scurrying about aboard them bawling at each other and carrying lanterns, all the men gathered down at the water's edge.

"Didn't know what?" Druz asked.

"That the world was so . . . big," Haarn whispered.

"Big?" Druz asked. "How big did you think Faerûn was? Or Toril for that matter?"

Haarn shook his head as if dazed. "I don't know. We aren't taught about the world outside our corner of it. I'd heard stories from merchants and sellswords, but I thought some of them were merely fantasies." He looked at Druz. "How big . . . how big is Turmish compared to the rest of the world?"

"Compared only to Faerûn," Druz said softly, "Turmish is small. There are a number of nations around the Sea of Fallen Stars that are much larger and more densely populated. When you get out to the west, to the Sword Coast, the cities are even bigger. The world goes there to study and trade."

Haarn tried to take it all in, but it was nearly too much. He gazed at the ships, knowing that what the woman said—as unbelievable as it sounded—had to be the truth.

Townspeople passed by them, giving Broadfoot plenty of room. The bear growled occasionally, letting Haarn know he was uncomfortable with the city as well. The bear wanted to get back to the forest and the life he knew best. Haarn felt that way too, but there was something inside him, perhaps something left to him by his mother's blood, that called him out toward the sea.

The druid stared out into the deepening night creeping in from the east. The ocean seemed to lift and flow outward from Alaghôn, bending over the horizon. He was intensely curious about what lay out there.

"The idea of seeing more of the world excites you, doesn't it?" Druz asked, interrupting his thoughts.

Haarn didn't say anything.

"That's why your father never brought you to the city, and why he spoke so harshly against them. He knew you, with your curious mind, would be tempted to go."

Shaking his head, Haarn said, "I can't."

It would be a dishonor to his father and there was all

his work to consider—work Silvanus had given him to do.

"Perhaps one day you'll change your mind," Druz suggested. "Come on. Ettrian is waiting for us again, and I don't want him to get the idea that standing here gawking was my idea."

She started off at once, but Haarn hesitated, trying to work through everything he was seeing and everything that had been said. He wanted to tell her he wouldn't be tempted, but he couldn't.

Broadfoot growled impatiently then nuzzled his wide head into Haarn's side, butting him in a bored fashion that suggested they start moving or start eating. With nothing more than a handful of scraps in his pouch, Haarn wisely considered that stopping to eat would be a mistake. He followed, staying a safe distance back from Druz so she wouldn't be asking any more questions and he could look at the city in relative peace.

Bells pealed, a rancorous clanging that set Haarn's teeth on edge.

"A ship!" someone shouted. "I see a ship!"

Glancing out toward the harbor, Haarn saw the tips of the sails come into view over the harbor. The ship sailed strongly, making good time.

"It's Borran Klosk!" another man yelled. "He's brung a ship full of dead men with him! Hurry! Someone get the watch!"

"The watch already knows, you damned fool!" someone else growled. "Who do you think is standing guard duty out there in them towers in the harbor?"

Further down the street, Ettrian broke into a run, making for the docks. Dozens of other citizens did the same. Wagons thundered across the cobblestone streets as drivers cracked whips above the heads of the pulling teams.

Haarn ran, urging Broadfoot to follow. The druid's scimitar was already in hand.

"There are two ships!" someone shouted. "Borran Klosk has done brought *two* ships back with him!"

Borran Klosk stood on the flying deck of *Mistress Talia* as storm winds blew them into Alaghôn's harbor. His rapacious tongue flicked out, tasting fear in the air.

Hundreds of lanterns and torches lined the dockyards. Men armed with bows occupied positions on top of the buildings. The men ringing the bells kept up their awful racket.

"It would have been better," Allis said, "if you had not let them see you coming."

"Sneaking back to Alaghôn like some thief in the night is not how I wanted to return in my moment of glory and triumph," Borran Klosk said, gazing at the sight of the frightened people taking a stance against him to save their city. He drank in their intoxicating fear. "All those years ago, they thought they had beaten me. They needed to know before I got back that they had failed."

The bells continued to ring, and the cacophony of harsh noise drew Borran Klosk's ire. Using the powers granted to him by the Glove of Malar, as he'd come to think of the device, he reached into the minds of some of the men aboard *Mistress Talia*.

Two dozen corpses leaped from the ship's side and hit the dark water. They disappeared without a trace, swimming deep.

The warning towers stood in the harbor, as they had when Borran Klosk preyed on Alaghôn in his human life. Crafted of mortised stone, the three towers stood as narrow pinnacles with lookouts for the harbor patrol and the watch stationed atop them.

With the military district so close by onshore, there was seldom any trouble in the harbor. Commerce was the primary interest in Alaghôn, and nothing was allowed to interfere with that.

Allis stood at Borran Klosk's side. Her features altered as she shifted into the half-human/half-spider shape. She wasn't like the rest of the dark troops the mohrg had gathered—she still feared death.

Borran Klosk enjoyed that savory tidbit from her, and it only whetted his appetite for what awaited him on shore and deeper into Alaghôn.

One of the warning tower bells started ringing in a haphazard manner, no longer bonging sonorously.

Turning his attention to the suddenly silent tower, Borran Klosk spied the drowned ones that had seized the two men manning the tower. The men screamed in terror, but it didn't last long.

The sea zombies easily overpowered both men. One of the drowned ones swung a man by his heels and smashed his head against the stone structure. Blood, the color of black bile, ran down the masonry. The drowned one tossed the dead man into the harbor. The two drowned ones, at Borran Klosk's silent command, cut the rope securing the bell and shoved it off into the water as well.

In short order, the other bells dropped into the harbor too, preceded by the men who stood guard there.

It was a waste, Borran Klosk reflected as he watched first one dead man then the other plunge below the surface of the dark water, but then, once he'd destroyed all of Alaghôn he would be able to raise up the newly-fallen dead and build an even larger army to take over all of Turmish.

Allis flinched as archers along the docks set fire to arrows and drew them back. When the archers unleashed their shafts, they leaped into the air like a hundred miniature comets. Some of the fire arrows went out before they reached the ships. Others missed the two vessels completely and extinguished in the harbor, but a number of the fiery projectiles found new homes in the sails, decks, and bodies of the undead.

Savage hunger filled the mohrg as he reached into the mind of the undead sailor manning the wheel. He made certain the man was staying on course. All the sails were up, and the storm winds blew them toward the harbor at top speed.

His long, purple tongue whipped the air before him, watching as the army standing along Alaghôn's docks waited to die. "These fools only see two ships filled with undead bearing down on them," Borran Klosk said. "Wait until they know the truth."

He plucked a flaming arrow from between his bare ribs and tossed it into the harbor.

CHAPTER TWENTY-THREE

"Hold the line, boys! Hold the line and drive those undead vermin back into the sea so the fish can choke on them!" a grizzled veteran of the Alaghôn Watch spat as he marched along the docks behind a contingent of his men only a short distance in front of Haarn.

Haarn stood ready in the line of warriors that faced Alaghôn's harbor. He couldn't believe all the sailors and warriors had gathered there on the spindly wooden docks. It was no place to fight even if they did have arrows. Haarn wanted the solid footing of the ground beneath him and room to move as he needed to instead of being packed in like one lemming among many.

Ettrian stood with the Elder Circle farther back from the line of piers. They conferred with watch commanders and other officials of the city. Haarn wasn't surprised to note that Shinthala Deepcrest, Ashenford Torinbow, and an elf woman he had to suppose was Lady Shadowmoon Crystalembers—the third member of the Elder Circle—all seemed to know the people of Alaghôn. He was surprised to see that his father was on quite comfortable terms with some people of Alaghôn as well.

Haarn glanced at Druz, who stood beside him. The warriors—men and women, humans and elves, with a few dwarves thrown in—all yelled threats at the approaching ships. It was a primitive defense,

Haarn knew, one that was ingrained into every species: act louder and bigger than the opposition, hoping to scare them away.

But how did they hope to scare dead men?

"This is wrong," Haarn said, loud enough to be heard over the crowd.

Druz looked at him from beneath the armored helm she'd been given. "If it's the crowd you don't like. . . ."

Haarn shook his head. The crowd made him claustrophobic, but that wasn't the problem.

"They're forgetting that they're not fighting flesh and blood men," Haarn said, glancing around.

The warriors had gathered with the druids, all of them figuring that a show of combined force would bring a swift end to Borran Klosk.

"It'll work," Druz said.

Haarn knew she was wrong. He looked over the heads of the warriors in front of him. The two small ships that had been hidden away at the sides of the inner harbor broke cover and raced to overtake the bigger ships. Only a handful of men crewed each of the small ships.

The Elder Circle had conspired with members of the Assembly of Stars based in Alaghôn to put the plan into operation. Shinthala Deepcrest had scried a glimpse of Borran Klosk at the Whamite Isles. They knew from her sighting that the mohrg had recruited troops from the sea zombies dwelling in the waters surrounding the island ruins, but it was only two shiploads. The general consensus was that they were hardly a threat, even though the zombies were difficult to kill.

A familiar scent stirred the air.

Haarn identified it almost immediately as the scent of the skeleton that had almost killed him. They'd never found its trail again, but it would be no surprise that the creature had made its way to Alaghôn to be with its master.

A rousing cheer went up through the crowd as the two small ships closed quickly on Borran Klosk's pirated vessels.

Putting his doubts aside for a moment, still curious about the scent of the skeleton, Haarn urged Broadfoot forward, breaking the line of warriors ahead of him so he had a better view.

Only a few feet away from the zombie-filled ships, the crew of the two smaller craft set fire to the oil-soaked payloads of tinder and pitch that they carried. Flames raged from prow to stern on the two smaller craft, sweeping as high as the masts, catching the oil-drenched sails afire as well.

As heavily laden as the two zombie ships were, they couldn't have taken evasive action even if skilled human crews had been aboard. The two ships careened forward, driven by the wind and tide. The crews of the fireships abandoned their vessels just before impact, diving into the water.

Smaller and lighter than the stolen frigates, the fireships struck and broke apart, smashing against the hulls of the bigger ships. The flames spread across the water, floating on the surface, and clung to the bigger ships.

Another rousing cheer went up from the warriors gathered along the dockyards.

"Haarn."

Turning, Haarn found his father standing behind him.

"When this happens," Ettrian said, his face grim, "stay close to me."

"Borran Klosk isn't going to stop," Haarn said, looking around at the cheering crowd.

"All he wants to do is find the five skeletons that carry the jewels," Ettrian said, "and he's going to kill as many of these people as he can to do it."

"We need to warn them!" Haarn shouted over the bedlam.

"There's no way," Ettrian said. "Not over this."

A thousand questions flooded Haarn's mind, but there was no time to ask any of them. He scented the air again, realizing that he had the skeleton's direction now, but he couldn't take his eyes from the carnage about to be unleashed on Alaghôn's dockyards.

Borran Klosk stood prominently on the flying deck of his commandeered ship. A woman stood at his side, but she was no normal woman.

All at once, the realization that Borran Klosk hadn't ordered the burning sails lowered or the anchor dropped spread through the crowd of warriors. A mass exodus of the front line began, but they had to try to fight their way through the people in back who hadn't yet seen that the mohrg had no intention of turning back.

Haarn was caught in the crowd, pushed and shoved as were Druz and Ettrian, moving but going nowhere.

"Grab onto Broadfoot!" Ettrian shouted over the yells and screams of the scrambling warriors.

Haarn knotted his fists in the bear's pelt, pulling himself close. They clung to the bear while the rest of the warriors abandoned their posts and moved around them like a raging ocean.

Broadfoot growled and swiped at people who came too close to him. His claws never broke skin, but Haarn knew there would be more than a few people with bruises in the morning—if they survived Borran Klosk's attack.

Haarn watched anxiously as the zombie ships bore down on the dockyards. Nearly all of Alaghôn's piers stood on pilings buried deep in the harbor mud, but none of them were strong enough to withstand the tonnage of ships hurtling at them.

The flaming sails of Borran Klosk's craft highlighted the zombies standing on the deck. None of them moved, even up to the point of impact.

The two ships struck the docks, reducing the piers to splinters, ripping through the pilings and shoving docks that weren't torn to pieces at once back into the shoreside warehouses. The groaning, shearing, crumbling carnage filled the harbor with deafening noise. Other ships lying at anchor against the docks caught fire as well when flaming debris from the two zombie ships flew onto their decks and into their rigging. In the space of a drawn breath, a dozen ships had caught fire and a conflagration began that looked as though it might well burn the harbor down.

Haarn fought to maintain his position at Broadfoot's side. The stained glass windows of the tall buildings overlooking the harbor caught the red and orange glow of the burning ships.

Borran Klosk's ships came apart. Zombies tumbled and were thrown onto the ground when the vessels rammed into the land behind the piers and finally stopped. Not much was left of either of them.

The shipwrecks put Haarn in the mind of anthills the way the zombies boiled from their holds. Borran Klosk must have stacked them on top of each other like sacks of grain in a merchant's wagon.

The zombies stumbled from the wrecks and from the sea, coming into the shore like a tidal wave of dead flesh. Warriors stood their ground where they could.

The battle, thought a certain victory by the living army of warriors and druids only moments before, swiftly became a bloodbath. Haarn watched in helpless frustration as the front line of Alaghôn's defenders went down under the hands and fangs of Borran Klosk's undead forces.

"Where is Borran Klosk?" Ettrian demanded, yelling to be heard above the sounds of the one-sided battle.

"I don't know!" Haarn shouted back. "I lost sight of him when the ships struck the docks."

He urged Broadfoot up and forward. The bear was more than equal to the task, shoving aside the warriors who didn't move readily enough for him.

When news of Borran Klosk's impending return had spread throughout Alaghôn, most of the populace had been of a mind to pack up and leave. Some of them had, but there were a number of others who rallied to the cause. The volunteer army had swiftly grown beyond the ability of the Assembly of Stars to control. When the flaming ships hit the docks, that volunteer army was the first, and least orderly, to beat a hasty retreat.

"A line is forming in front!" Ettrian cried over the roaring chaos.

"I see them!" Haarn shouted back.

His senses whirled, confused by the press of people around him, by the alien landscape of the city, and by sight of the zombies crawling out of the harbor and starting toward the city.

A ragged line of warriors made up of members of the Alaghôn city watch and the Emerald Enclave formed at the retreating backs of the last of the volunteers to escape the approaching zombies.

Haarn's heart swelled with pride as he watched the druids attack their undead foes. In the face of overwhelming odds, the druids stood their ground.

Broadfoot burst through the final ranks of the retreating would-be city champions and rose to his hind legs. Towering over the zombies, the bear laid waste to them. Massive blows from his front paws scattered the zombies in broken heaps of bone and torn flesh.

Haarn clutched his scimitar tightly and cut at a zombie to his left. The heavy blade connected and the zombie's head leaped from its shoulders.

Broadfoot roared again, dropping to all fours for an instant to regain his balance, then he surged up once more like a flesh and blood mountain and knocked a dozen zombies backward into each other. The first few were only bags of bones that were never going to be able to move again.

Magic shimmered through the air.

Great tentacles formed from thin air, and multi-colored rays touched zombies and reduced them to dust. Haarn grabbed the hand of another zombie as he drew the scimitar back, unable to get it into play quickly. Yanking on the zombie's hand, he pulled the foul thing off-balance then chopped the scimitar across its back, ripping through dead flesh and biting through its spine.

Black seawater boiled from the zombie's guts as its stomach opened and small crabs scuttled out.

Fighting revulsion, Haarn drew back his scimitar and cleaved the skull of another zombie. The creature continued to stare at the druid with hatred in its dead eyes, and it reached for him. Haarn slapped the creature's hand away with his free arm then stepped forward and to the side. He stamped and shattered the zombie's knee, driving it to the tilted wooden pier.

Only a short distance away, Druz Talimsir fought for her life. Her sword flew, gleaming as it reflected the flames that still burned in the ships, and zombie body parts dropped to the ground around her. Blood spattered her face and arms, and since the zombies didn't bleed, Haarn knew it was hers, though there were dead humans and elves at her feet as well.

A female druid came sprawling back out of the melee ahead of Haarn. He caught her and barely blocked a knife thrust in time that would have opened his throat for him.

"Sorry," she said then lunged back into the fray.

By the time she reached the line of undead staggering out of the water, she'd shifted into the form of a leopard. Her claws and fangs flicked into the zombies, slicing them to ribbons.

Haarn raced to aid Druz, getting there just in time to watch the mercenary skewer the last zombie in front of her with her long sword, then rip its throat out with her knife, decapitating it. She whirled on him, bringing her weapons to the ready.

"Are you all right?" Haarn asked.

Druz wiped the blood from her face. Only a few scratches showed and none of them looked serious.

"I'm fine," she said as she sheathed her dagger and leaned down, scooping up a round shield from a dead soldier.

Another lurch of zombies drew Haarn's attention back to survival. He fought with every trick and skill he knew. Anything mortal would have fallen before his blades a long time before. He thanked Silvanus that the zombies were so slow. He was tiring, but he was still faster than they were.

A whirlwind took shape near the water's edge, and Haarn knew that one of the elder druids had summoned it. The shrieking column of air danced through the zombies, picking them up and shooting them high into the air. The undead things fell back down onto the burning wrecks.

Farther out beyond the water's edge, four water elementals surged up from the roiling surface. They rose from the sea like storm-tossed waves, each with two deep green orbs that served as eyes. When the elementals encountered zombies, they wrapped their watery arms around them and dragged them under the sea. The water churned, then zombie pieces—no longer in any shape to be animated—floated to the top.

Broadfoot continued fighting, snapping off hands, arms, and the occasional leg as chance permitted. His huge basso growls flooded the air, but the noise didn't bother the advancing zombies.

"Have you seen Borran Klosk?" someone shouted above the din.

"Not since the shipwreck," someone else answered.

Haarn cut the legs from under a zombie and looked out to sea. The water elementals continued attacking the zombies coming out of the ocean, but they worked between floating pools of burning oil.

"Eldath preserve us!" a cleric wearing the Quiet One's colors on a blood-spattered robe said from only a short distance away. "There are more of them!"

Haarn watched in disbelief as the flickering lights of the burning ships and the flaming oil pools revealed the secret that Borran Klosk had kept even after the attack. Zombies marched from the harbor pulling huge fishing nets that were filled with even more zombies.

As Haarn battled, trying desperately to get to the nets and slay the zombies that pulled them to shore, the zombies inside the net began to stir. They opened their jaws and chewed at the nets. The ones that had teeth parted the strands and began crawling out.

"Fall back! Fall back!" a watch officer yelled. "We can't hold this position against the reinforcements. We'll hold them at the second line of defense!"

Haarn grabbed Broadfoot's fur and yanked the bear

backward. Growling and snapping his fangs, Broadfoot dropped to all fours and grudgingly gave ground.

"Haarn!" Druz called. "Look out!"

Spinning, Haarn tried to focus in the direction she'd indicated. He lifted his scimitar, but it was too late. A zombie hit him with a fist and the black talons opened a cut along the top of his shoulder. Blood covered his arm. Reeling from the impact, hardly aware of the pain, the druid stumbled back and tried to get his knife up to defend himself.

The zombie drew its fist back again, focusing its dead gaze on Haarn.

The druid knew he would never get the knife up in time and watched helplessly as the zombie's fist came crashing down.

Hip-deep in Alaghôn's harbor, surrounded by fire and the screams of dying men, Borran Klosk marched under the shattered remnants of the docks, praying to Malar that the sewer drains yet remained intact after the ships had torn the docks apart.

Allis splashed along after him, still in half-spider form.

"Where are we going?" she asked in her sibilant voice.

"To win the battle," Borran Klosk replied.

"We've gathered the zombies and loosed them on the city. They are winning the battle," Allis protested. "They need a leader with them."

"They need a leader who has possession of Taraketh's Hive," Borran Klosk argued, "not someone who would be destroyed with them. Don't forget that they are merely things. They are nothing like me."

He glanced under the sagging timbers of the pier, looking for an opening on the inclined land beneath the docks. Giving up, he seized an oil-soaked piece of timber that floated on top of the water and still maintained a flickering flame. When he lifted the timber from the water, the flame caught hold more strongly.

The flame also attracted the attention of one of the water elementals busy destroying the zombies he'd brought in from the Whamite Isles. Great green orbs turned in Borran Klosk's direction. Without hesitation, the water elemental started for the mohrg.

Harnessing the power of Malar's Glove, Borran Klosk spoke a spell to dismiss the elemental. He pointed at the creature and a bright orange light pulsed from his hand. When the light struck the elemental, the creature froze in place then became transparent, showing the burning ship only a short distance behind it. The elemental fought the power of the spell, roaring in rage and sounding like a crashing wave, but Borran Klosk, aided by the magic in Malar's Glove, was too strong. In the next moment, the elemental was completely gone.

Borran Klosk turned and retreated under the pilings again. Deep under the wreckage that remained of the pier, Borran Klosk paused and closed his eyes. The power he'd placed within each of the five skeletons allowed him to peer through their eyes. All of the skeletons had taken up positions around the docks and were watching the battle, and all of them were filled with the lust to join in the massacre.

Borran Klosk denied them their urges just has he had forced them to remain in seclusion inside Alaghôn. Most of them had been there for days, hiding in abandoned buildings, tool sheds, and cellars awaiting his return. One of them was severely damaged, though, missing an arm and a foot.

It had replaced the missing foot with a block of wood, and it stood perched on a rooftop, staring down at the warriors and druids retreating from the advancing lines of sea zombies. Somewhere in the dim recesses of emotion that its limited intellect clung to, the skeleton wanted vengeance for the injuries that had been dealt it.

Clamping down on the skeleton's dark desires, bending it more thoroughly to his will, Borran Klosk ordered it into motion again, heading it for the rendezvous point. The view through the skeleton's eyes shifted from the dockside battle to the jewel it clutched in its remaining hand. The crimson facets held a wet gleam. The skeleton's gaze swept on to the next rooftop. Even with one foot missing, it had enough power to jump between the buildings. The wooden block made landing difficult, but it was underway.

Borran Klosk opened his eyes and found Allis staring at him. Behind her, limned in the fire of the burning ships, the battle raged on as more of the zombies made their way to shore. He laughed at his own cleverness and knew the city's defenders had to have been shocked and dismayed to see still more troops coming up from the depths.

Turning, the mohrg plunged deeper under the dark recesses of the piers. The makeshift torch in his hand lit the way, bringing the mouth of the sewer at the end of it into sharp relief. The sewer was almost ten feet wide, big enough to get small boats down into it in order to clean the drains.

Crimson-eyed rats peered out at him from behind the rusting iron grate across the sewer's mouth. Green sewer water spewed into the harbor

"Here," Borran Klosk said, passing the torch back to Allis.

She took it grudgingly. "What are we doing here?"

The timbers supporting the pier overhead creaked and groaned as if it might give way. Being underneath the structure obviously made her nervous.

Borran Klosk growled as he seized the sewer grate. The rats squealed and plunged back into the dark throat of the sewer.

"We are going to destroy the Emerald Enclave by taking away the one thing they live for: the wild lands of Turmish."

"How?"

Borran Klosk grabbed the iron grate and yanked. The bolts set into the stone foundation him for the moment, but he heard the shrill of rusty metal turning loose. He bent to the task again.

"With Taraketh's Hive," he answered.

Allis shook her head, her many opal eyes glittering from the burning ships out in the harbor.

"I have read about the device," she said. "It was crafted by Taraketh Greenglimmer, an elf druid, who lived hundreds of years ago."

"More than a thousand," Borran Klosk corrected.

He yanked on the metal grate again, and this time it came free, giving them access to the sewer. He threw the grate into the water, then took the torch again from her hand.

"Taraketh Greenglimmer helped stock the insect population around the Sea of Fallen Stars," he said. "After the stars fell from the heavens and destroyed so much of the lands that had been here, and water filled in the depths left behind, nature was out of balance here. Taraketh corrected most of that imbalance and helped make these lands more hospitable to elves. Of course, the humans promptly moved in once the regions were arable and more comfortable."

"But Taraketh's Hive only summons insects," Allis protested, "and only a few of them at a time."

Borran Klosk stepped up into the sewer, noticing that his cloak dragged through the fouled water. He reached back and tore the cloak off. There was no longer any need for disguises. He plunged down the sewer, taking great strides that sent rats scattering in all directions.

After a moment's hesitation, Allis followed. Before she took more than a handful of steps into the sewer, the section of the piers they'd been standing under collapsed with a thunderous crash of splintering wood.

Borran Klosk only glanced back for a moment to make sure they weren't pursued. He didn't hesitate in his forward momentum. His future and the destruction of every living thing on the Turmish coastline and perhaps the Vilhon Reach itself lay ahead of him.

"What can you do with insects?" Allis asked. "You should be leading the army you brought back from the Whamite Isles. That's why Malar had the glove made."

Borran Klosk wheeled around on her, giving vent to

the anger that raged within him. His long, thick, purple tongue slid free of his jaws before he knew it. He almost sent it spiking into her face, stopping himself only at the last moment.

"I sought long and hard for my victory against the damned Emerald Enclave," he growled. "The cities along the Turmish coast were going to be mine. Mine! I had them all in the palm of my hand, but then the Emerald Enclave had to step in and ruin it."

Allis stepped back from him, drawing up to her full height.

The mohrg continued, "Now the Emerald Enclave will have to sit and watch as everything they have fought to build and preserve slowly dies and withers to ash. My vengeance will be complete, and it will be years in the making—not some invasion of Alaghôn that will bring about return attacks from the rest of Turmish. I learned that last time. You can't destroy living things. They have a tendency to unite, even when they are from disparate causes and normally hate each other. I taught them to hate me even more and to fear me. Give them something larger than themselves and they will rise to conquer it. Together."

Allis said nothing, and a moment passed before her footsteps started splashing in the muck after him.

"I would be a fool if I hadn't learned something during my incarceration," Borran Klosk said, reminding himself more than he was telling her. "Once I have assembled Taraketh's Hive and used its powers, all of these lands are doomed. I can hide and wait, though it may take a hundred years. As long as they do not destroy me, I can live forever. And I will." He thrust the torch ahead of him and continued on defiantly. "By all that is dark and unholy, they will die and—*I will live!*"

When she saw Haarn get hit by the zombie facing him then stumble back with blood gushing from his shoulder,

Druz stepped in, praying to Tymora that she would be in time. She slid her shield under the zombie's blow. The creature's fist would probably have cracked Haarn's skull, but the shield protected him. The shock dislocated Druz's elbow.

Biting back a yelp of pain, she stepped in again, still managing to hold the zombie's hand back. She shoved a hip into Haarn, knocking him out of the way. Reversing her sword, grabbing it so that it jutted down from the heel of her hand instead of up, she swept the blade across the front of the zombie. The practiced cuts sliced open the dead thing's unprotected stomach and spilled its guts in twisting coils to the pier. She pushed the shield up, crying out from the pain of the dislocated elbow, and brought the sword across the zombie's throat.

The thing's head flopped backward, blinding it to anything in front of it.

Druz raised a leg and kicked the zombie backward. Her opponent took three stumbling steps and fell, sprawling over two dead men in Alaghôn watch uniforms.

Even as the zombie fell, three more lurched in to take its place.

Druz's spirits fell. She hadn't hoped to hold the dockyards after the arrival of the zombie reinforcements. Her experience as a mercenary had made that plain, but she had hoped to live. Gritting her teeth, lifting her shield with her injured arm as best as she was able, she reversed her sword.

"All right then, you dried-up, diseased bastards," she growled, "come on and taste good Cormyrean steel. My father made this blade, and he made it to last."

Before the zombies could reach her, Broadfoot rushed in. The bear bled from a dozen wounds but was not slowed in the slightest. He snapped and swiped the zombies, breaking them into pieces, then growled in triumph, drawing cheers from the men struggling on either side of him.

"Come on," Haarn said.

She turned and found the druid behind her. Blood

covered his face, and more ran down his arm, which dangled at his side and looked barely strong enough to hold his sword.

"Come on," the druid said again. "Fall back to the second position with the others."

Druz followed him. She stumbled wearily up the incline leading down to the docks, following Haarn as they leaned on each other.

At least they were still faster than the zombies, but that blessing would be short-lived if the way her legs felt was any indication. The zombies never fatigued, and they never got weak from blood loss or hunger.

She glanced around at the warriors and druids retreating from the harbor. All of them wore horror-filled faces and bore wounds. The knowledge that the dead would rise up again at Borran Klosk's hand chilled her to the bone.

She gazed at Haarn, watching the scratches heal on his face under the layer of blood. His wounded shoulder knitted itself, rebinding muscle and tissue until only pink skin remained.

Haarn shook his head and spoke in a voice that sounded stronger than the hoarse one he'd addressed her with earlier.

"It's not my doing." He looked around at the crowd of warriors and druids running with them. "It's a druid. A mass healing."

The warriors and druids retreated into the alleys fronting Dockside, the street that ran roughly parallel to the harbor. The zombies came after them, and when they did, crews posted on the rooftops on either side of the alleys poured oil over them.

"Fire!" a watch officer yelled.

Flaming arrows sped from archers' bows and lit the oil. The twisting flames sucked at what flesh the zombies had left to them, drawing the cartilage tight as the moisture burned from their bodies.

Still, more zombies came on. There was no doubt that the second line of defense wouldn't hold either.

"Over there!" Haarn shouted, pushing Druz to the left as they cleared the alley.

Druz stared through the running figures and spotted Ettrian. The elf was retreating with a group of other men, helping load wounded onto wagons that had been commandeered to evacuate warriors too wounded to fend for themselves. The wagons were nearly full and still they kept piling wounded on while the horses stamped nervously.

"Father!" Haarn yelled, urging Druz to greater speed.

Ettrian looked up at his son. The elf was covered in blood and gore, and the left side of his face held blistered burns.

"You're still alive," the elf said. "Thank Silvanus, but I'd almost given up hope for you."

"And I you," Haarn said, hugging his father.

Ettrian shook his head. "We're not going to be able to hold the city. The Elder Circle has decided, along with the Alaghôn Watch, to abandon this place."

"What of Borran Klosk?" Haarn asked.

"No one has seen him since the ships crashed into the harbor."

Haarn's face hardened. "Borran Klosk wasn't destroyed."

"No one thinks that," Ettrian agreed, "but we can't fight him here."

"There's more to it," Haarn said.

Druz knew he was right. "Borran Klosk wouldn't have just disappeared during this fight," she said. "He has another agenda. Otherwise he'd be visible here, leading his damned zombies."

"What about the skeleton with the jewel?" Haarn asked.

"It's never been seen."

Haarn looked up, scenting the air like an animal. The wind swooping in off the harbor ruffled his hair, making it look feathery.

"I can track the skeleton. I have its scent." He glanced back at his father and added, "It will go to Borran Klosk. If I can follow it, I can find him."

Ettrian hesitated. "Haarn, I shifted earlier to avoid an attack. I can't shift again. Not this soon."

"Then I'll find a way to guide you there," Haarn promised. His form compressed and shifted, becoming that of an owl in the blink of an eye. The predatory bird beat his wings and flew into the sky, climbing over the rooftops and heading south.

"Ettrian!" Druz shouted over the confusion of the wounded and those trying to help them onto the wagons. "You can't let Haarn go alone. It's too dangerous."

The elf's face grew stern and he said, "He's my son, woman, and I won't suffer him to be lost without a fight."

He turned and called out names. Three nearby druids shifted into avian shapes—another owl, a hawk, and a falcon—and flung themselves into the sky. All of them winged after Haarn, who was already growing small in the dark sky, gone before Druz had time to realize it.

"One of them will come back," Ettrian said when he finished ordering another contingent of men to come to him. "If there's something that can be done then, we'll do it."

"If?" Druz screamed. "Damn it! There's no if! Haarn is already out there looking for Borran Klosk!"

"We have to marshal our forces, woman!" Ettrian shouted back. "This is no longer just a battle; this is a war, and a war needs careful—"

Broadfoot's growl broke Druz's attention, drawing her eyes to the bear loping through the crowd. She didn't bother to stay and hear the rest of Ettrian's speech.

She knew the elf was right, but after everything she'd been through with Haarn, and with the feelings he had so unknowingly stirred within her, she knew that her place—if she could find a way—was with him.

Druz went racing through the crowd in the bear's wake. Broadfoot had a connection to Haarn and they always seemed to know where the other was. She hoped it was still true. Pushing herself, she drew even with the bear as people scattered before them, then she knotted a fist in

Broadfoot's pelt, leaped, and pulled herself aboard the animal.

Broadfoot growled and turned back to face her.

Druz thought the bear was going to try to bite her face off, but Broadfoot turned and continued forward, moving into a run when the street cleared ahead.

Druz leaned over the bear, holding on tight, locking her legs around his barrel chest. His fur scraped her skin and the wind pushed into her face.

Glancing up, she thought she got a glimpse of the owl that was Haarn, but it was gone so quickly she couldn't be sure. She clung to the bear, feeling the huge muscles bunch beneath her.

Please, Tymora, she prayed silently. Please let me arrive in time.

CHAPTER TWENTY-FOUR

Haarn flapped his owl wings and stayed in a low glide above the tops of the buildings lining Alaghôn's southern section. The scent of the skeleton kept fading in and out, and he had to fly above some areas three times to pick up the trail again. His sense of smell wasn't as keen in owl form, but better vision offset that loss. The city spread out below him came through in sharp focus and he could see through most shadows.

The fire was still spreading along the harbor, and as Haarn glided across the rooftops he saw one of the warehouses collapse in on itself and smash to the ground. It was so far away and there was so much noise from the battle that it didn't seem to make a sound. Flames roiled up from the tumbling mass, chased by fiery embers that climbed into the sky like a meteor shower in reverse.

Farther out in the harbor, a fishing boat burned down to the waterline, the masts wreathed with fire and still stabbing into the dark, smoke-filled sky. The black sea sloshed over the boat's side and the harbor drank it down. The last things that disappeared were the flaming masts, looking like burning tapers until the water finally extinguished them.

The skeleton's scent drew Haarn's attention again. He stared down, gauging the wind, surprised to find that he could sort out the scent at all with the amount of smoke in the air. He banked in the air, dropping lower over the rooftops.

Motion caught Haarn's eye. Flying closer, below the level of the rooftops, Haarn saw a one-armed skeleton with a block of wood tied in place of a missing foot.

Light from the burning harbor reached the jewel the skeleton carried in its hand. The gem glowed red like fresh-spilled blood.

Hypnotized by his find, aware of the skeleton's odor deep in his nostrils, Haarn flew closer. He held his wings steady, knowing his approach was soundless as long as he didn't flap.

Something warned the skeleton, though, some inexplicable primitive instinct reserved for those who hunted and yet were hunted. The foul creature turned, keeping the jewel wrapped tightly against its broken rib cage. It lunged with its jaws. The gruesome mouth slammed shut less than an inch from Haarn's face.

Unable to stop, Haarn flapped his wings to gain speed and altitude. The cityscape, filled with unaccustomed hazards, threw him off. He crashed against a window with bruising force. Grateful that he hadn't broken a wing, he just managed to keep himself from smashing into the ground. Flapping again, Haarn drove himself up. As he came around, he spotted three other birds in the air. He girded himself for battle.

"Haarn," the falcon called. "Ettrian sent us to help you find Borran Klosk."

"The creature we seek is down there," Haarn said.

He banked again, turning all the way over this time, then swooped back toward the skeleton, marked by the jewel's distinctive red glow. He bore down on the creature, ready to shift back to his normal form and fight.

A ruby ray shot from the jewel.

Haarn twisted and maintained the owl form. The hot ruby beam shot past him and struck the owl that had come with the falcon and the hawk.

When the ruby beam touched the owl, it exploded into

a puff of feathers. Misshapen chunks of burned meat, neither owl nor man, hit the cobblestone street below.

Haarn led the other two birds away from the skeleton, planning to get a safe distance away and resume his form. He banked and came around, preparing to undo the spell. One of the other two birds became an elf female by the time she touched the cobblestones.

Thin and dark-haired, looking like little more than a waif, the elf gazed back at the skeleton and threw her hands out. Her voice rolled the words of a spell in a sharp, clear voice.

A pale green fire shimmered into being around the skeleton. The druid's spell highlighted the skeleton, making it stand out from the shadows that filled the street, and prevented any possible attempt to hide and make its escape using the cover of night.

The skeleton stood for a moment as if confused.

Holding his owl shape for the time, Haarn flew toward the skeleton.

The creature's head turned toward him, and the single hand remained like an eagle's claw gripping the red jewel as it pulsed with unholy light.

Anticipating the strike but not knowing if he could dodge the magic, Haarn dropped a wingtip to the right and dropped and banked. Light strobed from the jewel, but it struck the corner of a building instead of him. Brick and mortar blasted loose in a deafening explosion. Haarn felt several small pieces batter his feathers and strike his body hard enough to bruise.

He banked again, reclaiming control of his headlong flight. Glancing back at the skeleton, he saw it holding up the jewel, either by way of taunting him or to use its terrible powers, Haarn wasn't sure. He flapped his wings again, gaining altitude and skimming over a rooftop just as another beam flew from the jewel.

The beam smashed into the edge of the rooftop, blowing out a cloud of debris and smoke that took shape just behind Haarn. Counting on the amount of time it took for the jewel to ready itself for another blast, he flew over the edge of the building again and aimed himself at the skeleton.

The skeleton turned, bringing the jewel up in one hand.

As unflinching as an arrow driven from a bow, Haarn stayed on course. Silvanus willing, the jewel would not be ready to discharge again just long enough—

Haarn shifted, regaining his original form and weight, slamming into the skeleton feet first like a catapult load. He heard bone crack, saw the red jewel go spinning away, bouncing across the cobblestones, then he and the skeleton hit the street with blinding force.

Breath driven from him, aching all over, Haarn commanded himself to get up. Mud that had seeped between the cobblestones stained his face, tasted grainy inside his mouth, and salty. He'd split his lip when he hit the street. Raising his head, he searched for the skeleton.

The undead creature lay stretched out a few feet away. The red jewel, still pulsing with power, lay still farther away.

Haarn stood on trembling legs, his lungs burning, but the burn eased and his head cleared with every rapid breath.

The hawk dropped to the street, wings outspread and becoming human by the time he touched down. The druid was an older warrior, shaggy headed and bearded and human. He took a sickle from his side and advanced on the fallen skeleton.

"You've done your duty, lad," the druid said. "Lay there and leave off for a time. I'll finish the foul thing, then we'll see about doing for Borran Klosk as well."

Haarn gasped and stood on his weak knees. The druid maid remained on the other side of the street, a quarter-staff in her hands. A look of fear filled her face when she stared at the skeleton.

The human druid drew his hand back and swung the sickle. The keen blade rasped against the skeleton's spine but didn't quite cut through. Before the man could deliver another blow, the skeleton pulled one of its broken ribs free, rolled to its foot and wooden block, and brought the jagged bone in its fist around in a hard, tight arc that ended up under the druid's chin.

Pained surprise showed on the druid's face as he died with the bone shard driven deep up through his throat and curving into his brain.

"No!" Haarn shouted, moving toward the skeleton, but he knew he was too late to save the man.

The skeleton held the dead man at the end of its arm, then cast the corpse away and pulled another broken bone from its rib cage. It turned to face Haarn.

Haarn whipped his scimitar forward, slapping the skeleton's hand away and kicking the foul thing in the side of the head. Bound by the narrow spinal column and whatever magic had brought it to life, the skull rocked precariously but didn't snap off.

A new and eerie purple light filled the skeleton's eye hollows, warring with the green fire the druid maid had ensorcelled him with. Its mouth opened, dropping broken teeth out, and it spoke in a dry, hoarse voice.

"Don't fight. Run."

At first, Haarn thought that it was talking to him, trying to scare him, then he realized that the voice was someone else's. Someone else had entered the skeleton's skull through a magical link, and the instructions were *for* the undead thing.

The skeleton turned and ran away from Haarn, streaking for the jewel lying a short distance away on the cobblestones.

Body protesting, pain screaming in every joint, Haarn pursued the skeleton, overtaking it in five long strides even as it reached down for the jewel.

Haarn smashed into the skeleton with his shoulder, knocking it from its foot and wooden block. Landing on the ground, it seemed to bounce then turned over and flailed at him with its fist. The cracked knucklebones skidded across Haarn's face, opening cuts that stung like he'd brushed up against fireweed. Face aflame with pain, Haarn drew back his scimitar and brought it down, crushing the skeleton's skull and extinguishing the purple light in its eye hollows.

Gasping for breath and wary, struggling for control, Haarn crossed to the jewel.

"Be careful," the druid maid called from her position across the street.

Senses alive for the slightest danger, praying to Silvanus to guide his hands, Haarn dropped the scimitar and fell to his knees. Anxiety filling him, he cupped the jewel in his hands, finding to his surprise that it was cool to the touch for something that blazed so hot.

Concentrating on the task before him, he prayed to Silvanus and invoked a spell designed to seal the magic inside the jewel. With Silvanus's blessing, his own meager magical seal would hold the jewel dormant until he was able to turn it over to Ashenford Torinbow or one of the other members of the Elder Circle. Perhaps there was even a wizard in Alaghôn who could more properly deal with the device.

"Do you know what it is that you're holding, boy?" a harsh voice demanded.

Haarn looked up, and his blood ran cold.

Borran Klosk stood on the other side of the street. Naked to the world except for a sash and pouch girding his bony hips, the mohrg held the young druid maid against him like a shield. One of the skeletal hands was cupped under the girl's chin and the other pressed against the side of her head.

Four skeletons stood at Borran Klosk's side, flanking him. One of them held a large ruby jewel that looked like the piece Haarn held, but was four times as large.

Holding the jewel in one hand, Haarn reached for his scimitar with the other.

"No," Borran Klosk growled. He shook the young druid maid, making her yelp in pain.

"I'm sorry," the young druid said. "I didn't hear him. I should have been watching."

Haarn stayed his hand, his mind wrapping around all the possibilities left open to him. They were precious few. If he'd been in a forest or even a marsh, he would have had more options. The city was dead to him. Nothing lived that he could touch and use, and nothing lent itself to him for cover.

Moving with slow precision, Haarn stood, not wanting to face the foul undead thing before him on his knees. How many druids had died at Borran Klosk's hands this day alone? How many more would die if he surrendered the jewel?

Haarn said, "We're at an impasse."

"No," the mohrg replied. He moved his hands again, making the girl cry out. "If you make the wrong decision, half-breed, she dies." The creature set his teeth like he was grinning. "You hold her life, like that jewel, in your hands."

Haarn said nothing. The four skeletons at Borran Klosk's flank stepped forward. Matching them, giving no doubt as to what he would do, Haarn took a step back toward the only alley open to him. The alley led back to the harbor, but he was prepared to take his chances there.

"Wrong," Haarn said, "you hold her life in your hands." He raised the jewel in one hand. "While I am certain I hold the lives of several others in mine."

Borran Klosk seemed surprised, and if he'd had a face, Haarn felt certain that would have shown as well.

"You would run?" the mohrg asked in disbelief.

"Yes," Haarn replied without hesitation. "Sometimes, Borran Klosk, the few must be sacrificed so that the many may survive. That is nature."

"And have you no feelings for this poor child, boy?" Borran Klosk demanded.

"I will mourn her," Haarn said. He glanced at the druid maid as he spoke, offering his words to her. "And I will remember her to Silvanus."

"I understand," the girl said, struggling to get the declaration out through the skeletal hands that held her.

She straightened herself as best she could, but tears gleamed in her frightened eyes. The way Borran Klosk gripped her, she was helpless.

It was almost too much for Haarn to bear. Still, he'd

slit the throats of fawns that had ended up bereft of mothers in the dead of winter because there was no way to keep them alive, and he'd eaten their meat so they wouldn't go to waste and so the balance that Silvanus stood for would be maintained. Nature was hard and demanded such sacrifices so that only the fittest could survive. Those laws didn't go by the emotions of civilized men. Grief was still mixed in there, but above all was the balance.

"Malar's fangs, boy," Borran Klosk roared in inarticulate rage, "I don't understand. I don't understand at all how you could turn your back on her. By Malar, I despise you damned druids and your stupid ways!"

He snapped the girl's neck and let her fall, lifeless, to his feet.

"Now," the monster continued, "give me that damned jewel or I promise you I'll make your death much harder than the kindness I showed her!"

Steeling himself against the pained confusion that filled him at the sight of the girl's death, Haarn turned and fled as fast as he could toward the alley.

The shadows in the alley were off, all angles and lines that wouldn't have been found in nature, and as a result, he didn't see the spider web broaching the narrow throat of the alley until he was almost into it. He stopped just short of it, avoiding the sticky strands by perhaps another layer of skin.

Then he noticed the way the web quivered, the silken gossamer reflecting the orange flames of the ships and buildings burning in the harbor district.

Haarn looked up, knowing what he would see.

The giant spider, opal eyes blazing without pity as it slid down a single strand, dropped toward him, closing on him before he could run.

Broadfoot had arrived seconds before, so silent on his great padded paws that no one knew he was there. Druz had slid from the bear's broad back and crept as close to Haarn as she'd been able to. She'd seen the spider web a moment before Borran Klosk had murdered the young girl.

Broadfoot raced from the shadows, snarling and roaring, raising himself to walk on his hind legs, wobbling from side to side in a manner that would have been comical if the whole situation wasn't so filled with the threat of death.

Throwing herself the last few feet as Haarn stopped short of the spider web, Druz caught the druid around the waist with one arm and pulled him away. They hit the ground hard.

She was up before he was. Shaking off the effects of the harsh landing, she gripped her long sword and faced the spider, aware that her move might have saved Haarn from the arachnid but it had left them both open to attack from Borran Klosk.

The spider approached on all eight legs, standing taller than Druz. Her mandibles moved and dripped green ichor.

Broadfoot slammed into the skeletons, scattering them. The bear's undead foes jumped to their feet and fought again, protecting their master. Their bony fists sounded like mallets as they struck the bear, but Broadfoot gave as good as he got, smashing the skeletons and breaking pieces off of them with each swipe.

Haarn struggled to his feet while Druz slapped away the leg the spider-woman stretched toward them.

"Get up," Druz said to Haarn. "We've got to get out of here."

The spider-woman laughed, using both her front legs now to test Druz's defenses.

"You shouldn't have come," Haarn said.

"What was I going to do?" Druz asked.

She freed a dagger from her boot, blocking every attempt the spider made to reach her, but she couldn't maintain her position. The spider-woman kept forcing her back, and there was only the wall behind her.

Across the street, Borran Klosk turned and spoke a

word to Broadfoot. The bear had broken free of the skeletons, leaving at least two of them in broken shambles behind him. Before Broadfoot reached Borran Klosk, the mohrg flicked out a hand. Violet fire sparked from the skeletal hand touching the bear's broad head. Borran Klosk dodged away as Broadfoot became an inanimate lump that looked like a taxidermist's project. Without a sound, the bear smacked onto the cobblestones and lay there limp.

Carrion stench, the odor of dead things, filled the street, and Druz knew it came from the bear's body. Borran Klosk had slain the mighty ursine with just a touch. The cold realization of what she faced daunted her. She backed away from the spider-woman, but nausea welled up in her guts.

"Catch her," Borran Klosk commanded. "I want her alive."

Unable to compose herself against the carrion stench coming from the bear, Druz was no match at all against the spider-woman. Before Druz could move, the giant spider had her trapped in two strong, hairy legs. She tried to break free, but the nausea kept welling up in her and doubling her over. She tried to tell Haarn to run, but she couldn't even get that out.

Calculating and cold, Borran Klosk crossed the street.

We lost, Druz thought as her stomach tried to empty. She gazed at Haarn, who stood with his back against the wall. He held the jewel they'd come for in one hand. His scimitar was in the other. She knew he wouldn't give it up.

Borran Klosk stopped ten feet away. His thick purple tongue darted out from between his jaws, the length of it coiling in restless abandon in his hollowed-out stomach.

"If you give me the jewel," he suggested, "I might let you live."

Haarn shook his head. He stepped forward and threw his scimitar.

The blade whipped end over end, flying straight at Borran Klosk. The mohrg flicked out a hand and knocked the scimitar aside. The weapon clanged against the cobble-stones.

Haarn steadied himself with his free hand on the stone wall behind him.

"I don't suppose you'd give me the jewel if I told you I'd spare the life of the woman?" Borran Klosk said.

Druz wanted to tell Haarn not to agree. The mohrg was lying; he had to be. She didn't dare hope that he would let her go. The single possibility that remained was that Ettrian would arrive with help in time to save them, but the street remained empty at both ends and the spider web blocked the nearest alley.

"No," Haarn said in a flat voice.

Druz chose not to hold the answer against the druid. She might have answered the same way had their positions been reversed. Borran Klosk wanted the jewel, and maybe Haarn could destroy it. Maybe that was why the mohrg was hesitating.

"Then you can die," Borran Klosk said, gesturing and speaking words Druz didn't understand.

The mohrg opened his hand and a fireball formed there. He threw it at the druid and it swelled, growing larger and larger as it flew. It was almost as big as Haarn when it reached him.

Druz couldn't believe the druid made no move to flee. Maybe the carrion stench had made him sick as well, too sick to move with any real speed—or to move at all. It looked like the fireball drove him back against the stone wall.

It exploded, detonating in a sulfurous haze that threw heated air over Druz. At least the sudden blast of hot wind cleared the carrion stench from the street for a moment.

When the smoke dissipated, there was nothing left of Haarn Brightoak. He was gone. Only the red jewel, gleaming and unmarked on the cobblestones in front of the wall, remained.

Druz stared at the ground where Haarn had been, not believing he was gone. She had seen him fight slavers and

Stonefur, zombies and skeletons, and he'd survived. How could he not survive this? She felt cold and empty inside, and it wasn't just from the sickness that still twisted through her.

Excitement flared through Borran Klosk as he crossed the short distance to the fifth and final piece of Taraketh's Hive. He'd already assembled the other four jewels, but the magical device wouldn't work unless all of them were together.

He knelt and picked the jewel up then fitted it into place with the other four. He started the incantation, watching as the jewels glowed in an alternating pattern and dimmed as Taraketh's Hive fed on its five pieces.

He glanced up at the woman who remained in Allis's spidery grasp and said, "You're going to live, by the way." She looked like she didn't believe him, and he found that amusing. "I want someone to inform the Emerald Enclave that their doom is coming."

She swore an oath that surprised him.

"It isn't often that I pass up the chance to slay a woman," he said, "especially one as pretty as yourself, but I want the Emerald Enclave to know they and all of the Vilhon Reach are going to lose more than this city. I am going to take the life from this place, and—Malar willing—move on from here."

"They stopped you last time, Borran Klosk," the woman said, "and they'll stop you this time. This time they'll destroy you. There will be no mercy from Eldath or any other."

Borran Klosk ignored her. Instead, he watched the jeweled pieces cycle faster, blazing with color.

"With this device, Taraketh imported bees, which are the most important creature in the ecology of any land. Without bees, nothing gets pollinated. Without pollination, nothing grows. Without growth, everything dies."

His purple tongue flicked out toward her face to make sure he had her undivided attention.

The woman turned away in fear and disgust.

Appreciating both emotions, the mohrg pulled his tongue back and continued.

"I learned about my enemies. I found their weakness. If I found a way to destroy all the bees in these lands, the lands would die, and the people living here would be forced to move or die as well. So I tracked down Taraketh's Hive, and I found out how to call forth vangdumonders."

Her lack of comprehension showed on her face.

"Vangdumonders are parasitic creatures from another plane," Borran Klosk said. "They prey on bees and other pollinators, but they do not spread pollen themselves. Once I introduce the vangdumonders into this ecology, they will kill the bees and replace them, but they won't be taking care of the pollination. Everything—*everything*—will be unable to reproduce. There will be no fruit, no vegetables. In short order, no plant life at all."

"That can't happen," the woman argued, struggling against Allis's spider's legs.

"It can," Borran Klosk crowed in triumph, "and it will. You get to be the first to watch as I bring the vangdumonders into this world. Be sure to tell those damned druids what you see here."

The woman made another effort to free herself, but it was useless against Allis's greater strength.

Borran Klosk returned his attention to the incantation, mouthing the words he'd learned all those years before.

The lights flaring inside the jewel sped faster and faster, but instead of producing the first of the vangdumonders, they continued to gather speed. A humming noise flared to life, driving pain deep into Borran Klosk's bones.

Something was wrong. He could feel it. The connections that were supposed to be made weren't being made. It came to him in a rush. The damned druid had used magic to seal the fifth piece of the jewel.

Borran Klosk cursed. The druid's spell would have in no way withstood the powers he could bring to bear. Desperate, the mohrg tried to put a halt to the process his incantation had started, but it was too late.

Once initiated, the spell had to run its course, and it would fail. It would—

The explosion knocked Borran Klosk from his feet, driving him backward and blowing him end over end. His senses reeled, and he almost blacked out. Staggered, he forced himself up, peering through the smoky haze at the five pieces of Taraketh's Hive. The five jewels lay scattered across the cobblestone street, all of them inert and dark. He couldn't reach them with his mind.

A tingle made its way up his arm. He glanced down and saw that Malar's Glove lay in tiny coral pieces across the street from where he and the five jewels lay. The glove had somehow protected him from the full power of the spell's misfire.

Joy washed through Borran Klosk, then he saw the druid—the damned druid that he thought he'd already killed—step from the soot-blasted wall where the fireball had exploded.

Haarn ended the spell that had kept him safe from harm inside the solid stone wall and went into motion at once, flicking a pair of throwing knives at the giant spider's head. The blades whirled through the air and embedded in the werespider, one of them sinking through an opal eye.

The spider screamed in a woman's voice and drew back. Druz took advantage of the spider's painful distraction and freed herself. Before the werespider could react, Druz hacked off two of the legs on her left side, causing it to fall. While the spider scuttled, trying to get back to its remaining feet, Druz stepped in and hacked off its head.

Haarn was in motion, diving for the scimitar and dodging Borran Klosk's tongue as the spider's head bounced across the cobblestones and became a woman's head. The head wore a shocked expression.

As fast as he'd moved, even after healing himself while he was inside the stone wall, Haarn couldn't completely avoid Borran Klosk's barbed tongue. It ripped along his left shoulder, tearing and searing into the flesh. The druid came up in a roll, putting the pain out of his mind, focusing on the mohrg.

Borran Klosk succeeded in pushing himself to his feet, and the purple tongue darted out like a rapier, striking over and over again.

Haarn was hard-pressed to keep the tongue from piercing his throat or stabbing into his face. The blows he blocked brought fiery pain to his arms as he struggled to compensate against the undead thing's incredible strength. He had to keep the fight going; he couldn't allow Borran Klosk one moment's respite for the mohrg to use his magic.

Every time he swung his scimitar to block one of the mohrg's attacks, Haarn took a step forward, chasing his opponent back against the building on the other side of the street. The druid's advance was relentless, his swordplay the best it had ever been. He fought with memory of all those who had been ripped from their mortal coils that night, for those who had stood against Borran Klosk all those years before, and for the girl who had died only moments before.

And he fought for the preservation of all that Silvanus had entrusted him with. If Borran Klosk escaped, Haarn had no doubt the mohrg would take Taraketh's Hive and summon the vangdumonders. Borran Klosk had been right about that: if the bees died in a place, so did that place. A creature that any civilized person would take for granted was the basic ingredient of the chain of life Silvanus had taught his followers to so revere.

"Stand away, boy," Borran Klosk said, even though his tongue never once stopped flicking. The barbed end tore into Haarn's left thigh. "I've no wish to fight you. You can live."

"And you can die," Haarn growled, swinging the scimitar again.

His arms felt like lead and his breath came hard, burning the back of his throat and deep into his lungs.

Pressing his advantage, Haarn took two quick steps forward, slamming blow after blow at the mohrg, almost reaching him. Druz remained back, unable to get any closer. Haarn had to move so fast and so broadly there was no room for her to join the battle.

Blood dripped from Haarn's wounded shoulder, running down the length of his arm in crimson threads that made their way down to his hands and dripped on the cobblestones. His foot hit a patch of his own blood and he slipped. It wasn't much of a slip, but it was enough for Borran Klosk to try to seize the advantage.

Quick as a darting hummingbird, lethal as a striking viper, the mohrg's tongue leaped for Haarn's face. The druid knew he had no defense. He couldn't get the scimitar up at an angle to deflect the tongue, and he couldn't dodge, and sticking an arm in front of his face would only add one more layer of flesh and bone for the tongue to go through before it pierced his head.

Instead, Haarn lifted the scimitar and held it edge-out, concentrating on the tongue, making himself one with his weapon, keeping the balance between fear and hope as Silvanus's teachings instructed.

The tongue slammed into the scimitar, then split into halves. The horrendous wound spilled no blood, but Borran Klosk shrilled in surprised pain. Grabbing the retreating tongue with one hand, Haarn let the dreadful appendage pull him toward his opponent. Borran Klosk didn't see him coming until it was too late.

Putting his weight into the blow, Haarn drew the scimitar from under his wounded arm in a backhanded slash that caught Borran Klosk beneath the chin. The scimitar sliced through the long, purple tongue and it flopped to the ground like a dying snake. The heavy blade caught halfway through the mohrg's spine at the base of the skull.

No mercy in him, Haarn gripped the back edge of the scimitar blade, stepped forward, and twisted the sword as hard as he could.

Borran Klosk's head snapped free of the spine and sailed through the air. It bounced against the wall behind him then came to a rest at Haarn's feet.

Striding forward, Haarn shoved the rest of Borran Klosk's body down. He knelt beside the skull, looking into the lighted eye hollows, knowing that the evil entity that was the mohrg still dwelt somewhere inside. Using his scimitar as a prying instrument, Haarn pulled one of the big cobblestones from the street. He lifted it in both hands then smashed it into Borran Klosk's skull.

"Noooooo—"

The scream died midway through.

Bony splinters were all that remained of the skull.

"That won't get rid of him, you know."

Breathing hard, still bleeding a copious amount from his wounded shoulder, Haarn glanced up at Druz Talimsir.

"I know," he said, "but there was a certain satisfaction in breaking his head." He took a deep, shuddering breath. "My father and the others will know what to do with Borran Klosk's remains so that he can never return."

He opened the magical bag of holding at his waist and shoved the mohrg's skeleton into it. At least there—if Borran Klosk found a way to return to life in the next few minutes—the mohrg would be stuck in the neverwhere that the bag of holding gave access to.

Druz's gaze turned tender, and it was surprising to see how she could pull it off wearing a layer of soot and blood-stains.

"I thought you were dead," she said.

"Almost," he replied.

A few feet away, Broadfoot woke and gave an angry snuffle. The bear pawed with grave suspicion at the pile of skeletons he was lying on. When none of them moved, he pushed himself to his feet and stood swaying. He bawled, shook his head, and approached Haarn, butting his head into the druid.

Haarn scratched the bear's head, then he gazed up at Alaghôn. Gray smoke stained the black sky.

"Let's go," he said, pushing himself up. "There's still a battle to be won here."

The sun came up early in the eastern sky, turning it pink and purple. Haarn sat atop one of the buildings that had survived the night's fires and looked out over the Sea of Fallen Stars.

A growl echoed up the side of the building, but Haarn refused the call. Restless and irritable, Broadfoot padded at the base of the building. The great bear wanted to eat and sleep, but more than anything he wanted to get out of Alaghôn.

The excited yaps and growls of wild dogs and wolves filled the streets. After Borran Klosk's defeat, the sea zombies had abandoned the battle, withdrawing back to the sea. Whatever magic bound them to the ruins of the Whamite Isles still called them.

Letting out a deep breath to relax tired muscles that hurt all over, Haarn turned his face up to the sun. He took solace in the basking heat, which eased his troubled thoughts.

Ettrian and the Elder Circle had taken the bag of holding containing Borran Klosk's remains. Shinthala Deepcrest went back to the House of Silvanus in Ilighôn, saying that when she was finished with the mohrg's body, he would never come back again. Even the priests of Eldath remained quiet about her decision.

Priests sang in the streets below, joined by the townspeople. Their voices lifted with hope buoyed with sorrow. Wagons still gathered the dead.

Boats plied the harbor, salvaging what they could of the ships that had gone down.

The experience was different from anything Haarn had ever imagined when he thought about cities and the people who lived in them. He closed his eyes and let the sunrise play on the backs of his eyelids.

Footsteps sounded on the split wooden shingles that covered the rooftop.

Images of Borran Klosk's skeletons and sea zombies filled Haarn's head. He fisted his scimitar's hilt and came to his feet, taking one small step to the side.

Druz Talimsir stopped. She was dressed in the same smoke- and battle-damaged clothing she'd worn the night before, but her hair showed signs of an attempt to put it back into place. Her face was clean, but scratches showed on one cheek. She carried a small, covered basket in one hand.

"I thought you were asleep," she said.

Haarn put the scimitar away and felt a little foolish. The woman had a way of making him feel that way, and when they'd helped rout the last of the sea zombies and aided in putting out the various fires, that feeling had become even stronger.

"I knew you'd be up here," Druz said. "This was the only building with a bear under it."

Broadfoot growled, bemoaning his hunger and boredom.

Haarn nodded, not sure at all what to say.

Druz raised the basket and said, "I brought you something to eat. It's not much. You have to scramble for food down there."

Haarn waited.

"I mean, if you've already eaten," Druz said, "I'll take it away."

"No," Haarn said. "I haven't eaten."

Druz let out a deep breath. "Good. I'd have hated climbing up here for nothing."

She crossed the rooftop and sat on his side of it, on the side that slanted out toward the Sea of Fallen Stars.

Sitting cross-legged, she whisked the covering off the basket and revealed fresh fruit, salted meat, half a loaf of bread, and wedges of cheese.

Haarn joined her, sitting on the other side of the basket.

Druz chose a dark purple plum and bit into it with her clean white teeth. She wrapped her arms around her knees and looked out at the sea.

"So the world is much bigger than you thought," she said. "Does it scare you?"

"No." Haarn chewed on a piece of cheese and swallowed. "It just means the threat of civilization is much larger than I'd thought."

With the danger of Borran Klosk passed, the divisions between the druids and the citizens of Alaghôn started to become apparent again. Haarn had heard some of the brewing arguments about where the trees would be harvested to replace the burned buildings.

"They will rebuild here, you know," Druz said.

"I know."

"So where will you go?"

"Home," Haarn answered without hesitation. "There is still a lot of work I must do in the lands Silvanus and the Elder Circle have entrusted to me. I will want to check on Stonefur's cubs and make sure they're doing all right."

They ate in silence for a time as ship's bells rang over the harbor.

"Do you think," Druz asked in a quiet voice, "you'll ever come back this way?"

"Perhaps," Haarn said.

"If you do," Druz said, "and if I'm available, I'd like to show you more of this city, and perhaps even Suzail. Suzail puts this place to shame."

She looked at him and fell silent.

Prompted by a desire he didn't yet fully understand but was willing to explore, Haarn leaned across the food basket and took her face in his hand. He kissed her, just a tender caress of his lips against hers, and he used his power to heal the cuts on her face. When he pulled back from her, some of the pain and fatigue had dropped from her eyes.

"Well," she said in a husky voice. Her face flushed beneath the layer of soot. "That was unexpected."

The feeling that swept through Haarn was unexpected as well. It started in his stomach and went throughout his body.

"Yes," he agreed, "it was."

He took a plum from the basket and tossed it over the side, calling out to Broadfoot.

"Should you ever find yourself in the wilderness again," he said, "I would like to see you."

She looked at him, hugging her knees. "We're from two different worlds, Haarn. This could be hard."

"Nothing worth doing," Haarn said, "is ever easy."

She leaned in to kiss him, bearing him down to the sun-warmed wooden shingles, and he didn't resist.

R.A. Salvatore's
War of the Spider Queen

New York Times best-selling author R.A.
Salvatore, creator of the legendary dark elf
Drizzt Do'Urden, lends his creative genius to
a new FORGOTTEN REALMS® series that delves
deep into the mythic Underdark and even
deeper into the black hearts of the drow.

DISSOLUTION
Book I
Richard Lee Byers sets the stage as the delicate power structure
of Menzoberranzan tilts and threatens to smash apart. When
drow faces drow, only the strongest and most evil can survive.

July 2002

INSURRECTION
Book II
Thomas M. Reid turns up the heat on the drow civil war and
sends the Underdark reeling into chaos. When a god goes silent,
what could possibly set things right?

December 2002

The latest collections from best-selling author R.A. Salvatore

Now available in paperback!
THE CLERIC QUINTET COLLECTOR'S EDITION

Follow the tales of scholar-priest Cadderly as he is torn from his quiet life at the Edificant Library to fulfill a heroic quest across the land of Faerûn. This one-volume collection includes all five of the original novels, complete and unabridged, and an introduction by R.A. Salvatore.

January 2002

A new collectible boxed set!
THE ICEWIND DALE TRILOGY GIFT SET

A handsome hardside case houses the first three tales of Drizzt Do'Urden ever published – the novels that started it all! Follow the renegade dark elf and his companions as they pursue evil from the windswept reaches of Icewind Dale to the farthest edges of the desert. A must-have for any fan or collector.

September 2002

Shandril's Saga

*Ed Greenwood's legendary tales of Shandril
of Highmoon are brought together in this trilogy
that features an all-new finale!*

SPELLFIRE
Book I
"Director's cut" version in an all-new trade paperback edition!

The secret of Spellfire has fallen into the hands of Shandril of
Highmoon. Now the forces of the evil Zhentarim are after her.

April 2002

CROWN OF FIRE
Book II
All-new trade paperback edition!

Shandril and Narm are on the run from the Zhentarim. As
they make their way toward Waterdeep, aided by a motley
band of fighters and mages, the danger grows.

June 2002

New!
HAND OF FIRE
Book III
*Ed Greenwood's latest novel brings
Shandril's Saga to its thrilling conclusion!*

The forces of the Zhentarim and the terrifying Cult of
the Dragon converge on Shandril, but there may be a worse
fate in store for her.

September 2002

FORGOTTEN REALMS

For five hundred years, Elminster has fought evil in the FORGOTTEN REALMS.

Now he must fight evil in Hell itself.

ELMINSTER IN HELL
By Ed Greenwood

An ancient fiend has imprisoned the Old Mage in the shackles of Hell. Bent on supreme power, the demon is determined to steal every memory, every morsel of magic from the defender of the Realms. As the secrets of Elminster's mind are laid bare, one by one, he weakens unto death.

But Elminster won't go without a fight.

And that is one instance for which his captor may be woefully unprepared.

Available in paperback May 2002